Classified under codename AEDINOSAUR, it was the mission that would change everything.

THE AGENCY

first: that this was not just a book, but a weap

since Stalin's death

eeping epic about the doomed love between Yuri Zhivago

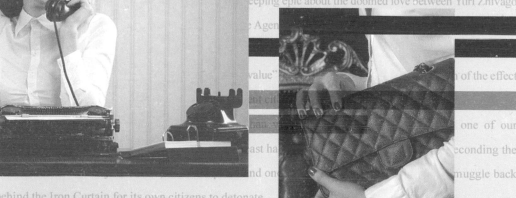

behind the Iron Curtain for its own citizens to detonate.

The Secrets We Kept

LARA PRESCOTT

Lara Prescott

HUTCHINSON
LONDON

Hutchinson
20 Vauxhall Bridge Road
London SW1V 2SA

Hutchinson is part of the Penguin Random House group of companies whose addresses can be found at global.penguinrandomhouse.com

First published ...

First published in the USA by Knopf in 2019
First published in Great Britain by Hutchinson in 2019

www.penguin.co.uk

A CIP catalogue record for this book is available from the British Library.

"I want to be with those who know secret things or else alone."

— Rainer Maria Rilke

Contents

The
Secrets
We Kept

PROLOGUE

THE TYPISTS

We typed a hundred words per minute and never missed a syllable. Our identical desks were each equipped with a mint-shelled Royal Quiet Deluxe typewriter, a black Western Electric rotary phone, and a stack of yellow steno pads. Our fingers flew across the keys. Our clacking was constant. We'd pause only to answer the phone or to take a drag of a cigarette; some of us managed to master both without missing a beat.

The men would arrive around ten. One by one, they'd pull us into their offices. We'd sit in small chairs pushed into the corners while they'd sit behind their large mahogany desks or pace the carpet while speaking to the ceiling. We'd listen. We'd record. We were their audience of one for their memos, reports, write-ups, lunch orders. Sometimes they'd forget we were there and we'd learn much more: who was trying to box out whom, who was making a power play, who was having an affair, who was in and who was out.

Sometimes they'd refer to us not by name but by hair color or body type: Blondie, Red, Tits. We had our secret names for them, too: Grabber, Coffee Breath, Teeth.

They would call us girls, but we were not.

We came to the Agency by way of Radcliffe, Vassar, Smith. We were the first daughters of our families to earn degrees. Some of us spoke Mandarin. Some could fly planes. Some of us could handle a Colt 1873 better than John Wayne. But all we were asked when interviewed was "Can you type?"

It's been said that the typewriter was built for women—that to truly make the keys sing requires the feminine touch, that our narrow fingers are suited for the device, that while men lay claim to cars and bombs and rockets, the typewriter is a machine of our own.

Well, we don't know about all that. But what we will say is that as we typed, our fingers became extensions of our brains, with no delay between the words coming out of their mouths—words they told us not to remember—and our keys slapping ink onto paper. And when you think about it like that, about the mechanics of it all, it's almost poetic. Almost.

But did we aspire to tension headaches and sore wrists and bad posture? Is it what we dreamed of in high school, when studying twice as hard as the boys? Was clerical work what we had in mind when opening

the fat manila envelopes containing our college acceptance letters? Or where we thought we'd be headed as
we sat in those white wooden chairs on the fifty-yard
line, capped and gowned, receiving the rolled parch-
ments that promised we were qualified to do so much
more?

Most of us viewed the job in the typing pool as
temporary. We wouldn't admit it aloud—not even to
each other—but many of us believed it would be a first
rung toward achieving what the men got right out of
college: positions as officers; our own offices with lamps
that gave off a flattering light, plush rugs, wooden desks;
our own typists taking down *our* dictation. We thought
of it as a beginning, not an end, despite what we'd been
told all our lives.

Other women came to the Agency not to start their
careers but to round them out. Leftovers from the OSS,
where they'd been legends during the war, they'd become
relics relegated to the typing pool or the records department or some desk in some corner with nothing to do.

There was Betty. During the war, she ran black ops,
striking blows at opposition morale by planting newspaper articles and dropping propaganda flyers from
airplanes. We'd heard she once provided dynamite to a
man who blew up a resource train as it passed over a
bridge somewhere in Burma. We could never be sure
what was true and what wasn't; those old OSS records
had a way of disappearing. But what we did know was
that at the Agency, Betty sat at a desk along with the

rest of us, the Ivy League men who were her peers during the war having become her bosses.

We think of Virginia, sitting at a similar desk—her thick yellow cardigan wrapped around her shoulders no matter the season, a pencil stuck in the bun atop her head. We think of her one fuzzy blue slipper underneath her desk—no need for the other, her left leg amputated after a childhood hunting accident. She'd named her prosthetic leg Cuthbert, and if she had too many drinks, she'd take it off and hand it to you. Virginia rarely spoke of her time in the OSS, and if you hadn't heard the secondhand stories about her spy days you'd think she was just another aging government gal. But we'd heard the stories. Like the time she disguised herself as a milkmaid and led a herd of cows and two French Resistance fighters to the border. How the Gestapo had called her one of the most dangerous of the allied spies—Cuthbert and all. Sometimes Virginia would pass us in the hall, or we'd share an elevator with her, or we'd see her waiting for the number sixteen bus at the corner of E and Twenty-First. We'd want to stop and ask her about her days fighting the Nazis—about whether she still thought of those days while sitting at that desk waiting for the next war, or for someone to tell her to go home.

They'd tried to push the OSS gals out for years—they had no use for them in their new cold war. Those same fingers that once pulled triggers had become better suited for the typewriter, it seemed.

But who were we to complain? It was a good job, and we were lucky to have it. And it was certainly more exciting than most government gigs. Department of Agriculture? Interior? Could you imagine?

The Soviet Russia Division, or SR, became our home away from home. And just as the Agency was known as a boys' club, we formed our own group. We began thinking of ourselves as the Pool, and we were stronger for it.

Plus, the commute wasn't bad. We'd take buses or streetcars in bad weather and walk on nice days. Most of us lived in the neighborhoods bordering downtown: Georgetown, Dupont, Cleveland Park, Cathedral Heights. We lived alone in walk-up studios so small one could practically lie down and touch one wall with her head and the other with her toes. We lived in the last remaining boarding houses on Mass. Avenue, with lines of bunk beds and ten-thirty curfews. We often had roommates—other government gals with names like Agnes or Peg who were always leaving their pink foam curlers in the sink or peanut butter stuck to the back of the butter knife or used sanitary napkins improperly wrapped in the small wastebasket next to the sink.

Only Linda Murphy was married back then, and only just married. The marrieds never stayed long. Some stuck it out until they got pregnant, but usually as soon as an engagement ring was slipped on, they'd plan their departure. We'd eat Safeway sheet cake in the break room to see them off. The men would come in for a slice and say they were awfully sad to see them go; but we'd catch that glimmer in their eye as they thought about whichever newer, younger girl might take their place. We'd promise to keep in touch, but after the wedding and the baby, they'd settle down in the farthest corners of the District—places one would have to take a taxi or two buses to reach, like Bethesda or Fairfax or Alexandria. Maybe we'd make the journey out there for the baby's first birthday, but anything after that was unlikely.

Most of us were single, putting our career first, a choice we'd repeatedly have to tell our parents was not a political statement. Sure, they were proud when we graduated from college, but with each passing year spent making careers instead of babies, they grew increasingly confused about our state of husbandlessness and our rather odd decision to live in a city built on a swamp.

And sure, in summer, Washington's humidity was thick as a wet blanket, the mosquitoes tiger-striped and fierce. In the morning, our curls, done up the night before, would deflate as soon as we'd step outside. And the streetcars and buses felt like saunas but smelled like rotten sponges. Apart from a cold shower, there was never a moment when one felt less than sweaty and disheveled.

Winter didn't offer much reprieve. We'd bundle up and rush from our bus stop with our head down to avoid the winds that blew off the icy Potomac.

But in the fall, the city came alive. The trees along Connecticut Avenue looked like falling orange and red fireworks. And the temperature was lovely, no need to worry about our blouses being soaked through at the armpits. The hot dog vendors would serve fire-roasted chestnuts in small paper bags—the perfect amount for an evening walk home.

And each spring brought cherry blossoms and busloads of tourists who would walk the monuments and, not heeding the many signs, pluck the pink-and-white flowers and tuck them behind an ear or into a suit pocket.

Fall and spring in the District were times to linger, and in those moments we'd stop and sit on a bench or take a detour around the Reflecting Pool. Sure, inside the Agency's E Street complex the fluorescent lights cast everything in a harsh glow, exaggerating the shine on our forehead and the pores on our nose. But when we'd leave for the day and the cool air would hit our bare arms, when we'd choose to take the long walk home through the Mall, it was in those moments that the city on a swamp became a postcard.

But we also remember the sore fingers and the aching wrists and the endless memos and reports and dictations. We typed so much, some of us even dreamed of typing. Even years later, men we shared our beds with would remark that our fingers would sometimes twitch in our sleep. We remember looking at the clock every five minutes on Friday afternoons. We remember the paper cuts, the scratchy toilet paper, the way the lobby's hard-wood floors smelled of Murphy Oil Soap on Monday mornings and how our heels would skid across them for days after they were waxed.

We remember the one strip of windows lining the far end of SR—how they were too high to see out of, how all we could see anyway was the gray State Department building across the street, which looked exactly like our gray building. We'd speculate about their typing pool. What did they look like? What were their lives like? Did they ever look out their windows at our gray building and wonder about us?

At the time, those days felt so long and specific; but thinking back, they all blend. We can't tell you whether the Christmas party when Walter Anderson spilled red wine all over the front of his shirt and passed out at reception with a note pinned to his lapel that read DO NOT RESUSCITATE happened in '51 or '55. Nor do we remember if Holly Falcon was fired because she let a visiting officer take nude photos of her in the second-floor conference room, or if she was promoted because of those very photos and fired shortly after for some other reason.

But there are other things we do remember.

If you were to come to Headquarters and see a woman in a smart green tweed suit following a man into his office or a woman wearing red heels and a matching angora sweater at reception, you might've assumed these women were typists or secretaries; and you would've been right. But you would have also been wrong. *Secretary*: a person entrusted with a secret. From the Latin *secretus, secretum*. We all typed, but some of us did more. We spoke no word of the work we did after we covered our typewriters each day. Unlike some of the men, we could keep our secrets.

EAST

1949–1950

CHAPTER 1

THE MUSE

When the men in black suits came, my daughter offered them tea. The men accepted, polite as invited guests. But when they began emptying my desk drawers onto the floor, pulling books off the shelf by the armful, flipping mattresses, riffling through closets, Ira took the whistling kettle off the stove and put the teacups and saucers back in the cupboard.

When one man carrying a large crate ordered the other men to box up anything useful, my youngest, Mitya, went onto the balcony, where he kept his hedgehog. He swaddled her inside his sweater, as if the men would box up his pet too. One of the men—the one who would later let his hand slide down my backside while putting me into their black car—put his hand atop Mitya's head and called him a good boy. Mitya, gentle Mitya, pushed the man's hand off in one violent movement and retreated into the bedroom he shared with his sister.

My mother, who'd been in the bath when the men arrived, emerged wearing just a robe—her hair still wet, her face flushed. "I told you this would happen. I told you they would come." The men ransacked my letters from Boris, my notes, food lists, newspaper clippings, magazines, books. "I told you he would bring us nothing but pain, Olga."

Before I could respond, one of the men took hold of my arm—more like a lover than someone sent to arrest me—and, with his breath hot against my neck, said it was time to go. I froze. It took the howls of my children to snap me back into the moment. The door shut behind us, but their howls grew louder still.

The car made two left turns, then a right. Then another right. I didn't have to look out the window to know where the men in black suits were taking me. I felt sick, and told the man next to me, who smelled like fried onions and cabbage. He opened the window—a small kindness. But the nausea persisted, and when the big yellow brick building came into view, I gagged.

As a child, I was taught to hold my breath and clear my thoughts when walking past Lubyanka—it was said the Ministry for State Security could tell if you harbored anti-Soviet thoughts. At the time, I had no idea what anti-Soviet thoughts were.

The car went through a roundabout and then the gate into Lubyanka's inner courtyard. My mouth filled with bile, which I quickly swallowed. The men seated next to me moved away as far as they could.

The car stopped. "What's the tallest building in Moscow?" the man who smelled like onions and cabbage asked, opening the door. I felt another wave of nausea and bent forward, emptying my breakfast of fried eggs onto the cobblestones, just missing the man's dull black shoes. "Lubyanka, of course. They say you can see all the way to Siberia from the basement."

The second man laughed and put out his cigarette on the bottom of his shoe.

I spat twice and wiped my mouth with the back of my hand.

Once inside their big yellow brick building, the men in black suits handed me off to two female guards, but not before giving me a look that said I should be grateful they weren't the ones taking me all the way to my cell. The larger woman, with a faint mustache, sat in a blue plastic chair in the corner while the smaller woman asked me, in a voice so soft it was as if coaxing a toddler onto the toilet, to remove my clothing. I removed my jacket, dress, and shoes and stood in my flesh-colored underwear while the smaller woman took off my wristwatch and rings. She dropped them into a metal container with a clank that echoed against the concrete walls and motioned for me to undo my brassiere. I balked, crossing my arms.

"We need it," the woman in the blue chair said—her first words to me. "You might hang yourself." I unclasped my bra and removed it, the cold air hitting my chest. I felt their eyes scan my body. Even in such circumstances, women appraise each other.

"Are you pregnant?" the larger woman asked.

"Yes," I answered. It was the first time I'd acknowledged this aloud.

The last time Boris and I had made love was a week after he'd broken things off with me for the third time. "It's over," he'd told me. "It has to end." I was destroying his family. I was the cause of his pain. He'd told me all this as we walked down an alley off the Arbat, and I fell into a bakery's doorway. He went to pick me up, and I screamed for him to leave me be. People stopped and stared.

The next week, he was at my front door. He'd brought a gift: a luxurious Japanese dressing gown his sisters had procured for him in London. "Try it on for me," he implored. I ducked behind my dressing screen and slipped it on. The fabric was stiff and unflattering, billowing out at my stomach. It was too big—maybe he'd told his sisters the gift was for his wife. I hated it and told him so. He laughed. "Take it off, then," he pleaded. And I did.

A month later, my skin began tingling, as if submerging into a hot bath after coming in from the cold. I'd felt that tingle before, with Ira and Mitya, and knew I was carrying his child.

"A doctor will visit you soon, then," the smaller guard said.

They searched me, took everything, gave me a big gray smock and slippers two sizes too big, and escorted me to a cement box containing only a mat and a bucket.

I was kept in the cement box for three days and given kasha and sour milk twice daily. A doctor came to check on me, though only to confirm what I already knew. I owed the baby growing inside me for preventing the more terrible things I'd heard happened to women in that box.

After the three days, they moved me to a large room, also cement, with fourteen other female prisoners. I was given a bed with a metal frame screwed into the floor. As soon as the guards closed the door, I lay down.

"You can't sleep now," said a young woman sitting on the adjacent bed. She had thin arms with sores on her elbows. "They'll come and wake you." She pointed to the fluorescent lights glaring above. "Sleeping is not allowed during the day."

"And you'll be lucky if you get an hour of sleep at night," a second woman said. She slightly resembled the first woman but looked old enough to be her mother. I wondered if they were related—or if after being in this place, under those bright lights, wearing the same clothes, everyone eventually resembled each other. "That's when they come get you for their *little talks.*"

The younger woman gave the older woman a look.

"What do we do instead of sleep?" I asked.

"We wait."

"And play chess."

"Chess?"

"Yes," said a third woman, who was sitting at a table across the room. She held up a knight fashioned from a thimble. "Do you play?" I didn't, but I would learn over the next month of waiting.

The guards did come. Each night, they'd pull one woman out at a time and return her to Cell No. 7 hours later, red-eyed and silent. I steeled myself each night to be taken but was still surprised when they finally did come.

I was awoken with the tap of a wooden truncheon against my bare shoulder. "Initials!" spat the guard hovering over my bed. The men who came at night always demanded our initials before taking us away. I mumbled a reply. The guard told me to get dressed, and he didn't look away while I did.

We walked the length of a dark hallway and down several flights of stairs. I wondered if the rumors were true: that Lubyanka went twenty floors below ground and connected to the Kremlin by tunnels, and that one tunnel went to a bunker equipped with every luxury, built for Stalin during the war.

I was led to the end of another hall, to a door marked 271. The guard opened it a crack, peeked in, then flung it open with a laugh. It wasn't a cell, but a storage room stocked with towers of canned meats and neatly stacked boxes of tea and sacks of rye flour. The guard grunted and pointed across the room to another door, this one with no number. I opened it. Inside, my eyes had trouble adjusting to the light. It was an office with posh furnishings that wouldn't be out of place in a hotel lobby. A wall of bookshelves packed with leather-bound books lined one wall; three guards lined another. A man wearing a military tunic was sitting at the large desk at the center of the room. On his desk were stacks of books and letters: *my* books, *my* letters.

"Have a seat, Olga Vsevolodovna," he said. The man had the rounded shoulders of someone who'd spent a lifetime behind a desk or bent over in hard labor; by his perfectly manicured hands wrapped around his teacup, I guessed the former. I sat in the small chair in front of him.

"Sorry to keep you waiting," he said.

I started in with the speech I'd had weeks to prepare: "I have done nothing wrong. You must release me. I have a family. There is no—"

He held up a finger. "Nothing wrong? We will determine that . . . in time." He sighed and picked at his teeth with the tip of his thick, yellowed thumbnail. "And it will take time."

I'd thought they'd let me out any day, that all would be resolved, that I would spend New Year's Eve sitting next to a warm stove toasting with a nice glass of Georgian wine with Boris.

"So what have you done?" He shuffled through some papers and held up what appeared to be a warrant. "Expressing *anti-Soviet opinions of a terroristic nature*," he read, as if reading a list of ingredients in a honey cake recipe.

One might think terror runs cold—that it numbs the body, a preparation for incoming harm. For me, it was a hotness that burned like fire traveling from one end to the other. "Please," I said, "I need to speak to my family."

"Allow me to introduce myself." He smiled and leaned back in his chair, the leather creaking. "I am your humble interrogator. Can I offer you some tea?"

"Yes."

He made no move to fetch me tea. "My name is Anatoli Sergeyevich Semionov."

"Anatoli Sergeyevich—"

"You may address me as Anatoli. We'll be getting to know each other quite well, Olga."

"You may address me as Olga Vsevolodovna."

"That is fine."

"And I'd like you to be direct with me, Anatoli Sergeyevich."

"And I'd like you to be honest with me, Olga Vsevolodovna." He pulled out a stained handkerchief from his pocket and blew his nose. "Tell me about this novel he's been writing. I've heard things."

"Such as?"

"Tell me," he said. "What is this *Doctor Zhivago* about?"

"I don't know."

"You don't know?"

"He's still writing it."

"Suppose I left you here alone for a while, with a little piece of paper and a pen—maybe you could think about what you do or don't know about the book and write it all down. Is that a good plan?"

I didn't respond.

He stood and handed me a stack of blank paper. He pulled a gold-plated pen from his pocket. "Here, use my pen."

He left me with his pen and his paper and his three guards.

Dear Anatoli Sergeyevich Semionov,

Do I even address this as a letter? How does one properly address a confession?

I do have something to confess, but it is not what you want to hear. And with such a confession, where does one even begin? Perhaps at the beginning?

I put the pen down.

The first time I saw Boris, he was at a reading. He stood behind a simple wooden lectern, a spotlight glinting off his silver hair, a shine on his high forehead. As he read his poetry, his eyes were wide, his expressions big and childlike, radiating out across the audience like waves, even up to my seat in the balcony. His hands had moved rapidly, as if directing an orchestra. And in a way, he had been. Sometimes the audience couldn't hold back and yelled out his lines before he could finish. Once, Boris had paused and looked up into the lights, and I swore he could see me watching from the balcony—that my gaze cut through the white lights to meet his. When he finished, I stood—my hands clasped together, forgetting to clap. I watched as people rushed the staged and engulfed him, and I remained standing as my row, then the balcony, then the entire auditorium emptied.

I picked up the pen.

Or should I begin with how it began?

Less than a week after that poetry reading, Boris stood on the thick red carpet in *Novy Mir*'s lobby, chatting with the literary magazine's new editor, Konstantin Mikhailovich Simonov, a man with a closet full of prewar suits and two ruby signet rings that clinked against each other when he smoked his pipe. It was not uncommon for writers to visit the office. In fact, I was often charged with giving the tour, offering them tea, taking them to lunch—the normal courtesies. But Boris Leonidovich Pasternak was Russia's most famous living poet, so Konstantin had played the host, walking him down the long row of desks, introducing him to the copywriters, designers, translators, and other important staff. Close up, Boris was even more attractive than he had been on stage. He was fifty-six but could've passed for forty. His eyes darted between people as he exchanged pleasantries, his high cheekbones exaggerated by his broad smile.

As they neared my desk, I grabbed the translation I'd been working on earlier that morning and began marking up the poetry manuscript at random. Under my desk, I wiggled my stockinged feet into my heels.

"I'd like to introduce you to one of your most ardent admirers," Konstantin said to Boris. "Olga Vsevolodovna Ivinskaya."

I extended my hand.

Boris turned my wrist over to kiss the back of my hand. "Pleasure to meet you."

"I've loved your poems since I was a girl," I'd said, stupidly, as he pulled away.

He smiled, exposing the gap between his teeth. "I'm actually working on a novel now."

"What is it about?" I asked, cursing myself for asking a writer to explain his project before he was finished.

"It's about the old Moscow. One you're much too young to remember."

"How very exciting," Konstantin said. "Speaking of which, we should chat in my office."

"I'll hope to see you again then, Olga Vsevolodovna," Boris said. "How nice I still have admirers."

It went from there.

The first time I agreed to meet him, I was late and he was early. He said he didn't mind, that he'd gotten to Pushkinskaya Square an hour early and had enjoyed watching one pigeon after the next take their place atop Pushkin's bronze statue, like breathing, feathered hats. When I sat next to him on the bench, he took my hand

and said he hadn't thought of anything else since meeting me—that he couldn't stop thinking about how it would feel to see me approach and sit down next to him, how it would feel to take my hand.

Every morning after, he'd wait outside my apartment. Before work, we'd walk the wide boulevards, through squares and parks, back and forth across every bridge that crossed the Moskva, never with any destination in mind. The lime trees had been in full bloom that summer, and the entire city smelled honey sweet and slightly rotten.

I'd told him everything: of my first husband, whom I'd found hanging in our apartment; of my second, who'd died in my arms; of the men I'd been with before them, and the men I'd been with after. I spoke of my shames, my humiliations. I spoke of my hidden joys: being the first person off a train, arranging my face creams and perfumes so their labels faced forward, the taste of sour cherry pie for breakfast. Those first few months, I talked and talked and Boris listened.

By summer's end, I began calling him Borya and he began calling me Olya. And people had begun to talk about us—my mother the most. "It's simply unacceptable," she'd said so many times I lost count. "He's a married man, Olga."

But I knew Anatoli Sergeyevich did not care to hear *that* confession. I knew what confession he wanted me to write. I remembered his words: "Pasternak's fate will depend on how truthful you are." I picked up the pen and began again.

Dear Anatoli Sergeyevich Semionov,
Doctor Zhivago is about a doctor.
It's an account of the years between the two wars.
It's about Yuri and Lara.
It's about the old Moscow.
It's about the old Russia.
It's about love.
It's about us.
Doctor Zhivago is not anti-Soviet.

When Semionov returned an hour later, I handed him my letter. He scanned it, turning it over. "You can try again tomorrow night." He crushed the paper into a ball, dropped it, and waved at the guards to take me away.

Night after night, a guard would come for me, and Semionov and I would have our little chats. And night after night, my humble interrogator would ask the same questions: *What is the novel about? Why is he writing it? Why are you protecting him?*

I didn't tell him what he wanted to hear: that the novel was critical of the revolution. That Boris had rejected socialist realism in favor of writing characters who lived and loved by their hearts' intent, independent of the State's influence.

I didn't tell him that Borya had begun the novel before we met. That Lara was already in his mind—and that in the early pages, his heroine resembled his wife, Zinaida. I didn't tell him that as time went on, Lara eventually became me. Or maybe I became her.

I didn't tell him how Borya had called me his muse, how that first year together he said he made more progress on the novel than he had in the previous three years combined. How I'd first been attracted to him because of his name—the name everyone knew—but fell in love with him despite it. How to me, he was more than the famous poet up on the stage, the photograph in the newspaper, the person in the spotlight. How I delighted in his imperfections: the gap in his teeth; the twenty-year-old comb he refused to replace; the way he scratched his cheek with a pen when thinking, leaving a streak of black ink across his face; the way he pushed himself to write his great work no matter the cost.

And he did push himself. By day he'd write at a furious pace, letting the filled pages fall into a wicker basket under his desk. And at night, he'd read me what he had written.

Sometimes he would read to small gatherings in apartments across Moscow. Friends would sit in chairs arranged in a semicircle around a small table, where Borya sat. I'd sit next to him, feeling proud to play the hostess, the woman at his side, the almost wife. He'd read in his excited way, words toppling over each other, and stare just above the heads of those seated before him.

I would attend those readings in the city, but not when he'd read in Peredelkino, a short train ride from Moscow. The dacha in the writers' colony was his wife's territory. The reddish-brown wooden house with large bay windows sat atop a sloping hill. Behind it were rows of birch and fir trees, to the side a dirt path leading to a large garden. When he first brought me there, Borya took his time explaining which vegetables had thrived over the years, which had failed, and why.

The dacha, larger than most citizens' regular homes, was provided to him by the government. In fact, the entire colony of Peredelkino was a gift from Stalin himself, to help the Motherland's handpicked writers flourish. "The production of souls is more important than the production of tanks," he'd said.

As Borya said, it was also a fine way to keep track of them. The author Konstantin Aleksandrovich Fedin lived next door. Korney Ivanovich Chukovsky lived nearby, using his house to work on his children's books. The house where Isaac Emmanuilovich Babel lived and was arrested, and to which he never returned, was down the hill.

And I didn't say a word to Semionov about how Borya had confessed to me that what he was writing could be the death of him, how he feared Stalin would put an end to him as he'd done to so many of his friends during the Purges.

The vague answers I did offer never satisfied my interrogator. He'd give me fresh paper and his pen and tell me to try again.

Semionov tried everything to elicit a confession. Sometimes he was kind, bringing me tea, asking my thoughts on poetry, saying he had always been a fan of Borya's early work. He arranged for a doctor to see me once a week and instructed the guards to give me an additional woolen blanket.

Other times, he attempted to bait me, saying Borya had tried to turn himself in, in exchange for me. Once, a metal cart rolled down the hallway, knocking into a wall with a bang, and he joked that it was Boris, pounding on the walls of Lubyanka trying to get in.

Or he'd say Boris was spotted at an event, looking fine with his wife on his arm. "Unencumbered" was the word he used. Sometimes it was not his wife, but a pretty young woman. "French, I think." I'd force myself to smile and say I was glad to hear he was happy and healthy.

Semionov never once laid a hand on me, nor even threatened to. But the violence was always there, his gentle demeanor always calculated. I had known men like him all my life and knew what they were capable of.

At night, my cellmates and I tied strips of musty linen around our eyes—a futile attempt to block out the lights that never shut off. Guards came and went. Sleep came and went.

On nights when sleep didn't come at all, I'd breathe in and out, trying to settle my mind long enough to open a window to the baby growing inside me. I held my hand on my stomach, trying to feel something. Once, I thought I felt something small—as small as a bubble breaking. I held on to that feeling as long as I could.

As my belly grew, I was allowed to lie down an hour longer than the other women. I was also given one extra portion of kasha and the occasional serving of steamed cabbage. My cellmates gave me portions of their food as well.

Eventually, they gave me a bigger smock. My cellmates asked to touch my belly and feel the baby kick. His kicks felt like a promise of a life outside Cell No. 7. *Our littlest prisoner,* they'd coo.

———⟨✦⟩———

The night began like the others. I was roused from bed by the poke of a truncheon and escorted to the interrogation room. I sat across from Semionov and was given a fresh sheet of paper.

Then there was a knock at the door. A man with hair so white it almost looked blue entered the room and told Semionov the meeting had been arranged. The man turned toward me. "You have asked for one, and now you have it."

"I have?" I asked. "With whom?"

"Pasternak," Semionov answered, his voice louder and harsher in the other man's presence. "He's waiting for you."

I didn't believe it. But when they loaded me into the back of a van with no windows, I let myself believe. Or rather, I couldn't suppress the tiny hope. The thought of seeing him, even under those circumstances, was the most joy I'd felt since our baby's first kick.

We arrived at another government building and I was led though a series of corridors and down several flights of stairs. By the time we reached a dark room in the basement, I was exhausted and sweaty and couldn't help but think of Borya seeing me in such an ugly state.

I turned around, taking in the bare room. There were no chairs; there was no table. A lightbulb dangled from the ceiling. The floor sloped toward a rusted drain at its center.

"Where is he?" I asked, immediately realizing how stupid I'd been.

Instead of an answer, my escort suddenly pushed me through a metal door, which locked behind me. The smell assaulted me. It was sweet and unmistakable. Tables holding long forms under canvas came into focus. My knees buckled and I fell to the cold, wet floor. Was Boris under there? Is that why they'd brought me here?

The door opened again, after what could've been minutes or hours, and two arms lifted me to my feet. I was dragged back up the stairs, down more seemingly endless corridors.

We boarded a freight elevator at the end of one hall. The guard closed the cage and pulled the lever. Motors came to life and the elevator shook violently but did not move. The guard pulled the lever again and swung the cage open. "I keep forgetting," he said with a smirk, pushing me out of the elevator. "It's been out of service for ages."

He turned to the first door on the left and opened it. Semionov was inside. "We've been waiting," he said.

"Who is *we*?"

He knocked twice on the wall. The door opened again, and an old man shuffled inside. It took me a moment to realize it was Sergei Nikolayevich Nikiforov, Ira's former English teacher—or a shadow of him. The normally fastidious teacher's beard was wiry, his trousers falling off his slight frame, his shoes missing their laces. He reeked of urine.

"Sergei," I mouthed. But he refused to look at me.

"Shall we begin?" Semionov asked. "Good," he said without waiting for an answer. "Let's go over this again. Sergei Nikolayevich Nikiforov, do you confirm the evidence you gave to us yesterday: that you were present during anti-Soviet conversations between Pasternak and Ivinskaya?"

I screamed but was quickly silenced by a slap from the guard standing next to the door. I was knocked against the tiled wall, but I felt nothing.

"Yes," Nikiforov replied, his head still bowed.

"And that Ivinskaya informed you of her plan to escape abroad with Pasternak?"

"Yes," Nikiforov said.

"It's not true!" I cried. The guard lunged toward me.

"And that you listened to anti-Soviet radio broadcasts at the home of Ivinskaya?"

"That's not . . . actually, no . . . I think—"

"So you lied to us, then?"

"No." The old man raised his shaky hands to cover his face, letting out an unearthly whine.

I told myself to look away, but didn't.

After Nikiforov's confession, they took him away, and me back to Cell No. 7. I'm not sure when the pain began—I had been numb for hours—but at some point, my cellmates alerted the guard that my bedroll was soaked with blood.

I was taken to the Lubyanka hospital and as the doctor told me what I already knew, all I could think of was how my clothes still smelled like the morgue, like death.

"The witnesses' statements have enabled us to uncover your actions: You have continued to denigrate our regime and the Soviet Union. You have listened to Voice of America. You have slandered Soviet writers with patriotic views and have praised to the skies the work of Pasternak, a writer with antiestablishment opinions."

I listened to the judge's verdict. I heard his words, and the number he gave. But I didn't put the two together until I was taken back to my cell. Someone asked, and I answered: "Five years." And it was only then that it hit me: five years in a reeducation camp in Potma. Five years, six hundred kilometers from Moscow. My daughter and son would be teenagers. My mother would be nearly seventy. Would she still be alive? Boris would have moved on—maybe having found a new muse, a new Lara. Maybe he already had.

The day after my sentencing, they gave me a moth-eaten winter coat and loaded me into the back of a canvas-topped truck filled with other women. We watched Moscow stream by through an opening in the back.

At one point, a group of schoolchildren crossed behind the truck, two by two. Their teacher called out for them to keep their eyes straight ahead, but a little boy turned and we made eye contact. For a moment, I imagined he was my own son, my Mitya, or maybe the baby I'd never know.

When the truck stopped, the guards yelled for us to get out and move quickly to the train that would take us to the Gulag. I thought of the early pages of Borya's novel, of Yuri Zhivago boarding a train with his young family, seeking safety in the Ural Mountains.

The guards sat us on benches in a car without windows, and as the train rolled out, I closed my eyes.

Moscow radiates out in circles, like a pebble dropped into still water. The city expands from its red center to its boulevards and monuments to apartment buildings— each one taller and wider than the next. Then come the trees, then the countryside, then snow, then snow.

WEST

FALL 1956

CHAPTER 2

THE APPLICANT

It was one of those humid days in the District, the air thick over the Potomac. Even in September, it still felt like breathing through a wet rag. As soon as I stepped out of the basement apartment I shared with my mother, I regretted wearing my gray skirt. With each step, all I could think was *wool, wool, wool.* By the time I boarded the number eight and took a seat in back, I could feel the sweat soaking through my white blouse. Worse yet, I felt as if there were two large sweat stains, one per cheek, on my behind. With our landlord threatening to raise our rent, I badly needed this job. Why hadn't I worn linen?

After a bus transfer and another three blocks of chafing, I arrived at Foggy Bottom. Walking down E, I discreetly attempted to check my rear in a Peoples Drug window. But I couldn't make anything out, on account of the sun's glare and the fact that I wasn't wearing my glasses.

I was twenty when I first saw an optometrist, but by that time, I was so used to life's dulled edges, when I finally saw the world as it really is, everything was far too vivid. I could see every leaf on a tree and each pore on my nose. I could see each strand of white cat fur on every article of clothing, thanks to my upstairs neighbor's cat, Miska. It all gave me a headache. I found myself preferring things as one fuzzy whole, not broken down by their clear parts, and so rarely wore my glasses. Or maybe I was just stubborn—I had an idea about how the world was, and anything contrary made me uneasy.

Passing a man on a bench, I could feel his eyes lingering. Was he looking at the way I slouched my shoulders and focused on the ground as I walked? I'd practiced correcting my posture by walking around my bedroom for hours with books on my head, but all the practice hadn't fixed it. Whenever I felt a man's gaze, I assumed he was looking at my awkward gait. The other possibility, that he might've found me attractive, never crossed my mind. It was always how I walked, or the homemade clothes I wore, or whether I accidentally stared too long at someone, as I'm prone to do. It was never that I was pretty. No, never that.

I picked up my pace, ducked into a diner, and went straight to the restroom.

No sweat stains, thank God. Everything else was another matter: my bangs were plastered to my forehead,

the mascara my mother had told me looked like something a mail-order bride would wear had run, and the
powder I'd delicately applied to what the Woolworth's
saleswoman called my "problem areas" was thick as
Bisquick. I splashed my face with water and was about
to towel it off when someone knocked on the door.

"Just a minute."

The knocking continued.

"Occupied!"

The person on the other side jiggled the knob.

Cracking the door open, I stuck my dripping face out.
"Be right out," I told the man with a newspaper tucked
under his arm, and slammed the door. Hiking up my
skirt, I wedged a folded-up paper towel between my
underwear and girdle and checked my watch: twenty-
five minutes until my interview.

Sidney, my ex-boyfriend, if you could call him that,
had first told me about the job opening one night over
pizza and beers at the Bayou. He was one of those D.C.
guys who pride themselves on being in the know, and
he knew I'd been trying to land a government gig since
graduating two years earlier. But entry-level positions
had become scarce and you usually had to know
someone who knew someone to get an in. Sidney was
my in. He had a job at the State Department and heard
about the open typist position from a friend of a friend.
I knew it'd be a long shot, as my typing and shorthand skills were just okay and my only other work
experience had been answering phones for an almost-retired

litigator who wore ill-fitting suits. But Sidney said I was shoo-in because he'd put in a word with someone he knew at the Agency. I suspected he didn't really know anyone at the Agency with whom to put in a word, but I thanked him anyway. When Sidney leaned in for a kiss, I extended my hand and thanked him again.

I left the bathroom, relieved to see that the man with the newspaper was gone. I ordered a large Coca-Cola and the little Greek man behind the counter gave it to me with a wink. "Rough start?" he asked. Nodding, I guzzled down the soda. "Thanks," I said, sliding a nickel across the counter. He pushed it back with one finger. "My treat," he said, and winked again.

I arrived fifteen minutes early at the black iron gates leading into the complex of large gray and red brick buildings on Navy Hill. Five minutes would've been respectable, but fifteen minutes early meant I had to walk around the block three times before entering. By then, I was a sweaty mess all over again. As I pushed the heavy door, I expected to be greeted with a blast of delicious air conditioning, but was hit only with more hot air.

After waiting in the inspection line, it was my turn to have my ID checked against the list of preapproved visitors. But as I went to get it, a white-haired man in round wire-rimmed glasses pushed past me, knocking into me and causing me to drop my handbag. My meager one-page résumé fell to the floor. The man who'd breezed past security turned and came back. He picked it up, handing me my now smudged and slightly embellished yet still meager list of accomplishments and qualifications with a "Here you go, miss." Then he was off before I could respond.

In the elevator, I licked my fingertip and scratched at the smudge on my résumé. It only made it worse, and I cursed myself for not bringing an extra copy. I'd written it with the help of a book I checked out from the library titled *How to Land the Job Fair and Square!* I formatted the résumé per the book's instructions, even paying extra for the heavier off-white paper stock. The smudged résumé was what the book would call "amateur hour."

To make matters worse, in the process of picking it up, I'd caused the paper towel I'd inserted in the bathroom to ride up, and I could feel it pressing against the small of my back. I told myself not to think of it, which made me think of it even more.

"Where you headed?" the woman next to me asked, her finger hovering over the buttons.

"Oh," I said. "Three. No, four."

"Interview?"

I held up the smudged résumé.

"Typist?"

"How'd you know?"

"I'm pretty good at making quick assessments." The woman extended her hand. She had wide-set eyes and full lips with waxy red lipstick that resembled two

Swedish Fish. "Lonnie Reynolds," she said. "Been at the Agency since before it was the Agency." She seemed simultaneously proud and tired of that fact. When she shook my hand, I noticed a band of white skin on her ring finger. She noticed me notice the missing ring and held my gaze for an uncomfortable moment. The elevator dinged at the fourth floor.

"Any advice?" I asked as she stepped out.

"Type fast. Don't ask questions. And don't take any shit." As two men got into the elevator, I heard her call out from behind them. "And that was Dulles who ran into you, by the way."

Before I could ask who that was, the doors closed.

On the fourth floor, the receptionist greeted me by pointing to the row of plastic chairs lining the wall where two women were already seated. I took a seat and felt the paper towel shift. I cursed myself for not coming up earlier when I'd had the chance.

To my right was an older woman wearing a heavy green cardigan that looked about two decades old and a long brown corduroy skirt. She was dressed more like a schoolmarm than a shorthand typist, or what I'd envisioned a shorthand typist to look like, and I scolded myself for being so judgmental. She held her résumé on her lap, pinched between her index fingers and thumbs. Was she as nervous as I was? Was she coming back to work after her kids had left the nest? Had she started a new career, taking business classes at night, wanting to do something new? She looked at me and whispered "Good luck." I smiled and told myself to knock it off.

I checked the time on the wall clock as an excuse to check out the petite brunette seated to my left. She seemed just out of secretarial school—twenty, maybe, but she didn't look a day over sixteen. Prettier than me, she wore a coat of glossy pink nail polish the color of ballet slippers. She had one of those hairstyles that looked as if it had taken a lot of time and bobby pins to achieve. And she wore an outfit that looked new: a long-sleeved dress with a white collar and hound's-tooth heels. It was the kind of dress I would've seen in a department store window and wished I could buy instead of having to go home and draw it on a piece of paper so my mother could make me a knockoff. My own blasted wool skirt was a copy of a lovely gray one I'd seen on a mannequin in a Garfinckel's widow display a year earlier.

I complained far too often that my clothes weren't store-bought or even in fashion, but after the litigator had fully retired and let me go, Mama's seamstress business was the only thing paying the rent for our basement apartment. She worked out of the dining room on an old Ping-Pong table we'd found on the curb. We removed the broken net and she positioned her pride and joy—a foot-pedal Vesta that was a gift from my father, and one of the only items she'd taken with her on the journey from Moscow—on the large green table. In Moscow, Mama had worked at a Bolshevichka factory, but she always had a black-market side business creating custom dresses and wedding gowns. She was a bulldog of a woman—in looks and temperament. She'd come to America during the last of the second wave of Russian immigrants to leave the Motherland. The borders were on the brink of closing, and if my parents had waited even a few more months, I'd have grown up behind the Iron Curtain instead of in the Land of the Free.

When they'd packed up their tiny room, in a collective apartment shared with four families, Mama had been three months pregnant with me and hoped to reach American shores in time for my birth. In fact, Mama's pregnancy was what motivated my parents to leave. As her belly swelled, my father had secured the necessary papers and a place to live temporarily—with second cousins who'd made a life for themselves in a place called Pikesville, Maryland. It sounded so exotic to Mama at the time, and she'd whisper it to herself like a prayer: "Maryland," she'd say. "Maryland."

At the time, my father had worked in an armaments factory, but before that, he'd attended the Institute of the Red Professors, where he studied philosophy. In his third year, he was dismissed for expressing *ideas which fell outside the designated curriculum*. The plan was for my father to seek work at one of the many universities in Baltimore or Washington, save up by living with our cousins for a year or two, then buy a house, a car, have another baby—the whole thing. My parents dreamed about the baby they'd have. They'd visualized its entire life: birth in a clean American hospital, learning its first words in both Russian and English, attending the best schools, learning to drive a big American car on a big American highway, maybe even playing baseball. In their dream, they'd sit up in the stands and eat peanuts and cheer. And in their future home, Mama would have a room of her own to make her dresses, and maybe even start her own business.

They said goodbye to their parents and siblings and everyone and everything they'd ever known. They knew that once they left, they'd never be able to return, their citizenship stripped permanently for the pursuit of the American dream.

I was born at Johns Hopkins Hospital, and my first word was a Russian *da,* followed by an English *no.* I did attend an excellent public school and even played softball and learned to drive in my cousin's Crosley. But my father never saw any of it. It took years for Mama to tell me why I never met him, and when she did, she blurted it out in one rapid speech, as if she had something to confess. As she told it, they'd gotten in line to board the steamship that would take them across the Atlantic when two uniformed men approached and demanded that my father show them his papers. They'd already gone through this process with the other uniformed men, so Mama hadn't immediately sensed the danger that Papa had when he pulled the papers out of his jacket. Without even looking at the travel documents, the men had taken hold of my father's arms, saying their superior needed to have a look—in private. Mama grabbed hold of Papa, but the men yanked him away. She screamed and Papa calmly told Mama to board the ship—that he'd be along shortly. When she protested, he said again, "Board the ship."

As the steamer whistled that it was about to leave, Mama didn't run to the railing to see if my father was running up the ramp at the last minute; she already knew she'd never see her husband again. Instead, she collapsed on the cot reserved for her in the third-class bunk. The cot next to hers would remain empty for the remainder of the journey, my steady kicks inside her belly her only companionship.

Years later, when we received a telegram from Mama's sister in Moscow saying that Papa had died in the Gulag, Mama spent exactly one week in bed. I was only eight at the time, but I carried on with the cooking and cleaning, getting myself to and from school, and finishing Mama's small sewing jobs—repairing torn sleeves and hemming pants and then delivering the finished items.

Her first job in America had been at Lou's Cleaners & Alterations, where she pressed and ironed men's shirts all day, coming home each night with her hands stained and cracked from the harsh chemicals. Only occasionally did she have the meager opportunity to take out her needle and hem a pair of pants or repair a jacket button. But a week after hearing about my father's death, Mama got out of bed, put on a full face of makeup, quit her job at Lou's, and went to work. Stitch after stitch, bead after bead, feather after feather, she applied the full extent of her grief to making dresses. She barely left the house for two months, and when she was done, she'd filled two trunks with gowns more beautiful than anything she'd ever produced. She persuaded the priest at Holy Cross Russian Orthodox Church to allow her to set up a small table at their annual fall festival. She sold every dress within hours, even the showpiece—a bridal gown that a woman bought for her eleven-year-old daughter to wear sometime in the future. When she was finished, we had enough money to move out of our cousins' crowded house in Maryland, to put first and last months' rent down on an apartment in D.C., and for Mama to get her dress business off the ground. She'd have her American dream, even if she had to do it by herself.

She set up her shop—*USA Dresses and More for You*—in our basement apartment, and word of her talents spread. First- and second-generation Russian Americans sought her out for the intricate work she could do for a wedding or funeral or any special occasion. She boasted that she could stitch more sequins onto a bodice than anyone else on the continent. Soon enough she was known as the second-best Russian seamstress in the District. Number one was a woman named Bianka, with whom Mama had a bit of a rivalry. "She makes cuts," she'd tell anyone who'd listen. "Her needlework, it's sloppy. Her hems fall out if the wind blows. She has been in America far too long."

Mama supported us with her business, even paying for my college tuition when I received only a partial scholarship to Trinity. But when our landlord threatened to raise our rent, it became critical that I get a job. As I sat in reception, surveying my competition, the thought settled in my chest and I pressed my hand against my sternum to suppress it.

Just as I was about to ask the receptionist where the ladies' room was—so I could finally fix the paper towel that was now midway up my back—a man entered. He clapped his hands as if killing a fly. Then I recognized him: it was the same man who'd been waiting at the diner bathroom with the newspaper under his arm. My stomach fell through a hidden trapdoor.

"This it?" the man asked.

We all looked at one another, not knowing whom he was addressing.

The receptionist looked up. "Indeed."

I felt like hiding behind the coat rack.

We followed the man down a hall and into a room arranged with rows of desks. On each one sat a type-writer and a stack of paper. I sat in the second row, not wanting to seem too eager. It seemed no one else wanted to appear too eager either, so the second row turned out to be the front row after all.

The man's face—well, his nose anyway—made him look as if he'd once played hockey or boxed. He gave me a once-over as I took my seat but still didn't seem to recognize me from the diner, thank God. He removed his suit jacket and rolled up his light blue sleeves.

"I'm Walter Anderson," he began. "Anderson," he repeated. I half-expected him to turn around, pull down a chalkboard, and write his name in cursive. Instead, he opened his briefcase and removed a stopwatch. "If you pass this first test, I'll learn your names. If you can't type fast, I recommend you leave now."

He made eye contact with each of us and I looked right back at him the way Mama had always taught me to do. "They won't respect you if you don't look them in the eyes, Irina," she'd told me. "Especially men."

Some women shifted in their seats, but no one got up.

"Good," Anderson said. "Let's begin."

"Excuse me," the older woman in the heavy cardigan asked. She had her hand raised and I burned with embarrassment for her.

"I'm not your teacher," Anderson said.

She dropped her hand. "Right."

Anderson looked to the ceiling and exhaled. "Did you have a question?"

"What will we be typing?"

He sat at the large desk in the front of the room and removed a yellow book from his briefcase. It was a novel: *The Bridges at Toko-ri*. "Any literature fans?"

We all raised our hands.

"Good," he said. "Any James Michener fans?

39

"I saw the movie," I blurted out. "Grace Kelly was wonderful."

"Good for you," Anderson said. He opened the book to the first page. "Shall we begin?" He held up his stopwatch.

After, standing in the crowded elevator, I subtly plucked my blouse from my sweaty back. I reached underneath and fished around. Nothing. It was gone. Had the paper towel fallen out in the elevator? Or, God forbid, had it fallen out when I stood up after the test? Was Walter Anderson looking at the disgusting thing at that very moment? I thought about going back and retracing my steps to see where it might've come out but decided it didn't matter. I wasn't going to get the job anyway.

I was the second-slowest in the group, which I knew because Walter Anderson had tabulated, then read the results aloud.

"Well, that's it, I guess," the pretty young brunette named Becky said as the elevator descended. She'd been the slowest.

"There'll be other opportunities," said the older woman in the cardigan. She tried suppressing it, but I heard a tinge of joy in her voice—she had the best score by far.

"That guy seemed like a total creep, anyway," Becky continued. "Did you see how he looked at us? Like a steak dinner." She looked at me. "Especially you."

"Yeah, right," I said. I had noticed Anderson looking at me, but I thought it had just been in an interview kind of way. But that was always the case with me and men. If a man found me attractive, I was always the last to know. A man would have to tell me directly for me to believe it—and even then, I only half-believed it. I thought myself rather plain—the kind of woman you might pass on the street or sit down next to on the bus without a second glance. My mother always said I was the type of woman you had to get a good look at to appreciate. And to tell you the truth, I preferred fading into the background. Life was easier being unnoticed—without the whistles that trailed other women, the comments that made them cover their chest with their purse, the eyes that followed them everywhere.

There was a slight disappointment, though, when, at sixteen, I realized I wasn't going to turn out to be the kind of beauty my mother had been in her youth. Whereas Mama was all curves, I was all angles. When I was a girl, she'd wear a shapeless housedress during the day while she worked. But sometimes, at night, she'd change into her handmade creations and model the dresses she'd made for wealthy women. She'd twirl and make the full skirts fly in our kitchen, and I'd tell her the dress would never again look as beautiful.

I'd seen a photograph of her at my age, wearing her factory uniform—an olive-green smock with matching cap. We couldn't have looked more dissimilar. I looked so much more like my father. After he died, Mama kept a photograph of him wearing his army uniform in her bottom dresser drawer. Sometimes, when she was out of the house, I'd pull the trunk out and stare at that photograph, telling myself that if I ever forgot what he looked like, an empty space would open inside me that could never be closed again.

The applicants parted outside the Agency's gates with a wave. The older woman who'd bested us all called out "Good luck!"

"I'll need it," said the woman who'd sat next to me during the test, as she lit a cigarette.

I needed it too, although I didn't believe in luck.

Two weeks passed and I found myself back at the kitchen table circling want ads while drinking tea. Mama was at the Ping-Pong table working on a dress for our land-lord's daughter's Quinceañera in hopes of buttering him up not to raise our rent. She was telling me for the second time that day a story she'd read in the *Post* about a woman who'd given birth to a baby girl on the Key Bridge. "They couldn't make it to the hospital in time, so they stopped the car and delivered the baby right there! Can you believe this?" she called out from the next room. When I didn't answer, she repeated the story, but two decibels louder.

"I heard you the first time!"

"Can you believe this?"

"I can't."

"What?"

"I said, I can't!"

I needed to get out of the house—to go for a walk, to go anywhere. Mama had me running errands for her, but besides that I didn't have much to do. I'd responded to a dozen ads but secured only one interview for the following week. As I put on my coat, the phone rang. I ran into the living room just in time to see Mama pick up the receiver. "What do you say?" she said in the extra-loud voice she reserved for telephone calls.

"Who is it?" I asked.

"Irene? There is no Irene here. Why are you calling here?"

I grabbed the phone. "Hello?" Mama shrugged and went back to the Ping-Pong table.

"Miss Irina Droz-do-vah?" a woman's voice asked.

"Yes, this is she. I'm sorry about that. My mother doesn't—"

"Please hold for Walter Anderson."

"What?"

Classical music switched on, and my stomach muscles clenched. After a moment, the music stopped, cut off by Mr. Anderson's voice. "We want you to come back in."

"I thought I scored second to last?" I asked, then gritted my teeth. Did I really have to remind him of my mediocrity?

"That's correct."

"And I thought there was only one position open?" Was I trying to self-sabotage?

"We liked what we saw."

"I got the job?"

"Not yet, Speedy," he said. "Or should I come up with a better nickname for you, given your typing skills? Can you come in at two?"

"Today?" I was supposed to go to a fabric store in Friendship Heights to help Mama pick out some silver sequins for the Quinceañera dress. Mama never liked to go to the fabric store alone because she thought the woman who owned it was prejudiced against Russians. "She charges me twice, no, three times as much!" she'd told me the last time she went by herself. "She looks at me like I'm about to drop the bomb on the store. Every time!"

"Yes. Today," he said.

"At two?"

"Two."

"Two?" Mama appeared in the entryway. "We have to go to the Friendship Heights at two."

I waved her away. "I'll be there," I said, but was met with silence. Anderson had already hung up. I had one hour to get dressed and get downtown.

"So?" Mama asked.

"I have another interview. Today."

"You already did the typing examination. What else do you they want you to do? Perform gymnastics? Bake a cake? What else do they need to know?"

"I don't know."

She looked up and down at the flowered housedress I was wearing. "Whatever it is, you can't go looking like that."

This time, I wore the linen.

I was early again, but was escorted into Walter Anderson's office as soon as I arrived. What he asked first was not a question I'd anticipated. He didn't ask where I saw myself in five years, what I thought my biggest weakness was, or why I wanted the job. And he didn't ask if I was a Communist, or if I had any allegiance to the place of my birth. "Tell me about your father," he began as soon as I sat down. He opened a thick folder with my name on it. "Mikhail Abramovich Drozdov." My chest tightened. I hadn't heard his name spoken in years. Despite the linen, I could feel beads of sweat collect at the nape of my neck.

"I never knew my father."

"One moment," he said, and pulled back from his desk. He removed a tape recorder from the bottom drawer. "I'm always forgetting to turn this thing on. Do you mind?" Without waiting for me to answer, he clicked the button. "Says here he was sentenced to hard labor for illegally procuring travel documents."

So that was it: that was why they'd taken him at the docks. But why had they let my mother go? I asked Anderson the question as soon as I thought it.

"Punishment," he said.

I stared at the coffee stains on his desk, overlapping like Olympic rings. A flush of heat ran down my arms and legs and I felt unsteady. "I was eight when I found out," I managed to say. For eight years, we knew nothing. As a child, I'd imagined the moment I'd be reunited with my father—what he'd look like and how he'd scoop me up into his arms and whether he'd have a certain smell to him, like tobacco or aftershave, as I'd imagined.

I scanned Anderson's face for sympathy, but all I got was slight annoyance, as if I should've known what the Big Red Monster was capable of. "I'm sorry, what does this have to do with the typing position?"

"It has everything to do with your working here. If you'd like to stop now, if you find it too uncomfortable, that's fine with me."

"No, I . . ." I wanted to scream that it was all my fault, that it was I who'd caused his death, that if I hadn't been conceived, they wouldn't have risked so much. But I composed myself.

"Do you know how he died?" Anderson asked.

"We were told he had a heart attack in the tin mines at Berlag."

"Do you believe that?"

"No. I don't." I'd always felt the answer buried deep inside but had never said it aloud, not even to Mama.

"He never made it to the camps. He died in Moscow." He paused. "During interrogations."

I wondered what Mama knew, and what she didn't. Had she believed what was in the telegram from her sister about my father's death? Or had she known better? Had she pretended all this time for my sake?

"How does that make you feel?" Anderson asked.

This was not a question I'd prepared for. I fixed my gaze on the coffee rings. "Confused."

"Anything else?"

"Angry."

"Angry?"

"Yes."

"Look." He closed the folder with my name on it. "We see something in you."

"What is this about?"

"We're good at spotting hidden talents."

CHAPTER 3

THE TYPISTS

Fall had come to Washington. It was dark when we woke and dark when we left the office. The temperature had dropped twenty degrees and during our commute we'd walk with our heads down to avoid the wind whipping through the spaces between buildings, careful not to slip on wet leaves or roll our heels on the slick sidewalks. On mornings like that—when the thought of getting out of a warm bed to go stand on a crowded streetcar under some man's armpit just to spend the day in a drafty office under harsh fluorescent lights almost made us call in sick—we'd meet at Ralph's for coffee and doughnuts before work. We needed those twenty minutes, that dose of sugar—not to mention a better cup of coffee. The Agency's own brew, though brown and hot, tasted more like the Styrofoam cups we drank it from.

Ralph was actually a little old Greek man named Marcos. He'd come to the States, he told us, just for the chance to fatten up pretty American girls like us with the pastries he woke up at four o'clock each morning to bake. He'd call us "beautiful" and "exquisite," although he could hardly see us through his cataracts. Marcos was a shameless flirt, even though his wife—a white-haired woman named Athena with a bosom so large she had to take a step back when opening the register—was always right behind the counter. Athena didn't seem to mind, though. She'd roll her eyes and laugh at the old man. We'd laugh in return and touch his arm, hopeful he'd put an extra powdered doughnut in our bag and hand it to us with a cloudy-eyed wink.

Whoever arrived at Ralph's first would get us a booth in the back. It was important to get a booth in back so we could keep an eye on the door to see who came in. Ralph's was not the closest coffee shop to HQ, but the occasional officer would wander in from time to time, and much of what we said during our morning meetings we did not want overheard.

Gail Carter would usually get there first, having walked only three blocks from her studio apartment above the hat shop on H Street. Gail roomed with a woman who was a third-year intern on the Hill and whose wealthy father owned a textile factory in New Hampshire and paid all her living expenses.

That particular Monday morning in October started out with the same back-and-forth. "Pure hell," Norma

Kelly said. "Last week was pure hell." At eighteen, Norma had moved to New York with dreams of becoming a poet. Irish American with the strawberry blond hair to prove it, Norma had gotten off the bus at the Dixie Bus Center on West Forty-Second and, suitcase in hand, made her way to Costello's to rub elbows with the Madison Avenue ad men and freelance writers for *The New Yorker*. She eventually figured out that both were more interested in what was in her pants than in the words she wanted to put on paper. But it was at Costello's that she also met a few Agency men. They'd encouraged her to apply for a job only as a way of flirting, but she needed a paycheck so pursued it anyway. Norma tucked a strand of hair behind her ear and stirred three sugars into her coffee. "No, this week was worse than hell."

Judy Hendricks cut her plain doughnut into four equal pieces with a butter knife. Judy was always on some sort of fad diet she read in *Woman's Own* or *Redbook*. "What's worse than hell?" Judy asked.

"This week, that's what." Norma took a sip of coffee.

"I don't know," Judy said. "Last week was pretty bad. I mean, that meeting about the new Mohawk Midgetapes? I think we can understand how to click *Record* without a two-hour orientation. If that man pointed to that diagram one more time, my eyes would've rolled right out of their sockets." She wiped an invisible crumb from her lip, though she had yet to touch her doughnut.

Norma put her napkin to her chest. "But how on earth are we supposed to understand unless a man thoroughly explains it?" she asked, doing her best Scarlett O'Hara.

"It can always get worse," Linda said. "You can't let that little stuff get you down. You have to save the headache for the bigger stuff. Like the fact that they haven't filled the Kotex machine since Truman was in office."

Linda was only twenty-three, but once she got married, she started speaking as though she was wise to the world in a way we single gals couldn't possibly fathom—like we were still virgins or something. It got on our nerves, but we still looked to her as a kind of mother figure: the first to calm us when we wanted to tell off one of the men, or to smooth a flyaway hair. The one who'd tell us the appropriate time to let a man know he could get somewhere with us, and what to do if he didn't call the next day.

"If I have to listen to Anderson tell me one more time that my voice sounds too gravelly when I answer the phone, I swear to God," Gail said. Walter Anderson, a bear cub of a man with perpetually uneven sideburns who looked as though he once played college football but had come to consider his walk from the bus stop to the office his daily exercise, oversaw the typing pool and other administrative operations in SR. He had been in the field during his OSS days and was assigned an office job shortly after the Agency formed in '47. Never quite at home behind a desk, Anderson would pace the floor, seeking something or someone to take his pent-up frustrations out on. But after he did let someone have it, he was often remorseful, and overcompensated with boxes of doughnuts and fresh flowers in the break room. He preferred that we call him Walter, so we called him Anderson.

Gail dabbed a twisted paper napkin into her water glass and blotted a spot of pink jelly on the cuff of her blouse. "Us government gals are relegated to the type-writer while overgrown children like Anderson tell us what to do." Gail didn't have a chip on her shoulder; it was more like a cement block. After earning an engineering degree from U.C. Berkeley, she had applied to NSF and Defense, only to be turned away for her "lack of an advanced degree"—code for her being a black woman. Gail knew for a fact that several former white, male students with the same degree were already working there—and moving up in the ranks. With her savings low, she applied for typist positions and bounced around from one government gig to the next. By the time she got to the Agency, she was fed up that her real skills hadn't been noticed. "And the other day, you know what he said to me?" Gail continued. "That he and his wife *just love The Nat King Cole Show*, and that I must be *very proud* to see him on television. When I asked what exactly I should be proud of, he just mumbled something and shuffled away." She took a sip of coffee. "I *am* proud, but wasn't about to let him know that."

"At least the hours are good," chimed in Kathy Potter. Our eternal optimist with a four-inch shellacked bouffant, Kathy had come to the Agency with her older sister, Sarah, who had married an officer three months into the job and moved with him to a foreign station. With Sarah gone, Kathy was particularly quiet, but whenever she did speak, it was always to remind us the glass was half full.

"Well, I'll toast to nine to five," Norma said, raising her mug, though no one else followed. She set it back down.

"And the benefits," Linda added. "When I worked in that dentist's office after college, I didn't even get dental insurance. Can you believe it? He replaced my cracked filling under the table, after hours, if you know what I mean. And that's only because he wanted to, as he put it, *get to know me better*, and thought the laughing gas would help."

"Did it?" Kathy asked.

"Well . . ." she took a bite of her doughnut.

"Well?" Norma prodded.

Linda swallowed. "That stuff really does put you in a good mood."

After Ralph's, we took our time walking to 2430 E Street. Agency HQ, set back from the street, was in a complex that used to house the OSS during the war. We passed through a black iron gate and went up the walkway. It would be two years before the Agency would move to Langley. In the meantime, HQ was spread across several of these nondescript buildings overlooking the National Mall. We called them "tempos," because they'd been telling us we'd be moving soon since we started. The tin-roofed buildings were hard to heat in the winter, and the air conditioning worked just about as well as anything in Washington.

Norma had this recurring gag where she'd hesitate before going through the heavy wooden doors into the lobby. "I won't go," she said that Monday, holding on to a bald cherry tree next to the door. We pulled her in with us and got into the inspection line, our laminated badges in hand, our pocketbooks open and ready to be prodded with a dowel.

<hr />

We knew her name before she arrived. Lonnie Reynolds in Personnel had told us the Friday before she started. "Irina Drozdova. Anderson will bring her around and introduce her Monday morning."

"Another Russian," Norma said, voicing what we'd all been thinking. It wasn't unusual for Russians to come over to our side—in fact, SR had so many defectors, we joked that the water cooler was full of vodka. Dulles hated to use the term "defectors," preferring to call them "volunteers." Regardless, the Russians were usually men, not typists.

"Be nice," Lonnie said. "She seems like a good kid."

"We're always nice."

"Whatever you say," Lonnie said, and left the Pool. We never liked Lonnie.

Irina was already at her desk by the time we came in that Monday. Thin as a birch tree, medium-length blond hair, debutante-straight posture. We ignored her for a good hour, going about our day as usual while she made slight adjustments to her chair and typewriter, played with the buttons on her brown jacket, and moved paper clips from one drawer to another.

We weren't trying to be rude. But this new girl was replacing Tabitha Jenkins, one of the longest-standing members of the Pool. Tabitha's husband had retired from Lockheed and they'd skedaddled down to a bungalow in sunny Fort Lauderdale. Now this Russian was sitting at her desk.

We put off the usual niceties for a little longer than usual. As the clock ticked past ten, it became more uncomfortable. Someone had to say something, and it turned out Irina was the one to break the ice. She stood, and all eyes looked up and down her svelte figure.

"Excuse me," she said, more to the floor than to anyone in particular. "Where can I find the ladies'?" She picked a piece of string off her jacket. "It's my first day," she added, blushing at the obviousness. She had a peculiar way of speaking: no trace of an accent, but slightly unnatural, as if she had to think about each word before saying it.

"You don't sound Russian," Norma said, instead of pointing her to the bathroom.

"I'm not. Well, not exactly. I was born here, but my parents are from there."

"All the Russians working here say that," Norma said, and we all tittered. "I'm Norma." She extended her hand. "Born here too."

Irina shook Norma's hand. We felt the tension drop. "Nice to meet you all," she said. She looked across the typing pool and made eye contact with each of us.

"Down the hall, make a right, then another right," Linda said.

"What?" Irina asked.

"Little girls' room."

"Oh, yes," she said. "Thank you."

We watched until she disappeared down the hall before we discussed: her Russianness (or lack thereof), her hair color (not from a bottle), her strange way of speaking (like a budget Katharine Hepburn), her slightly outdated fashion (bargain basement or homemade?).

"She seems nice," Judy concluded.

"Nice enough," Linda said.

"Where'd they find her?

"The Gulag?"

"I think she's pretty," Gail said.

We had to agree on that. Irina's was not the type to win any beauty contests, but it was there—a subtler kind of beauty.

Irina returned to the Pool, walking shoulder to shoulder with Lonnie. "I trust the girls are making you feel welcome?" Lonnie asked.

"Oh, yes," Irina replied without a hint of sarcasm.

"Good. These gals can be a tough group to crack."

"I heard Personnel is where they keep all the crack-ups," Norma said.

Lonnie rolled her eyes. "Anyways, since Mr. Anderson has failed to grace us with his presence this morning—"

"Is he out sick?" Linda interrupted. We took extra-long lunches when Anderson was out.

"He's out. That's all I know. Whether he's passed out on a park bench somewhere or is having his tonsils removed, it's none of my business." Lonnie positioned herself in front of Irina, her back to us. "Anyways, I'm supposed to make sure you have everything you need, then I'm to"—she held up her fingers in air quotes—*"fetch you for a meeting down South."*

Irina told Lonnie she had everything she needed, then followed her out. As soon as they left, we retired to the ladies' room for more in-depth speculation. "A meeting?" Linda asked. "Already?"

"Think it's with J.M.?" Kathy asked, referring to SR's Chief, John Maury.

"She said *down South*," Gail said. Down South referred to the ramshackle wooden tempos near the Lincoln Memorial. "That's Frank."

Norma lit a cigarette. "A Moscow mystery?" She took a puff, then exhaled. "Of course it's with Frank."

Frank Wisner was the boss under the big boss, and the father of the Agency's clandestine ops. A founding member of the Georgetown Set of influential politicians, journalists, and Agency men, Wisner—with his Southern accent and charm—was known to conduct most business during his famous Sunday night suppers. It was at these parties, after the pot roast and apple pie had been served and the group was thoroughly buzzed from cigars and bourbon, that a vision for a new world had taken shape.

Why would Irina be meeting with Frank? And on her first day? It didn't take a genius to put it together: Irina hadn't been hired for her words per minute.

The routine was for the Pool to treat the new gal to a lunch at Ralph's—to warm her up, and to find out her stats: NW or NE? College or typing school? Single or attached? Sober or fun? Then we'd quiz her on where she got her hair done, what she liked to do on weekends, why she came to the Agency, her thoughts on the new policy of not being allowed to wear flats or sleeveless dresses. But when our lunch hour came and went and Irina still hadn't returned, we had to settle for a quick bite in the cafeteria without her.

She returned that afternoon carrying a stack of handwritten field reports to type up—her demeanor unchanged. If nothing else, we were professionals. So we didn't ask how her meeting went or what special skills she must possess or what other duties she might've been assigned.

It was four thirty—right about the time our typing would slow and we'd begin filing away our unfinished work and start looking at the clock every three minutes. But Irina was still typing away with gusto. We were pleased to see the new gal had a solid work ethic, in addition to whatever hidden talents she might possess. A weak link in the Pool would only create more work for the rest of us. At five on the dot, we stood and asked Irina to join us at Martin's.

"Martini? Tom Collins? Singapore Sling?" Judy asked. "What's your poison?"

"I can't," Irina said, gesturing toward a stack of papers. "I have to catch up."

"Catch up on work?" Linda said when we were finally outside. "On her first day?"

"Did *you* meet with Frank on *your* first day?" Gail asked.

"Hell, I *still* haven't met with Frank," Norma said.

Cold stones of jealousy rattled in our stomachs and we wanted to know more. We wanted to know everything about the new Russian gal.

Irina took to the job quickly. Weeks passed and she never once asked for help. And thank God, as we didn't have time for handholding. Tensions had increased threefold in SR that November, after news spread of the failed uprising against the Soviet Union in Hungary—and our role in it. Encouraged by Agency propaganda efforts, Hungarian protesters had taken to the streets of Budapest to oppose their Soviet occupiers. They'd been under the impression that reinforcements would come from Western allies. No reinforcements came. The revolution lasted just twelve days before the Soviets put a violent end to it. The number of Hungarians the *Times* reported killed was horrifying, but the number we typed in our reports was even worse. They thought they were doing the right thing, that their well-laid plans would work. Our best men were on it. How could it fail? But the country was in ruins. The Agency *had* failed. Allen Dulles—the spy chief we'd see only when those of us with high enough clearance were asked to take notes at an important meeting—demanded answers, which the men struggled to provide.

We were asked to work late, to sit in during after-hours meetings. If we stayed past the time the buses and streetcars ran, they'd pay for our taxis home. Going into Thanksgiving, we feared they'd cancel our holiday time. Thankfully, they didn't.

Those of us whose families were a plane ride away would usually stay in Washington over the holiday, saving our paychecks for Christmas travel. We'd throw a potluck at whoever's apartment was the largest, or whoever's roommate was out of town. We'd bring a chair and a covered dish and even though we'd try to plan who brought what, we'd always end up with at least four pumpkin pies and enough turkey to last a week.

Those of us whose families were just a train or a bus ride away would go home. Our parents and siblings always welcomed us back like prodigal daughters. For them, Washington was more than a world away—it was a place where the nightly news was made. We'd be purposefully vague about our job duties, and our families thought our lives to be much more exciting than they were. We'd drop names like Nelson Rockefeller, Adlai Stevenson, and the impossibly handsome senator from Massachusetts, John Kennedy, saying we'd met these movers and shakers at various parties and events, though we were lucky if we knew someone who knew someone who'd met them.

For those of us who'd go back to our hometowns, the night before Thanksgiving always meant a big meet-up at a local bar. The old high school crowd would gather over cocktails and we'd wear our best heels and our softest cashmere and make sure our hair was done and that we had no lipstick on our teeth. Forgetting their wedding rings, the popular boys who'd ignored us in high school would tell us how great it was to see us and that we should come home more often. In D.C., we were part of the throngs of government gals, but in our hometowns, we'd made it.

We'd say our goodbyes to our old classmates with a "See ya next year" and go home, slightly tipsy, to at least one of our parents who'd tried waiting up for us but had fallen asleep on the couch. The next day, we'd cook turkey, then eat turkey, then nap, then eat more turkey, then nap again. *It was good to be home*, we'd tell our aunts and uncles and cousins. But within two days we'd be back on the bus or train to D.C., a turkey sandwich packed in our pocketbook.

When we returned the Monday after this particular Thanksgiving, we'd forgotten about Irina and were surprised to see her sitting at Tabitha's old desk. We were polite, asking what she'd done over the holiday, and she told us that she and her mother didn't really celebrate Thanksgiving, but that she had picked up two Swanson Hungry-Man turkey dinners, and that they were surprisingly good. "My mother ate half my peas and mashed potatoes when I got up to get another glass of wine," she said. We hadn't known Irina lived with her mother. And before we could ask any more questions, Anderson came by with bundles of paperwork. "Christmas came early, girls," he said.

We moaned. We envied our counterparts on Capitol Hill, who enjoyed long breaks when Congress wasn't in session. We had no such luck; the Agency never slept.

"Lotta work to catch up on, girls. Let's hop to it, huh?"

"Lotta stuffing you ate last week, huh?" Gail muttered when Anderson walked away.

We eventually got back to work, and the rest of the morning dragged. By eleven, we were already on our fifth Virginia Slim and looking at the clock. By noon, we were practically jumping out of our chair for lunch. Most of us had leftover turkey sandwiches, and Kathy had brought a Thermos of turkey noodle soup. But it was just one of those days when we had to get out of the office. The first day back from vacation, even a short one, was always the worst.

Linda stood first and cracked her knuckles. "Cafeteria?"

"Really?" asked Norma.

"Hot Shoppes?" Norma suggested. "I could go for an Orange Freeze."

"Too cold out," Judy said.

"Too *far*," said Kathy.

"La Niçoise?" Linda suggested.

"Not everyone has the luxury of a husband's salary," Gail said.

We looked at each other and said it together: "Ralph's?"

Not only did Ralph's serve the best damn doughnuts in the District, it also had the most delicious French fries, and ketchup that was made in house. Plus, the men never lunched there. They preferred the Old Ebbitt Grill, where they could feast on oysters and drink their fill of ten-cent martinis. Sometimes the men would invite us if they were feeling generous or amorous or both. They'd order trays of oysters and rounds of martinis for the table, even though Kathy had a shellfish allergy and Judy refused to eat anything hauled out of the ocean.

We asked Irina if she wanted to join us, because she was finally talking and we wanted to keep her talking. To our surprise, she agreed, even though we'd seen her put a sandwich dinner in the break room fridge that morning.

On our way out, Teddy Helms and Henry Rennet were coming in. We liked Teddy, but Henry was another matter. The men at the Agency thought we were just sitting in the corner typing away quietly. But we weren't just taking memos—we were also taking names. And Henry's was at the top of our list. Why Teddy and Henry were friends, we hadn't a clue. Henry was the kind of man whose confidence, not his looks, got him much in life—too much. Women, a high-ranking job right out of Yale, all the right Washington invites. Teddy was his opposite—someone who thought before he spoke, who was pensive and a little mysterious.

"You haven't introduced me to the new girl," Henry started in, even though we'd avoided eye contact with him. Teddy stood beside him, his hands in his pockets, looking sideways at Irina.

"The sharks have already begun to circle," whispered Kathy.

"Were you expecting an invitation to her coming-out party?" Norma asked, not exactly disguising her disdain for Henry. The previous summer, there'd been a rumor circling SR that he'd slept with Norma after a barbecue at Anderson's house. In reality, Henry had offered Norma a ride home and, at a stoplight, reached under her skirt and grabbed her. Norma didn't say a word. She just opened the car door and stepped out into the middle of traffic. Henry yelled out the window for her to stop being stupid and get back in the damn car as other drivers honked for her to get out of the way. She ended up walking the four miles home, and she didn't tell us for months about the incident.

"Of course," Henry said. "It's my business to know everything going on here."

"Is it?" Judy asked.

"I'm Irina." She extended her hand and Henry laughed.

"How quaint," Henry said, shaking her hand in that bone-crushing way of his. "Henry. Pleasure." He turned to Norma. "Now, that wasn't too hard, was it?"

"Teddy," Teddy said, extending his hand to Irina.

"Pleasure to meet you." It was clear Irina was just being polite, but judging from Teddy's shuffling schoolboy posture, he seemed smitten from the get-go.

"Well," Norma said, tapping an invisible watch. "Our lunch hour is now our lunch half hour."

Outside, we were met with a blast of wind. We tightened our scarves and Irina draped a fringed shawl over her head, then wrapped it around her neck. We wondered just how much of the old country was left in her. We wanted to warn Irina about Henry and also find out what she thought of Teddy right away but, not wanting anyone else to hear, decided to save it for Ralph's.

Christmas wreaths and garlands on every lamppost had already replaced the last traces of fall. We passed Kann's and stopped to watch as a young woman put the finishing touches on an elaborate winter wonderland display in the store's window. She placed individual pieces of silver tinsel on a bare cherry blossom branch, then stood back to admire her work. "So pretty," Irina said. "I just love Christmas."

"I thought Russians don't celebrate Christmas?" Linda asked. "The no religion thing and all?"

We looked at each other, unsure if Irina was offended by the remark. She tightened her shawl around her face, then said in a thick Russian accent, "Well, I was born here, wasn't I?" She smiled. We laughed, and felt the subtle walls of our group begin to expand.

CHAPTER 4

THE SWALLOW

"Remember the snake?" Walter Anderson asked, balancing his champagne over the railing of the *Miss Christin,* spilling it into the Potomac. Red-cheeked, more from the booze than from the brisk fall air, Anderson was holding court in front of six people who'd heard the story many times, myself included.

"Who could forget the snake?" I asked.

"Certainly not you, Sally." He gave me an exaggerated wink.

I loved teasing Anderson, and he loved dishing it right back. We'd both been stationed in Kandy during the war, working Morale Operations to steer the message toward the greater good. In other words, we were propagandists. Back then, he'd given his all to trying to get cozy with me, and when I rebuked him for the tenth time, he settled into a big brother role.

"Got something in your eye?" I asked. Most people found him obnoxious, but I thought Anderson was harmlessly corny.

The crowd ate it up. It was always like that: any time we all got together, the old stories would start up as the drinking wound down. After the war, most of them had moved on, creating new stories they were forbidden to speak about. So they told the old stories—the stories they'd told a hundred times before. The snake tale was an old standby of Anderson's. After his time in the OSS, rumor had it he'd attempted to write scripts in Hollywood. We'd heard he'd worked on a series of *Cloak and Dagger* meets *It Came from Outer Space* type treatments that got him some early meetings with producers but never got off the ground. He'd then decided to spend his days perfecting his backswing at the Columbia Country Club, but that got boring, and after a month or two, he knocked on Dulles's door—his actual door, in Georgetown—and asked for a job at the Agency. In his early fifties, Anderson was given an administrative role, although he'd begged to be put back into the field.

The old gang had gathered to celebrate an anniversary of sorts. Eleven years earlier, we'd left our posts in Ceylon, the war already over. The future of the OSS and American intelligence had remained uncertain. It'd be two years before the Agency would be created—two years before a home would be given to wayward OSS officers who'd grown tired of raking in the dough at their New York law firms and brokerage houses and wanted, even more than to serve their country again, the power that came from being a keeper of secrets. It was a power that some, myself included, found more intoxicating than any drug, sex, or other means of quickening one's heartbeat. We'd planned on celebrating our tenth anniversary, but it was postponed again and again until someone just set a date.

"Anyway," Anderson continued. "Honest to God, the fucker was twelve meters long."

"Thirty-nine feet?" one of the younger Agency men piped in.

"That's right, Henry, my boy. Mark my words, she was a man-eater. Killed half a dozen Burmese by the time I got called in."

"How do you know she was a *she*?" I asked.

"Believe me, Sally, only a female could've wreaked such havoc. And they needed a man to put her in her place."

"So why were *you* called in?" I said.

"Community relations," he said, straight-faced. "The snake was a menace. I'm telling you, she was something out of a horror flick. I swear to God, that snake still makes the occasional cameo in my nightmares. Just ask Prudy." He pointed to his wife, a petite woman with large yellow plastic earrings that made her earlobes droop, keeping warm inside the yacht's saloon with the other wives. She looked out the window and gave a little wave. "Anyway, she wouldn't come out of her hole— "

"Like this story!" someone yelled from the back of the crowd.

"It was more like a cave than a hole, really," he continued, ignoring the heckler. "She'd be in there for months. Sleeping, waiting. Then one day, she'd slither out and saddle up next to a cow. Then bam!" He clapped his hands for effect. "She'd drag the poor bovine back down the hole without so much as a moo. Really put a hurting on the village's economy. And we didn't want that, right?"

"Wouldn't be a horrible way to go," Frank Wisner said, joining the group. The circle split so the boss could take a front row seat for Anderson's story. Frank was the one who'd paid for the boat we were standing on, the alcohol we were drinking, and the shrimp cocktail we were eating. "Wouldn't know it was comin'," he continued in his Mississippi lilt. "Just standing in a grassy field somewhere, chewin' on some cud, perhaps contemplating whether to go down to the stream for a drink, and then—"

"Don' be morbid, Frank," Anderson said. "Jesus."

Anderson had started slurring his words—and when he slurred his words, the words he did manage to get out usually got him in trouble. With the boss in the mix now, I motioned for him to hurry up and finish the goddamn story.

"I oversaw the whole operation."

"Operation Kaa?" my friend Beverly asked. She half-laughed, half-hiccupped, and the crowd tittered.

"For the love of God, can I please go on?"

"No one's holding you back," Bev said, her voice high and throaty, indicating she was one too many glasses of bubbly over her limit. She was wearing a black Givenchy sack dress, bought on a recent trip to Paris. After the war, Bev had married an oil lobbyist, who kept her dressed in the latest fashions as long as she turned her head when he came home smelling like bourbon and knock-off Chanel No. 5. She hated the guy's guts, so she made sure the trade was as even as possible by buying everything as soon as it stepped off the runway, not to mention having the occasional dalliance of her own with her old OSS beaux. The sack dress did nothing to flatter her figure, but I gave her credit for attempting it.

Someone handed Anderson a flask. He took a swig and coughed. "Anyway. I brought ten men with me to the cave, hole, whatever you call it. Plan was to smoke her out, then bag her."

"What kind of bag's gonna hold a forty-foot snake?" Frank asked. He was smiling, egging Anderson on. They'd entered the OSS together, but Frank had risen to the top while Anderson stayed stuck in the middle. Frank was still handsome, still maintained the physique of the college track star he'd been thirty years earlier. He was the kind of man who believed anything was possible—especially with himself at the helm. But there was something off about him that night. Twice I'd seen him standing apart from the guests, looking out over the slowly churning Potomac. I wondered if the rumors were true that he'd suffered a breakdown after the Soviets put an end to the Hungarian uprising he'd helped orchestrate.

Anderson took another swig from the flask and cleared his throat. "Good question, boss. We sewed a bunch of burlap sacks together, then rigged a giant zipper down the middle."

Frank grinned. He already knew the ending, of course. "And it held?"

Anderson took another swig. "I had five guys holding the bag, two to zip it up when the snake came out, two standing by with pistols, and me supervising—just in case something went wrong."

"What could go wrong?" I asked.

"What couldn't?" Frank said, and the crowd laughed louder than the boss's joke warranted.

"I'll tell you!" Anderson answered. But before he could continue, the *Miss Christin* lurched and the engine stopped. Someone went to ask the captain what was going on and found him not on the bridge, but enjoying a drink in the saloon surrounded by the wives. The captain went to check with the engineer, who confirmed that a fuse had blown and said he'd call the marina for a tow back to the dock. Frank told the captain to wait another hour before calling, and the party continued, unmoored.

As we bobbed along, Anderson continued. He said they smoked the snake out of its hole with a tear gas canister and when the snake came out, they zipped her up in the bag, but the snake, a fighter, busted out within minutes. But not to worry, Anderson was standing by with his pistol. "Right between the eyes," he concluded.

"Poor thing," I said.

"Bullshit," Frank said.

Anderson placed his hand over his heart. "Swear to God."

Fact was, Anderson's wife, Prudy, had corroborated the story the first time I heard it—over a steak dinner at the Colony—confirming that the snakeskin was indeed stored away in their basement, slowly disintegrating in an old refrigerator box. "Why he ever brought that nasty thing home, I have no idea," she'd told me.

I squeezed Anderson's arm and excused myself and joined Bev on the stern.

She leaned in and lit my cigarette. "Hey, stranger," she said. "Story over yet?"

"Finally."

The Jefferson Memorial was lit up in the distance, the District asleep behind it. Under the orange night sky, the city looked peaceful, the power plays and constant angling at rest for the night.

"This isn't so bad, is it?" Bev asked.

"Not bad at all, Bev." I'd surprised myself by actually having a good time. After the war, I'd come back to Washington with the promise that I could land a job at the State Department. And I did. But instead of a cushy job at State with my own office, they stuck me in the basement sorting records. I could only take it for six months before I quit, after which, I distanced myself from the old boys' club.

I'd been many things, but I was no record keeper. I couldn't even pretend. I'd been a nurse, a waitress, an heiress. I once posed as a librarian. I'd been someone's wife, someone's mistress, fiancée, lover. I'd been Russian, French, and British. I'd been from Pittsburgh, Palm Springs, and Winnipeg. I could become just about anyone. I had one of those faces—the wide eyes, the ready smile that suggested I was an open book, someone who had no secrets to keep, and if she did, wouldn't be able to keep them anyway. That, and with the rise in popularity of actresses with more generous waistlines like Marilyn Monroe and Jayne Mansfield, my figure, which I'd attempted to diet away as a teenager, worked to my advantage in prying secrets out of powerful men.

I walked right out of there with my head held high, then rallied the girls for drinks followed by dancing at Café Trinidad until closing—which, in D.C., was unfortunately at midnight. But the next day, after I nursed my hangover with a cold compress and a Bloody Mary, I had a minor breakdown at the realization I had no job, no income, and no savings. The last due to one of my blessings and curses: a heightened appreciation for beautiful things. The blessing was that my innate sense of style made people think I was born with a silver spoon in my mouth in a place like Grosse Point or Greenwich, and not a clapboard row house in Pittsburgh's

Little Italy. The curse was that my good eye often exceeded my means.

I knew I needed to formulate a plan before my bank account dwindled to Code Red level. There was no running to Mommy or Daddy, as some of my friends had the luxury of doing when times got tough. That evening, I'd flipped through my little black book and set up a stream of dates with the D.C. lobbyist and lawyer set, an occasional diplomat, and one or two congressmen. The dates were tedious and exhausting, but at the end of the day, the rent was paid on my Georgetown apartment, I'd gotten some nice dinners out of them, and the men whose company I'd pretended to enjoy kept me in couture that rivaled Bev's. I was not attracted to them, and yet how easy it had been to convince them that I was.

That line of "work" suited me fine. But after a while, I grew bored with the taxi, dinner, hotel, taxi, dinner, hotel rotation. That and the high level of personal upkeep were wearing me out. The brushing, tweezing, plucking, dyeing, waxing, bleaching, squeezing—even the endless shopping—were beginning to take their toll.

I thought of becoming a stewardess. For one, I'd look great in Pam Am's signature blue. Plus, I loved to travel. It's what I liked most during the war—the possibility of being uprooted to a new place every few months. But they'd take one look at my age—thirty-two if I was being honest or thirty-six if I was *actually* honest—and say I was "overqualified" for the position.

The truth was, I missed intelligence work, missed being in the know. So when Bev rang one last time to beg me to go to the party, I said yes.

"So many familiar faces," Bev said, scanning the crowd. The music had started up again and people were dancing and spilling their gin fizzes on one another. I spotted Jim Roberts across the deck, breathing down some poor girl's neck. Jim had once cornered me at an embassy party in Shanghai, putting his hands around my waist and saying he wasn't going to let me go until I gave him a smile. I did smile, then I kneed him in the groin.

"Maybe a few too many familiar faces."

"I'll toast to that," she said. Bev leaned over the rail and brushed a piece of her dark brown hair out of her face. Bev was the kind of woman whose beauty came late, passing over her high school years, college years, and early twenties entirely, only to arrive in her late twenties and not reach its full glory until her thirties. Bev had had many Jim Roberts experiences herself. "But still," she continued. "I wish all the girls could've been here."

"Me too." Bev and I were the only two of our old crew still living in Washington. Julia was in France with her new husband, Jane was in Jakarta with someone else's husband, and Anna was in either Venice or Madrid, depending on what mood she was in that month. Our group had first met on the *Mariposa*, a former luxury liner recommissioned to shuttle GIs to the front line. The only women on board, we shared a cramped cabin outfitted with metal bunks, one toilet, and a tub that sputtered cold salt water. Despite the camp-like conditions and the seasickness, we all got along famously. We were in our early twenties and ready to take on the world. We were the kind of girls who'd grown up reading *Treasure Island* and *Robinson Crusoe*, then graduated to H. Rider Haggard's *She* in high school. We bonded over the belief that a life of adventure wasn't reserved for men, and we set out to claim our piece of it.

Most important, we shared a similar sense of humor, which went a long way when sharing one toilet with questionable flushing abilities—especially when the ship hit rougher seas. Julia loved to play pranks and once started a rumor that we were a group of Catholic nuns headed to Calcutta. The men, who'd been catcalling us any chance they could get, became reverent when passing us in the corridors. One soldier had even asked if we'd pray for his sick dog. I made the sign of the cross and Bev burst out laughing.

By the time the *Mariposa* made landfall in Ceylon, we were inseparable, and held tight to each other in the back of a thick-wheeled truck that jettisoned us through the jungle to the port at Kandy. Surrounded by tea plantations and electric green terraced rice paddies that spilled down from the hills, Kandy, though just across the bay from the terror unfolding in Burma, felt as far away from the war as one could get.

Many of us would remember our time in Kandy fondly. And when we'd write each other—or, if we were lucky, catch up in person—we'd reminisce about the many nights spent under a sky so large and so dark the stars would reveal themselves in layers. We'd recount slicing papayas off the trees surrounding the thatched-roofed OSS offices with a rusty machete, or the time an elephant got into our compound and had to be enticed out with a jar of peanut butter. We'd recall the all-night parties at the Officers' Club, dangling our legs in blue-green Kandy Lake and yanking them back out when we disturbed some bubbling creature lurking beneath. There were the throngs of monks making their way to and from the Temple of the Sacred Tooth Relic, the sweaty weekends in Colombo, the leaf monkey we'd named Matilda who'd given birth in our food hut.

I'd started out as MO support staff—filing papers, typing, that sort of thing. But my career trajectory changed when I received an invitation to attend a dinner at Earl Louis Mountbatten's lavish residence up on the hill, overlooking the OSS compound. It was the first of many parties I'd attend and the first time I'd discover that powerful men would willingly give information to me, whether I asked for it or not.

That's how it started. That first party, I'd squeezed myself into a low-cut black evening gown Bev had packed "just in case," and by the end of the night, a Brazilian arms dealer who'd been chatting me up let slip that he believed there was a mole within Mountbatten's staff. I reported the tip to Anderson the next day. What the OSS did with that information, I have no idea. But I was soon inundated with more dinner invitations, set up with visiting people of import, and given questions to ask loose-lipped men.

I got good at my new job—so good I was given a stipend to purchase gowns we'd have shipped in with our toilet paper, Spam, and mosquito repellent. The funny thing was, I never thought of myself as a spy. Surely the craft took more than smiling and laughing at stupid jokes and pretending to be interested in everything these men said. There wasn't a name for it back then, but it was at that first party that I became a Swallow: a woman who uses her God-given talents to gain information—talents I'd been accumulating since puberty, had refined in my twenties, and then perfected in my thirties. These men thought they were using me, but it was always the reverse; my power was making them think it wasn't.

"Wanna dance?" Bev asked.

I wrinkled my nose as Bev shimmied her hips. "To this?" I yelled over the Perry Como. Bev didn't care. She took hold of my arms and moved them back and forth until I gave in. Just as I was getting into the swing of things, someone shut off the record player with a scratch. From the back of the crowd, someone clinked his fork against a glass, and the rest of the crowd joined in until the entire boat sounded like a chandelier in a windstorm.

"Oh boy," Bev said. "Here we go."

The men began with the toasts: *To Frank! To Wild Bill! To the Old Standby Stooges! To the Otherwise Sad Sacks!* Then came the songs we used to close out the night with back in Kandy: "I'll Be Seeing You" and "Lili Marlene," followed by their not-so-secret clubs' songs from Harvard and Princeton and Yale. Bev and I always snickered at the drunken musicale that rounded out every party—but that night, we couldn't help but link arms and join in.

The toot of an approaching tugboat come to tow us back to the marina interrupted the third round of Yale's " 'Neath the Elms." We yelled for the tug captain to come join us for a nightcap. Not very happy to be dragged out of bed to come and rescue the drunken lot of us, he and another man went to work tethering the *Miss Christin.*

Back on dry ground, the men debated whether to head to the Social Club on Sixteenth or the twenty-four-hour diner on U Street. Bev and I said our goodbyes in front of the black sedan her husband had sent, promising not to let so much time pass before seeing each other again. "Are you sure you don't need a ride?" she asked.

"I could use the air."

"Suit yourself!" She blew me a kiss from the open window as the car pulled away.

Someone tapped me on the shoulder. "Can I walk with you?" asked Frank. "I could use some air too," he said, his breath minty with a hint of tobacco. He seemed perfectly sober. I wondered if he'd been sipping Coca-Cola the whole night. "We're going in the same direction, right?"

Frank lived down the street from me, but in terms of real estate, his Georgetown townhouse was light-years away from my small apartment above a French bakery. "Indeed we are," I said. Frank wasn't the kind of man who'd ask to walk a girl home with ill intentions; he'd never made a pass at me as long as I'd known him. If Frank said he wanted to talk, he usually wanted to talk business. He signaled to his driver, who was standing by the open door of his black sedan. "I'll be walking tonight," he called out. The driver tipped his hat and closed the door.

We walked away from the Potomac, through downtown Washington's sleeping streets. "I'm happy you came," he said. "I hoped Beverly could talk you into coming."

"She was in on it?"

"Is she ever *not* in on it?"

I laughed. "No, I suppose not."

He was silent again, as if he'd forgotten why he'd asked me to walk with him.

"You could've told your driver to go home earlier, before making him wait all night."

"Didn't know I was gonna want to walk," he said. "Not until I made up my mind."

"Made up your mind?"

"Do you miss it?"

"All the time," I said.

"I envy that. I really do."

"Do you wish you'd stopped? After the war?"

"I never used to think about the *what ifs*," said Frank. "But now . . . I'm not so sure. Things aren't as black-and-white as they used to be."

We arrived at the bakery. The lights were on, the morning baker already loading baguettes into the oven. I'd chosen to live there not only because it was in my price range when I started at State, but also because I love the smell of fresh-baked bread even more than I like eating it.

"I hear you're looking for a new line of work."

"Can't keep a secret from you, Frank."

He laughed. "No, you really can't."

"Why? Have you heard of something?"

He gave a tight-lipped smile. "Well, I've got something that may be of interest."

I tilted my ear toward him.

"It's about a book."

EAST

1950–1955

CHAPTER 5

~~THE MUSE~~

THE REHABILTATED WOMAN

Respected Anatoli Sergeyevich Semionov,
  *This is not the letter you've long sought. This is not
about the book. This is not the confession that would
prove the crimes you've assigned to me. Nor is it a plea
for my innocence. I am innocent of what I've been
accused of, but not of everything. I've taken a man for
my own, knowing he had a wife. I've failed at being a
good daughter, a good mother—my own mother left to
pick up the pieces I've left behind. All that is over now,
and yet still I feel the need to write.*
  *You may believe every word I write with this pencil
I traded two sugar rations for, or you may take it for
a work of fiction. No matter. I'm not writing for you;
you are only a name at the top of my letter. And I will*

never send this letter. Each page will be burned as I finish. Your name is a mere salutation to me now.

You said I didn't tell you everything during our nightly talks, that I left great holes in my "stories." As an interrogator, you must know how unreliable memory can be. One's mind can never get the entire story straight. But I will try.

I have this one sharpened pencil. It is smaller than my thumb, and my wrist already aches. But I will write until it wears down and turns to dust.

But where to start? Should I begin with this moment? How I spent my day, my eighty-sixth of the 1,825 days it will take to make me a rehabilitated woman? Or should I start with what has already transpired? Do you want to know about my 600-kilometer journey to this place? Have you been on the trains that go to nowhere? Have you visited the windowless wooden boxes they kept us shivering in while we waited to be shuttled to the next location? Do you know what it's like to live on the edge of the world, Anatoli? So far from Moscow, from your family, from every warm thing and every kindness?

Do you want to know that during the final stage of our journey, the guards forced us to walk? How it was so cold that when the woman walking next to me collapsed and they pried her boot from her foot, she left her smallest toe inside? Or how I shared a train compartment with a woman with two skinny braids that ran the length of her long back who claimed to have drowned her two small children in the bath? How when someone asked her why she did it, she replied that a voice that still won't shut up had told her to? Should I tell you how she woke up screaming?

No, Anatoli, I won't write to you of these worries. Really, for what you must know, these details would likely bore you, and I do not wish to bore you. What I wish is for you to keep reading.

Let me go back.

After Moscow, we arrived first to a transit camp, run by female guards—a slight improvement over the conditions where you and I met. The cells were clean and cement-floored, and they smelled of ammonia. Each woman in our cell, Cell No. 142, had her own mattress, and the guards turned the lights off at night and let us finally sleep.

But not for long.

Days after arriving, they came at night and emptied out Cell No. 142. They boarded us onto the trains and told us the next stop, the only stop, was Potma. The train was dark and smelled like rotting wood. Iron bars separated each compartment from the corridor, so the guards could see us at all times. There were two metal buckets in the corner—one our toilet, the other full of lye with which to cover our mess. I claimed a spot on an upper berth, where I could lie down and stretch my legs. And if I tilted my head just so, I could see a sliver of sky through the cracks in the ceiling. If it wasn't for that tiny sky, I wouldn't have known when it was day or night, or how many days and nights had passed since we boarded.

It was night when the train came to a stop.

It looked more like a manger than a train station. But instead of sheep or donkeys, men in worn army uniforms with dogs that resembled stout lions awaited us on the platform. The guards yelled for us to get out, and we looked at each other wildly. When no one got up, a guard grabbed a young woman with short red hair by the arm and told her to get in line. We followed in silence.

The guard at the front held up a hand and the march commenced. As we left the platform, we realized there would be no other train or truck to take us the rest of the way. I pulled the sleeves of my coat to cover my balled-up hands. They were warm then, but they wouldn't be for long.

We cut a path through the virgin snow, following the train tracks until they stopped and disappeared into white. No one asked how long the march would be, but that's all we could think about. Would it be two hours or two days? Or two weeks? Instead, I attempted to focus on the footsteps of the woman in front of me, whose name I never knew. I tried to fit my own foot-prints neatly inside the ones she'd left behind. I tried not to think of the way my toes and fingers had begun to tingle, how the snot in my nose dripped and froze in the dimple above my upper lip—the same dimple Borya often touched with a fingertip when teasing me.

It was something out of Doctor Zhivago. Yes, Anatoli, something out of the book you long to read. Our march felt as if it had sprung from Borya's mind. The moon was full and illuminated the snow-covered road, casting a silvery glow on our footprints. It was a deathly beauty, and maybe if I'd had any sense left in me, I would've run out into the woods that lined the road, running and running until my body gave out, or until someone stopped me. I think I would've liked to die there, in that place that felt as if it were conjured from Borya's dreams.

First, the guard towers—each capped with a dull red star—peeked out from the tops of the tall pines in the distance. Then, as we got closer: the barbed wire fence, the barren yard, the lines of barracks, a thin plume of smoke connecting the gray sky to each building's chimney. A malnourished rooster walked the fence's perimeter, its beak cracked, its red comb mangled.

We'd arrived.

I cannot speak for all of us, but I'd spent every second, every minute, every hour, every day of our four-day march dreaming of warmth. And yet, when they herded us through the barbed wire fence and we were allowed to warm ourselves by the fires burning in tin drums in the courtyard, I'd never felt colder.

On the far side of the yard, forty or fifty women stood in a line, holding metal plates and mugs, awaiting dinner. They turned when we approached and appraised our pale faces, our full heads of hair, our hands: frost-bitten, yes, but uncalloused. We looked at their jaundiced faces, their kerchiefed or shaved heads, their broad, hunched shoulders. Soon it would be like looking into a mirror. Soon it would be us standing in line for dinner while a new group of women began their rehabilitation.

A dozen female guards appeared and the men who'd marched us there turned and silently walked back into the snow. We were led into a long building with a cement floor and stove. There, the guards instructed us to strip. We stood naked, shivering while they ran their fingers through our hair, then across our bodies, lifting our arms and checking under our breasts. They made us spread our fingers, our toes, our legs. They stuck their fingers in our mouths. I began to warm up, but not from the wood stove. I burned with an anger I still have not yet begun to process. Have you felt such an anger, Anatoli? An anger burning somewhere inside you that you can't pinpoint but that can overtake you like a match to petrol? Does it come for you at night, as it comes for me? Is that why you're in the position you are in now? Is power, no matter the cost, the only cure?

After the search, we got in another line. There's always another line in the Gulag, Anatoli. They handed us pieces of lye soap, just slivers, and turned on the showers. The water was cold but felt scalding hot on our frozen skin. We air-dried and were dusted with a powder to kill whatever we may have brought with us.

A Polish woman with beautiful wisps of flaxen hair framing her otherwise bald head sat at a table mending smocks the color of an overcast day. She looked us each over and pointed to either the stack of smocks on her right or the stack on her left: large and larger.

Then a woman with prominent ears and an even more prominent nose who didn't even attempt to guess our right size gave us shoes. I stepped into the black leather shoes, and as I went to walk, my heels came out. It would take a month of saving up my sugar rations until I could barter with another prisoner—not for a new pair of shoes, which would have cost me at least three months of sugar, but for a ream of tape with which to fasten them to my feet.

The guards split the line into three and I followed my line into Barrack No. 11. I'd live there for the next three years, Anatoli, shuffling my feet so I didn't lose a shoe.

Barrack No. 11 was empty, its current residents still at work in the cornfields. A guard pointed to the empty bunks, three layered on top of each other, in the back of the room, farthest from the wood-burning stove. We ducked under the clothesline strung from wall to wall, where women had hung their washed but stained socks and underthings. The building smelled of sweat and onions and warm bodies. It smelled of the living; a small comfort.

I placed the wool blanket I'd been given onto the top bunk, second from the back. I chose that bunk because a petite woman I'd noticed on the train took the one below it. I guessed her to be around my age, midthirties, with black hair and delicate hands, and I thought perhaps we could become friends. Her name was Ana.

I never made friends with Ana. Nor did I make friends with any of the other women in Barrack No. 11. At the end of each day, we were exhausted and needed to conserve our energy to get out of bed and do it again the next day.

That first night in Potma was quiet. All nights were like that, only the howls of the wind to soothe us to sleep. Sometimes we could hear the cry of a woman who'd succumbed to loneliness ring out across the camp like an air raid siren. The woman would be quickly quieted—how, we could only imagine. And although no one spoke of those cries, we all heard them, and we all silently joined in.

My first day in the fields, the earth was hard and frozen, and the pick too heavy for me to raise above my waist. My hands were blistered within half an hour. I used all my strength just to pierce the soil—just a chip, the width of a finger. The woman next to me was having better luck, having been given a shovel that she could step on, so that her weight would force its tip into the ground. But I had only a pick, and a few cubic meters of earth to be upturned before I'd be given my ration for the day.

That first day of my rehabilitation, I didn't eat anything.

My second day of rehabilitation, I didn't eat again.

On my third day, I still could make but a few dents in the earth, so was denied rations yet again. But a young nun broke off a piece of her bread and handed it to me as I passed her in line for the bathhouse. I was thankful, and for the first time since the men had taken me in my apartment in Moscow, I thought that maybe I should start praying.

The nuns of Potma fascinated me, Anatoli. They were a small group from Poland and tougher than the most hardened criminals. They refused to back down when they didn't agree with a guard's order. They prayed aloud during morning reveille, which infuriated the guards but gave me comfort, despite not being an overly religious woman myself. Sometimes the guards would make an example of their insolence by dragging one out of line by her smock and making her kneel in front of us. One nun was forced to kneel like that for an entire day, her bare knees pressed into the rocky soil. But she never gave in, never asked to stand—praying the whole time with the serene smile of a Holy Fool. They used their fingers to count beads on invisible rosaries, even as their faces burned under the unforgiving sun, even as urine trickled from their smocks and cut a path through the dirt.

Once or twice, the guards threw the whole lot of them into the punishment block—the first barrack built at the camp, where the roof had half caved in and the cold air rushed in, along with insects and rats.

It was hard not to be jealous of the nuns, even though their sentences far exceeded my own. They had one another, and no need for word from the outside world, something the rest of us craved. Even when they were separated, they never succumbed to the dark loneliness that plagued us all. They had the company of their God. My only faith was put into a man: my Borya, a mere mortal, a poet. And having been unable to contact him since the men took me from my apartment, I didn't know whether he was dead or alive.

By the fourth day of my rehabilitation, a thick callus had developed on my once soft hands and I could finally grip the pick. I swung it overhead and into the earth with surprising force. By day's end, I'd turned over my assigned piece of earth and was finally given rations, of which I could eat only a few bites. My body had adapted faster than my mind. Isn't that the way it always works, Anatoli?

Those first few terrible days, then weeks, then months, then years, passed—not in days on a calendar but in holes dug, number of lice picked from my hair. They passed in blisters cracked and calluses made from shoveling, in cockroaches killed under our bunks, in the number of visible ribs. And there were only two seasons: summer and winter; each as punishing as the other.

I learned what human bodies need to survive, how very little we require. I could survive on 800 grams of bread, two cubes of sugar, and soup so thin it was hard to tell whether it was actual food or seawater.

But the mind takes so much more to survive, and Borya was never far from mine. I used to think I could feel it when he thought of me—that the tingle I felt whispering across the back of my neck or down the length of my arms was him. I felt it for months. Then one year passed without that feeling, that tingle, then another. Did that mean he was dead? If they sent me to the Gulag, surely what they did to him must've been even worse.

Anatoli, I can tell you now that my five-year sentence was a blessing and a curse. Only bourgeois Muscovites had such pitiful sentences, a fact I was reminded of again and again by our barrack brigade leader—a Ukrainian woman named Buinaya, who was sentenced to ten years for stealing a sack of flour from her collective farm. She was strong and severe and everything I was not. Over time, I grew stronger in the field, but I was still one of the slowest workers, and Buinaya made a point of making me the primary recipient of her sharp tongue.

Once, after coming in from the fields, I was too tired to bathe and went directly to my bunk, so exhausted I didn't even remove my dirt-encrusted smock. Just as I shut my eyes, I heard Buinaya's unmistakable voice. "Number 3478!" she called out like a magpie with a cough, using my prison number as the guards did.

I didn't stir. But she called out my number again, and Ana tapped the underside of my bed. When I didn't respond, she kicked it. "Answer her or there'll be trouble," she whispered.

I sat up. "Yes?"

"I thought you Muscovites were a cleanly people. You smell like shit."

A ripple of laughter erupted across Barrack No. 11 and I felt the burn of embarrassment spread across my chest and up my neck to my cheeks. I did smell, although there were women in the barracks who smelled far worse.

"I was born in a dugout," she continued, "and even I was taught to wash my crotch at least once a week. No wonder only traitor poets will go near yours. Isn't that why you're here?"

The laughter rose as I swung my legs over the edge of the bunk and got down. My legs shook so hard I was sure they were vibrating the floorboards. I could feel every eye on me, awaiting my response. But I hesitated, and turned to face the wall, which made Buinaya, then the rest, laugh even harder. She picked up a small pile of her dirty underthings and marched down the middle of the barracks until she reached my bunk. "Here," she said, dumping the clothes on the floor. "While you're cleaning your filthy body, you don't mind washing some of my things as well? Of course not."

Anatoli, I'd like to report that I turned away from the wall and threw Buinaya's dirty things back in her face. That I stood my ground and slapped her, which provoked a fight that left me bruised the next day. That although I'd lost the fight, I'd gained Buinaya's respect.

But I didn't. I took her dirty things to the wash basin and scrubbed them with my lye ration, then carefully hung them to dry in the best spot next to the wood-burning stove. Then I stripped and washed myself in the cold, cloudy water. Then I slept. Then it happened again the next day.

If I were to give you now what you'd asked for during our late-night chats in Lubyanka, Anatoli, would it do me any good? Would my sentence be lessened if I cooperated now? If I were to confess to every last charge, could I leave this place? If I took the sharp end of my pick and used all my force, could I end things for good?

One might think winter would be worse, but the summers are what wore us down most. As we worked the fields, digging or pulling or hauling, sweat pooled under our gray smocks. We called those smocks "devil's skins" as they didn't allow our skin to breathe and the pools of sweat wouldn't evaporate. We developed sores and rashes and attracted black flies with vicious bites. To shield us from the sun, we stretched gauze over rusted wire to fashion hats that resembled a beekeeper's. Other women, their hide already tanned from a decade or more in the fields, laughed at our hats, at our precious porcelain Muscovite skin. They were thirty or forty but looked sixty or seventy. They knew it would be only a matter of time before we'd give up trying to block the sun—before we'd turn our faces up and let the rays take from us the last remainder of the people we were before coming to Potma.

We were in the fields twelve hours at a time, Anatoli. I'd pass those hours reciting Borya's poems in my head—timing the rhythm of each line, each break, with the clang of my shovel.

In the evenings, when we came back from the fields and they ran their hands over our bodies to ensure we hadn't brought anything back to the barracks, I ran Borya's words through my mind, deadening what was happening to my body.

I'd also compose poems of my own, the lines appearing in my head as they would on paper. I'd say them to myself again and again until they were cemented. But for some reason I cannot recite them now, when I have the paper to write them down. Maybe certain poems are meant only for oneself.

They called for me one evening after I'd finished washing Buinaya's dirty clothes. I was about to lie down when a new guard, who hadn't quite mastered the tone of voice the other guards used when barking orders, entered the barracks and called out my number in her singsong way. I put on my smock and shoes and followed her out the door.

When the guard turned left at the end of the path that cut through the barracks, I realized where we were going: the small cottage whose upkeep was given to prisoners who'd gained favor with the camp's Godfather.

The style of the cottage did not fit with the rest of the camp, and the first time I saw it, I thought I might've been hallucinating. It resembled a grandmother's dacha—bright green with white trim and neat flower boxes lining the windows.

In one window, I could see the glow of a red-shaded lamp. Beyond that, I could see, sitting at a desk, the Godfather—a man I'd seen only once before, standing at the center of a semicircle of lower-level government officials who'd once toured Potma. Even from a distance, I could see his thick white eyebrows. They seemed to stretch up his forehead, almost touching the white hair he'd combed down across his bald spot. He looked friendly, seated there at his desk like any dedushka. But I knew from some of the other women that he was no harmless grandfather. The Godfather's job was to inter-rogate prisoners and recruit informers. He was also widely known to have taken several camp wives—women who were called into the green cottage and given the option of either letting him do whatever he wanted with them or face the rest of their sentences in another camp, where the most violent offenders were taken.

The camp wives were identifiable by the silk robes they'd wear after bathing and the large straw hats they wore to shield their faces from the sun. They were also taken out of the fields to work the easier jobs in the kitchen or laundry. Or they simply spent hours tending to the cottage's hedges and flowers—and then whatever else needed tending to on the inside. Each of the camp *wives was beautiful, the prettiest among them an eighteen-year-old named Lena. I never saw Lena, but her famed black hair, long and sleek as an orca's back, was talked about across the camp. It was rumored that Lena had been given special shampoo the Godfather had smuggled in from France, and a pair of calfskin gloves to protect her slender fingers, as she had been a promising pianist in Georgia before her arrest. It was also rumored she was pregnant once, and a babki was brought in with her knitting needles to perform the abortion.*

These were rumors, only rumors, I told myself as the guard pointed her truncheon at the cottage door. I told myself I was too old for the Godfather's taste, which I'd heard was for women who'd yet to have children or reach the age of twenty-two—whichever came first.

I entered the two-room cottage and stood at the door. The Godfather sat at his desk, writing. I wanted him to speak, but all he did was point his fountain pen to the chair in front of his desk. Ten minutes passed before he put down his pen and looked at me. Without a word, he opened his desk drawer and handed me a parcel. "For you. These cannot leave this office. You must read them here." He pushed a piece of paper toward me. "And when you're finished, you will sign that you've seen it."

"What is it?"

"Nothing of importance."

Inside the parcel was a twelve-page letter and a small green notebook. I opened it, but the words didn't register.

All I could see was the handwriting—his handwriting—broad scrawls that always reminded me of soaring cranes. I flipped through the notebook, then the letter, and the words started to register. Borya was alive. He was free. And he'd written me a poem.

I won't share the poem with you, Anatoli. Did you think I would? I read it over and over again until I committed it to memory, then I never saw the actual pages again. Maybe you've already read them, but I will pretend you haven't—that his words are mine and mine alone.

In the letter, he wrote he was doing everything in his power to get me out, and if he could change places with me, he would do so gladly. He said the guilt was a weight on his chest that grew heavier each day. He said he feared the weight would become so heavy, his ribs would crack and he'd be crushed to death.

Reading the letter, I felt something I think only the nuns of the camp could understand—the warmth and protection of faith.

Why was I allowed to read what Borya had written me, Anatoli? Why had the Godfather given the letter to me after all that time? Perhaps he wanted something in return. Whatever it was, I knew then that I would do it. I'd become an informer, I'd become a camp wife—whatever it took as long as I could hear from him.

But, Anatoli, the Godfather never asked that I become his wife, nor did he groom me to become an informer. Only later did I discover that Borya had demanded proof I was still alive, and that they had sent him some months later the piece of paper I had signed that night after reading his letter.

It was rumored that Stalin was sick and his reins were loosening. After my night in the cottage, I was allowed to receive mail from my family and Borya. He wrote of his heart attack, a condition he attributed to my arrest, and how he spent months in a hospital bed fearing he'd never see me again.

He wrote of his renewed obsession with finishing his novel now that he was well again and could be in contact with me. He said he'd finish it at all costs, and nothing—not the authorities who were likely reading his letters, nor his bad heart—would keep him from doing so.

Dear Anatoli, do you remember the night before Stalin died? I dreamed of birds that night. Not the white doves I'd been longing for—which the women of the camp believed signaled one's imminent release—but of black crows, thousands sitting in rows like chess pawns in an empty concrete lot. The crows barely appeared to be breathing, and when I walked toward them and clapped my hands, they remained still. I clapped and clapped until my hands were raw. And when I turned to walk away, some inaudible signal propelled them to take flight. They swarmed into a beating cloud that covered the moon. I watched as the cloud shifted to the right, then left. Then, all at once, the cloud dissipated in all directions, each bird going her own way.

The next morning, the music started before dawn, blaring from the camp's loudspeakers. We all seemed to sit up at once, squinting until our eyes adjusted to the darkness. Funeral music—they were playing funeral music. No one in Barrack No. 11 said a word. No one asked who had died. We already knew.

As the music continued, we splashed cold water on our faces from the bathing trough and dressed in our smocks, not knowing if we'd be summoned. When no roll call came, we sat on our bunks and waited in silence. Buinaya went to the door, cracking it open and sticking her head out. "Nothing," she said, shaking her head.

The music stopped and the loudspeakers crackled. We heard the needle hit a record, then our national anthem began. We looked around, not knowing whether to sit or stand and sing. A few women stood, then the rest of us followed. The anthem finished and we remained standing. There was a moment of silence before the speakers crackled again and the familiar, deep voice of Radio Moscow's Yuri Borisovich Levitan announced, "The heart of the collaborator and follower of the genius of Lenin's work, the wise leader and teacher of the Communist Party and of the Soviet people, has stopped beating."

The recording ended and we knew we were supposed to cry. And we did. We cried until our eyes were swollen and throats raw. But not one tear dropped for him.

Soon after the Red Tsar fell, my five years were cut to three. I'd be home by 25 April. Stalin's death prompted *our new leaders to release 1.5 million of us. When I received the letter stating the date of my release, I went back to Barrack No. 11 and looked into the jagged piece of mirror hanging above the bathing trough. I had the bronzed look of someone who'd spent years in the camps. My eyes were still cornflower blue, but framed by wrinkles and dark bags. My nose was spotted from sunburns. My figure was not the picture of health but of survival: my clavicle sticking out, each rib visible, my thighs thin as sticks, my blond hair dull and lifeless, my front tooth chipped from a pebble in my soup.*

What would Borya think? I thought back to the time he told me he feared seeing his sisters again after years of being apart, after they'd emigrated to Oxford. He said he almost preferred to not see them again, to keep the pretty young visions he had of them intact. Would he feel the same way about me? Would he look at me as he had his wife—someone he no longer shared a bed with? Would he compare me with my own daughter, someone he'd seen grow into a beautiful young woman while I aged beyond my years? "Ira's become the very picture of her mother," he'd written me in a postcard.

Buinaya, who had yet to receive amnesty, walked behind me as if going to wash her face, then turned and pushed me into the makeshift mirror. Shards of glass dropped to the floor and I stumbled back, a thin line of blood dripping from my forehead. She smiled at me and I smiled back, blood trickling into my mouth. She scowled and walked away. And that was the last I saw of her. But when I heard that those who had not received amnesty eventually rose up—and that during that uprising, the fields and the Godfather's cottage and the whole camp had burned to the ground—I imagined Buinaya was the one who'd lit the match.

I boarded the train to Moscow a rehabilitated woman, Anatoli. The city had grown in bounds during the three years I'd been gone. Cranes hoisted steel beams. Factories had taken the place of fields. Between the old two-story buildings made from logs, blocks of apartments had sprung up with thousands of windows and thousands of laundry lines stretching across their thousands of balconies. Stalin's baroque and gothic vysotki reached for the sky with their star-topped towers, changing the cityscape and announcing to the world that we, too, could build buildings that touched the clouds.

It was April and the city was on the brink of spring. I'd come home just in time for the purple lilacs and tulips and beds of red and white pansies to emerge from their winter slumber. I imagined walking along Moscow's wide boulevards with Borya again. I closed my eyes to savor the picture, and when I opened them again, the train had arrived. I looked anxiously down the tracks. He said he'd be waiting for me.

CHAPTER 6

THE CLOUD DWELLER

Boris wakes. His first thought is of a train lighting a path through the countryside, bound for the White-Stoned Mother. Under a thin quilt, he flexes his feet and pictures Olga's rounded cheek pressed against the train's window. How he'd loved watching her sleep, even the way she snored, soft as a distant factory whistle.

In six hours, the train carrying his beloved will pull in to the station. Olga's mother and children will wait at the edge of the tracks, standing on tiptoes to be the first to see her step off the train. In five hours, Boris is to meet her family at their apartment on Potapov Street, so that they may all go to the station together.

Three years since he heard her voice. Three years since he touched her. The last time was on a bench in the public gardens outside the editorial offices of *Goslitizdat*. As they made plans for the evening, Olga had remarked on the presence of a man in a leather duster who seemed to be listening to their conversation. Boris had looked the man over and decided he was just a man sitting on a bench. "That's all," he told her.

"Are you sure?"

He squeezed her hand.

"Maybe you should stay with me instead of going home?" she asked.

"I must work, my love, but will see you tonight in Peredelkino. She's in Moscow for two days," he said, careful to never speak his wife's name in Olga's presence. "We can relax and have a late supper. And I'd like to get your thoughts on a new chapter."

She agreed to the plan and kissed him on the cheek in the chaste way she did in public. He hated it when she kissed him like that, feeling more like an uncle, or, worse, her father.

Had he known their meeting on the park bench would be the last time he'd see Olga in three years, he would've turned his head and kissed her on her lips. He wouldn't have rushed home to work. He would've believed her about the man in the leather coat. He wouldn't have let go of her hand.

That evening, Boris waited for Olga to arrive at his dacha, but after many hours passed with no sign of her, he knew something was wrong. He went straight to Olga's apartment, where her mother was sitting—nearly catatonic and fingering a giant slit in the sofa cushion. She looked up blankly when Boris entered the room, and answered his questions in pieces. "Men in black suits," she said. "Two . . . no, three . . . all of her letters, her books . . . a black car." Boris didn't need exact answers to know who the men were or where they'd taken Olga.

"Where are the children?" he'd asked.

She picked up a black-and-white goose feather from the erupting cushion and rubbed it between her fingers.

"Are they here? Are they safe?"

When Olga's mother didn't answer, Boris went to the children's bedroom, and he was both relieved and heartbroken to hear Mitya and Ira's muted crying from behind the closed door.

He turned and was surprised to see Olga's mother standing in the hallway behind him. Before he could ask another question, she pelted him with her own. "You will go and get her, won't you? To demand her release? To undo everything?" She waved the goose feather in his face. "To make up for everything you've done. The danger you've put her in."

Boris had promised Olga's mother he'd go straight to Lubyanka and do everything in his power to save her daughter. He hadn't told her that he had no power at all, that it would be futile to knock on Lubyanka's gates and demand Olga's release. That his status as Russia's most famous living writer could do nothing when their intentions were to hurt him through her. That if anything, they'd lock him up too.

He went home, not to his dacha in Peredelkino, but to his Moscow apartment, to his wife. Zinaida was seated at their kitchen table, smoking and playing cards with friends. "You look like you've seen a ghost," she said when he came in.

"I've seen many ghosts," he told her. She'd recognized the look on her husband's face. It was the same look he'd had many times throughout the Purges. During the Great Terror, thousands had been imprisoned, nearly all perishing in the camps. Poets, writers, artists. Boris's friends, Zinaida's friends. Astronomers, professors, philosophers. A decade had passed and the wounds still hadn't healed—memories as bloody and red as the flag. She knew better than to ask what was wrong.

By the time Olga's train arrives, she will have been traveling for four days. From Potma, she will have walked, then taken a train, then another train before reaching Moscow.

Boris gets out of bed and dresses in a clean white Oxford shirt and brown homespun pants with suspenders. Careful not to wake his sleeping wife, he walks down the stairs, slips on his rubber boots, and leaves the dacha through the side porch.

The sun's crown appears over the tips of the budding birch trees as Boris walks the mulch path through the forest. He hears a pair of magpies chattering somewhere in the branches and pauses to look up but can't locate them. The path weaves its way toward a stream that's risen considerably from the newly melted snow. Boris stops on the narrow footbridge and takes a deep breath. He loves the smell of the cold water flowing below.

From the sun, Boris estimates the time to be six o'clock. Instead of walking through the cemetery, around the perimeter of the Patriarch's summer residence and down to the writers' club, as he usually does, Boris cuts over to the main road to take the faster route back home. He wants at least an hour or two to write before leaving to meet Olga's family in Moscow.

There's a light on in the kitchen as he approaches. Zinaida's heating up the stove and cooking Boris's usual breakfast: two fried eggs with dried dill. Despite a chill in the air, Boris strips and washes himself in his outdoor tub. Even after his dacha was winterized with a new bathroom and hot water, Boris still prefers to bathe outside, the cold water a pleasant shock to the system.

As Boris dries off with a musty towel, his old dog greets him by licking the drops of water trailing down his long, skinny legs. Boris pets Tobik's head and chides the half-blind mutt for not joining him on his morning walk yet again.

Boris's ears are assaulted by the sound of the television as he enters the dacha. Zinaida had insisted on having a television installed. He'd fought it for months but gave in when she threatened to stop preparing his meals. The television, a luxury, is replaying Stalin's funeral for the hundredth time. Boris pauses to watch as the camera focuses on the most grief-stricken faces in the crowd. He grimaces, then turns it off.

"What's that?" Zinaida calls from the kitchen.

"Good morning," Boris answers. He's not hungry but sits anyway. She sets his plate down and pours him a cup of tea. She doesn't join her husband at the table, instead turning back to the sink to wash the frying pan while smoking a cigarette, letting the ashes fall into the drain.

"Could you open the window, Z?" Boris asks. He hates the smell of cigarettes, and although Zinaida promised to cut back, she has yet to. She sighs, stubs it out, and finishes washing the dishes. Boris looks at his wife in the morning light streaming in from the window above the sink. The lines on her forehead and rolls of skin banding her neck are blurred for a moment and she looks just the picture of the woman he'd married twenty years earlier. He thinks about telling her she looks lovely, but a pang of guilt because he's about to meet Olga stops him.

The clock in the hallway chimes seven. Olga's train arrives in four hours. Boris forces himself to finish his breakfast. Swallowing the last bite of eggs, he pushes his chair back from the table.

"Off to write?" Zinaida asks.

With the question, Boris begins to suspect his wife already knows his plans. "Yes," he answers. "As always. But just an hour or so. I have business in the city."

"Weren't you just there yesterday?"

"That was two days ago, dear." He pauses. He's out of practice in lying to his wife. "I'm meeting with an editor at *Literaturnaya Moskva*. He's interested in some new translations."

"Perhaps I'll join you," she says. "I have some shopping to do."

"Next time, Zina. We'll make a day of it. Maybe take a walk and smell the budding lime trees."

Zinaida nods. She takes his plate and washes it in silence.

Boris sits at his writing desk. From the wicker basket at his feet, he takes the pages he wrote the day before. He frowns and strikes through a sentence with a fountain pen, then a paragraph, then a page. He pulls out a fresh sheet of paper and attempts the scene again.

The desk had belonged to Titsian Tabidze, the great Georgian poet and his dear friend. In '37, during the height of the Purge, Titsian was taken from his home one autumn evening. His wife, Nina, had run into the street, chasing after the black car in her bare feet. When they charged him with treason for committing *anti-Soviet activities*, Titsian named his favorite eighteenth-century poet, Besiki, as his only accomplice.

Boris has imagined many times what happened to Titsian after the black car took him away, believing that if he doesn't imagine his friend's fate, Titsian will have suffered alone. He often tells himself there's still a possibility his friend is alive, but Nina gave up such hope long ago. When she gave Boris her husband's desk, she told him he must continue her husband's good work. "Write the great novel you've dreamed of," she told him. Boris accepted Nina's gift, but he never felt worthy of it.

Titsian wasn't the first of Boris's friends to have been taken. Boris often pictures them at night, when he can't sleep, running their fates through his mind one at a time. There was Osip, shivering in a transit camp, knowing his end was near. Paolo, walking up the steps of the Writers' Union and standing still for a moment before putting a gun to his head. And Marina, tying the noose, then throwing the rope up over a ceiling beam.

It was well known that Stalin had enjoyed Boris's poetry. And what did it mean to have such a man find kinship through his words? To what had the Red Tsar connected? It was a hard truth, knowing he no longer owned his words once they were in the world. Once published, they were available for anyone to claim, even a madman. And it was even harder knowing he'd been struck from Stalin's list, the madman having told his minions to leave the Holy Fool, the Cloud Dweller, alone.

Boris hears the muffled chimes of the downstairs clock strike eight. Olga's train arrives in three hours, and he's yet to write a single word. The scene that flowed so easily the day before now refuses to appear.

He began *Doctor Zhivago* almost ten years earlier, and although he's made much progress, he still wishes he could go back to the days when the novel first came to him, when it was still pouring from some untapped pool inside him. It had felt like finding a new lover—the obsession, the infatuation, his thoughts on nothing else, his characters infiltrating his dreams, his heart weightless with every new discovery, every sentence, every scene. At times, Boris had felt it was the only thing keeping him alive.

Shortly before Olga's arrest, the authorities had pulped twenty-five thousand copies of Boris's *Selected Works*. When he couldn't sleep, Boris would often imagine his words dissolving into the milky slush.

The increasing censorship, in combination with his lover's arrest, inflamed Boris to finish *Zhivago*. He'd retreated to the country to write but found himself unable to. This block provoked an anxiety that felt like needle pricks across his chest. Eventually the needles became knives, and he soon found himself confined to a hospital bed. He'd had a heart attack, and there, with tubes hooked up to him and a bedpan by his side, Boris wondered who would inherit the desk Nina had given him. Would Titsian's desk be passed down to one of his sons? Or perhaps to another writer? Or would someone take an ax to it for firewood, to keep his widow and children warm when he'd failed to? They could add his unfinished novel to the pyre.

Boris recovered from his heart attack in time to witness the end of an era. Stalin was dead and Olga would return to him. Things could go on as they had before.

Boris goes to his standing desk, thinking the change in posture will inspire movement in his pen. But it doesn't. He looks out the window. The sun slants across the lower half of his garden and he estimates Olga's train will arrive in two hours. He must leave within the hour to be on time to meet her family. He watches a small flock of ducks land in the yard and begin picking for worms in the newly upturned earth.

Boris neglected the garden for those three years that Olga was in Potma. The first spring after Olga was taken, Zinaida took it upon herself to clear the weeds for planting. Boris had been out on his morning walk when Zinaida began the task, and when he returned to the dacha, she was halfway through cutting the net of weeds with pruning shears. He'd called out to her to stop, but she pretended not to hear him. He opened the gate and ran into the garden. "No," he insisted, taking the shears from her hand.

Zinaida dropped to her knees. "The world hasn't stopped," she cried out. "It's here. It's right here!" She yanked a fistful of weeds from the earth and threw them at his feet.

Zinaida never attempted to clear the weeds again, and each time she passed the garden she refused to even look at it. Soon the garden became so overgrown that even Boris had trouble deciphering its original perimeter.

That is, until Boris read Olga's postcard and saw the date: *25 April*. That very afternoon, he spent hours turning up the newly thawed earth with a shovel. The next day, he burned the leaves and weeds in a small fire at the edge of his property and filled a wheelbarrow with rocks that had migrated into the garden. He fertilized the soil by burying a few trout a meter deep. He repaired the wooden bench that had fallen into disrepair. Sitting on it for the first time in three years, he mapped out which crops he'd plant and where. First red kale and spinach. Then dill, strawberries, currants, gooseberries, and cucumbers. Then squash, potatoes, and radishes. Then onions and leeks. After solidifying his garden plans, Boris began contemplating what Olga's homecoming would entail.

Three years earlier, Boris couldn't have imagined a world without Olga at its center. And although there was never a day in which he hadn't thought of her, the longing he felt lessened over time, and he'd begun to appreciate how simple his life had become. How he no longer felt the guilt of lying to his wife, the embarrassment of people talking, of Zinaida's knowing but never addressing the matter. He no longer felt the anxiety that came with Olga's many changing moods, and the helplessness he felt in not being able to give her everything she demanded.

After that day in the garden, Boris went back and forth on the reasons to stay with Olga and the reasons to distance himself. Without Olga, he'd never experience the same highs he had when next to her, but he'd also avoid the devastating lows. He'd never feel that same burning desire, but he'd also not be subjected to her fits, her threats, her moods.

During these equivocations, Boris read a piece of *Onegin's Journey* and wrote Pushkin's words on a scrap of paper. He'd looked at the lines for days, contemplating whether to throw it away or include it in his novel.

> *My ideal now is a housewife,*
> *My desire is for peace,*
> *A pot of soup, and my fine self.*

In the end, he decided to include it, and to end things with Olga. A week before he was to meet her at the train station, Boris asked Ira to meet him in Pushkinskaya Square, the place where he had first asked Olga to meet him seven years ago.

Boris was the first to arrive. He sat on a bench and watched an elderly man throw sunflower seeds to pigeons. When the man ran out of seeds, he threw torn bits of newspaper, hoping the birds wouldn't know the difference and stay near him just a while longer. But after a few pecks, the birds moved on.

Ira turned the corner and spotted Boris sitting on the bench. She waved and her face broke out in a grin.

When Boris had first met Olga's daughter she was but a girl, still in pink bows and white shoes. He remembered the first time he met Ira and Mitya at Olga's apartment. How the conversation had been slow at first, but the children began to open up after he'd peppered them with questions: *How do you like school? Do you know any songs? Do you like cats? Do you prefer the city or the country? Do you like poetry?*

"Oh, yes," Ira had replied to the last question. "I write poems."

"Would you be kind enough to recite one for me?"

Ira stood and recited a poem about a toy horse who came to life and galloped across Moscow only to fall into a hole in the frozen river. She'd recited it from memory with a passion and animation that took Boris aback.

Now Ira was a young woman of fifteen, wearing her mother's silk scarf around her shoulders. Boris admired her beauty, and he was ashamed to feel the familiar stir of passion Olga had caused when he'd first seen her at *Novy Mir.*

"Let's walk," Ira had said, taking Boris's arm. She'd often told him that he was her *almost father,* a compliment that both delighted him and filled him with apprehension. "Such a beautiful day." She began talking rapidly, telling him of all the preparations they were making for her mother's return. She said they'd planned a party, that she and her grandmother had already begun preparing the feast, and that a neighbor had given them two bottles of cognac to celebrate. "Of course, besides Mama, you'll be the guest of honor. I'm even tracking down some of those hazelnut chocolates you like."

"I'm afraid I can't attend," Boris told her.

Ira stopped walking and turned to him. "What do you mean?" she asked.

"I'm not sure I can climb the stairs." He placed his hand over his heart. "I'm still not well."

"Mitya and I will help you. We help Babushka up and down the stairs twice a day."

"My schedule has become quite full. With the novel. And I'm working on a new translation. I barely have enough time to comb my hair." He patted his silver hair for the joke, but Ira didn't laugh. Her face darkened and she asked what could be more important than seeing her mother's return, after all she'd been through.

"I'll never abandon your mother, nor you and Mitya. But it's over now."

"Your heart has gone cold after just a few years?"

"We must adjust to this new reality. You must tell your mother that we can have a friendship, but only that. After my illness, I've realized I need to stay with my family."

"You've told me. You've told Mitya. You've told my grandmother. You've told my mother that *we* are your family."

"You are. Of course, but—"

"Why are you telling this to me, and not my mother?"

"I need your help convincing her that this is for the best. For all of us."

"I'll leave it up to my mother to decide what's best for her," Ira said.

"Please understand—"

"I've never understood." She untangled her arm from his. "Never."

"I don't want to leave things on these terms."

"Then you will meet my mother at the train station with us. You will embrace her. After all she's been through—for you. It's the very least you can do. Then you can tell her what you need to yourself."

Boris agreed, and they parted ways. As he watched Ira walk away, he thought how the back of her head looked so much like Olga's. He wanted to call out to Ira—to tell her he'd been wrong, that he hadn't meant what he'd said, that of course things would return to the way they were. How could they not?

Instead, he walked back to his bench and saw a new old man take the former old man's place feeding the pigeons. He wondered how many years he had left until he'd take that old man's place, his own coat pockets filled with birdseed.

Olga was likely awake now. He wonders what she looks like. Is she still beautiful? Or have the camps changed her? And what will Olga think when she sees him again? He's lost weight, lost hair, and for the first time in his life has begun to feel his true age. The one improvement he's made while she was gone was to get a set of porcelain veneers. But even with his perfect new teeth, when he looks in the mirror now, he sees an old man, diminished, with a weak heart.

Boris puts the thought out of mind and turns back to his work. Finally he hits upon the right sentence and the rest of the words flow. The paper fills and he drops it into the wicker basket, then pulls out another. He knows he needs to leave in the next few minutes to avoid being late, but he keeps writing.

When he looks up again from his work, the room has darkened and he can smell the chicken Zinaida is roasting. He pulls the chain of the small lamp on his desk and continues to write.

When he finally goes downstairs for dinner, Zinaida smiles at her husband. She puts out her cigarette and lights the two candles in the center of the table. She doesn't say anything about Boris not going into Moscow, nor does he. They eat together in silence, and he feels a tension in his shoulders release that he hadn't known he was holding. This is how he should spend the rest of his days, he thinks: writing, being productive, sharing a hot meal with his wife. He asks for some wine, and his wife fills his glass.

He tells himself not to think of Olga and what she's doing. Is she eating the feast with her family, or has she lost her appetite? Will she sleep tonight? He tries not to think of the way her face must have looked as she saw her family standing on the platform waiting to greet her—how it looked when she realized he wasn't there.

Boris wakes. It is still dark. He dresses and leaves the dacha for his morning walk, careful not to wake his sleeping wife. As he passes his garden, he sees a few bright spots of green poking up from the earth. He sets off down the hill, passes the stream, and goes up through the cemetery, then into the village. He finds himself waiting at the station for the morning train into Moscow.

It isn't until he's on Olga's street that he makes up his mind to see her. He slowly ascends the five flights of stairs, holding the handrail as he climbs. At each landing, he tells himself he will see her for only a moment, just a moment, to tell her what he told Ira in the park. She deserves to hear it from him, he tells himself when he reaches her door. He steadies his heart by pressing his hand to his chest. He takes a deep breath before he knocks, but she opens it before he can raise his fist. It has been seven years since they met, and three since he's seen her. She's aged twofold in that time: her blond hair, half-tucked under a headscarf, looks as dull as straw; her curves have straightened; wrinkles now radiate from her mouth, across her forehead, and from the corners of her eyes; her skin is marked with sun spots and unfamiliar moles.

And yet he falls to his knees. She is even more beautiful than before.

Boris no longer questions what to do. He rises and kisses her—and she lets him for a moment, before stepping back. Olga retreats into her apartment but leaves the door open. Boris follows, reaching for her embrace. She holds out her hand to stop him. "Never again," she says.

"Never again?" he asks.

"Will you keep me waiting."

"Never," he says. "Never."

CHAPTER 7

~~THE MUSE~~
~~THE REHABILITATED WOMAN~~
THE EMISSARY

How many times had I imagined our reunion? Pictured Borya waiting, hat in hand, looking up the tracks? How many times had I thought of that first embrace? Rubbed my arms and squeezed my shoulders while lying alone on my bunk to simulate how it would feel?

Three and a half years had passed since we had shared a bed, and we didn't waste time. His touch shocked me. It had been so long since I had been touched. We came together like crashing boulders that echoed across Moscow.

After, I laid my head down on his chest to listen to the beat of his heart. I joked that after two heart attacks, he had a new rhythm. "And your teeth." His large, yellowed teeth with the gap in the middle were now gleaming white porcelain.

"You don't like them?" he asked. He closed his mouth, and I used my pinky finger to pry it open again. He pretended to bite it.

He held on tighter, not letting go as easily as he had before. He didn't want to leave my apartment except to write and sleep. In my absence, he'd moved full time to his dacha in Peredelkino, which, in the years I'd been gone, had been expanded with three new rooms, gas heat, running water, a new clawfoot tub. While I was living in the barracks, he was living in a retreat in the woods most Russians could only dream of.

After Potma, I asked freely and without guilt for him to share his good fortune—money for clothing, books, food, school supplies for the children, a new bed.

There were other things too.

He left all business pertaining to his writing to me: the contracts, the speaking engagements, payments for his translation work. If an editor called for a meeting, it was I who would attend. I became his agent, his mouthpiece, the one people went to if they wanted to get to him. I finally felt useful to him as Zinaida was. But instead of cooking and cleaning, I was the person who ushered his words out into the world. I became his emissary.

Almost daily, I'd take the train from Moscow to Peredelkino and we'd meet in the cemetery. We could be alone there to discuss *Zhivago* or just sit together. Our only company was the occasional widow or widower carrying plastic flowers, or the caretaker, who usually stayed in his shed smoking cigarettes and reading. Sometimes I'd bring small pieces of meat wrapped in a cloth napkin for the two large dogs who'd greet me at the iron gates.

Our place was on the sloping hill in the unused part of the cemetery. If the weather was pleasant, we'd sit on one of my scarves spread out on the grass.

"I want to be buried here in this very spot," he told me more than once.

"Don't be morbid."

"I thought it romantic."

Once, as we sat in our place on the hill, Borya spotted Zinaida walking up the main road toward their dacha. She looked like an old woman—walking slowly, her hair covered in a plastic babushka, both arms laden with shopping bags. She paused, set down the bags, and lit a cigarette. I sat up to get a better look. Borya gently pushed me back down.

That summer, to be closer to him, I rented a house across Lake Izmalkovo, a thirty-minute walk from his dacha. Borya wouldn't live with me, but it would be a place of our own, a place for a new start.

The children took one bedroom, and I made the glassed-in veranda mine. Mama mostly stayed behind in Moscow, saying the country was only good in small doses.

How I loved that glass house. How the roots of the poplars made natural steps leading up to my door. How the veranda was all light, and how I could see Borya approach along the path while lying in bed.

But when Borya first saw the cottage, he scolded me, saying a glass house offered no privacy when the whole point of my moving closer was to afford us more. That afternoon, I took the train into the city and bought red and blue chintz. I spent the evening making drapes that would convert my room of light into a den.

That summer was hot. Wild roses erupted in pockets of reds and pinks along the path and the skies opened up with daily thunderstorms. The glass walls of my room condensed from the trapped heat. I cracked every window, but it brought little relief. Borya and I sweated through my sheets, and I joked that we could turn my bedroom into a greenhouse and grow tropical fruits like mangoes and bananas. Borya didn't think it funny. He hated that glass house.

But Mitya loved the glass house, just as I did. He took to country life quickly, spending his days traipsing around the forest, bringing home plants and rocks and frogs in his pockets. He made a home for his frogs in a tin bucket filled with grass and pebbles and the top of a jelly jar, for water. He wiped mud underneath his eyes and fashioned a bow and arrow from a stick and string to become Robin Hood.

Ira was another matter. She refused to play with her brother, having grown out of such games while I was gone. She complained about being stuck inside the tiny cottage all day while her friends were back in Moscow. "There's nowhere to even get ice cream here," she said. When I made her plombir ice cream with fresh mint from Borya's garden, she spat it out. "Tastes like dirt," she said, pushing the bowl away. "Give it to your patron."

I scolded her for speaking ill about Borya, and she got up and left. When she didn't come home that evening, I went to the train station and found her sitting on a bench, alone but for the station manager sweeping his broom.

"I wanted to go home," she said. "But I didn't have any money."

"Home is here. With me and Mitya."

"And Boris."

"Yes. Boris too."

"For now."

Before I could say another word, Ira got up and started back toward the cottage. I sat on the bench alone, watching the station manager sweep the platform clean.

By summer's end, when the children needed to return to Moscow for school, Borya worried I'd also leave. "I'll be alone again," he complained, on the brink of tears. I enjoyed it, and willed his tears to fall. And when they did, I felt a sudden shift of power. I liked the feeling, and didn't tell him for weeks that I'd already decided to stay, even if it meant I'd see the children only on weekends. I'd always known I'd stay; I just wanted him to beg.

Ira had her things packed two days in advance of their leaving, but Mitya put it off until an hour before their train was to leave. Each item I folded and placed in his suitcase, he removed. "Mitya, please," I said.

"Where's *your* suitcase?" he asked.

"You know you are going home to Moscow."

"But you said *this* was home."

"There is no school here. Don't you want to see your friends again? And Babushka?"

"Where's *your* suitcase?" he asked again, his eyes welling.

I soothed him by kissing his forehead and promising he could take his pet frog Erik—the only one to survive the summer—back to Moscow if he promised to take very good care of him.

The children left, and I stayed in the glass house until late autumn. It wasn't insulated for winter, so Borya ultimately got his way. I moved to another small home, even closer to Borya's. We called it Little House, and his dacha Big House.

I took great pleasure furnishing Little House, hanging up my curtains, laying down thick red rugs. Most of my books had been confiscated and were rotting in some damp storage room in Lubyanka, so

Borya restocked my library, even building the book-shelves himself.

When all was finished, I happily gave Borya the grand tour, making sure to point out *our* bed, *our* table, *our* shelves. "We'll build our garden right there come spring," I said, pointing out the window that faced the yard.

Every space Borya and I inhabited became ours. If I said it wasn't easy to put my old life in Moscow out of mind as well—my children, my mother, my respon-sibilities—I'd be lying. Once, I overheard Mitya acci-dentally call my mother *Mama,* and instead of feeling like a betrayal, it was a relief.

That winter felt so far from my days spent in dark-ness. Friends came, and the readings of *Doctor Zhivago* started up again. Every Sunday, Mitya and Ira and our friends would take the train in from Moscow. We'd dine, then Borya would read, I the hostess at his side once again.

The novel was almost finished. Borya worked at a furious pace, as he had when we'd first fallen in love. He'd write in Peredelkino in the mornings then walk to Little House. I'd help edit and retype in the afternoons.

Zhivago was ever present, especially as he neared its completion. If you asked him about the weather or how he'd enjoyed his dinner or whether he thought aphids were the reason his summer squash had withered on the vine, he'd find a way to bring the conversation back to the book. Sometimes he'd even dream of Yuri and Lara. "They are as clear to me as anyone living," he said. "It's as if they once existed and their ghosts are speaking to me."

But as Yuri and Lara were ever on his mind, Big House was ever on mine. He wrote there. He ate there. He slept there. She cooked for him and mended his socks. She watched television there. She played cards with the neighbors on nights he was gone. She nursed him when he had a headache or upset stomach or fretted about his heart.

She entered his study only to clean and never interrupted his work. She created the perfect conditions for his writing. Although he never told me, I believe that's why he stayed. At the time, I told myself it was his obsession to finish the novel that kept him there.

I wondered whether they slept together. I didn't think so, but still, the thought was an ink spot on a white tablecloth. What would they look like intertwined? His long, lean torso pressed against the folds of her belly. His strong hands lifting her breasts to the position they once occupied. Part of me wanted it to be true. In a strange, twisted way it reassured me he'd still want me when I was old. Once, I asked whether they did still sleep together, and Borya assured me it had been years. "How many?" I asked. "Did you sleep with her while I was gone?"

"Of course not. We are not that way anymore."

"Did you sleep with anyone?" I asked. "I'll understand if you had," I added, though I didn't mean it. He told me I had nothing to worry about, that my place in his life was forever cemented. That he kept company only with Lara during my absence.

And still I persisted, still I pushed. "No one?"

<hr />

"He's dead," Borya said over the telephone.

I tightened my grip on the receiver. "Who is dead?"

He groaned as though he had stomach cramps. "Yuri," he finally got out.

Tears came to my eyes. "He's dead?"

"It's done. My novel is complete."

I arranged for the manuscript to be edited, retyped, and bound with a leather cover. I went into Moscow to pick up three copies from the printer and carried the box back on the train, the weight of Borya's words heavy on my lap.

He was waiting for me at Little House. When I handed him the box containing his life's work, he held it in his hands for a moment, then set it down and spun me around the room. We danced without music. As we spun, I saw myself in the oval mirror, and I, too, looked happy—but as a mother looks after she's given birth: elated and exhausted, happy and pained, peaceful and at the same time terrified.

"Perhaps it *will* be published," Borya said.

I thought of Anatoli Sergeyevich Semionov sitting at his large desk inquiring about *Doctor Zhivago*. I thought about the State's obsession with what he had written. But I said nothing.

I scheduled meetings with every literary magazine, every editor, every publishing house, anyone who might publish *Zhivago*. I went alone to speak on Borya's behalf. When pushed to describe his work, defend it, or even promote it, he felt he couldn't. "It's as if my own words are lost somewhere between putting them to paper and seeing them in print," he told me.

So I spoke for him.

The editors met with me, but none made promises. A few said they'd possibly be interested in publishing the poems that came at the end of the novel, but my questions about publishing the book in full were never answered directly.

Many nights, Borya waited for me on the train platform for news of how my meetings in Moscow had gone. I tried to frame everything positively, talking more excitedly than was warranted about *Novy Mir*'s interest in publishing some poems, but Borya knew better. He'd walk me back to Little House in silence, his arm tightly intertwined with mine, as if I were holding him up.

Once, on my return from another fruitless trip, Borya stopped in the middle of the road and announced he no longer believed *Zhivago* would be published. "You mark my words. They will not publish this novel for anything in the world."

"You must be patient. You don't know that yet."

"They'll never allow it." He scratched his eyebrow. "Never."

I started to think he might be right. After yet another meeting with yet another publisher, Borya met me in Moscow so that we could attend a piano recital. We arrived early and sat on a bench under a chestnut tree.

A man who I thought I'd seen on the Metro stood at the end of the pond in front of us, watching the ducks. The man was young, wearing a long brown overcoat despite the heat.

"I feel as if we're being watched," I told Borya.

"Yes," he replied, matter-of-factly.

"Yes?"

"I assumed you knew." The man standing at the pond noticed us looking at him and walked down the path, disappearing from view. "Shall we go?" Borya asked. "We don't want to be late."

Borya maintained that the surveillance didn't bother him. He'd even joke about it, addressing whoever was listening by speaking into a lamp or to the ceiling.

"Hello? Hello?" he asked no one. "How are you today?"

"I'm fine, thank you," he answered himself.

"Are we boring you?" he asked a light fixture. "Maybe instead of what we're having for dinner tonight, we should talk about something more interesting."

"Will you stop?" I asked. I didn't find his jokes funny, and I told him as much. "I've faced them before," I said. "And I won't do it again."

He took my hand and kissed it. "We must laugh at it all," he said.

"It's all we can do."

WEST

FEBRUARY-FALL 1957

CHAPTER 8

~~THE APPLICANT~~

THE CARRIER

As the taxi turned left onto Connecticut, I pressed two fingers to my wrist the way Mama had taught me when I was a child and carsick. The feeling intensified when we hit Dupont Circle. I thought about getting out and walking, but that wasn't the plan. I couldn't deviate from the plan—not unless I was being followed.

I was told to hail a taxi at the corner of Florida and T at seven forty-five and take it to the Mayflower Hotel. The hotel was only a short walk from there, but the *optics*, they said, were better if I got out of a taxi.

I was told to avoid wearing anything that would make me stand out: flashy jewelry, too much makeup, an ostentatious hat, ostentatious shoes, anything ostentatious. I thought of all those sequined gowns filling our basement apartment, of all the women coming by to try them on and buy them from Mama. I didn't own a single item of clothing that could be classified as ostentatious. My instructions were to dress well but not too well, to look nice but not too nice. I was to look like the type of woman who frequented the Mayflower's bar, the Town & Country Lounge. The tricky part was that I was the type of woman who hadn't even heard of the Mayflower Hotel, let alone the Town & Country Lounge.

For the night, I was no longer Irina; I was Nancy.

The taxi came to a full stop midway through the circle and I checked my hair in my compact, still unsure I'd gotten the look right. I wore Mama's old fur, which I'd spritzed with Jean Naté—an attempt to mask the mothball smell. I wore the periwinkle and white polka dot dress I'd worn to every wedding I'd attended for the last five years. My hair was pulled back into a French twist and secured with a silver comb, another item borrowed from Mama. Reapplying the new shade of orange-red lipstick I'd purchased from Woolworth's, I frowned into the mirror. Something was still off. It wasn't until the taxi pulled up to the hotel and a doorman opened my door that I looked down and realized it was my shoes: dull black pumps. Dull black pumps with a scuffed left heel. And I hadn't even thought of shining them. The kind of women who went for drinks at the Town & Country on a Wednesday night wouldn't be caught dead in anything dull. As I entered the Mayflower's grand lobby, decked out in red and white roses for Valentine's the next day, I couldn't stop thinking about my shoes. At least I'd been given a nice purse—a quilted black leather Chanel bag with a double flap and a gold chain, large enough to hold an envelope.

I told myself to project confidence, to become someone who belonged with the well-heeled set—to become my cover, to become Nancy. Gripping the Chanel like a talisman, I passed the bellboys in their tasseled caps, the honeymooners checking in, the huddled men conducting after-hours meetings, the glamorous brunette waiting for one of those men to take her upstairs, the large potted palms lining the mirrored corridor. I walked through the lobby and into the Town & Country like the kind of person whom the bartender knew by name.

I already knew the bartender's name. It was Gregory, and there he was: prematurely gray hair, white shirt and black bow tie, standing behind the bar pouring a Gibson.

The lounge was busy, but the second-to-last high-backed chair at the bar was free, as they said it would be.

"What'll it be?" Gregory asked, his nametag confirming what I already knew.

"Gin martini," I said. "Three olives, with one of those little red swords." *One of those little red swords?* I scolded myself for going off script.

In front of me was a thin glass vase containing a single white rose. I picked it up, turned it clockwise in my hand, sniffed it, and put it back—as instructed. Then

I hung the Chanel by its gold chain on the chair back's left side. Then I waited.

The man to my left hadn't so much as glanced my way when I sat down. He was reading the sports section of the *Post* and looked like every other man in the place—a lawyer or businessman on a one-night trip in from New York or Chicago or wherever those types came to the District from. The word to describe him would be *nondescript,* and I wondered if he'd describe me that way too. I hoped so.

Gregory set my drink down on a white napkin with the Mayflower's gold insignia, and I took a sip. "You make a damn fine martini," I said. I hated martinis.

I'd been told there wouldn't be any sign of it—that the man sitting next to me would slip the envelope into my purse without detection, that if I didn't notice it, he'd done his job. The man closed his newspaper, swallowed the last of his Scotch, threw down a dollar, and left.

I waited fifteen minutes then finished my drink and told Gregory I was ready to settle-up.

Reaching for the Chanel, I half expected it to feel different. But it didn't, and I wondered if I'd done something wrong—that maybe the man reading the sports section was just a man reading the sports section. I resisted the urge to check and left the Town & Country, passing the potted palms, a man waiting for the elevator with the glamorous brunette, a retired couple checking in, the tassel-hatted bellboys.

Walking up Connecticut, I did my best to keep my cool, to not let the adrenaline cause me to break into a sprint. Stopping at P Street, I looked at my watch, a Lady Elgin given to me along with the Chanel. Within seconds, the number fifteen bus pulled up to the curb. I took the second-to-last seat in the back, in front of a man holding a green umbrella in his lap. As the bus passed the two stone lions guarding the entrance to the Taft Bridge, the man behind me tapped me on the shoulder and asked the time. I told him it was a quarter after nine. It wasn't. He thanked me and I set the Chanel down and pushed it back with my heel.

I got off at Woodley Park and walked toward the zoo. At a red light, I held out my hands to let the newly falling snowflakes hit my gloves, then dissolve into minuscule puddles. I wondered: Is this what's it like to have an affair, to have a secret? I felt a rush and could see why Teddy Helms had told me that one could get addicted to this line of work. I already was.

I'd applied to be a typist, but they gave me another job. Had they seen something in me that I hadn't seen in myself? Or maybe they just looked to my past, to my father's death, and knew I'd do whatever was asked of me. Later, I was told that such deep anger ensures a type of loyalty to the Agency that patriotism never can.

Whatever they'd seen in me, for my first few months at the Agency, I couldn't shake the feeling that they'd chosen the wrong person for the job.

The Mayflower test changed that. For the first time in my life, I felt as if I had a greater purpose, not just a job. That night, something unlocked in me—a hidden power I never knew I had. I discovered I was well suited to the work of a Carrier.

During the day, I took dictation, transcribed notes, stayed quiet during meetings, and typed and typed and typed—all the while making certain I didn't retain any of the information I was typing. "Just picture the information passing through your fingertips to the keys to the paper and then disappearing from your mind forever," Norma had instructed me on my first and only day of training. "In one ear and out the other, you know?" And all the typists said the same thing: *Don't retain what you type; you'll type faster if you're not thinking about what you're typing; it's classified information, so even if you remember it, you'd better pretend you don't.*

"Fast fingers keep secrets" was the Pool's unofficial motto. And yet I wasn't sure any of them followed their own credo. Even in my first few weeks, as I was just getting to know the girls, it was clear they knew everything about everyone.

Did they know everything about me, too? Did they know about my other position? The extra fifty dollars per paycheck? Did my typewriter dinging a beat slower than theirs make them wonder? Did they notice I drank two more cups of coffee than they did and had bags under my eyes?

Mama sure noticed. She brewed a pot of chamomile tea and froze it into ice cubes to place on my eyelids. She thought I was dating a new man, and implored me to bring him home to meet her before I disgraced her name in the neighborhood.

But what did the women in the typing pool think?

Was it the reason they hadn't exactly accepted me into their ranks? Of course, they were always polite and friendly, saying *Hello* in the morning and a *Have a good weekend* on Fridays. But I can't say they were overly welcoming. I wanted to be part of the group, but didn't want it to *seem* like I wanted to be part of the group. One might think this scenario plays out only in high school or college, but the politics of friendship is tricky at every age.

The Pool invited me to lunch with them a few times, but that was before my first paycheck, when I had only enough money for my bus commute. By the time I did have money to spare, the lunch invites had dried up.

I wanted to believe their standoffishness was a product of my having taken their friend Tabitha's place, though couldn't help but think it was something else, something that had plagued me my entire life: the feeling of being a constant outsider, of being most comfortable alone. Even as a child, I preferred to play alone. I'd pretend our small kitchen pantry was a fort. I'd create elaborate plays with puppets cut from brown paper bags and glued to Popsicle sticks. I was happiest playing by myself. When my little cousins would try to play with me, I'd end up scolding them for messing up one of the puppets or not playing the character exactly how I'd wanted them to. They'd get mad and leave, and I'd tell myself that that was fine. It was easier to convince myself that it was I who didn't want to play with them, rather than the reverse.

Regardless of feeling out of place, I took to the day job fast. And although I typed slower than the other women, I was steady and accurate.

There was more of a learning curve with my after-hours work.

On my first day, when I asked just how I'd be trained, I was given a slip of paper with the address of an unmarked tempo office that overlooked the Reflecting Pool—the office where I was to meet the officer Teddy Helms each day after I clocked out.

The first time I met Teddy, I was struck by how much he resembled a movie star playing a spy. He was a few years older than I—tall, with brown hair, long delicate fingers, and handsome in the way men like that are expected to be. Several members of the typing pool were absolutely gone for Teddy, but I never really saw him like that. He did look like the type of man I'd fantasized about as a young girl, though—not as a lover or boyfriend, but as the older brother I'd always wanted. Someone who'd teach me how to fit in, how to be less painfully awkward, someone to protect me from the high school boys who'd flip up my skirt in the hallway. Someone to help support Mama and ease our financial burdens that came and went with each spent paycheck.

Teddy was quiet at first, saying I was the first woman he'd ever trained. In the OSS days, women had been entrusted with blowing up bridges, but just a few years later, the Agency was still testing the waters to see what we were capable of.

Teddy was different. "If you ask me, women are well suited to be Carriers," Teddy said. "No one suspects that the pretty girl on the bus is delivering secrets."

Teddy and I got to know each other well in those first few weeks of '57. He was the kind of man one feels comfortable with from the get-go—someone you'd find yourself telling more in the space of an hour than people you'd known your whole life.

Teddy had come to the Agency after being recruited by one of his lit professors at Georgetown. He studied political science and Slavic languages and spoke fluent Russian with a practiced accent that could fool any Muscovite. During our trainings, Teddy would switch between English and Russian, saying he enjoyed any opportunity to practice. It was a joy to be able to talk to him in the language I used only with Mama. He'd ask question after question: about my mother's dress business, my childhood in Pikesville, my college days at Trinity, my shyness. No one had ever asked me questions like that before, and at first I balked at his boldness. But before long, I found myself unspooling my personal history to him.

Perhaps I felt so comfortable because he had offered up facts of his life so willingly. I discovered he had an older brother who'd died a few years back. How Julian had returned from the war a hero just to get drunk one night and wrap his car around a tree. How Teddy felt that he'd never live up to the reputation his brother had left behind, how his parents chose to remember only the hero Julian had been by enshrining his photo above the mantel next to the folded flag they'd been given. Teddy said he initially wanted to follow his brother's footsteps and enlist in the Army, or join his father at the law firm that carried their last name, but ended up drawn more to literature. As a result, his college mentor guided him toward a different profession.

Teddy would pour us whiskeys from the bottle he kept in his desk and wax poetic about the role he believed art and literature played in spreading democracy, how books were key to demonstrating that great art could come only from true freedom and how he joined up with the Agency to spread that message. He'd say Russians valued literature as Americans valued freedom: "Washington has its statues of Lincoln and Jefferson," he said, "while Moscow pays tribute to Pushkin and Gogol." Teddy wanted the Soviets to understand that their own government was hindering their ability to produce the next Tolstoy or Dostoyevsky—that art could thrive only in a free nation, that the West had become the king of letters. This message was akin to sticking a knife between the Red Monster's ribs and twisting the blade.

During the day, Teddy treated me as he treated all the typists when passing through SR: a nod in the morning, maybe a wave goodbye at night. But after hours, he'd give me his full attention in training me to pick up and deliver internal messages for the Agency.

He'd have me practice putting an envelope under a table, bench, chair, barstool, bus seat, toilet. He started me out with the standard white letter envelope. Then I graduated to pamphlets and manila folders, then books, then packages. He compared what we were doing to a magic trick, telling me the Agency had studied the sleight-of-hand greats like Walter Irving Scott and Dai Vernon, adapting their techniques. He showed me how to let a package slide down my leg and hit the ground without a sound. "It's all a trick," he said.

He taught me how to tell if someone was following me—to look out for anyone suspicious, anyone watching, and especially to be careful of LOPs. "Little Old People have a lot of time on their hands," he explained. "They sit in parks for hours and will call the cops at the drop of a hat if they see something out of the ordinary."

When I'd make a mistake, he'd tell me that all it takes is practice. And practice I did. Every night, when Mama was asleep, I locked my bedroom door and practiced sliding envelopes of various sizes into books, my purse,

Mama's purse, a suitcase, and every pocket in my wardrobe. When I demonstrated for Teddy how I could slip a tiny scroll of paper from a hollow lipstick tube into his jacket pocket, he told me I was ready for a real test.

"You sure?"

"Only one way to find out."

That was the Mayflower drop: not a real mission, but a test to see if I was ready. Teddy told me he'd be watching, although I wouldn't see him. And he was right; there'd been no sign of Teddy that night at the Mayflower. But the next day, I came into the office to find a white rose propped against my typewriter with a tiny red plastic sword sticking out of its stem like a thorn.

"Secret admirer?" Norma asked.

"Just a friend," I said.

"A *friend*, huh? Not a secret Valentine?"

"Valentine?"

"It's today, you know."

"Oh," I said. I'd forgotten. Thankfully, Norma got called into a meeting before she could ask another question. But the mystery of the rose was revisited again that afternoon. "I hear you're dating Teddy Helms," Linda said, peeking over the partition that separated our desks. When I looked up, the entire typing pool was standing there, waiting for an answer.

"What? No. We're not." I was taken aback, worried I'd blown my cover.

"Gail said Lonnie Reynolds said she saw Teddy leave the white rose this morning."

"I mean, he wasn't exactly keeping it hush-hush," Gail said.

"When did you two start dating?"

Overwhelmed, I excused myself to the ladies', hopeful they'd forget all about the rose by the time I got back. They hadn't, and they continued peppering me with questions I had no answers to until it was time to clock out.

"Wanna come to Martin's with us?" Norma asked. "Two-for-one oysters and a bartender who pours us doubles 'cause he has a thing for Judy. And seeing how you say you're still single, you probably won't have Valentine's Day plans, right?"

"I can't," I said. "I do have plans, but not a date. Not anything like that."

"Uh-huh," Norma said.

I was furious at Teddy for putting me in the typing pool's crosshairs. Why had he done it? What was he getting at? I made up my mind to ask as soon as I saw him, but lost my nerve when he greeted me with a glass of whiskey and a toast to a job well done at the Mayflower.

"You did good, kid," he said, clinking my glass. "There are a few things we need to work on, but you did a damn fine job. Anderson's pleased. We think you'll be ready for the field soon, for a real mission coming down the pipeline."

"Got it," I said, knowing not to ask for details but not knowing what else to say. "And thank you." I could tell Teddy wasn't sure if I was thanking him for his compliment or for the white rose. An awkward pause opened between us.

"By the way, you didn't say anything," Teddy said, breaking the silence.

"About?" I asked dumbly.

"The rose."

"The typing pool was quite enthralled."

"But you weren't?"

"I don't . . . I don't really like being the center of attention."

Teddy laughed. "The talent you were hired for," he said. "But really. Sorry about that. People here latch on to a rumor like a dog to a mailman."

"A dog?"

"I mean, I'm sorry. I thought it would be nice."

"It was nice . . . it's just that . . . do we want people knowing we know each other?"

He scratched his chin and leaned forward. "Maybe it could work as a cover. If people think we're dating, they won't suspect anything out of the ordinary if they see us together. Nothing serious—no harm done, right? Unless you have a real boyfriend who might get upset?"

"I don't have a boyfriend, but—"

"Perfect," he said. "Wanna start now? We could get a drink at Martin's. Don't they all congregate there?"

"I don't know."

Teddy held up the now empty glass. "Let's just stop by for a minute."

"Isn't that the kind of thing that's frowned upon in the workplace?"

"Pardon my French, but half the Agency wouldn't get laid if we didn't date each other. Besides, we're not really dating, are we?"

Teddy took my hand as we crossed the threshold into Martin's. The bar was crowded with K Street lobbyists—Teddy said you could pick them out by their finer suits and shoes so new they still squeaked on the waxed floor. They took up real estate at the bar while their poorly dressed government counterparts occupied the tables. Law interns mingled at the buffet, loading up on oysters. And the typing pool was still there, sitting at a booth to the left of the bar.

"How 'bout we sit there?" I asked, pointing at a two-top across the room.

"Let's grab a drink at the bar first."

"They have waitresses, I think."

"This'll be quicker." We squeezed ourselves in and Teddy signaled for the bartender to bring us two whiskeys. He paid and held up his glass. "To new friends," he said. And just as we clinked, I felt a tap on my shoulder.

"Irina," Norma said. "You finally made it to Martin's. Come on over and join us." She looked at Teddy. "You, too, Teddy."

"It was a last-minute sorta thing," Teddy said. "We have dinner reservations at Rive Gauche. Just stopped in for a drink."

"Rive Gauche? How'd you land that on Valentine's?"

"Friend owed me a favor."

"Why don't you join us for your drink? There's plenty of room at our table."

We looked over at the table and the girls looked away. "Sure," I said. "Why not?"

"Look who the cat dragged in," Norma said, escorting us to the booth. The girls scooted around to make room. I took a seat, but Teddy remained standing. "Excuse me for a moment, ladies." We watched as he went to the jukebox and started feeding it change.

Judy elbowed me. "Nothing going on with you two, huh?"

Norma gave Judy a told-you-so look. "White rose on the desk in the morning? Rive Gauche at night?"

"Rive Gauche?" Kathy said. "Fancy."

Teddy returned just as the jukebox clicked on a record. He took his jacket off and handed it to Judy, who forced a smile. Was she jealous? Of me? "Wanna dance?" he asked.

"But no one's dancing," I said.

"They will be," Teddy replied, extending a hand. "Come on! This is Little Richard!"

"Little who?" Without waiting for my answer, he took my hand and led me to the dance floor: a square of parquet with no tables on it. I was never a very good dancer—all arms and legs that never seemed to co-operate with each other—but I still loved to try. And boy, could Teddy dance. Not only was every pair of eyes in the typing pool on us, it seemed everyone in the place was watching. Teddy spun me around as if he were Fred Astaire and I felt I was playing a role—and playing it well. I ate up the feeling just as I had at the Mayflower drop. Teddy pulled me closer. "They've bought it," he whispered.

After another dance and another drink, we left the bar. Out on the sidewalk, I said goodbye. Teddy interrupted. "You don't want to grab some dinner?"

"I thought that was just something you said."

"What if I said I really do have reservations at Rive Gauche?"

I thought of the leftover borscht Mama would be reheating, then looked down at the pea-soup-colored dress I'd worn that day. "I'm not really dressed for that kind of place."

"You look beautiful," he said, and held out his hand. "Let's go."

CHAPTER 9

THE TYPISTS

Another Friday morning at Ralph's. Another doughnut, another mug of coffee. By the time we left the diner, the chilly fall morning had turned mild. We molted our hats and scarves and opened our jackets as we made our way down E Street.

First thing in the morning, SR was usually bustling with people settling in at their desks or grabbing coffee in the break room or rushing into one of the many morning briefings that started promptly at nine fifteen. The phone at reception would already be ringing, the chairs in the waiting area already filled. But not that day in early October. That day, reception was empty, as was the break room, as was every desk surrounding the typing pool.

"What's going on?" Gail asked Teddy Helms, who was half-walking, half-running toward the elevator. He stopped short and stumbled over a bump in the ancient beige carpet.

"Meeting upstairs," Teddy said, which was code for Dulles's office, which was really downstairs. Teddy hurried off and we went to our desks, where Irina was sitting behind her typewriter.

"Teddy say anything?" Gail asked.

"We lost," Irina said.

"Lost what?" Norma asked.

"Unclear."

"What are you talking about?" Kathy asked.

"I can't explain the science of it."

"Science? Of what?"

"Something they shot into space," Irina said.

"They?"

"*They*, they," she whispered. "Just think of it . . ." she trailed off and pointed to the asbestos-tiled ceiling. "It's up there. Right now."

It was the size of a beach ball and weighed as much as the average American man but had the impact of a nuclear warhead. The news of Sputnik's launch spread across SR hours before the Russian state news agency, Tass, announced that the first satellite to reach space was now nine hundred kilometers above Earth, circling the planet every ninety-eight minutes.

Even with all the men gone, it was impossible to get any work done. We cracked our knuckles and looked around the empty office. Kathy peeked over the partition. "What kind of name is Sputnik, anyway?"

"Sounds like a potato," Judy said.

"It means *fellow traveler,*" said Irina. "I think it's quite poetic."

"No," Norma said. "It's terrifying."

Gail stood up, closed her eyes, and drew invisible calculations in the air with her finger. She opened her eyes. "Fourteen."

"Huh?" we asked.

"If it's circling at that speed, it's passing over us fourteen times a day."

We all looked up.

After lunch, we gathered around the radio in Anderson's empty office. No one had any real information, and the announcer said frantic reports were coming in from all over the country about possible sightings—from Phoenix, Tampa, Pittsburgh, both Portlands. It seemed everyone but us had seen the satellite.

"But it wouldn't be visible to the naked eye," Gail said. "Especially not during the day."

Just as the Alka-Seltzer jingle came on, Anderson walked in. "I could use one of those myself," he said. "Looks like we're hard at work here."

"Plop, plop, fizz, fizz," Norma said under her breath.

Kathy turned the volume down. "We wanted to know what's going on," she said.

"Don't we all," Anderson said.

"Do you know?" Norma asked.

"Does anyone know?" said Gail.

Anderson clapped his hands like an exuberant high school basketball coach. "All right, time to get back to work."

"How can we work with that thing flying over our heads?"

Anderson turned off the radio and shooed us away like pigeons. As we headed out, he asked Irina if she could stay behind for a minute. His request was not unusual, as Irina wasn't just another member of the typing pool. Since she'd started, we'd suspected she had special duties at the Agency, *extracurricular* activities. But what they were, we didn't know. Whether Anderson wanted to chat with her about those after-hours activities, and if they had anything to do with Sputnik, we had no idea. But that didn't keep us from speculating.

News reports throughout the weekend ranged from the exaggerated (*Russia Wins!*) to the absurd (*End Days?*) to the practical (*When Will Sputnik Fall?*) to the political (*What Will Ike Do?*). By Monday morning, the inspection line into Headquarters was just a trickle, as large contingents of men were off to meetings at the White House and on the Hill, assuaging fears that all was lost. The men who remained looked as though they hadn't been home since Friday—their white shirts yellowed at the armpits, their eyes bleary, their shadows far past five o'clock.

On Tuesday, Gail came in to work with one of the Mohawk Midgetapes we used to record phone calls.

She took off her hat and gloves and set the recorder in front of her typewriter. She motioned for us to come over to her desk. We gathered around as she flipped the switch to *Play*. We leaned in. Static.

"What are we listening for?" Kathy asked.

"I don't hear anything," Irina said.

"Shhh," Gail snapped.

We leaned in closer.

Then we heard it: a weak, continuous beeping, like the heartbeat of a frightened mouse. "Got it," she said, and clicked the recorder off.

"Got what?"

"They said you could hear it if you dial in to twenty MHz," she said. "But when I tried, all I got was static. So I figured I needed more power. Wanna guess what I did?"

"I have no idea, because I have no idea what you are even talking about," Judy said.

"I went to my kitchen window and removed the wire screen. My roommate must've thought I'd lost my marbles."

"She may have been right," Norma said.

"Then I ran a wire from the screen to the radio, dialed back to twenty megahertz, positioned the microphone just right, and that was it." She lowered her voice. "Contact."

"With what?"

"Sputnik."

We all looked at each other.

"You may want to keep this conversation for after hours," Linda said, looking around.

Gail snorted. "It's practically child's play."

"What does it mean?" Judy whispered.

Gail shook her head. "Don't know." She motioned to the row of offices behind her. "That's for them to find out."

"Maybe a code?" Norma said.

"A countdown?"

"What happens when the beeping stops?" Judy asked.

Gail shrugged.

"It means you have to get back to work," Anderson said from behind. We scattered, except for Gail, who remained standing. "And, Gail," we heard Anderson say, "I'll see you in my office."

"Now?"

"Now."

We watched her trail Anderson into his office; then we watched as she left it twenty minutes later, holding her white hankie to her nose. Norma stood up, but Gail waved her away.

October passed. The leaves turned orange, then red, then brown, then fell. We hauled out our heavier coats from the backs of our closets. The mosquitoes died off, bars began advertising hot toddies, and everywhere, even downtown, the city smelled of burning leaves. Someone brought in a jack-o'-lantern with a hammer and sickle carved into it to display at reception, and the men had their annual trick-or-treat around SR, going desk to desk taking shots of vodka.

November came in with a bang—or rather, a blast. The Soviets shot Sputnik II into space—this time carrying a dog named Laika. Kathy hung a Lost Dog poster with a picture captioned MUTTNIK: LAST SEEN ORBITING THE EARTH in the break room, but it was promptly removed.

Tension at the Agency increased, and we were asked to stay late for the men's after-hours meetings. Sometimes they'd pick up a pizza or sandwiches if we had to stay past nine. But often there were no breaks and no food, and we made sure to pack extra lunches, just in case.

The Gaither Report soon followed, informing Eisenhower of what he already knew: that in the space race, nuclear race, and almost every other race we were further behind the Soviets than we had thought.

But as it turned out, the Agency already had another weapon in its pipeline.

They had their satellites, but we had their books. Back then, we believed books could be weapons—that literature could change the course of history. The Agency knew it would take time to change the hearts and minds of men, but they were in it for the long game. Since its OSS roots, the Agency had doubled down on soft-propaganda warfare—using art, music, and literature to advance its objectives. The goal: to emphasize how the Soviet system did not allow free thought—how the

Red State hindered, censored, and persecuted even its finest artists. The tactic: to get cultural materials into the hands of Soviet citizens by any means.

We started out stuffing pamphlets into weather balloons and sent them over borders to burst, their contents raining down behind the Iron Curtain. Then we mailed Soviet-banned books back behind enemy lines. At first, the men had the bright idea to just mail the books in nondescript envelopes, cross their fingers, and hope at least a few would make it across undetected. But during one of their book meetings, Linda piped up, suggesting the idea of affixing false covers to the books for better protection. A few of us gathered every copy we could find of less controversial titles like *Charlotte's Web* and *Pride and Prejudice*, removed their dust jackets, and glued them to the contraband before dropping them into the mail. Naturally, the men took the credit.

And it was around that time that the Agency decided we ought to dive even deeper into the war of the words, graduating several men within the ranks to create their own publishing companies and found literary magazines to front our efforts. The Agency became a bit of a book club with a black budget. It was more appealing to poets and writers than book readings with free wine. We had our hands so deep in publishing you'd have thought we got a cut of the royalties.

We'd sit in on the men's meetings and take notes while they talked about the novels they wanted to exploit next. They'd debate the merits of making

Orwell's *Animal Farm* the subject of their next mission versus Joyce's *Portrait of the Artist as a Young Man*. They'd talk books as if their critiques would be printed in the *Times*. So serious, and yet we'd joke that their conversations felt like ones we'd had back in our undergrad lit classes. Someone would make a point, then someone else would disagree, then they'd go off on some tangent. These discussions went on for hours, and we'd be lying if we said we hadn't caught ourselves nodding off once or twice. Once, Norma interrupted the men by saying she firmly believed the themes Bellows explores far outweigh the sheer beauty of Nabokov's sentences, and that was the last book meeting she ever took notes at.

So there were the balloons, the false covers, the publishing companies, the lit mags, all the other books we'd smuggled into the USSR.

Then there was *Zhivago*.

Classified under code name AEDINOSAUR, it was the mission that would change everything.

Doctor Zhivago—a name more than one of us had trouble spelling at first—was written by the Soviet's most famous living writer, Boris Pasternak, and banned in the Eastern Bloc due to its critiques of the October Revolution and its so-called *subversive* nature.

On first glance, it wasn't evident how a sweeping epic about the doomed love between Yuri Zhivago and Lara Antipova could be used as a weapon, but the Agency was always creative.

The initial internal memo described *Zhivago* as "the most heretical literary work by a Soviet author since Stalin's death," saying it had "great propaganda value" for its "passive but piercing exposition of the effect of the Soviet system on the life of a sensitive, intelligent citizen." In other words, it was perfect.

The memo passed through SR faster than word of a break room tryst during one of our martini-soaked Christmas parties and spawned at least half a dozen additional memos, each seconding the first: that this was not just a book, but a weapon—and one the Agency wanted to obtain and smuggle back behind the Iron Curtain for its own citizens to detonate.

EAST

1955–1956

CHAPTER 10

THE AGENT

Sergio D'Angelo awoke to his three-year-old son beside his bed babbling on midsentence about a dragon named Stefano—a large green-and-yellow papier-mâché creature they'd seen at a puppet show back in Rome. "Giulietta!" Sergio called to his wife, hoping she'd take pity on him and fetch their child so that he could sleep another hour. Giulietta ignored his pleas.

Sergio's mouth was dry and his temples throbbed from too many vodka shots the night before. "To the Italians!" his coworker Vladlen had cried, raising a glass to the group gathered for the Radio Moscow party. Sergio laughed and drank without pointing out that he was but one *Italian*, not plural *Italians*. Sergio led the charge to the dance floor. Handsome and dressed as though he'd stepped off an Italian film set, he had his choice of dancing partners. And he chose them all, until

Vladlen tapped him on the shoulder to tell him the music had ended a half hour ago and the café owner was throwing them out. A petite woman with whom Sergio was dancing to no music invited them back to her apartment to continue the revelry, but Sergio declined. Not just because his wife was waiting for him at home, but because, despite the next day being Sunday, he had work to do.

Sergio translated bulletins for Radio Moscow's Italian broadcast, but he'd also come to the USSR for another reason: he was a would-be literary agent. His employer, Giangiacomo Feltrinelli—the timber heir and founder of a new publishing company—wanted to find the next modern classic and was convinced it had to come from the Motherland. "Find me the next *Lolita*," Feltrinelli had instructed.

Sergio had yet to find the next smash hit, but a bulletin that had come across his desk the previous week offered a promising lead: *The publication of Boris Pasternak's* Doctor Zhivago *is imminent. Written in the form of a diary, it is a novel that spans three quarters of a century, ending with the Second World War.* Sergio telegraphed Feltrinelli and was given the go-ahead to attempt to secure the international rights. Unable to get hold of the author by telephone, Sergio made plans with Vladlen to visit Pasternak at his dacha in Peredelkino that Sunday.

That morning, with his son still at his heels, Sergio splashed cold water on his face at the sink and wished he'd asked Vladlen to make the trip the following weekend instead. Entering the kitchen, which was half the size of his kitchen back home, his wife sat at the table drinking a cup of the instant espresso she'd brought with them from Rome. His four-year-old daughter, Francesca, sat across from Giulietta and mimicked her mother, bringing her own plastic cup to her lips and setting it gently down. "Good morning, my darlings," Sergio said, and kissed them both on their cheeks.

"Mama is angry with you, Papa," Francesca said. "Very angry."

"Nonsense. Why would she be angry if there's nothing to be angry about? Your mother knows I must work today. I'm paying the most famous poet in the Soviet Union a visit."

"She didn't say why she is angry, just that she is angry."

Giulietta got up and put her cup into the sink. "I don't care who you are visiting. As long as you don't stay out all night again."

Sergio dressed in his best suit—a custom-tailored sand-colored Brioni, a gift from his generous employer. By the door, he polished his shoes with a horsehair brush. Throughout what had seemed like an endless Russian winter, Sergio had worn the same black rubber boots all Russians wore. Now that spring had come, Sergio felt a jolt of joy as he slipped his feet into his fine leather shoes. Clicking his heels, he bid his family goodbye and was out the door.

Vladlen was waiting for Sergio at track number seven, holding a paper bag full of onion-and-egg piroshki for their short journey. The two men shook hands and Vladlen held out the paper bag. Sergio held his stomach. "I can't."

"Hung over?" Vladlen asked. "You'll need to practice if you want to keep up with us Russians." He opened the bag and shook it. "An old remedy. Take one. We're about to meet Russian royalty, and you need to be at your very best."

Sergio pulled out a pastry. "I thought the Russians killed off all their royals."

"Not yet." Vladlen laughed, a piece of hard-boiled egg falling from his mouth.

The train pulled out of the station, and as the many tracks narrowed to one, Sergio held on to the top of the open window, letting the warm air kiss his fingertips. The spring weather felt magnificent after he had been covered head to toe all winter. He was also excited to see the countryside, as he hadn't yet ventured out of Moscow. "What are they building over there?" he asked his companion.

Vladlen flipped through Pasternak's first book of poetry—*Twin in the Clouds*—which he'd brought along in hopes the author might sign it. "Apartments," he replied without looking up.

"But you didn't even look."

"Factories, then."

The passing landscape changed from recently constructed buildings to buildings under construction to countryside—dotted with spring-green trees and the occasional village marked by an Orthodox church and small country homes, each sectioned off with a fence and its own plot of land. Sergio waved at a young boy on the side of the tracks holding a speckled chicken under his arm. The boy didn't wave back. "How long does it go on like this?" Sergio asked.

"Until Leningrad."

The two men disembarked at Peredelkino. It had rained during the night, and as soon as they crossed the railroad tracks, Sergio stepped in mud. He cursed himself for wearing his good shoes. He sat on a bench and tried to remove the muck with a lace handkerchief, but stopped when he realized he was drawing the attention of three men on the side of the road. The men were trying to hitch an elderly mule to the front of a dilapidated Volga. Sergio and Vladlen made for an odd sight. The blond Russian in his oversized pants—cuffed at the bottom—and tight-fitting vest looked like any man from the city. He was a head taller than the Italian and twice as wide. And Sergio, in his slim-cut suit, was clearly a foreigner.

Sergio dropped the useless handkerchief and asked Vladlen if there was a café nearby where he could properly clean his shoes. Vladlen pointed to a wooden building resembling a large shed across the street, and the two men went inside.

"Toilet?" Sergio asked the woman behind the counter. She had the same expression as the men hitching the mule to the car.

"Outside," she said.

Sergio sighed and asked for a glass of water and a napkin instead. The woman left, then returned with a piece of newspaper and a shot of vodka. "This isn't going to—"

"*Spasibo,*" Vladlen interrupted, and downed the shot, pounding his palm on the counter for another.

"We have important work to do," Sergio said.

"We don't have an appointment. The poet can surely wait."

Sergio forced his friend off his stool and out the door.

Outside, the trio of men had successfully hitched the mule to the car. A small child was now behind the wheel and steered as the men pushed. They stopped and stared as Sergio and Vladlen crossed the street and proceeded up the path that ran alongside the main road.

Passing the Russian Patriarch's summer residence—a grand red and white building behind an equally grand wall—Sergio wished he'd brought his camera. They crossed a small stream, swollen with melted snow and rain, and trudged their way up the small hill and down a gravel road lined with birch and pine trees.

"A place fit for a poet!" Sergio remarked.

"Stalin gave these dachas to a handpicked group of writers," Vladlen replied. "So that they may better *converse with the muse.* That, and it makes it easier to keep track of them."

Pasternak's dacha was on the left and reminded Sergio of a cross between a Swiss chalet and a barn. "There he is," Vladlen said. Dressed like a peasant, Pasternak was tall with a full head of gray hair falling in his face as he bent over his garden plot with a shovel. As Sergio and Vladlen approached, Pasternak looked up and shielded his eyes from the sun to see who'd come to visit.

"*Buon giorno!*" Sergio called out, his enthusiasm betraying his nervousness. Pasternak looked confused, then smiled broadly.

"Come in!" Pasternak replied.

As they got closer to the famous poet, Sergio and Vladlen were struck by how attractive and young Pasternak looked. A handsome man always sizes up another handsome man, but instead of provoking jealousy, the outmatched Sergio looked at the writer with awe.

Pasternak leaned his shovel against a newly pruned apple tree and approached the men. "I had forgotten you were coming," he said, and laughed. "And please forgive me, but I've also forgotten who you are. And why you've come."

"Sergio D'Angelo." He extended his hand and shook Pasternak's. "And this is Anton Vladlen, my colleague at Radio Moscow."

Vladlen, whose eyes were focused on the dirt in front of his shoes instead of at his poet hero, could only muster a grunt.

"What a beautiful name," Pasternak said. "D'Angelo. Such a pleasant sound. What does it mean?"

"Of the angel. It's actually quite common in Italy."

"My surname means parsnip, which I suppose is suitable given my love of toiling in the earth." Pasternak ushered the men to an L-shaped bench at the perimeter of the garden. They sat and Pasternak wiped his brow with a sweat-stained handkerchief. "Radio Moscow? You're here to interview me, then? I'm afraid I haven't much to contribute to the public discussion at the moment."

"I've not come on behalf of Radio Moscow. I've come to discuss your novel."

"Another topic on which I haven't much to say."

"I represent the interests of the Italian publisher Giangiacomo Feltrinelli. You may have heard of him?"

"I have not."

"The Feltrinelli family is one of the wealthiest in Italy. Giangiacomo's new publishing company recently published the autobiography of the first Indian prime minister, Jawaharlal Nehru. You may have heard of it?"

"I've heard of Nehru, of course, but not of his book."

"I'm to bring Feltrinelli the very best new work from behind the Iron Curtain."

"Are you new to our country?"

"I've been here less than a year."

"They don't care for that term." Pasternak looked to the trees as if addressing someone watching. "Iron Curtain."

"Forgive me," Sergio said. He shifted on the bench. "I'm in search of the best new work from the Motherland. Feltrinelli is interested in bringing *Doctor Zhivago* to an Italian audience, then perhaps beyond."

Boris brushed a mosquito from his arm, careful not to kill it. "I've been to Italy once. I was twenty-two and studying music at the University of Marburg. During the summer, I toured Florence and Venice, but I never made it to Rome. I ran out of money. I wanted to visit Milan and go to La Scala. I dreamed of it. I still dream of it. But I was a student, poor as a pauper."

"I've been to La Scala many times," Sergio said. "You must go someday. Feltrinelli can get you the best seat in the house."

Boris laughed, his gaze downward. "I long to travel, but those days are behind me now. Even if I wanted to, they make it so hard for us." He paused. "I wanted to be a composer then, when I was a young man. I had some talent, but not as much as I would have liked. Isn't that always the case with such things? One's passion almost always outweighs talent."

"I'm very passionate about literature," Sergio said, attempting to bring the conversation back to *Doctor Zhivago*. "And I've heard your novel is a masterpiece."

"Who told you that?"

Sergio crossed his legs and the bench wobbled. "Everyone's talking about it. Isn't that right, Vladlen?"

"Everyone is talking," Vladlen said, his first words to Pasternak.

"I haven't heard a word from the publishing houses. I've never had to wait a day to hear word about my work." Pasternak stood from the bench and walked down the center row of his garden, between freshly tilled soil on the left and freshly seeded soil on the right. "I think their silence is clear," he said, his back to the men still sitting on the bench. "My novel will not be published. It does not conform to their *cultural guidelines*."

Sergio and Vladlen got up and followed. "But its publication has already been announced," Vladlen said. "Sergio translated the bulletin for Radio Moscow himself."

Pasternak turned back toward them. "I am not sure what you've heard, but the novel's publication is impossible, I'm afraid."

"Have you received an official rejection?" Vladlen asked.

"Not yet, no. But I've already put the possibility out of my mind. It's best that way, you see. Otherwise I'd drive myself mad." He laughed again, and Sergio wondered if that outcome had already occurred.

Sergio had not anticipated that *Doctor Zhivago* might be banned in the USSR. "That's impossible," he said. "They surely wouldn't suppress such an important work. What about this *thaw* we've heard rumors of?"

"Khrushchev and the rest can make their speeches and their promises, but the only thaw I'm concerned about pertains to my spring planting," Pasternak replied.

"What if you were to give me the manuscript?" Sergio asked.

"For what purpose? If they won't allow it to be published here, it cannot be published anywhere."

"Feltrinelli could get a head start on the Italian translation, so when it does come out in the USSR—"

"It won't."

"I believe it will," Sergio continued, "and when it does, Feltrinelli will be ready at the printing press. He is a member in good standing of the Italian Communist Party, and there will surely be no reason to stall its international publication with him at the helm," Sergio said. He was the consummate optimist, believing nothing impossible. "*Zhivago* will be in the window of every bookshop from Milan to Florence to Naples, and then onward. The whole world needs to read your novel. The whole world *will* read your novel!" It didn't matter that Sergio had never read *Doctor Zhivago* and couldn't comment on its literary merit, and he was well aware he was making promises he wasn't sure he could keep, but he went on and on, as flattery did seem to have a positive effect on the writer.

"One moment," Pasternak said. He walked toward his dacha, taking off his rubber boots before going inside. The two men remained standing in the garden.

"What do you think?" Vladlen asked.

"I don't know. But I do think the novel will come out."

"You are not Russian. You don't understand how things work here. I don't know what he's written, but if it goes against cultural norms, no *thaw* will allow it to be published. If the State bans it here, it will be illegal for Pasternak to publish his book—anywhere. Not now, not ever."

"He hasn't been rejected yet."

"It's been months, and he hasn't heard a response. They don't have to say it to make the message clear."

"That's true, but I also know that history doesn't stand still."

There was movement in the downstairs front window. An older woman peered at them through parted curtains, then disappeared. "The wife?" Sergio asked.

"Must be, although I've heard he has a much younger lover who he doesn't hide away. A public mistress who lives a short walk from here. She's always on his arm, they say. All over Moscow. And his wife doesn't put an end to it."

The dacha's door opened and Pasternak emerged holding a large brown paper package. He walked across the yard barefoot, then paused for a moment in front of his visitors before speaking. "This is *Doctor Zhivago*." He held out the package and Sergio went to take it, but Boris didn't let go. The two men held the package for a moment before Pasternak dropped his hands. "May it make its way around the world."

Sergio turned the package over in his hands, feeling its weight. "Your novel is in good hands with Signore Feltrinelli. You shall see. I will be hand-delivering this to him in person within the week."

Pasternak nodded but looked unconvinced. The three men said their goodbyes. As Sergio and Vladlen set off down the road to the train station, Pasternak called after them, "You are hereby invited to my execution!"

"Poets!" Sergio laughed.

Vladlen said nothing.

The next day, *Doctor Zhivago* was on its way to West Berlin—where Sergio was to hand off the manuscript to Feltrinelli himself, who would take it the rest of the way to Milan.

After a train, a plane, another train, three kilometers of walking, and one bribe, Sergio arrived safely to his hotel on Joachimstahler Strasse. The Kurfürstendamm was bright and showy and thumping with capitalism—everything Moscow wasn't. Smartly dressed men and women walked arm in arm, going out to dinner or dancing or to one of the many *kabarett* that had reopened across the city. Volkswagen Beetles and motorcycles skidded around the wide boulevards with teenagers riding hunch-backed. Neon signs lit up one after the next: NESCAFÉ in yellow, BOSCH in red, HOTEL AM ZOO in white, SALA-MANDER SHOES in blue. Tables lined the sidewalks of the many cafés and restaurants dotting the street. The sound of a piano drifted out of a cocktail lounge where a striking black woman resembling a curvier Josephine Baker was enticing passersby to come in.

Once in his room, he opened his suitcase and removed the tailored Oxford shirt and paisley-patterned silk pajamas that covered the manuscript, still wrapped in its brown paper. Twice he'd averted having his suitcase searched when crossing from East to West Berlin by making friendly conversation with soldiers on both sides and having the kind of face some people trusted and the kind of pockets that made the doubtful trust again. He kissed the manuscript, placed it inside the dresser's bottom drawer, and covered it with the pajamas.

Sergio took a long shower. The hot water lasted only four minutes, which was three minutes longer than it lasted back in Moscow. After, he drip-dried while shaving in the bathroom mirror, happy he'd brought his own razor.

Although he craved Orecchiette alla Crudaiola and any wine made from Italian grapes, he settled for pilsner and schnitzel at the hotel bar. He knew that when Feltrinelli arrived the next day, his employer would know exactly where to go and celebrate the procurement of Pasternak's novel; he'd have secured the best tables at the finest restaurants and the best Chianti moments after stepping off the plane.

After a breakfast of liverwurst, a boiled egg, herbed cheese, and a roll with marmalade, Sergio double-checked with the man at the front desk to ensure that Feltrinelli's presidential suite would be ready for him.

"Do you have the cognac?"

"*Ja.*"

"The cigarettes?"

"We've located a box of Nazionali Esportazione for Mr. Feltrinelli."

"The sheets . . . they're untucked at the end as he prefers?"

"I believe so."

"Can you check then with the maid?"

"*Ja.* Can we do anything else for you?"

"Taxi?"

"Of course."

At Tempelhof Airport, Sergio watched Feltrinelli's plane touch down and come to a stop. A mobile staircase was driven up to its door. He stepped out with a *Corriere della Sera* newspaper tucked under his arm and paused at the top of the stairs to survey the Fatherland. His tan suit jacket opened and his tie flew back behind his shoulder with a gust of wind. Spotting his agent waiting for him below, he descended.

The publisher greeted Sergio warmly, kissing him on both cheeks, then shaking his hand. Sergio had met Giangiacomo Feltrinelli only a handful of times, but he had always been struck by his magnetism. Slimly built with dark hair styled back to reveal a high widow's peak, Feltrinelli was the kind of man both women and men found themselves drawn to. Even his signature thick black glasses did nothing to hide the vitality in his eyes. Maybe it was his enormous wealth that earned him such attention. Or maybe it was the confidence that accompanied that wealth. Or it could be his collection of fast cars and custom-made suits, or the beautiful women who flocked to him. Whatever it was, Feltrinelli had it in spades.

Sergio took Feltrinelli's calfskin bag and Feltrinelli took his arm as though they were school chums. Sergio suggested they go to a restaurant for lunch, but Feltrinelli shook his head. "I'd like to see it right away."

Feltrinelli paced the hotel's burnt-orange carpeting as Sergio fetched the manuscript. He handed *Doctor Zhivago* to his boss, and Feltrinelli held it in his hands as if he could feel its significance by its weight. He flipped through the novel, then held it to his chest. "I've never wanted to be able to read Russian more than now."

"It is sure to be a hit."

"I believe it will be. I've arranged for the best translator to take a look at it as soon as I get back to Milan. He's promised to give me his honest opinion."

"There's something I haven't told you."

Feltrinelli waited for him to continue.

"Pasternak believes the Soviets will not allow its publication. I couldn't say this in my telegram, but he thinks it doesn't fit—how did he put it?—their *guidelines*."

Feltrinelli brushed it off. "I've heard the same, but let's not think of that now. Besides, once the Soviets find out I have it, they might just change their mind."

"There was something else. He mentioned he was giving himself a death sentence by handing over the novel. Surely he was joking?"

Feltrinelli put the book under his arm without answering. "I'm here for only two days. We must celebrate."

"Of course! What would you like to do first?"

"I want to drink good German beer, and I want to dance, and I want to find a few girls. And I'd like to purchase a pair of binoculars from a shop in Kurfürstendamm I've heard makes the best in the world." He took off his glasses and pointed to his nose. "They take the measurements from the bridge of your nose to the outer corners of your eyes to create the exact fit. They'll be perfect for my yacht. I must have them."

"Of course, of course," Sergio said. "I suppose my job is done, then."

"Yes, my friend. And mine is just beginning."

CHAPTER 11

~~THE MUSE~~
~~THE REHABILITATED WOMAN~~

THE EMISSARY

My train pulled in to the station after four fruitless days in Moscow, after more fruitless attempts at persuading publishers to print *Zhivago*. I saw Borya sitting alone on a bench. It was late May and the sun had just begun to dip below the tree line. In the golden light, his white hair looked blond and his eyes seemed to sparkle even through the dirty train window. I felt a pain in my chest. From a distance, he looked like a young man, even younger than I. We'd been together nearly a decade and that pain was still there. He stood as the train doors opened.

"Something most unusual happened this week," he said, taking my bag and slinging it over his shoulder. "I had two unexpected visitors."

"Who?"

Borya pointed to the path that ran along the tracks, where we'd walk if we had something important to talk about. He took my hand and helped me cross. A train passed, going in the opposite direction, and rustled the bottom of my skirt with a gust of air. I could tell from his gait, a step faster than usual, that he was both excited and anxious. "Who visited you?" I asked again.

"An Italian and a Russian," he said, his speech matching his pace. "The Italian was young and charming. Tall with black hair, very handsome. You would've liked him very much, Olya. He had such a wonderful name! *Sergio D'Angelo*. He said it's quite a common surname in Italy, but I've never heard it. Beautiful, isn't it? *D'Angelo*. It means *of the angel*."

"Why did they come?"

"You would've been delighted by him—the Italian. The other, the Russian, I don't recall his name—he didn't speak much."

I took hold of his arm, forcing him to slow down and tell me what he had to say.

"We had the most wonderful conversation. I told them about my time studying in Marburg as a young man. How much I had enjoyed traveling to Florence and Venice. I explained how I'd wanted to go to Rome as well, but—"

"Why did the Italian come?"

"He wanted *Doctor Zhivago*."

"What did he want with it?"

Like a confession, Borya told me the story—about D'Angelo and the Russian and a publisher by the name of Feltrinelli.

"And what did you tell him?"

We stopped speaking as a young woman hauling a rickety cart filled with petrol cans passed us, then he continued. "I told him that the novel would never be published here. That it doesn't conform to cultural guidelines. But he pressed on, saying he thinks the book could still be published."

"How could he think such a thing if he's never read it?"

"That's why I gave it to him. To read. To get an honest assessment."

"You gave him the manuscript?"

"Yes." Borya's demeanor changed, and he looked his age again. He knew he'd done something that was not only irreversible, but dangerous.

"What have you done?" I tried to keep my voice down, but it came out like steam escaping a kettle. "Do you even know this person? This foreigner? Do you have any idea what they'll do when they intercept it? Or maybe they have it already. Did you think of that? What if this *D'Angelo* of yours isn't even really an Italian?"

He looked like a spanked child. "You are thinking too much of this." He ran his hand through his hair. "It will be fine. Feltrinelli's a Communist," he added.

"Fine?" My eyes watered. What Borya had done was akin to treason. If the West was to publish the novel without permission from the USSR, they would come for him—for me. And a brief stay in a labor camp wouldn't be punishment enough this time. I needed to sit, but there was nowhere to sit except in the mud. How could he be so selfish? Had he thought of me even once? I turned and began walking back.

"Stop," Borya said, coming after me. A shade fell across his bright eyes. He knew exactly what he'd done. "I wrote the book to be read, Olga. This could be its only chance. I'm ready to accept the consequences, whatever they may be. I'm not afraid of what they might do to me."

"But what about me? You may not care what happens to you, but what about me? I've gone away once . . . I can't . . . They can't take me again."

"They won't. I'll never allow it." He put his arms around my shoulders and I leaned against his chest. It was as if I could feel a new separation between our heartbeats. "I haven't signed anything yet."

"You gave them permission to publish. We both know that. And that's *if* they are who they said they are. There is no good outcome. I can't go back there," I said, wiping my eyes. "I won't."

"I'd rather burn *Zhivago* than let that happen. I'd rather die." His words felt like running a hand under cold water after burning it on the stove—the pain might be soothed while the water runs, but as soon as you turn off the faucet, the throbbing continues. And in that moment, for the first time, I lost faith in him.

"This book will take us down a spiral from which there will be no return."

"Let's see. I can always tell him I made a mistake," he said. "I can always ask for it back."

"No," I said. "*I* will ask for it back."

I traveled to Moscow and, having pried the address from Borya, knocked on D'Angelo's door, unannounced. An elegant woman with dark brown hair and arresting blue eyes answered. The woman introduced herself in broken Russian as D'Angelo's wife, Giulietta.

D'Angelo came to the door and kissed my extended hand. "How wonderful to meet you, Olga," he said, smiling rakishly. "I've heard rumors of your beauty, but you're even more beautiful than they've said."

Instead of thanking him, I launched right in. "You see," I finished, "he didn't understand fully what he was doing. We must have the manuscript back."

"Let us sit," he said, taking my hand and leading me back into the sitting room. "Would you like anything to drink?"

"No," I said. "I mean, no thank you."

He turned to his wife. "Darling, will you bring me an espresso? And one for our guest?"

Giulietta kissed her husband's cheek and went into the kitchen.

D'Angelo rubbed his hands across his thighs. "I'm afraid it is too late."

"What is too late?"

"The book." He was still smiling, as people in the West do—out of politeness, not happiness. "I've delivered it to Feltrinelli. And he loved it. He's already decided to publish it."

I looked at him incredulously. "But it's been only a few days since Borya gave it to you."

He laughed too loudly for my liking. "I was on the first plane to East Berlin. Well, two trains, a plane, then so much walking that I needed to purchase a new pair of shoes by the time I reached West Berlin. Signor Feltrinelli flew in himself to meet me. We had quite a time there—"

"You must get the manuscript back."

"That's impossible, I'm afraid. The translation has already begun. Feltrinelli said so himself, that it would be a crime not to publish this novel."

"A *crime*? What do you know of crimes? What do you know of punishment? The crime is for Boris to have it published outside the USSR. You must understand what you've done."

"Mr. Pasternak gave me his permission. I wasn't aware of any danger." He stood and retrieved his briefcase from the entryway. Inside was a black leather journal. "See, I wrote it down the day I visited him in Peredelkino. I'd found his words so eloquent."

I looked at the open page. Inside, D'Angelo had written: *This is Doctor Zhivago. May it make its way around the world.*

"See? Permission. And besides"—he paused, and I sensed the Italian did feel some culpability—"even if I wanted to bring it back, it's out of my hands now."

It was out of my hands as well. Borya *had* granted his permission, and had lied to me about having done so. *Zhivago* had made its way out of the country, and things were in motion. All I could do was try to push forward with the plan to have the book published in the USSR before Feltrinelli published it abroad. It was the only way to save him, to save myself.

Borya signed the contract with Feltrinelli a month later. I was not there when he signed his name. Nor was his wife, who, for the first time, was in total agreement with me: the novel's publication could only bring us pain.

He told me he thought a Soviet publisher would publish with the added pressure from abroad. I didn't believe him. "You haven't signed a contract," I said. "You have signed a death warrant."

I did my best. I pleaded with Sergio D'Angelo to pressure Feltrinelli to return the manuscript. And I saw every editor who'd meet with me to ask if they'd publish *Zhivago* before Feltrinelli could.

Word had gotten out the Italians had the novel, and the Central Committee's Culture Department demanded its return from Feltrinelli. I found myself in the new position of having to agree with the State. If *Zhivago* was to be published, it *must* be published first at home. But Feltrinelli ignored the requests, and I feared what might come next. So I met with the Department's head, Dmitri Alexeyevich Polikarpov, to see if I could soften their position.

Polikarpov was an attractive man whom I'd seen many times at events in the city but had never spoken with. He wore Western-cut suits with pegged trousers that brushed the sides of his shiny black loafers. He was known as an enforcer within the Moscow literary community, and my breath shortened as Polikarpov's secretary ushered me into his office. But even before I sat down, I took a deep breath and began the plea I'd rehearsed on the train. "The only thing to do is publish the novel before the Italians do," I reasoned. "We can edit out the parts deemed anti-Soviet before publication." Of course, Borya knew nothing of my negotiation. I knew better than anyone that he'd rather his novel not be published at all than have it hacked apart.

Polikarpov reached into his jacket pocket and pulled out a small metal tin. "Impossible." He took out two white pills and swallowed them dry. "*Doctor Zhivago* must be returned at all costs," he continued. "It cannot be published as is—not in Italy, not anywhere. If we publish one version and the Italians another, the world will ask why we published it without certain sections. It will be an embarrassment to the State and to Russian literature as a whole. Your *friend* has put me in a precarious position." He put the tin back in his pocket. "And you as well."

"But what is to be done?"

"You can ask Boris Leonidovich to sign the telegram I will give you."

"What does this telegram say?"

"That the manuscript Feltrinelli possesses is but a draft, that a new draft is forthcoming, and that the original manuscript must be returned posthaste. The telegram is to be signed within two days or else he will be arrested."

That was the stated threat. The unstated threat was that my arrest would soon follow. But I knew Feltrinelli wouldn't refrain from publication even if he received such a telegram. Borya had arranged to communicate with the Italian only in French and had instructed the publisher to disregard anything sent under his name in Russian. Plus, I knew it would cause Borya much shame to sign such a document. "I will try," I said.

And I did. I asked him. I asked him to send the telegram to Feltrinelli asking for his manuscript back, as Polikarpov had instructed. I asked the man I loved to stop the publication of his life's work. And when I did—over dinner at Little House—he just sat back in his chair. His hand went to his neck as if he were suffering a muscle spasm and he was quiet for a long moment. Then he spoke.

"Years ago, I received a phone call."

I put my fork down. I knew where he was going.

"It was shortly after Osip had been arrested for his poem against Stalin," he continued. "He hadn't even written it down, only committed it to memory. But even that proved to be a grievous mistake. Even the words in one's head could be an arrestable offense during those dark times. You were but a child, too young to remember now."

I refilled my wineglass. "I know how old I am."

"One night he recited the poem to a group of us on a street corner, and I told him it was akin to suicide. He didn't heed my warning, and of course they soon arrested him. Not long after, I received the phone call. Do you know who it was?"

"I've heard the stories."

"Of course you have. But never from me."

I moved to refill his wineglass, but he waved me away. "Stalin began without greeting, his voice immediately familiar. He asked if Osip was my friend, and if he was, why I hadn't petitioned for his release. I had no answer for him, Olya. But instead of making the case for Osip's freedom, I made excuses. I told the head of the Central Committee that even if I had petitioned on Osip's behalf, it would never have reached his ears. Stalin then asked if I thought Osip was a master, and I told him that was beside the point. Then do you know what I did?"

"What, Boris? Tell me what you did." I drank the rest of my wine.

"I changed the subject. I told Stalin I'd long wanted to have a serious conversation with him about life and death. And do you know how he responded?"

"How?"

"He hung up."

I rolled a pea around my plate with the back of my knife. "But what does this have to do with now? That was years ago. Stalin is dead."

"I've long regretted what I did. Or, rather, what I didn't do. I was given the chance to stand up for my friend, to save him, and I didn't take it. I was a coward."

"No one blames you for—"

Borya pounded his fist on the table, rattling the plates and silverware. "I won't be a coward again."

"This is not the same—"

"They've asked me to sign letters before."

"This is different. Feltrinelli already knows to ignore anything you send that's not written in French. You've prepared for this. It won't be a lie. It's simply a measure of protection."

"I don't need protection."

My anger grew. "What about me, then, Boris? Who will protect me?" I paused before unleashing everything. "They sent me to the Gulag once before. Because of you." I'd never laid the blame for my arrest directly at his feet, and he looked aghast. I said it again: "They sent me to that place because of you. Do you want to be responsible for sending me back there?"

Boris went quiet again.

"Well? Do you?"

"You must think very little of me," he finally answered. "Where is it?"

I went to my bedroom and returned with Polikarpov's telegram. He took it from me, and without reading it, signed his name. I sent it to Milan first thing in the morning, followed by a telegram to Polikarpov saying it had been done.

Borya and I didn't speak about the telegram again after that, and in the end, it didn't matter anyway. Feltrinelli ignored it, as we knew he would, and a date for publication in Italy was set for early November, 1957.

I had tried my best, but my best was not enough. *Doctor Zhivago* was a speeding train that could not be stopped.

WEST

FALL 1957–AUGUST 1958

CHAPTER 12

~~THE APPLICANT~~

THE CARRIER

Sally Forrester arrived on a Monday. I'd gone to Ralph's with the typing pool, at Norma's pleading. I knew she was only interested in getting the scoop on my relationship with Teddy, but I'd agreed when she offered to buy me a burger and a chocolate malt, knowing I had soggy tuna on Wonder Bread waiting for me at my desk.

The typing pool's usual booth was a tad cramped, so I sat with my long legs turned out to the aisle. As soon as we ordered, Norma volleyed questions at me. "Come on, Irina. You've been dating for what, a year? And you don't tell us anything. We don't know anything."

"Eight months," I said.

"I was engaged to David after three," Linda chimed in.

I smiled politely. Fact was, Teddy and I had become a real couple without my even realizing it. Our first dinner at Rive Gauche turned into dinner and a movie the following weekend, which turned into dinner and dancing, which turned into dinner at his parents' expansive home in Potomac. Teddy had introduced me as his girlfriend, and not wanting to hurt his feelings, I hadn't corrected him—even after months passed. Maybe it was because we got along well, or because Mama loved him and he had an impressive knowledge of Russian culture and mastery of the language. "You speak better Russian than my cousins, and they were born there!" she'd told him.

Plus, I was comfortable with him in a way I'd longed to be with a friend my entire life. I didn't have to analyze my every word and move with him. It was a friendship, but I hadn't yet given up hope that it could turn into something more. I was waiting for that lightning bolt, that electric shock, that weak-knees moment—every cliché I'd only read about.

There were other perks too. Teddy was seen as an up-and-comer at the Agency, a potential member of an inner circle that, as a woman, I could only hope to see the outskirts of. He'd take me to the Sunday dinner parties in Georgetown and the fancy cocktail parties at the Hay-Adams Hotel. And he wouldn't send me off to chat with the wives and girlfriends; he'd pull me from conversation to conversation with the men, and squeeze my hand when he felt proud of a point I'd made.

Teddy was a Catholic and never pressured me to do anything I wasn't ready for. It wasn't that he was against sex before marriage—he'd lost his virginity to a substitute teacher his senior year at prep school and had three more partners in college—but he was respectful of my boundaries. I wasn't against sex before marriage either, although I'd let him believe I was more of a prude than I actually was. Teddy didn't know it, but I was no virgin. I'd lost—or rather, given away—my virginity to a friend my junior year. I'd approached it as something to get over and done with, and invited him to my dorm when my roommate was away. He came through the door and I asked if he'd have sex with me. Poor guy was so taken aback, he initially tried to talk me out of it, but he relented when I took off my blouse.

I'd always approached sex as an anthropologist. Instead of turning the gaze on myself, I was most interested in observing the man and his reactions. And I liked how Teddy responded to touching me—even more than how it made me feel. His restrained desire made me feel powerful, and that was a revelation. Teddy was everything I should've hoped for—and yet.

Norma's questions came to a halt when Sally breezed into Ralph's. Linda alerted the group by widening her eyes. "Who is *that*?"

I looked at the same time the rest of the Pool did.

"Way to be inconspicuous."

Ralph's was a place for regulars: the typing pool gossiping in the back booth, the old-timers dipping their toast in their sunny-side-up eggs at the counter; the college students studying at the round-tops, having ordered only a coffee or a chocolate malt; the occasional lawyer or lobbyist who took clients there when they wanted to be incognito. Any newcomer to Ralph's got the Pool's attention—but this woman demanded it.

Judy pretended she was getting something out of her purse. "She looks familiar."

Marcos had already come around from behind the counter and was pointing out each and every pastry in the case to the woman. Athena leaned against the register, her eyes on her husband, his eyes on the woman. She was of medium height but wore heels that hiked her up a few inches. She looked young but was far too sophisticated for someone in her twenties in her bright blue knee-length coat with red silk lining and fox fur collar. Her hair was a deep red and perfectly curled—the kind of hair that makes you want to say the color aloud. My own hair resembled the color of an underbaked oatmeal cookie.

"Politician's wife?" Norma asked.

"Downtown at this hour?" Linda added. She wiped ketchup from the corner of her mouth with the tip of her napkin.

"Besides," Kathy jumped in, "those heels sure as hell don't belong to a politician's wife."

Judy dangled a French fry from her finger like a cigarette. "That's an understatement."

"Is she famous?" I asked. From where I was sitting, the woman could've passed for Rita Hayworth, but when she turned and I got a better look at her face, I realized she didn't look like Rita at all—her beauty was her own.

"Hmmm," appraised Linda. "Was she in that movie? The one that was banned? *Baby Doll*?"

"You're thinking of Carroll Baker," I said. "She's blond, but I guess she could've dyed her hair."

"Too old," Kathy said at the same time Judy said, "Too curvy."

Norma licked a spot of mustard off her finger. "That's no Carroll Baker. Was she in that Garfinckel's ad? You know, the one with the"—she lowered her voice— "magic inserts?"

"She doesn't look like she needs any magic inserts," I said, then covered my mouth as the typing pool burst out laughing.

The woman pointed to a cherry turnover and Marcos boxed up two. She paid Athena and shot Marcos a wink. She turned to leave, but not before a quick nod to our table. We all looked away, pretending we hadn't been looking in the first place.

That was the first time I saw Sally Forrester, before I knew her name.

The second time I saw Sally Forrester was at HQ. We'd returned from Ralph's and there she was, standing at reception chatting up Anderson. Anderson, who usually greeted us with some reference to working off the calories we'd consumed at lunch, didn't give us a second glance as we passed and went to our desks.

"Why's *she* here?" Judy asked.

"Someone important?" Norma said.

"One of Dulles's?" Linda asked with a smile. The spy chief's dalliances were no secret, and his affairs numbered well into the dozens. It was even rumored he'd dipped into the typing pool. But if that was true, none of us ever owned up to it.

"If that's the case, no way she'd be standing in SR with Anderson," Gail said. Anderson had eaten one of the woman's cherry turnovers, evidenced by a glob of jelly on his baby blue sweater vest. He leaned against the reception desk, trying to look important or maybe casual—a sad attempt at flirting. But the woman wasn't rolling her eyes like we would've. She just smiled and laughed and touched his arm.

She took off her blue coat and handed it to Anderson, who draped it over his arm like a waiter. Underneath, she wore a woolen mauve dress with a gold braided belt. I looked down the front of my navy shift dress and noticed a stain smack in the center of my chest, remnants of toothpaste I thought I'd gotten out that morning. I opened my bottom drawer and took out the brown cardigan I kept for when the building's heat got spotty. Horrid, I thought, putting it on and rolling the sleeves into cuffs.

"New typist?" Gail asked.

"Nah," Kathy said. "We're full now with the Russian."

"Russian American," I corrected.

Judy tossed a broken eraser at me. "Go find out, Anna Karenina."

But Anderson and the redhead were already moving toward us. He led the way, pointing out mundane features of the office, stating that the Xerox machine was "a year away from being released to the public" and the water cooler distributed "both hot *and* cold." They reached my desk first.

"Sally Forrester," the woman said and stuck out her hand.

I shook her hand. "Sally," I said.

"You're Sally too?"

"This is Irina," Anderson said for me.

Sally smiled again. "Pleasure."

I nodded dumbly, and before I could say it was a pleasure to meet her as well, they'd already moved on down the line, shaking hands with every member of the Pool.

"Miss Forrester is our new part-time receptionist," Anderson said to everyone. "She'll be in the office occasionally, helping out as needed."

We debriefed in the ladies' room.

"Those clothes!"

"That hair!"

"That handshake!"

Sally's handshake had been firm. Not like some of the men whose grips crushed our fingers, but enough to make us notice. "Firm, but not too firm," Norma said. "That's how the politicians do it."

"But why's she here?"

"Who knows."

"Well, I know they don't put women like that behind a reception desk," Norma said. "And if they do, it's for a reason."

After work, I took the long route home so I could pass Hecht's. Their elaborate window displays were my favorite in the city: mannequins dressed for the ski slopes atop a tiny hill of cotton snow in winter, searching for Easter eggs in their prettiest pastel frocks in spring, lounging in their bikinis by a blue cellophane pool in summer.

As I passed, a man with a tape measure in his back pocket was arranging a trio of mannequins dressed as witches behind a black plastic cauldron. I told myself I was just going to pass the window and be on my way. When I went inside, I told myself I was just going to browse. When I started browsing, I told myself I'd just look to see if I could afford anything that didn't look handmade—something that looked like something Sally Forrester might wear.

I passed my hands over the racks, fingering the silks and linens between my fingers, and ran my hand along a skirt's perfect stitching. If my mother had been with me, she'd have shown me how machines had cheaply achieved this uniformity and how, over time, the seams would fray, the buttons would fall off, and eventually the ill-informed shopper who'd purchased the overpriced skirt would come to her so she could fix it. She'd have held up a calloused sewing finger and told me there's no replacement for hard work.

As I pressed a red blouse with a red-and-white paisley scarf under its Peter Pan collar against my chest, a salesgirl asked if I needed help. "Just looking," I said. Salesgirls always intimidated me, which is why I hardly ever went into department stores in the first place—that, and I never had the money to spend.

"Lovely blouse," the salesgirl continued. She was dressed in a fit and flare black skirt and white blouse, her bangs shellacked into a high arch above her forehead. "It would look fabulous on you. Like to try it on?" She took the hanger from me before I could respond, and I followed her to the dressing room. She placed the blouse on a hook. "Let me know if you need another size."

Before undressing, I checked the price tag. I couldn't afford it, but I stayed in the dressing room for a few minutes to make her think I at least tried it on. I'd tell her red just wasn't my color. But when I opened the door, I found myself saying, "I'll take it."

Mama inundated me with questions when I walked through the door. "Where were you? On a date with

Teddy? Has he proposed yet?" Any time Mama brought up Teddy, I felt unnerved.

"I went for a walk."

"Has he broken up with you? I knew this would happen."

"Mama! I just wanted to go on a walk."

"Such a long walk! Always such long walks for you these days. God only knows what you're up to."

"You don't believe in God."

"No matter. You shouldn't walk so much. You're already too skinny. And who has time to walk anyway? I needed your help finishing the beading on Miss Halpern's prom dress. This is a big opportunity for me to get into the American teen market. I do a dress for Miss Halpern and all her friends see her in it, and then they want one too. Next thing you know, a *USA Dresses and More for You* dress will be on *American Bandstand* next to that handsome Richard Clark."

"*Dick* Clark?"

"Who?"

I sat at the kitchen table next to her, careful to place my purse under my feet so she wouldn't see the bit of tissue paper sticking out of the zipper. "Wait," I said. "I know that dress. Yellow chiffon, right?"

"Not a good color for such a pale girl, but who am I to say?"

"But that dress doesn't have much beading. Just a little on the straps. You can finish something like that in an hour." Instead of answering, Mama got up from the table. "Are you feeling okay?" I asked.

She turned and looked at me, her brow furrowed. "I'm just tired."

I wore my new red blouse to work the next day, hiding it under an oversized beige sweater before leaving. Mama didn't see the blouse, although she did comment on the sweater. "That ugly old thing?" she asked. She pretended to look out one of the half windows of our basement apartment. "Is it snowing outside? You're not going skiing, are you?"

"You're back to your old self."

"What other self would I be?"

I kissed her cheek and hurried out.

Sweating, I waited until I reached the bus stop before taking the sweater off. I held my coat between my thighs and wiggled out of it. A woman passing with her two children dressed in Catholic school uniforms gave me a look. It wasn't until I was on the bus that I realized my blouse was misbuttoned and a portion of my bra was exposed.

The elevator dinged and I stepped out into reception with my coat draped over my arm, my shoulders back, looking straight ahead instead of at my feet in an attempt to convey that I was as breezy and confident as the woman in the Ban Roll-On Deodorant ad. I glanced toward reception, ready to say hello to Sally, but was disappointed to see the regular receptionist.

"Cute blouse," she said. "Red's a lovely color on you."

"Thanks," I said. "Got it on sale." I was always doing that. If someone told me they liked my new haircut, I'd tell them that I wasn't sure about the length. If someone said they liked an idea I had or a joke I told, I'd attribute it to someone else.

Sally didn't come in the next day, nor the day after that. Every time I stepped out of the elevator, I braced myself to see her; but still no Sally. And I wasn't the only one who noticed. The typing pool took her absence as proof she had another role at the Agency. "Part-time receptionist my ass," Norma said. I laughed with the rest of them, though I couldn't help but wonder what they might say about me behind my back.

A week passed, but I still found myself thinking of her. Something about Sally Forrester lingered.

Another week passed and I'd given up on seeing her again. But when the elevator opened, there she was, seated at the reception desk doodling on a yellow steno pad. She waved hello and I faked a coughing fit to cover my reddening face.

I sat at my desk and went right to work, telling myself not to look in her direction. Even without looking, I could feel her presence all morning. When I got up to use the restroom, I was keenly aware how my body moved, how I held my head, what I looked like walking across SR. It was as if I was seeing myself through someone else's gaze. Then it happened: she spoke to me. I thought she was speaking to someone else, but it was my name she'd called out.

"Oh, I didn't know you were talking to me," I said instead of saying hello.

"Are there many Irinas in SR?"

"I don't think so. No. Maybe?"

"I'm teasing. Anyway, since I'm the new gal in town, I was thinking maybe we could grab lunch. You could give me the lay of the land."

"I brought my lunch," I said. "Tuna." *Stop,* I told myself, *just stop.*

"Eat it tomorrow." She picked a piece of lint from the front of her fuzzy chartreuse sweater. "Show me what's good around here."

We walked in the direction of the White House, Sally leading the way although she'd been the one who'd asked me where to go. "I know a great deli nearby. A rarity in Washington, believe me," she said. "They slice the ham paper thin and pile it six inches high. Only people from here know of it, and no one is actually *from* here. You know what I mean? Do you have to get back soon? It's still a bit of a walk."

"We have an hour for lunch, so we have about forty-five, maybe forty minutes left."

"You think Company boys look at their watches during their liquid lunches?"

"No, but . . ." I paused a beat too long, and Sally turned on her heels as if heading back toward the office. "No," I said. "Let's go."

She looped her arm through mine. "That's the spirit." I could feel the hot stares of men as we passed, and even a few women looked our way. I was with her. I liked being with her. My surroundings blurred as if we were no longer in the city—the endless car honking and bus screeching and jackhammers pummeling concrete ceased. It was noon on a Thursday, and the world slowed on its axis.

We passed a tour bus stopped at a light and I could hear the guide's microphoned voice direct the attention of the passengers toward the famous Octagon House. Sally surprised me by waving to the tourists, who enthusiastically waved back. One took a picture of her. She put her hand behind her head to pose. "Still can't get used to this city," she said. "Everyone flocks to the seat of power."

"Have you lived here long?"

"On and off."

We turned down an alley of P Street I'd never noticed. Narrow brownstones with ivy-covered chimneys lined the street. Halloween was approaching, and the residents had decorated with cotton spider webs spread across their hedges, paper black cats and skeletons with movable joints hung in the windows, and yet-to-be-carved pumpkins on their stoops. On the corner was the deli. Over the door hung a green and white-tiled sign: FERRANTI'S.

A bell tinkled as we opened the door. The owner, a man as long and thin as the dried sausages hanging from the deli's ceiling, slapped a sack of semolina flour and a tiny cloud erupted from the bag. "Where have you been all my life?" he asked.

"Off somewhere waiting for a better line than that," Sally said. The man kissed Sally on both cheeks with big, wet smacks.

"This is Paolo."

"And who is this exquisite creature?" Paolo asked. It took me a moment to realize he was talking about me.

Sally playfully slapped away my extended hand. "What do I get if I tell you?"

Paolo held up a finger, then disappeared into the back room. He emerged holding two wooden chairs, which he placed in the small space between the front window and the shelves filled with canned tomatoes, glass jars of bright green olives, and stacks of packaged noodles.

"No table?" Sally asked.

"Patience." He left and returned with a round table, just big enough to seat two. Like a magic trick, he reached behind his back and pulled out a small red-and-white-checkered tablecloth. He spread it over the table and gestured for us to take a seat.

"What, no candle?"

Paolo threw up his hands. "What else? Linen napkins? Salad forks?" He pointed to the ceiling. "Perhaps I should invest in a tiny chandelier?"

"That would be a start, but we're actually getting our food to go. It'd be a sin to be inside on such a gorgeous fall day."

He pretended to wipe a tear from his eye with the corner of his apron. "What a disappointment. But of course I understand." He moved a wax-coated cheese wheel aside to get a better look out the window. "I'd be out there myself if I could. Actually, maybe I'll close early and join you two ladies for a sandwich. Reflecting Pool? Tidal Basin?"

"Sorry, this is a business lunch."

"Such is life."

We ordered: turkey and Swiss on rye with a dill pickle plucked from a barrel for me, and an olive tapenade and some kind of meat I'd never heard of on a baguette for Sally. Paolo handed us our sandwiches in a brown paper bag. We said our goodbyes, and as we left, I turned back. "I'm Irina," I said.

"Irina! Sally broke her deal with me, didn't she? Such a beautiful name. I'll see you back again with Sally soon?"

"Yes."

We walked for another fifteen minutes, not thinking of the time left in our lunch hour. Sally stopped at the foot of an enormous building on Sixteenth I'd never noticed before. It looked like something out of ancient Egypt. Two giant sphinxes flanked the marble stairs leading up to a large brown door. "Museum?" I asked.

"House of the Temple. You know, Freemason secret society kinda stuff. I'm sure there's a lot of funny hat wearing and chanting and candle lighting going on in there. Just ask a few of the men we work with. To me, these steps are just the perfect place to have some lunch and watch the world pass by."

As we ate, I could feel myself becoming more comfortable, though still keenly aware of her presence. Sally finished her sandwich and wiped the corners of her mouth. She ate nearly twice as fast as I did. "How do you like the typing pool?"

"I like it. I think."

She opened her pocketbook and pulled out a compact and red lipstick. She puckered her lips. "Any on my teeth?"

"Oh, no. It looks perfect."

"So, you like it?"

"Red's a great color on you."

"I mean the Pool."

"It's a good job."

"Do you like the typing or the other stuff better?"

A flash of heat traveled down my throat to my stomach. I looked at Sally with what I thought was a blank stare, though I must have looked nervous.

"Don't worry," she said, placing her hand on mine. She had the softest hands, her nails painted the same shade of red as her lips. "You and I are the same. Well, almost."

"What do you mean?"

"Anderson told me when I joined back up. But he didn't really have to tell me. I could tell from the moment we met that you were different."

I looked from side to side, then behind us. "You carry messages too?"

"More of a message *sender*." She squeezed my hand. "Us gals gotta stick together. There aren't many of us. Right?"

"Right."

The day after our lunch on the Temple steps, Anderson informed me that instead of my meeting with Teddy, as I'd been doing, Sally would continue my training. "Surprised?" he asked.

"Yes," I said, biting my lip to keep from smiling.

The day after that, Sally stood outside the Agency's black iron gates, applying her red lipstick in the driver's side mirror of a pale yellow Studebaker. She looked impeccable in a tartan wool cape and long black calfskin gloves. She saw me approach in the mirror and turned, lipstick applied to only her bottom lip. "Looks like it's just you and me now, kiddo," she said and pressed her lips together. "Let's go for a walk."

As we made our way through Georgetown, Sally pointed out the stately homes of some of the Agency's higher-ups. "Dulles lives up there," she said, pointing to a red brick townhouse obscured by a wall of maple trees. "And that big white one with the black shutters across the way? That's Wild Bill Donovan's old house that the Grahams bought. Frank lives on the other side of Wisconsin. All of 'em spitting distance from each other."

"Where do you live?"

"Just up the street."

"To keep tabs on the men?"

She laughed. "Smart girl."

We took a left into Dumbarton Oaks and walked the park's winding path into the gardens. Descending the stone steps, Sally pulled on a dead wisteria vine hanging from the wooden arbor. "In the spring, this whole place smells absolutely delicious. I open my windows and hope for a breeze."

We walked until we reached the swimming pool, which had been drained for the season. We sat on a bench across from an elderly man who was working on a crossword puzzle in his wheelchair, parked next to his milk-faced caretaker. Two young mothers wearing almost identical belted red princess coats smoked and chatted at the pool's far end while their toddlers, a boy and a girl, tossed pebbles into the pool, screaming with glee when their stones reached the small puddle in the center. A pensive-looking young man sat in a black iron chair near the fountain at the pool's head reading a copy of *The Hatchet*.

"See that man over there?" Sally asked, without looking.

I nodded.

"What do you think his story is?"

"College student?"

"What else?"

"College student with a clip-on tie?"

"Nice eye. And what do you think that clip-on tie means?"

"He doesn't know how to tie a real one?"

"And what does that mean?"

"He's never been taught?"

"And?"

"He doesn't have a father? Maybe he doesn't come from money? He definitely doesn't have a girlfriend or a mother close by to tell him that clip-ons look ridiculous. Perhaps he's from out of town? On scholarship maybe?"

"Where?"

"Given our location? Georgetown. But given his choice of newspaper? I'd say George Washington."

"Studying?"

I looked the man over: clip-on, cowlick, maroon sweater vest, dull brown leather shoes, smoking Pall Malls, legs crossed, his right foot turning slow circles. "Could be anything, really."

"Philosophy."

"How do you know?"

Sally pointed to his open leather knapsack and the book inside it: Kierkegaard.

"How did I miss that?"

"Obvious things are the hardest to spot." Sally stretched her arms over her head to take off her cape, and the space between her blouse's buttons parted to reveal black lace. "Wanna do another?"

I looked away. "Sure."

I said the mothers were childhood friends who'd grown distant after marrying and having kids. "It's the way they smile at each other," I told Sally. "Like they're forcing some previous connection." The elderly man was a widower, clearly in love with his caretaker, who didn't share his feelings. When a gardener appeared and carefully plucked leaves out of the fountain, I suggested he was a leftover from the days when the garden was owned by the Bliss family, perhaps the only household employee to have been kept on. "That explains his diligence," I finished. Sally nodded approvingly.

Was this part of my training? If so, what exactly was Sally training me to do? It wasn't as if we could confirm the stories I'd manifested for these strangers. So what did it matter? "How do we know if we're right?" I asked when we'd gone through everyone.

"It's not about being right. It's about knowing enough to be able to quickly evaluate what kind of person someone is. People give away a lot more than they know. It's so much more than how you dress, how you look. Anyone can put on a nice blue and white polka dot dress and clutch a Chanel, but that doesn't mean she's become a new person." I blushed at the mention of my Mayflower outfit. "The change comes from inside and reflects every move, every gesture, every facial tic. You must adopt a certain understanding of who someone is in order to judge how he might act in different circumstances." She looked right at me. "And how you might act if you had to really *become* someone new. Everything would change—how you hold your cigarette, how you laugh, how you might blush at the mention of a Chanel purse." She poked my shoulder. "You understand what I'm telling you?"

"It starts from within," I said.

"Exactly."

Our training continued. Each day we'd meet after work, and during more long walks around the District, Sally would teach me everything she knew. Knowing what made herself stand out, she taught me how not to. She showed me what clothes drew the least attention. "They can't be too old or too new, too bright or too dull." On what hair color won't provoke the male gaze: "You'd think blondes get the most attention, but it's redheads. You'll be fine as long as you don't go platinum." How to stand: "Not too straight, not too slouched." How to eat: "Steak. Medium rare." How to drink: "Tom Collins, extra lime, extra ice. Won't stain if you spill, and won't get you too drunk."

Between her lessons, she'd tell me about her time spent in the OSS—how she first took up with the Old Boys' Club, how she'd managed to survive it. She told me about the person she'd been—a poor kid from Pittsburgh—and all the people she'd become since: a zookeeper's assistant, the second cousin of the Duchess of Aosta, an appraiser of Tang Dynasty porcelain, the heiress to the Wrigley's gum empire, a receptionist. "They got less creative over time," she said.

"Who do they want me to become?" I asked.

"That's not for me to decide, honey."

Sally had gone on a trip. She didn't tell me where she was going, and when I inquired, she just said "Overseas."

"Yeah, but where overseas?" I asked.

"*Overseas* overseas."

She couldn't tell me where she was going, but promised she'd call when she returned. That week dragged on, and when she finally did call, Mama answered. I hissed her away from the receiver as soon as I heard her say "Sally? I don't know of any Sally."

Sally skipped the small talk and immediately invited me to a Halloween party. Up to that point, all our contact had been work-related, so the invite caught me off guard. Plus, Halloween had passed. "But Halloween was last week," I said.

"It's actually a *post*-Halloween party."

When I told her I didn't have a costume, she said she'd take care of everything. We made plans to meet at a secondhand bookstore in Dupont and go from there.

The bookshop was narrow, with long shelves arranged not by author or genre, but by topic: Spiritualism &

the Occult, Flora & Fauna, Elder Issues, Nautical Tales, Mythology & Folklore, Freud, Trains & Railways, Southwestern Photography. The first to arrive, I walked the aisles, looking for the paperback section. "Excuse me, where are the novels?" I asked the bohemian-looking man behind the counter, who pointed toward the back of the store without looking up from his book.

"Do you have the time?"

He looked as if I'd asked him to explain Wittgenstein's *Tractatus*. "I don't wear a watch."

To spite him, I asked if he'd open the case of rare books for me. The man sighed. He closed his book, stubbed out his cigarette, and slid off his stool. Before he fished out the key from his pocket, he asked if I was really going to buy something.

"How do I know before I see it?"

"What is it you want to see?"

I panned the shelf and said the first thing I saw: *The Light of Egypt*.

"One or two?"

"What?"

"Volume. One or two?"

"Two," I said. "Of course."

"Of course."

Convinced Sally wasn't going to show, I rambled on about my love for archaeology and the pyramids and hieroglyphics as he went to put on his white gloves to handle the book.

Finally Sally came in, holding two shopping bags. The bookseller slapped his white gloves to his thigh. "Sally," he said. She presented both cheeks for a kiss. "Where have you been, darling?"

"Here and there," she said, her eyes directed toward me. "I see you already met my friend."

"Of course," he said, his voice taking on a warmer hue. "She has excellent taste."

"Would I associate with anyone who didn't?" She held up the shopping bags. "Can we use the little girls' room?"

He bowed with his hands folded in front of him. It took everything in me not to roll my eyes.

"Thanks, love," she said. I trailed her into the back room. "Lafitte's such a pill," she said as soon as we closed the bathroom door, which doubled as a janitor's closet.

"Lafitte?"

"Not his real name. He's from Cleveland, but lets people think he's from Paris. The type who goes on vacation and comes back with an accent, you know?"

I nodded as if I understood.

"But I still love this place," Sally continued, handing me one of the shopping bags. "One of my favorite places in this artistically impaired city. Wanna know a secret?"

"Yes."

"My dream is to open a bookshop of my own someday."

It was hard to picture Sally sitting behind a counter, her head buried in a book, and I wanted to know more about this person who wouldn't look out of place on a Hollywood red carpet but dreamed of running a bookstore. I wanted to dig into that space between the contradictions.

She placed her shopping bag on the back of the commode and turned around. "Do you mind?" She brushed her red curls away from her neck and I took hold of the zipper, trying to gently ease it down. It didn't budge. She took a deep breath. "Try now." The zipper came down and she stepped out of the dress in one motion, not catching her heels on the fabric. She was wearing a black slip, her body an exaggerated version of my own. But I wasn't jealous in the way other girls in my high school gym class had made me feel. Their bodies had been something to measure against—we'd disrobe and quickly calculate who had the largest breasts, whose stomach jiggled, whose legs bowed out. Seeing Sally wasn't like that; it was something different altogether. I wanted another look, but focused on my own undressing. She handed me a shopping bag.

Inside was a bundle of metallic fabric. "What is it?"

"You'll see."

I stepped into the jumpsuit and zipped it up. She handed me a headband with two fuzzy brown triangles glued to the top. Looking in the mirror, I started laughing.

"Wait!" she said, and reached into her bag. "The finishing touch." She carefully pinned a red CCCP patch over my heart.

"I wanted to use a fishbowl as the helmet, but I couldn't figure out how to drill holes in it so we wouldn't suffocate."

"You made this yourself?"

"I'm pretty handy." She joined me at the mirror, pulling a compact out of her purse and dabbing the shine off her nose. "You can be Laika if you want. I'll be one of the nameless dogs who perished among the stars."

Music spilled from the four-story Victorian row house off Logan Square. It was one of those grand D.C. homes I'd walked by a thousand times but had never been inside—with its iron-railed steps and front-facing bay window, its red bricks and sage-green witch's hat turret. The windows were open but the curtains drawn, and I could see the silhouettes of people dancing: people I didn't know and who didn't know me, people who might think me a bore or not notice me at all. The palms of my hands tingled. Sally must've sensed my apprehension. She straightened my fuzzy ears and told me what a gas the party would be now that I was arriving.

A ripple of confidence bolstered me as she reached for the doorbell and buzzed it three times, paused, then buzzed it again. A tall man in a black mask covering half his face opened the door partway.

"Trick or treat!" Sally said.

"Which do you prefer?"

"Neither. I prefer broccoli."

"Doesn't everyone?" The man opened the door and ushered us in, locking the door behind us before disappearing back into the crowd.

"Was that a password? Is this a work party?" I asked.

"Quite the opposite."

Instead of jack-o'-lanterns and apple bobbing, the house was decorated more like a gothic masquerade ball. Antique candelabra with flaming black candles were perched on every available surface. Black velvet drapes covered the built-in bookshelves. The dining room table featured an array of elaborate sequined masks for the taking. A large Siamese cat clad in a collar made from lavender ostrich feathers slunk through the legs of party guests. The first floor was packed with people dancing, smoking, picking at hors d'oeuvres, dipping bread cubes into pots of fondue.

"What's that green stuff?" I asked.

"Guacamole."

"What's that?"

She laughed. "Leonard goes all out, doesn't he?"

"The man who answered the door?"

"No." She pointed to a woman wearing a lacy-necked Southern debutante ball gown with a red belt. "Scarlett O'Hara over there." Scarlett, or Leonard, saw Sally and waved her over.

"Gorgeous as always," Sally said, kissing Leonard's hand. "You've really outdone yourself."

"I try." Leonard looked Sally over. "Foxy alien?"

"We're Muttniks, thank you very much."

"How trendy."

"You know me." She pulled me closer. "This is Irina."

"Enchanted," he said, and kissed my hand. "Welcome. Now, I need to see about this appalling music." He went to the record player and lifted the needle. The crowd groaned. "Patience, my children!" He slipped a new record out of its sleeve and moments later "Sh-Boom" was playing. The crowd groaned again. Undeterred, Leonard led a man dressed as Frankenstein's monster with two empty thread spools painted black and stuck to his neck to the middle of the floor. Several other couples joined in, and soon the dance floor was going again.

Sally wove her way through the crowd toward the kitchen, and a woman dressed as Annie Oakley caught her hand and spun her once around. Dog ears askew, Sally returned with two glasses of red punch topped with lime sherbet. "How 'bout we get some air?" she asked, handing me a glass.

Except for two women sitting on the porch swing—one dressed as Lucille Ball and the other as Ricky Ricardo—Sally and I were alone in the expansive backyard. We walked out into the grass, the ankles of our jumpsuits soaking through with dew. The yard was decorated with tiny white lights strung up in the towering oak trees and red paper lanterns hanging like ripened fruit from the lower branches. The sky was orange, the moon an almond sliver, and somewhere, someone was burning leaves.

"What do you think of all this?" she asked.

"I had no idea yards like this existed in D.C."

"I mean, all of *that*," she said, gesturing toward the house. "Not your average shindig."

"I love it!" I said, but wanted to say so much more. I knew a world like that existed, but at the same time, I had no idea. And what I had heard was nothing at all like this. It was like stepping inside the wardrobe and emerging in Narnia for the first time. "I mean, I love Halloween."

"Me too. Even if it *is* a week late."

"You can be whoever you want."

"Exactly. I'm happy Leonard got to have his party after all. It's a bit of a tradition for him. And he's not one to waste a good costume. Shame it was canceled on actual Halloween."

"Why was it?"

"Someone tipped off the police."

I had so many questions. The secret garden, the secret world—I wanted to know everything, but decided to wait. We were quiet, listening to the sounds of traffic on the other side of the garden wall, the honk of a car horn, the distant wail of a siren. Lucy and Ricky went back into the house, their arms wrapped around each other's waists. Sally watched as my eyes followed them. "So . . . Teddy Helms?" she asked.

"Yes," I said, with a pang of sadness I hadn't felt before.

"How long?"

"Nine months. No. Eight. No, nine-ish."

"Are you in love?"

With the exception of Mama, people were never that direct with me. "I don't know."

"Honey, if you don't know by now . . ."

"I do like him. I mean, I really like him. He's funny. Smart. So smart. And kind."

"Sounds like you're reading from his obituary."

"No," I said. "I didn't mean—"

"I'm only kidding." She poked me in the ribs. "What about his friend? Henry Rennet? What's he like?"

"I don't know him that well." I didn't tell her he seemed like a jackass and that I had no idea why Teddy was even friends with him. "Are you interested in him?" I envisioned a double date—me and Teddy, Sally and Henry—and the thought made my stomach flip.

"Darling." She reached for my hand and gave it a squeeze. "No." She held on, and something inside me, from a location hard to pinpoint, bloomed.

CHAPTER 13

THE SWALLOW

She was no mole—I was sure of that. A few months prior, Frank had asked me to suss out Irina and ensure her naïveté was not a put-on. It wasn't, I'd told him. "Good," he said. "We want her on the book project. Train her up, Sally. You know the drill."

Befriending Irina may have been a setup and training her part of the job, but it had turned into something else—something I could've put my finger on but wasn't about to just yet.

The Tuesday after Leonard's party—my own test of sorts—I stopped by her desk and asked if she wanted to see *Silk Stockings* that night. I'd planned on asking her to a Sunday matinee a few days earlier but lost my nerve mid-dial and hung up.

We walked to the Georgetown Theater after work, stopping at the Magruder's for some candy to sneak in—Irina's idea. I rarely ate candy other than chocolates, but decided to get a box of Jujubes just for the hell of it. Irina picked up two boxes of Boston Baked Beans, and we got in line to pay. "Hold my place for a second?" she asked.

She came back a minute later carrying a large bouquet of beets.

"Interesting snack choice."

"They're for my mother. She makes a vat of borscht once a month and asked me to pick some up at Eastern Market. She's convinced the beets sold by this elderly Russian man are superior to the beets sold at a regular store." She held up a finger. "It's worth the extra nickel for the quality," she said in a Russian accent.

I laughed. "Can she really tell the difference?"

"No! I always get them at Safeway and just take them out of the bag before I get home."

We paid for our movie contraband and Irina stuck the beets inside her purse with the green ends sticking out. After purchasing two tickets, we made our way into the theater.

Seeing a picture was one of my greatest pleasures, and one I almost always chose to do alone. If I had the money to spare, I'd take myself to the movies once or twice a week. Sometimes I'd see the same movie two or three times, sitting in the balcony's front row, where I could lean against the gold railing and rest my chin atop my hands.

I loved everything about it: the Georgetown's neon sign glowing red, waiting in line for the person in the glass booth to hand you your ticket, the smell of popcorn, the sticky floors, the ushers directing you to your seat with their small flashlights. I even had a habit of singing "Let's all go to the lobby" in the shower. But my favorite part has always been the space between when the lights go down and the film begins to flicker— that brief moment when the whole world feels that it's on the verge of something.

I wanted to share all this with Irina. I wanted to find out if she, too, felt on the verge of something. The lights dimmed, and when she looked at me with wide eyes after the MGM lion roared, I knew she did.

I don't remember much about the movie. But I do remember that about a quarter of the way through, Irina opened her purse and poked around the beets to find her Boston Baked Beans. The candy rattled and she cursed when the beets fell to the floor. She made such a commotion that a man smoking a cigar turned around to shush us. I found it charming.

And when Fred Astaire stomped on his top hat at the end of his "Ritz Roll and Rock" number, Irina gasped and touched my hand. She removed it right away, but the feeling lingered until the lights came back on.

When we left the theater, it was raining. We stood under the awning watching water pour off in sheets.

"Should we wait it out?" I asked. "We could run across the street and get a hot toddy."

"I better brave it." She patted her purse. "Mama's expecting her beets."

I laughed but felt a stab of sadness. "Rain check, then?"

"Deal."

Irina ran out to the turquoise-and-white streetcar idling on the corner. She boarded and I watched as it turned the corner and disappeared from view. The sky opened up with a crack of lightning. I leaned against a movie poster for *Jailhouse Rock* and it started to pour.

In the weeks following the movie, I took Irina to my favorite bookstores, going over each shop's pros and cons and what I'd do differently if I owned it. We saw the *West Side Story* premiere at the National and sang "I Feel Pretty" at the top of our lungs the entire walk home. We went to the zoo but left after Irina saw a lion who'd paced so long in her cage she'd worn a narrow path alongside the bars. "It's a crime," she said.

In all that time, we hadn't so much as let a hug linger a second too long, but it didn't matter. It had been so long that I didn't recognize it at first. Not since my Kandy days had I let someone get so close so fast. I'd built up a wall after Jane—a Navy Corps nurse with Shirley Temple hair and teeth white as soap—broke my heart.

Really, more than the heart breaks. When Jane told me our "special friendship" would be over as soon as we stepped back onto American soil and chalked it up to just one of those things that happened during the war, my chest felt as if it was caving in and my legs, my arms, the top of my head, even my teeth hurt. I vowed never to put myself in harm's way like that again, and I had been relatively successful.

Plus, I knew there was no path that wouldn't dead-end. I'd had friends who were picked up during their late-night walks in Lafayette Square, locked up, their names printed in the newspaper. I'd had friends who were fired from their government jobs, their reputations destroyed, disowned by their families. I'd had friends who convinced themselves the only way out was to step off a chair, a noose wrapped around their neck. The Red Scare had dwindled, but a new one had taken its place.

And yet I kept going. I kept asking her to grab lunch at Ferranti's, or check out the new Korean art exhibit at the National Gallery, or try on hats and fascinators at Rizik's.

I kept seeing how far I could go before needing to step back.

So when Frank asked me for another favor, I told myself that work would be a good distraction, a necessary distraction.

———✦———

The night before I left for my next job, I put on a Fats Domino record and felt a jolt of happiness every time I placed an item inside my mint-green Lady Baltimore luggage. After years of last-minute jaunts, I'd learned the art of packing light: one black pencil skirt, one white blouse, one nude bra and panty set, one cashmere wrap for the flight, black silk hose, my Tiffany cigarette case, toothbrush, toothpaste, Camay rose soap, Crème Simon face cream, deodorant, razor, Tabac Blond, notebook, pen, my favorite Hermès scarf, and Revlon lipstick—in Original Red. The gown I'd wear to the book party would be waiting for me when I arrived. After years away, it felt good to be back in the game, to know secrets, to be useful.

I arrived the next evening at the Grand Hotel Continental Milano, just hours before the party started. Minutes after I entered my hotel suite, there was a knock on the door and a bellhop brought in my gown. I pointed for him to lay it on the bed, and he did so as gently as laying down a lover. I tipped him generously, as I always did when someone else was footing the bill, and sent him on his way. I'd ordered the red-and-black floor-length Pucci as soon as I heard the words *Milan* and *party*. Running my hand across the silk, I was quite pleased I'd secured a clothing budget from the Agency. After a bath, I applied a drop of Tabac Blond to each side of my neck, then to my wrists, then under my breasts, and slipped on the gown that had been tailored to my exact measurements.

That was the best part: the moment you become someone else. New name, new occupation, new background, education, siblings, lovers, religion—it was easy for me. And I never broke my cover, even down to the smallest details: whether she ate toast or eggs for breakfast, whether she took her coffee black or with milk, whether she was the type of woman to stop in the street to admire a crossing pigeon or shoo one away in disgust, whether she slept nude or in a night-gown. It was both a talent and a survival tactic. After assuming a cover, I found it harder and harder to go back to my real life. I'd imagine what it would be like to completely disappear into someone new. To become someone else, you have to want to lose yourself in the first place.

I'd timed my entrance to exactly twenty-five minutes after the party began. A waiter handed me a flute of bubbly as I entered the gilded room and I immediately located the guest of honor: not the author of the novel whose publication was being celebrated, as he could not possibly attend, but the novel's publisher. Giangiacomo Feltrinelli stood in the middle of Milan's finest-dressed intellectuals, editors, journalists, writers, and hangers-on. He wore thick black glasses, had a high widow's peak, and was slightly too thin for his height. But all the women, and more than one man, couldn't take their eyes off him. Feltrinelli's nickname was the Jaguar, and indeed, he moved with the confidence and elegance of a jungle cat. The majority of the party guests were in black tie, but Feltrinelli wore white trousers and a navy blue sweater, the corner of his striped shirt beneath untucked. The trick to pinpointing the man with the biggest bank account in the room is not to look to the man in the nicest tux, but to the man not trying to impress. Feltrinelli pulled out a cigarette, and someone in his orbit reached to light it.

There are two types of ambitious men: those bred to be ambitious—told from a very young age that the world is theirs for the taking—and those who create their own legacy. Feltrinelli was cut from both cloths. Whereas most men born into great wealth carry the burden of preserving their inherited legacy, Feltrinelli hadn't started a publishing company just as another notch in his empire, but because he truly believed literature could change the world.

In the back of the room was a large table covered in books stacked into a pyramid. The Italians had done it: *Doctor Zhivago* had made it into print. Within a week, it would be in every bookstore window across Italy, its name splashed across every newspaper's front page. I was to take one of those books and hand-deliver it to the Agency so they could have it translated and determine if it was indeed the weapon the Agency thought it might be. Frank Wisner had also tasked me with getting close to Feltrinelli to see what we might find out—about the book's publication and distribution, about the publisher's relationship with Pasternak.

I took a copy of *Il dottor Živago* and ran my fingers across its glossy cover: a design of white, pink, and blue scribbles hovering above a tiny sleigh making its way to a snow-covered cottage.

"An American who reads Italian?" a man standing on the other side of the book pyramid asked. "How fetching." He wore an ivory tuxedo with black pocket square and tortoiseshell glasses with frames too small for his broad face.

"No." In truth, I could read Italian and was conversationally fluent. When I was young, back before I'd changed my name from Forelli to Forrester, my grandmother had lived with our family. First generation Italian American, Nonna spoke hardly a word of English—just *yes, no, stop it,* and *leave me be*—and I learned how to converse with her over card games of Scopa and Briscola.

"Why take a book you can't read?" His accent was hard to place. Italian, but a practiced Italian. He either wasn't Italian or was attempting a Roman accent to appear posher than he was.

"I love a first edition," I said. "And a good party."

"Well, if you need help reading it . . ." He tipped his glasses downward, and I noticed a small red mark on the bridge of his nose.

"I might just take you up on that."

He waved a waiter over and handed me a glass of Prosecco without taking one for himself.

"Nothing for the toast?"

"I'm afraid I must go," he said, and touched my arm. "If you ever get a spot on that pretty gown of yours, look me up back in Washington. I own a dry cleaning business and we can get any spot out, I assure you. Ink, wine, blood. Anything." He turned and left, a copy of *Il dottor Živago* tucked under his arm.

KGB? MI6? One of our own? I looked around to see if anyone had noticed the strange interaction as Feltrinelli clinked his glass with a spoon. The publisher stepped atop an overturned wooden crate as if about to make a stump speech. Had he brought the crate himself for the effect? Or had the hotel provided it? Regardless, the look fitted him.

"I'd like to take a moment to thank everyone for being here tonight on this momentous occasion," he began, reading from a piece of paper he'd pulled from his pocket. "Over a year ago, the winds of fate brought me Boris Pasternak's masterpiece. I wish those very winds could be here to celebrate with us tonight, but alas, they cannot." He grinned and few people in the audience laughed. "When I first held this novel in my hands, I could not read one word of it. The only Russian word I know is Stolichnaya." More laughter. "But my dear friend Pietro Antonio Zveteremich"—he pointed to a sweater-vested man puffing on a pipe toward the back of the crowd—"told me that to not publish a novel like this would constitute a crime against culture. But even before he read it, I knew just by holding it in my hands that it was special." He dropped the piece of paper he was reading from and let it flutter to the ground. "So I took a chance. It would be months before Pietro would complete his translation and I could finally read these words." He held up *Zhivago*. "But when I did, the Russian master's words burned themselves into my heart forever, as I'm sure they will into yours."

"Hear, hear!" someone called out.

"I never intended to be the first to bring this work to an audience," Feltrinelli continued. "It was my intention to secure the foreign rights after it was published in its native land. But of course life doesn't always go according to plan."

A woman at Feltrinelli's feet raised her glass. *"Cin cin!"*

"I've been told it would be a crime to publish this work. I've been told that to publish this book would be the end of me." He looked around the room. "But I hold in my heart the truth Piertro spoke when he first read it, that *not* to publish this novel would be an even greater crime. Of course, Boris Pasternak himself asked that I delay publication. I told him that there was no time to waste, that I needed to bring his words to the world posthaste. And I did." The crowd erupted. "Please raise your glasses for a toast to Boris Pasternak, a man I've yet to meet but feel tied to by fate. A man who created a work of art out of the Soviet experience, a life-changing—no, a life-*affirming*—work that will stand the test of time and place him firmly in the company of Tolstoy and Dostoyevsky. To a man much braver than I. *Salut!*"

Glasses were raised and drinks downed. Feltrinelli stepped off the crate and was absorbed back into his crowd of well-wishers. Moments later, he excused himself and made his way to the restroom. I positioned myself at a telephone in the lobby so he'd have to pass me on his way back.

He did, and I hung up the phone timed to the second he noticed me. "Having a pleasant time, I hope?" he asked.

"A wonderful time. A beautiful night."

"Unbearably so." He took a step back, as if to admire a piece of art from another angle. "We've never met?"

"The universe hasn't willed it, I suppose."

"Indeed. Well, I'm happy the universe has made a point of correcting its grievous mistake." He took my hand and kissed it.

"You are the reason the book has come to print?"

He placed his hand over his heart. "I accept sole responsibility."

"The author didn't have a say in it?"

"No, not exactly. It wasn't possible for him."

Before I could ask if Pasternak was still in danger, Feltrinelli's wife—a dark-haired beauty wearing a sleeveless black velvet gown and matching jeweled choker—approached. She took her husband firmly by the arm and escorted him back to the party. She looked back at me once, in case I hadn't gotten the point.

As the party wound down, the red-jacketed wait staff began clearing away the mounds of uneaten stuffed mussels, beef carpaccio, and shrimp crostini, along with the copious number of empty Prosecco bottles littered across the room. Mrs. Feltrinelli had left in a limousine moments earlier, and Feltrinelli called out to the dwindled crowd to join him at Bar Basso. As he left, followed by a throng of hangers-on, he turned abruptly to me. "You'll be joining us, no?" he asked. He didn't stop to wait for my answer, already knowing what it would be.

A silver Citroën and a small fleet of black Fiats awaited us at the front of the hotel. Feltrinelli and a young blonde who'd arrived just minutes after Mrs. Jaguar left got into the Alfa Romeo, and the rest of us piled into the Fiats. Feltrinelli revved his engine and sped away, while we got stuck behind two men carrying dates on Vespas— tourists, judging by the fact that they drove slowly and steadily instead of weaving in and out of traffic like locals.

Our group spilled out of the cars and pushed its way inside Bar Basso, shouting out drink orders at the white-jacketed bartenders. I found a spot along a mirrored wall and scanned the bar for Feltrinelli. No sign of him. A short man with an undone bow tie and red-wine-stained lips passed me carrying an oversized cocktail glass. I recognized him as one of the photographers from the party. "Would you like a drink?" He held out the glass. "Take mine!"

I kept my hands to my sides. "Where is the guest of honor?"

"In bed by now, I imagine."

"I thought he was coming here."

"How do you Americans say? Plans are made to be rearranged?"

"Changed?"

"That's it! I believe he decided to have a more private celebration." The photographer put his arm around my waist, the tips of his fingers drifting below the small of my back. Shuddering, I removed his hand from my body and left the bar.

I'd succeeded in obtaining the book, which I placed in my hotel room's small safe before heading back out. But I'd failed at getting more information out of Feltrinelli. It seemed he'd been protecting Pasternak, but why? Was the author in more danger than we thought? The blonde Feltrinelli had taken off with was at least fifteen years younger than I, and I couldn't help but think if I were that age, I'd have been the woman he pulled into his sports car and told his secrets to.

Taxis passed, but I decided to walk. I wanted to enjoy the fresh air. And I was hungry. My first stop was at a gelato cart attached to an old mule. The teenager manning the cart told me the mule's name was Vicente the Majestic. I laughed, and the boy said that my laugh was just as beautiful as my red dress and my red hair. I thanked him, and he handed me the lemon gelato, *"Offerto dalla casa."*

The free gelato helped soothe my damaged ego but didn't keep me from wondering if I was getting too old for this job. It used to be so easy. Now my skin glowed only with the application of expensive creams that made more promises than they could keep, and the sheen on my hair came from a bottle of pricey exotic oils bought in Paris. And when I lay down at night sans bra, my breasts gravitated to my armpits.

When I turned thirteen, boys and men alike began to notice me, the anonymity of my prepubescent form having disappeared over the course of one summer. My mother was the first to notice. Once, after she caught me looking at my profile in the reflection of a store window, she stopped and told me a beautiful woman needs to have something to fall back on when the beauty fades, or she'll be left with nothing. "And it will fade," she said. Would I have nothing to fall back on? How much longer did I have until I was forced to find out?

Unlike Feltrinelli, my ambition didn't come from my wallet. It stemmed from a delusion that I was someone special, and the world owed me something—perhaps because I was brought up with nothing. Or maybe we all hold that delusion at some point—most of us giving it up after adolescence; but I never let it go. It gave me an unwavering belief that I could do anything, at least for a while. The problem with that type of ambition is that it requires constant reassurance from others, and when that assurance doesn't come, you falter. And when you falter, you go after the lowest-hanging fruit— someone to make you feel wanted and powerful. But that type of reassurance is like the brief buzz of alcohol: you need it to keep dancing, but it only leaves you sick the next day.

The lemon gelato tasted like summer and I told myself to stop the self-loathing. I changed my mind about going straight back to the hotel and stopped in the Piazza della Scala to see the Leonardo da Vinci monument.

The piazza was aglow. A small team of men were hanging white Christmas lights from the trees encircling the monument at the square's center. One man in brown coveralls was holding the ladder with one hand and smoking with the other, while a man atop the ladder was trying to undo a knot in the wires. The other men stood to the side, arguing over the best way to undo such a significant knot.

A middle-aged couple sat on one of the concrete benches near Leonardo's feet. Their faces were close and intense, and I couldn't tell whether they were about to break up or kiss.

I thought of Irina. I thought about how we could never be that couple—kissing, or even fighting, right out there in the open for all to see. The thought came over me like news of someone's sudden death, and I realized I had to put a stop to whatever was happening between us and just mourn what could have been.

I walked to the edge of the square and hailed a taxi.

"Signora, si sente bene?" the taxi driver asked when we'd arrived at the hotel. I'd fallen asleep, and the driver spoke to me with such tenderness, I surprised myself by tearing up. He looked so concerned. He held out his hand and helped me out of the car. *"Starai bene,"* he said. *"Starai bene."*

I thought about asking him to come up to my room with me—this prematurely balding young man who smelled of fresh mint. I didn't want to sleep with him, but I would if he'd tell me that I'd be fine, *starai bene*, I'd be fine, over and over, until I fell asleep. Instead, I went up to my room alone and lay down atop the covers in my wrinkled gown.

In the morning, after two Alka-Seltzers and room service, I removed my copy of *Zhivago* from its safe. Before placing it in my suitcase, I opened the book. As I flipped through the pages, a business card fell out. No name, no telephone number, only an address: SARA'S DRY CLEANERS, 2010 P ST. NW, WASHINGTON, D.C. I knew the spot: a squat yellow brick building with a royal blue hand-painted sign, a stone's throw from where Dulles lived. I folded the card in half and placed it in my silver cigarette case.

CHAPTER 14

THE COMPANY MAN

I went to London to see a friend about a book. After settling in for the eleven-hour flight, I signaled for the stewardess to hang up my suit jacket and bring me a whiskey—with ice, seeing how it was still before noon. Kit wore Pan Am's blue and white uniform with the capped hat and white gloves well—the type of woman who'd place second or third in any Midwestern beauty pageant. "Here you go, Mr. Fredericks," she said with a wink.

I'd gone by many names: names given to me and names given to myself. My parents named me Theodore Helms III. In grade school I became Teddy. In high school I went by Ted, but was back to Teddy by college.

To Kit, or anyone who asked over the next two days, my name would be Harrison Fredericks, or Harry to friends. Twenty-seven and from Valley Stream, New

York, Harrison Edwin Fredericks was an analyst for Grumman Aerospace Corp. who—get this—hated to fly. He always made a point to keep the window shade closed and preferred not to sit next to anyone. If by chance you were to look in his pockets, you'd find a receipt from a Texaco five miles from his house, a half pack of Juicy Fruit, and a handkerchief with *HEF* embroidered on it.

I placed my briefcase on the empty seat next to me. My father had had it custom made in Florence: fine chestnut-brown leather with a single brass lock. He'd given it to me when I graduated from Georgetown, twenty-two years to the day after he'd graduated from Georgetown. He'd handed it to me, unwrapped, after a quiet dinner with mother at the Club and said he envisioned me carrying it into the Senate chamber one day, or to the Supreme Court, or to the law firm that carried our last name. What my father hadn't known at the time was that by my junior year, I'd switched from prelaw to Slavic languages.

It was the summer after my sophomore year when I knew for sure I didn't want to join our family's firm. But I didn't know what I wanted to do instead. That feeling of being lost, compounded with my older brother's death, brought on a depression that came over me like a cloud shadow moving across a sunbather. I stopped leaving the house and picked at my meals. After I dropped down to my high school freshman weight and my skin took on the color of a city sidewalk, it wasn't my parents or the doctor they forced me to "just talk to" that pulled me out of it; it was *The Brothers Karamazov.* Then *Crime and Punishment,* then *The Idiot,* then everything the man ever wrote. Dostoyevsky threw me a rope in the fog and began to tug. When he wrote that a Russian is either an apocalypticist at the positive pole or a nihilist at the negative, I thought *Yes! This is it!* I was convinced, as only a young man can be, that deep down I had the soul of a Russian.

I poured myself into studying the Greats. After Dostoyevsky came Tolstoy, Gogol, Pushkin, Chekhov. When I finished the geniuses of old, I went to the under-grounds, those rejected by the great Red Monster: Osip Mandelstam and Marina Tsvetaeva and Mikhail Bulgakov. And when I returned to school in the fall, the fog, though still there, had lifted a bit. That semester, I left prelaw and enrolled in Russian.

Six years later, the briefcase carried not legal memos or briefs, but the primary source of my anxiety: my own unfinished novel.

I took a sip of whiskey and reached into the briefcase. Instead of pulling out my novel as the plane left the ground, I pulled out someone else's: Jack Kerouac's *On the Road.* He was rumored to have written it in a three-week, Benzedrine-induced sprint on one continuous roll of paper. Maybe that's what I was doing wrong. Maybe I needed drugs and scrolls. I cracked it open and read the first few sentences, then closed it. I gulped down my drink and dozed off.

When I awoke, we were over the Atlantic. I decided I could finally take a look at my draft. The night before, after an early dinner with Irina, I'd started on a revised plot, tacking up notecards on my bedroom wall to see if I could make sense of the thing. I could, almost, and thought that maybe I was on the path to becoming a real writer. Or maybe not.

I never told anyone about my novel—or that I even aspired to be a writer. Not my parents, not Irina, not even Henry Rennet, who'd been my closest friend since Groton. Some people thought Henry was a striving brownnoser, and others thought he was just a jerk. And they might've been right. But he was also there for me when my brother died. When the months following Julian's death seemed to stretch as long and gray as a Russian landscape, Henry would sit in my apartment and drink whiskey with me and talk for hours.

My original plan was to publish my debut novel a year after college, surprising everyone with it. My parents had never said as much, but I could tell they were disappointed that I never went into the family business. A novel would be something they could brag to their friends at the Club about, an accomplishment they could actually hold.

But that didn't happen. The summer after graduation, I began a hundred novels, never getting beyond the first twenty pages. I did manage to make a career out of my love of books, though—well, that and being fluent in Russian. And my connections. Professor Humphries had recruited me at Georgetown. One of Frank Wisner's old OSS buddies, Humphries resumed his position as a professor of Slavic linguistics after the war and became one of the Agency's top talent scouts. I wasn't the first man Humphries recruited, nor the last. The higher-ups referred to us as Humphries' Boys, a nickname that made us sound more like an a capella group than spies.

The Agency wanted to stack its ranks with intellectuals—those who believed in the long game of changing people's ideology over time. And they believed books could do it. I believed books could do it. That was my job: to designate books for exploitation and help carry out their covert dissemination. It was my job to secure books that made the Soviets look bad: books they banned, books that criticized the system, books that made the United States look like a shining beacon. I wanted them to take a good hard look at a system that had allowed the State to kill off any writer, any intellectual—hell, even any meteorologist—they disagreed with. Sure, Stalin was dead, his body embalmed and sealed under glass, but the memory of the Purges was also preserved.

Like a publisher or editor, I was always thinking of what the next big novel would be and how to get it into as many hands as quickly as possible. The only difference was that I wanted to do it without any fingerprints.

My jaunt to London wasn't just about a book; it was about *the* book. We'd been after *Doctor Zhivago* for months. We had obtained the first printing in Italian and decided it was indeed all it had been cracked up to be. It was deemed an operational imperative to get the manuscript in its native Russian, "lest any of its potency be lost in translation." I didn't know if the concern had more to do with ensuring maximal impact on Soviet citizens or preserving the purity of the author's words. I liked to think it was the latter, or at least a bit of both.

My job was to convince our friends the Brits to hand their Russian language copy over to us—or at least to let us borrow it for a while. A tentative deal had been made, but they'd been dragging their feet, probably to buy some time so as to determine whether they could do something with it first. I was sent to the Big Smoke to put the matter to bed.

Not that I minded. I needed to get out of the swamp and clear my head. Irina had been distant, whereas I had thought we were headed down the aisle. I'd even asked my mother for my grandmother's ring and planned to pop the question over Christmas. But after some canceled dates and the feeling that something was off, I wasn't so sure it was the right move. And when I asked Irina about it, it only seemed to make things worse. I'd never met anyone like her. Up to that point, every girl I'd dated only had ambitions of landing my grandmother's ring. Irina wanted what I wanted: to move up in the Agency, to be treated with respect, to do her job well and be patted on the back for it. She was my equal, and someone who challenged me. I knew if I married one of the girls I'd dated back in college I'd be bored before the first child was born, and I didn't want to turn into the cliché Agency man with a woman or two on the side.

And she was Russian! How I loved her Russianness, although she claimed to be even more American than I. Eating homemade pelmeni in their quaint basement apartment; Mama—which she insisted I call her from day one—poking fun at my patrician Russian accent every chance she could get; I loved it all.

But when she pulled away, I'm ashamed to say I even tailed her home once or twice—to see if she was meeting another man. She wasn't. But still.

So yeah, it was good to get away, and I was happy my destination was London. I loved the city: Noël Coward at the Café de Paris, rain jackets, rain bonnets, rain boots, Teddy boys, Teddy girls. Of course, I also loved the literature. I wished I could stay a week and visit the house where H. G. Wells died or the pub where C. S. Lewis had pints with Tolkien. But if all went according to plan, I'd get the job done in one night and be on a plane back to the States the following morning.

The friend I was meeting, code name Chaucer, wasn't really a friend. I knew him, yes, and our lives had crossed over the subject of books several times. He was of medium height and medium build, and unremarkable in the ways we spooks strove to be. The one exception was his teeth: so white and straight you'd think he'd grown up in Scarsdale, not Liverpool. He could also switch accents to suit his company: posh among the posh, working-class among the working-class, Irish if speaking to a redhead. People found him charming, but I could only stand him for an hour or so.

Chaucer was twenty minutes late to our meeting at the George Inn. Making me wait, I was sure, was some sort of MI6 psych shit. I wouldn't be surprised to learn he'd arrived early and been watching me from a distance as I entered the pub, that he'd checked his pocket watch—definitely a pocket watch—and waited twenty minutes before entering. They were always pulling petty stuff like that and were quick to remind us lowly Americans at every opportunity that the Brits had hundreds of years over us in perfecting the craft. As Chaucer would say, he'd been in the game since I was in diapers.

Rumor had it that MI6 had acquired *Zhivago* in its original Russian when a plane carrying Feltrinelli was grounded in Malta after a sham emergency landing. Word was, officers posing as airport employees escorted Feltrinelli off the plane while another officer photographed the manuscript. I didn't know if it was true, but it sure made a hell of a story.

I sat at the two-top under the head of a glass-eyed stag and downed two Irish whiskeys—my own psych move, I guess. The barman plunked down my fish and chips and mushy peas just as Chaucer stepped in from the rain, the collar of his black overcoat pushed up to his ears. He took off his hat and shook it, wetting the two French tourists sitting next to the door. He bowed in apology, then lumbered over to my table. I noticed he'd gained a little weight since the last time I'd seen him.

He noticed me looking him up and down. "You look thin," he said.

"Thank you."

He held up his left hand. "Married now."

"That explains it."

"That infamous dry Yank wit. How I've missed it." He took a seat. "Heard you're engaged yourself."

"Not quite yet, but I'll drink to it anyway." I raised my glass and downed my whiskey.

"Want another glass of that Irish swill?" Before I could reply, he got up and went to the bar. He brought back two pints and handed me one. "They no longer carry Bushmills," he said. "You know, Dickens used to frequent this place." He reached for a soggy chip on my plate and pointed at the other end of the pub with it. "That was his spot. Wrote about it, even. *Bleak House*."

"I think I read that somewhere."

"Of course you did. What's that motto you Americans have? *Be prepared*?"

"That's the Boy Scouts. And the Dickens novel you're thinking of was *Little Dorrit*."

"Yes!" he said leaning back in his chair. "Clever boy. I've missed our repartee." He sighed. "But look at this place now. Just us tourists, overfoamed pints, soggy chips." He reached for another. "Speaking of great works, how's yours coming along?"

I wasn't surprised he knew of my failing aspirations. After all, I knew many things about him, too—like that he was indeed recently married but had continued to sleep with his longtime clerk, Violet, without pause, except for the two weeks he spent honeymooning in Bali. It just annoyed me that he was familiar with my major weakness. "Very well, thank you," I replied.

"Bloody fantastic," he said. "Can't wait to read it."

"I'll be sure to sign a copy for you."

He put a hand to his heart. "I'll surely treasure it."

"Speaking of books," I said, wanting to get on with it, "read any good ones lately?"

"*Diamonds Are Forever*. Have you read it? Bloody brilliant."

"No," I said. "Not my taste."

"A Fitzgerald type, I suppose."

"Compared to Fleming?"

"That Daisy! What a gal! I practically fell in love with her myself."

"I think men are really more in love with Gatsby than they care to admit."

"Not love. But we do want to be him. All men, all women, for that matter, secretly long for some great tragedy. It sharpens the lived experience. Makes for more interesting people. Wouldn't you agree?"

"Only privileged men romanticize tragedy."

He slapped his meaty thighs. "I knew we had something in common!"

My fish sat cold on my plate, the breading soggy with grease, but I slowly cut off a piece and swallowed it. "I *am* looking to pick something up for the trip home, though. Know of any good bookshops around here?"

He stood up, downed his pint, and wiped away his foam mustache with his sleeve. "Fancy a game?" We headed to the back of the pub. I was terrible at darts but beat him handily, which I took as his way of saying he was willing to do business.

"Well, then," he said after I bested him again. "Looks like I'm a little rusty." He pulled out his pocket watch and I couldn't help but smile at having called his choice of timepiece. "Have to be going. Taking the little missus to see *Uncle Vanya* at the Garrick."

"I love a good Russian play," I said.

"Who doesn't?"

"Good reviews?"

"It's closing in London soon, but should be on in the States next year. You know how it goes. We Brits like to test things here before handing them over to you lot."

Finally, we're getting somewhere. "When does it open?"

"Early January." He put on his coat and hat. "But they haven't announced the exact date yet."

"December would be ideal. I love taking in a good show around the holidays."

"I don't make the schedule," he said.

"Well, I'll keep my ear to the ground."

"I know you will."

He left, hurrying through the rain to an idling car parked out front. I went back in and ordered Bushmills, then settled up—Chaucer having left his bill to me, of course.

It started pouring as soon as I stepped outside. I arrived back at my hotel soaking wet and left a message at the front desk not to let any calls be put through to my room. "Tell them I've taken on a bit of jet lag and need my rest," I said—code to let the Agency know the Russian *Zhivago* was as good as ours.

CHAPTER 15

THE SWALLOW

December came and a layer of fresh snow blanketed the District. I'd left *Il dottor Živago* in the designated confessional at St. Patrick's the day I returned from Milan and had gone into a tempo office for debriefing the day after that. I told Frank everything—who'd attended, what the press was saying, what snippets of conversation I'd overheard, and, most important, what Feltrinelli had said in his speech. I went over every detail, except for the encounter with the man who'd managed to slip his card into my copy of the novel. Upon returning, I'd taken the card out of my cigarette case and placed it under a loose tile in my bathroom. Secrets were insurance in Washington, and a girl always needs a few in her back pocket.

Irina and I made plans to meet at the Reflecting Pool—to skate and then have dinner back at my apartment. After renting skates from a ski-masked man out of the back of his station wagon, we trudged our way through the snow toward the rink, but we never made it onto the ice. As we sat on the steps of the Lincoln Memorial undoing our boots, Irina blurted it out: Teddy had asked her to marry him. She didn't tell me she'd said yes, but she didn't have to. As she spoke, she fixed her gaze on the Washington Monument and never once turned to look at me.

I'd known it was a possibility. I'd known others who'd gotten engaged and married and even had children to cover their tracks, to avoid arrest, to live a "normal" life. Hell, I'd thought about doing the same once or twice. And after returning from Italy, I'd tried to end things with her a dozen times, but a dozen times just dug in deeper. I'd known it could happen—and yet. When I heard the words spill from her lips, I found myself unprepared. It was as if someone had removed a stone from my foundation and I wasn't sure exactly when I'd collapse. But in the moment, I managed to keep it together. Kept my cool as I'd been trained to do under any circumstance. I congratulated her, saying I'd love to be the one to throw the happy couple an engagement party. Taken aback, she said, in a voice as small as a comma, that that wouldn't be necessary. When I'd told Irina I didn't feel like skating after all, that I had a headache and should probably go home and get some rest, she got up and left me on the cold steps. I watched her red hat become a smaller and smaller dot in the white landscape.

That evening, Irina showed up at my apartment, still dressed for skating. She looked as if she'd been walking since she left me on the steps—her nose red, her body shivering. She pushed her way into my apartment, shedding her boots, her hat, her scarf, her coat. When I told her I'd been sleeping, that I thought I might be coming down with a cold and that she shouldn't get too close, she pressed her cold hands against my cheeks. "Listen," she said, but didn't say anything else. She kissed me, her lips adjusting to mine until they clicked into place. The kiss made me feel like crying; I felt a sense of loss as soon as she removed her mouth. "Listen," she said again. Her words made me want to look away, but she wouldn't let me. She stepped closer, her stockinged toes atop mine. Even without heels, she was taller than me by a forehead, and she held on to my face as if inspecting it.

She kissed me again, then slipped her cold hands into my robe. Her confidence took me aback. Was she pretending to be someone else, or had she actually become someone new and I just hadn't noticed?

A tremor moved through my legs, and I sank to my knees on the pink carpet. She followed. My robe now open, she kissed my stomach, and a noise escaped my lips, an embarrassing sound. She laughed, which made me laugh. "Who are you?" I asked. She didn't answer, concentrating instead on tracing the line of my pelvic bone. Maybe it was the reverse. Maybe I was the one who couldn't recognize myself. I'd always maintained the upper hand with sex. I'd gauge my partners' reactions and move, pose, and moan accordingly. This was different. She didn't expect anything of me. I was powerless.

I kept thinking we would stop—that she'd come to her senses, that I would come to mine. That she'd back down. When I voiced this, she said it was too late. "No going back."

She was right. It was like watching a film in Technicolor for the first time: the world was one way, and then everything changed.

We fell asleep on the carpet, my robe our blanket, my chest her pillow. I stirred with the sounds and smells of the bakery opening downstairs. I went to the bathroom to splash water on my face and brush my hair. The morning light coming through the small window above my shower looked harsh, my image in the mirror jarring. I thought of Irina and Teddy—what their wedding would look like, what she would look like walking down the aisle. And my new Technicolor world returned to black-and-white.

When I emerged, Irina was in the kitchen looking in the refrigerator. She brought out a half carton of eggs and asked how I liked them.

"I don't know. How does Teddy like his?"

She said nothing. When I asked again, she grabbed my hand and told me we'd think of something. When she said she loved me, instead of telling her the truth—that I loved her too—I pulled away and said I wasn't hungry, that she probably should just go. And she did.

Freezing rain the last night of the year. Standing in my kitchen, I unwrapped a foil package resembling a swan and heated up leftover filet mignon. I opened the window to my fire escape and pulled in the bottle of '49 Dom Pérignon that Frank had given me for a job mostly well done in Milan.

I ate my dinner standing in front of the open oven to warm my back, and the champagne was indeed as delicious as Frank had promised.

Earlier in the day, I'd gone alone to the matinee showing of *The Bridge on the River Kwai*. But I'd found it difficult to concentrate and left early. The sky was already dark, the rain had started to fall. By the time I got home, our white Christmas had been reduced to brown slush. The snowman some kids had built in the park across the street had turned into solid ice, its carrot nose replaced with a cigarette, its scarf missing. I hated New Year's Eve.

To make matters worse, my apartment was freezing—my breath visible in the frigid air, the radiator cold to the touch. I cursed my landlord, a man who owned half the buildings on the block but was too cheap to hire a super.

I drew a hot bath and sank in, careful not to wet my hair. When the water turned tepid, I turned the faucet back on with my toes, a process I repeated twice before finally getting out. Assaulted by cold air, I wrapped myself in an oversized terry cloth robe. I wanted to just slip into bed and fall asleep listening to Guy Lombardo ring in 1958 on the radio. But I couldn't. I had to dress, put on my face, and eat something before the black car arrived to shuttle me to the party in an hour. I had to work.

After Milan, when Frank and I debriefed, he'd looked pleased but distracted, as if he'd already known the details—which he probably had. He didn't seem to mind that I hadn't gotten closer to Feltrinelli. At first, I thought he might've shared my assessment that maybe I should've stayed in retirement, that maybe I didn't have what it takes anymore; but instead of politely sending me on my way, he said there was something else I could help with.

"I could use another favor."

"Anything."

The rain let up just as my black car arrived. I wrapped myself in my white mohair swing coat, leaving my fur in the closet, as I'd done since Irina had told me fur gave her the creeps. "Poor rabbits," she'd said, running her hand down my sleeve.

The driver, his patent-leather-billed cap in one hand, held the car door open for me with the other. "Gal like you doesn't have a date on New Year's?"

I slipped into the backseat.

The District streamed by, a sliver of moon visible in the fleeting spaces between buildings. I wondered if Irina could see the moon from where she was. She was spending the last night of the year with Teddy and his rich family at their chalet in the Green Mountains. Irina couldn't even ski. I hoped it was cloudy, that the freezing rain had made its way to Vermont.

The New Year's Eve party was at the Colony, a French restaurant downtown considered among D.C.'s finest, which wasn't saying much. Hosted by a Panamanian diplomat, the party was basically an office party sans office. This was an inner-circle, invite-only affair. The whole gang would be there: Frank, Maury, Meyer, the Dulles brothers, the Grahams, one Alsop brother, everyone in the Georgetown set. But I wasn't there to talk with them. I had other work to attend to.

The bas-relief statues of mythological figures lining the dining room wall were outfitted with party hats, the lounge with silver streamers and gold tinsel. A net of white balloons ready for the clock to strike twelve hovered above the crowded dance floor. A large banner hung across the main bar: CANNOT WAIT FOR '58! A brass band with a satin-dressed singer played in front of a giant clock, its movable hands set at ten. As I handed the coat check girl my wrap, a waitress dressed like a Rockette with a tiny top hat bobby-pinned to the side of her head presented me with a silver tray of noisemakers and hats. I selected a horn with metallic purple fringe but passed on the hat.

"Where's your holiday spirit, kid?" Anderson asked from behind me. He was wearing two pointed hats atop his head like devil's horns, the elastic digging into his double chin. His suit jacket was already off, the back of his tuxedo shirt translucent with sweat.

"Will Baby New Year be making another appearance tonight?" I asked, referring to the time he'd stripped down to a white sheet wrapped around his crotch, stuck a giant pacifier in his mouth, and clutched a bottle of whiskey at our New Year's Eve celebration in Kandy.

"The night's still young!"

"Speaking of holiday spirits, where can a girl get a drink?" My insides were already warm from the three glasses of Dom Pérignon I'd drunk at home, but I wanted to keep the feeling from dissipating; I wanted to keep my thoughts of Irina at bay, at least temporarily.

Anderson handed me his half-full punch glass. "Ladies first."

I downed it, blew my horn at him, then waved to the waiter with a fresh tray of drinks. Anderson asked if I wanted to dance, and I told him maybe later. I'd already spotted the man Frank wanted me to get to know better across the dance floor.

I watched Anderson go back to a table full of people who cheered his return, then turned my attention back to my man. Henry Rennet stood catercorner to the stage, watching the Eartha Kitt knock-off sing "Santa Baby." I bypassed Anderson's table, skirted the dance floor, and found a spot opposite the stage from Henry. Then I waited. The band finished the song and the singer sashayed over to the clock to move its hands to ten thirty. The crowd cheered; Henry snickered, but he raised his glass to the last hour and a half of 1957 anyway. Then he looked my way.

What I knew about Henry Rennet: Yale boy. Grew up in Long Island but said "the City" when asked. Just five years and three months into the Agency, his meteoric rise within SR raised suspicions. Lived alone in a one-bedroom walk-up across the bridge in Arlington paid for by his parents. A linguistics man—fluent in Russian, German, and French. Spent the year between Yale and the Agency "backpacking" across Europe—which really meant hopping from one five-star hotel to the next on his parents' dime. Orange-haired, freckled, and thick-necked, but did better with women than one might suspect. Had dated two members of the typing pool—in the loosest imaginable terms—neither of whom was aware the other had also dated him. Best friends with Teddy Helms, for reasons Irina did not understand. But I understood. Those Ivy League boys always stuck together.

The other thing about Henry Rennet, and the reason I was at the party, was that Frank thought he might be a mole. Frank had first told me about his suspicions months earlier, shortly after enlisting me for the book mission, and I'd put out a few feelers. When I returned from Italy, he asked that I get to know Henry better.

See, all Agency men had big egos—but usually flexed them only within their own circles. Henry had the type of ego that could get him into trouble. He was seen as a braggart. That and his known drinking problem were enough to raise a few flags.

I didn't bring it up, and I hoped the rumors weren't true, but I'd heard rumblings that Frank's mental faculties had recently been called into question—some saying he just wasn't the same after the failed mission in Hungary, some attributing his obsession with rooting out a Soviet mole to his diminishing competency.

After some chitchat by the stage, a few spins around the dance floor, and two glasses of punch, Henry suggested we go somewhere private to talk. The singer had already moved the hands of the clock to eleven forty-five and the crowd was readying itself with poppers, cranks, and drink refills for the midnight toast. We slipped away, and on our way out, he plucked a bottle of champagne from a silver bucket. "For our own toast," he said, holding it up like a trophy.

"Where we headed?"

Henry didn't answer, walking two paces in front of me. Normally, I was the one to take the lead, and as I quickened my pace, I tripped on a bump in the carpeting and went down. Henry turned to help me up, and the blood rushed to my head as I stood.

"Don't tell me a gal like you can't hold her booze?"

"I can hold it just fine, thank you."

He raised the bottle again. "Good." He looked at his watch. "Seven minutes till midnight." He put his arm around my waist, his thumb digging into the small of my back, and guided us toward the exit.

"I don't have my coat," I told him.

"Oh, we're not leaving."

We passed the doorman slouched on his stool, looking as though he'd indulged in a nip or two himself. Henry took my hand and danced us into a corner. His breath smelled like a bar floor, and I knew he was perhaps drunk enough to be loose-lipped. I straightened his tie—a narrow, ugly thing—and looked toward the doorman, who was pretending not to watch us. "I thought we were going somewhere quiet to talk?"

He reached behind me, and the wall turned into a door. "Well, what do you know?" he said, backing me into an unused coat-check room. The tiny room was empty except for a few white uniforms on wire hangers, a broken chair, and an old vacuum cleaner.

"Not exactly the cozy spot I had in mind."

"I know a girl like you is used to"—he pointed the champagne bottle toward the broken chair—"more ambiance and all that. But it's quiet, right?" He popped the cork, which landed in an empty hat cubby, and took a swig. "And private."

He offered me the bottle but I declined, feeling I was already just one drink away from losing the upper hand. "Maybe a sip at midnight."

He looked at his watch again and tapped its face. "Three more minutes."

"Any New Year's resolutions?" I asked.

"Just this." He put his sweaty hand against my cheek and leaned in to kiss me. I took a step back, my head brushing the closet rod behind me.

"Tell me something first," I said.

"You're beautiful." He moved in again.

I pushed him away with my index finger. "You'll have to do better than that."

He snickered in a way that made me cringe. "I like that. I like a challenge."

"Tell me something . . . interesting." I held his gaze, an old trick to get people to talk.

"Me? I'm an open book." He looked at the ceiling and exhaled. "I think you're the one with secrets."

"Every woman has her secrets."

"True, but I happen to know yours."

My mouth felt dry, my tongue heavy as a sandbag. "And what's that?"

"You want me to say it?"

"Say it."

"You don't think I know why you chatted me up?" he said. "You just happened to take a sudden interest in a man, what, a decade younger than you? You think

I don't know what you are? I know you've been asking questions about me. About my loyalties."

I eyed the door.

"What you don't know is that I have more friends here than you do."

I'd stepped right into it, too distracted and drunk to see it. I moved to leave, but he blocked me. "I'll scream."

"Good. They'll just think you're doing a job well done."

I pushed him away, and he pushed back. My head hit the closet's metal rod with surprising force. Before I could move, he crushed his body into mine and pressed his mouth to my lips so hard I tasted blood when he pulled away. I tried to push him off me but he did it again, forcing his tongue into my mouth. When I tried to knee him, he swept my legs out from under me. I went to the floor. He followed. I tried to get up but he forced my hands over my head and held them in one of his. I screamed but was drowned out by the crowd on the other side of the door beginning its countdown to midnight. *Thirty!* I could hear the side of my gown rip. "This is what you do, isn't it? How they use you?" *Twenty-three!* I spat at him and he wiped my spit from his face with a smirk I wished I could take a brick to. He pressed his forehead to mine. *Fourteen!* "So the other rumors are true, then?" His breath was hot and sour. "You're some kind of queer? Shame if that got out." *Three! Two! One!*

The crowd roared "Happy New Year!" and the band began playing "Auld Lang Syne." I closed my eyes and thought of the L-Pills from our survival kits back in Kandy—white and oval, in a thin glass vial encased in brown rubber. If need be, we were to bite down, crushing the glass and releasing the poison. When the poison is released, the heartbeat stops within minutes; death is fast and supposedly painless. It never crossed my mind that I might be captured so far from the battlefield.

He left me in the closet. I didn't think about getting up. I didn't think about crawling out. I didn't think about getting help. I didn't want to think at all. I wanted to sleep.

He returned with my coat and helped me to my feet. Anderson and his wife were leaving as we exited the coatroom—Henry first, me staggering a few steps behind him. But Anderson didn't approach, didn't call out "Happy New Year," didn't say anything. He looked at my smeared makeup, my torn dress, and he didn't say a word.

Henry was right. I was nothing to them. Even Anderson couldn't look at me. I wasn't their colleague, their peer. I certainly wasn't their friend. They'd all used me. The whole time, they'd been using me. Frank, Anderson, Henry, all of them. And I was certain they'd continue to use me until the honey dried up.

Henry put me in a car, kissed my cheek like a gentleman, and told the driver to drive carefully.

The driver escorted me to my door, and I walked up the steps to my apartment clinging to the railing. I could still feel him. I could still smell him.

The apartment was still cold. The half bottle of Dom Pérignon still sat on my glass coffee table next to the empty foil swan. The pair of heels I'd tried on with my gown but hadn't worn still sat at the foot of my floor-length mirror. The Christmas card Irina had mailed me still sat alone on my mantel.

I removed my shoes. I removed my makeup. I removed my gown. I stood in my tub and let the scalding water run over my body. Then I got into bed and slept—into the day, and into the next night.

When I awoke, I went into the bathroom and knelt on the cold floor. Counting six tiles from the wall, I pried my fingernail under the one loose tile. My red nail broke. I bit the rest off and spat it onto the floor. Removing the tile, I picked up the business card: SARA'S DRY CLEANERS, 2010 P ST. NW, WASHINGTON, D.C.

Turning the card over, I thought of Irina. I wanted to remember everything. I wanted to catalog, then file away my memories of her so I could pull from them in the future, protect them from the influence of others, protect them from the cruel distortion of time, protect them from the person I knew I'd have to become.

Once I made the call, there would be no turning back. A *double* is a bit of a misnomer: one person doesn't become two. Rather, one loses a part of herself in order to exist in two worlds, never fully existing in either.

I remembered seeing Irina at Ralph's: how she sat on the edge of the booth, her legs half in the aisle, when she turned her head in my direction for the first time. I remembered the pink bubble gum she bought at the gas station in Leesburg on our way out to a vineyard that turned out to be closed. How we went sledding the night of the first snow at Fort Reno, the District's highest point. How I balked when I met her in Tenleytown and she held up two pea-soup-colored trays she'd taken from the Agency's cafeteria. I pointed at my heels and told her I couldn't possibly. How I relented when she asked if I'd try just once. How the wind felt in my face as we rushed down the icy hill.

The time we ran into a Safeway ten minutes before it closed, in search of a birthday cake. It wasn't my birthday, or hers, but Irina insisted we get it, even asking the baker, who'd already undone his apron for the night, if he could please write my name on it, with an exclamation point, in blue icing.

When we watched airplanes land at National from Gravelly Point. How we huddled together under a blanket when a flash of light appeared in the distance. How the sound of the planes' engines grew louder and louder until they appeared overhead. How they looked so close we felt we could reach up and touch their bellies.

I even wanted to remember that morning in my apartment after we'd made love—when everything unraveled
like a loose string on a sweater. After she left, I went
to my closet, where I'd hidden a gift I'd bought her: an
antique print of the Eiffel Tower. After seeing *Funny
Face,* she'd said that we must go to Paris together
someday. The tiny tower was the size of my palm, its
intricate lines drawn by dipping the tip of a needle in
ink. I'd had it framed and wrapped it in butcher paper,
tied with red string. I had planned on giving it to her
for Christmas, but it remained in the back of my closet.

I held the business card in my hand. I memorized the
address, lit a match, and watched it go up in flames.

CHAPTER 16

~~THE APPLICANT~~

THE CARRIER

The Bishop's Garden was empty, the side gate unlocked. The bare trees formed black shadows against the illuminated National Cathedral. The cherub-covered fountain was turned off for winter, except for a steady drip to keep the pipes from freezing, the garden's famed rosebushes just thorny shrubs.

Three footlights along the path hugging the stone wall were burned out—as they said they'd be—but with the full moon and the lit-up cathedral looming over the garden, I had no trouble navigating along the path and through the stone arch to the wooden bench under the tallest pine.

I brushed off the thin layer of snow and dead pine needles and took a seat. A sudden movement behind me caused the hairs on the back of my neck to stand at attention. I looked around: nothing. Had I been followed? I looked up: Two yellow lanterns hung high in the towering pine. An owl steadied herself on a branch that seemed much too small to hold her. She swiveled her head, surveying the garden for an unlucky mouse or chipmunk. She was a regal bird, there on her throne, poised to pass judgment and carry out the sentence herself. She paid me, a commoner, no mind as she patiently waited for her dinner to appear. To operate fully under instinct was a gift given to the animals; how much simpler life would be if humans did the same. The branch creaked as the owl shifted her weight. With a flap of her wings, she coasted up and over the garden's wall. It wasn't until she was gone that I noticed I'd been holding my breath.

I pushed my red glove back and looked at my watch: seven fifty-six. Chaucer was due in four minutes. If he was late, I was to leave immediately and take the number ten bus to Dupont Circle. If he was on time, I was to take a small package from him, two rolls of microfilm containing *Doctor Zhivago* in its native Russian, then board the number twenty bus and deliver the film to a safe house on Albemarle Street.

It started snowing and I watched the flakes dance in the spotlights pointing at the Cathedral. My thighs began to itch, as they did whenever I was cold, and I tightened the belt of the long camel-hair coat Sally had insisted on buying me when she noticed the cigarette burn on my old winter jacket—a small gift from a man who'd bumped into me on the bus. I took off my red leather gloves and blew hot air into my balled-up fists. When I released my fingers, my engagement ring slipped off and clinked to the cobblestones. It was two sizes too big, and I hadn't gotten around to having it properly fitted. But my, it was beautiful. Teddy's grandmother had given it to him when he was a boy, telling him that someday the woman he'd love for the rest of his life would wear it. He remembered telling her he'd never marry—he'd be far too busy fighting Nazis, like Captain America. His grandmother patted him on his head. "Just you wait," she'd told him.

Teddy recounted this story before he got down on one knee at his parents' house the day after my twenty-fifth birthday, just before the strawberry short-cake was served. Instead of looking at Teddy, I looked at my mother, who beamed with a look of pride I'd never before seen in her. Then I looked at his parents across the table, smiling as if their baby boy had taken his first steps. Then I looked back at Teddy and nodded.

It was a beautiful ring, but I hated wearing it. Wearing it felt like a cover.

I knew that what I really wanted was impossible. But I wanted it anyway. I wanted the excitement, the home, the adventure, the expected, the unexpected. I wanted every contradiction, every opposite. And I wanted it all at once. I couldn't wait for my reality to catch up to my desires. And that need was my constant companion, the underlying current of nerves that caused me to overanalyze every interaction and question every decision—the source of the never-ending conversation in my head that kept me up nights while Mama snored softly on the other side of the thin wall separating our bedrooms.

I knew what people called it: an abomination, a perversion, a deviance, an immorality, a depravity, a sin. But I didn't know what to call it—what to call us.

Sally had shown me a world that existed behind closed doors, but it still didn't feel like my world, my reality. All I knew was that I hadn't seen Sally since the night I spent at her apartment two weeks and three days earlier, and that in those two weeks and three days, I hadn't spent one waking hour not thinking of her.

I picked up the ring and put it back on as the cathedral bells rang out eight times. After the final bell, Chaucer appeared, as planned. There had been no sound—not of the gate opening, nor of footsteps. He arrived silent as snow, wearing a long black coat and a plaid hat with flaps that covered his ears. With his funny hat and curious expression, he reminded me of a basset hound. "Hello, Eliot," he said.

"Hello, Chaucer."

"Lovely night for a stroll." His accent dripped with the articulations of a high-class Londoner.

"Indeed."

He remained standing, and a beat of silence passed between us. He made no move to hand me the package, but turned and looked up at the cathedral. "Impressive structure. You Americans do love making new buildings look old."

"I suppose so."

"Take bits and pieces from the Old Country, cobble them together, and put the old American stamp on it, isn't that right?"

I wasn't about to debate him, nor did I understand why he seemed to want to debate me. Maybe this was what the men did when they met like this, but I had no time for the volley of clever banter. There was a job to be done.

He looked hurt at my nonresponse and reached into his coat, handing me a small package wrapped in newspaper.

I placed the package in my Chanel purse.

"Let's do this again sometime." He tipped his hat and remained standing there as I left.

The thrill never dampened—like the moment when a roller coaster crests at the top of the hill and pauses just before it lets gravity pull it down. I walked to the corner of Wisconsin and Massachusetts. But instead of boarding the number twenty bus as I was supposed to, I walked the twenty minutes to the large Tudor house at 3812 Albemarle. If I couldn't have everything my heart desired, at least I had that moment, that feeling—and I wanted to savor it as long as possible.

After slipping the package into the safe house mail slot, I continued down the hill to Connecticut Avenue, where I caught a bus to Chinatown.

A wall of warm air and the smell of fried rice greeted me when I walked into Joy Luck Noodle. The host pointed to a back table, where Sally was pouring herself a cup of steaming tea from the small iron kettle kept warm by a flickering tea light. She hadn't noticed me enter, and when we made eye contact, I felt that familiar inner gasp.

Two weeks and three days since I'd seen her—since the day I told her Teddy and I were engaged, since the night we made love. That night I'd felt I'd been changed from the inside out—into the kind of person who is confident in her every action, someone who doesn't question her every thought, every move. But seeing her sitting there made me want to retreat to the bathroom and steady my nerves. When Sally gave me that smile of hers as I took off my coat and hung it over the back of my chair, for a moment I relaxed.

She looked beautiful as always, except for the caked makeup she'd attempted to cover the bags under her eyes with. She wore a brocaded green silk turban, but the strands of her red bangs peeking through appeared stringy and unwashed. As she reached for her teacup, I noticed her shaking hands.

"Tired? Hungry?" she asked in our own coded language.

"Hungry," I said. "And I need a drink."

We never talked specifics of our missions, but *tired* meant things hadn't gone well, *hungry* meant things had, and *need a drink* meant exactly that.

She signaled for the waiter to bring us two Mai Tais. "I went ahead and ordered us the cashew chicken and pineapple fried rice."

"Perfect." I took off my gloves and set them on the table. Sally's eyes drifted to my left hand for a moment before looking away. She let the silence linger—an old trick she must've forgotten she'd told me about, something she picked up during the war to get people to start talking. *People will do anything to fill an uncomfortable silence,* she'd said. I sipped from my Mai Tai and remembered Sally had prefaced her invitation to a late dinner by saying we needed to talk. I'd thought nothing of it then, but now it was all I could think about. "You wanted to tell me something?" I fished out the blue paper umbrella from my drink and popped the cherry on the tiny sword into my mouth.

"Nothing big." She sipped her drink through the blue straw, careful not to disturb her lipstick. "Just wanted to find out how your New Year's Eve was."

"Two turns down the bunny slope and I was done. Spent most of the night in the lodge sipping hot cocoa by myself."

"I imagine Teddy's a fine skier. The naturally athletic type." She rarely mentioned Teddy, and certainly never complimented him.

"I suppose so."

"Well, my New Year's Eve was as lovely as ever," she said after another long sip. "Went to a party. Danced all night. Drank a little too much, you know how it goes."

She was punishing me. "Sounds like a gas."

The waiter came with our chicken, and again I was thankful for a chance not to talk. Sally wielded her chopsticks like a pro. I reached for a fork and stabbed a piece of pineapple.

After the waiter took away our plates, Sally took a deep breath and said in rapid succession that we could no longer see each other, that she was thankful for the time we'd had together and for our friendship but it would be better for both of us if we went our separate ways, that she was about to be too busy with work and wouldn't have much time for socializing anyway.

Her words felt like kicks to the stomach, again and again, and I could hardly breathe by the time she was finished. The word "friendship" stung the most. "Of course," she concluded, "we'll remain on professional terms at work." It seemed she wanted to say more, but didn't.

"Professional," I repeated.

"Glad you agree." Her indifference was cruel. I wanted to tell her I didn't agree. No, I wanted to scream it. The thought of no longer spending time with her, of having to treat her professionally, of having to pretend there was never anything between us, made me sick. I wanted to tell her I'd rather walk barefoot across barbed wire than make polite chitchat with her in the elevator. And I wanted to ask her how she could—how it was so easy for her to turn off the switch.

But I didn't say anything. And it wasn't until after I stood up, after my knees hit the underside of the table, spilling the pink Mai Tai on the tablecloth, after I turned to leave, after I heard her tell the waiter I wasn't feeling well, after I stormed out, after my walk broke out into a run—it wasn't until after all that that I realized my silence was also an answer.

CHAPTER 17

THE TYPISTS

We'd speculated about Irina since she'd arrived at the Agency. And our suspicious were confirmed shortly after Sputnik took to the skies and Gail saw her name on a memo pertaining to the *Zhivago* mission. She never spoke of the work she did after hours, and we never asked. Like a good Carrier, Irina said nothing of the secrets she carried. But still, it wasn't long before we found out the rest.

What made Irina stand out in the typing pool was precisely that Irina didn't stand out in the typing pool. Despite the winning lottery of ingredients comprising her physical appearance, she had the ability to go unnoticed. Even a year after her joining the Agency, she still managed to fly under our radar. We'd be reapplying lipstick in the ladies' room when she'd startle us from behind, saying that that shade of pink was a nice color for spring. Or we'd be toasting during happy hour at Martin's and she'd clink our glasses a beat after we thought we'd clinked with everyone. At lunch in the cafeteria, she'd get up to say she had to return to work when no one remembered her having sat down with us in the first place.

Her talent for going unnoticed did not go unnoticed; and with her father having died at the hands of the Red Monster, she had the makings of a perfect asset. After some training, a memo went through the chain of command and Irina was put into the field. And she was good at her job. Irina's first missions consisted of delivering internal messages around town, but as she proved herself, her assignments carried increased importance. That cold January night in the Bishop's Garden was her first with the *Zhivago* mission.

After leaving HQ that evening, she took the number fifteen bus to the corner of Massachusetts and Wisconsin, walked around St. Albans School to the cathedral grounds' back entrance, and slipped into the garden through the iron side gate.

Irina was likely wearing her new long camel-hair coat with the brown collar and the red leather gloves Teddy had given her. The day after she received the gloves, Irina had shown them to us. "Aren't they pretty?" she asked, fanning her fingers as we stood in line to have our hats, coats, and pocketbooks inspected on our way into HQ. "A little small, but they'll break in." We all agreed that they were very chic and that Teddy had excellent taste. All except for Sally Forrester, who took one look and said they were knock-offs.

Under the red gloves would have been Irina's new diamond ring, which Teddy had given her the day after her twenty-fifth birthday. It was a tasteful Art Deco number with a diamond whose size surprised us. We knew Teddy came from a wealthy family, but we had no idea they were *that* wealthy. The stunner was too large for her ring finger, and she'd yet to get it resized. During work hours, she put it inside her desk drawer so it didn't fall off when she was typing, sometimes even forgetting to put it back on again at the end of the day. If it had been one of us, we would've had it resized the day we got it. But Irina wasn't the flaunting type.

A wedding in the typing pool always warranted much discussion, but Irina hadn't seemed interested in discussing hers.

"Will you come back to work?" Gail asked.

"Why wouldn't I?"

"What are your thoughts on taffeta?" Kathy asked.

"Pro, I guess?"

We learned that Irina's mother was planning the big day, using it to purge the last vestiges of her Russianness by throwing the most American of weddings. "She wants to have red, white, and blue carnation centerpieces," Irina told us. "She's planning to spray-paint the blue ones herself."

To celebrate the engagement, we each pitched in two dollars to purchase a black lace negligée from Hecht's.

We wrapped it in silver tissue paper and placed it on her desk before she arrived. When she sat down, she picked up the package and looked around the room as we pretended to work. She tore a small corner of the tissue paper and a black silk strap spilled out. Irina tried to push it back inside but only tore the paper more. She started to cry. We froze, not knowing what to do. One of a typist's golden rules is never to let them see you cry. Of course, we'd all done it—but from the relative privacy of the ladies' room, or in the stairwell at least. At our desks? Never.

We wondered whether Irina was thinking of the black negligée as she waited for Chaucer to arrive that night in the Bishop's Garden. Was that the start of her cold feet? Or had the second thoughts already begun—long before the negligée, before Teddy had proposed, before he'd told her he loved her during their walk around the Tidal Basin as the cherry trees clung to the season's last pink petals?

It's hard to say. We can't know everything.

But we do know that Chaucer arrived right on time and that Irina collected the two rolls of Minox film containing *Doctor Zhivago*. And we do know she took the number twenty bus to Tenleytown, where she delivered the package to a safe house on Albemarle Street.

The first stage of the mission was complete, thanks in part to Irina. The men patted themselves on their backs for finding such an unexpected asset. But it wasn't a man who'd developed Irina's talent; it was Sally Forrester.

Sally was officially a part-time receptionist, but it didn't take a genius to figure out she was much more. Soon after Anderson brought her around HQ, we discovered it was common knowledge among those in the know that Sally was a Swallow who'd been flitting around since her OSS days. When not sitting behind the reception desk, which was most of the time, Sally traveled the world, using her "gifts" to gain information. Unlike Irina, Sally could never be invisible. Everything about her screamed *Look at me! Look at me! I am the one who should be looked at!* Her hair was cut in the Italian style—soft red curls framing her heart-shaped face—and her figure always seemed to threaten the integrity of her tight woolen skirts and cardigans. And she always overdressed: fuchsia designer trapeze dresses, white satin swing capes, a rabbit fur coat rumored to have been a gift from Dulles himself.

One of the men had taught Irina how to take a package from a passerby on K Street during rush hour and keep walking without looking back; how to leave a hollow book under a bench in Meridian Hill Park and leave without someone's jumping up to say *Hey, Miss, you forgot your book;* how to slip a piece of paper into the pocket of a man sitting next to her at Longchamps. But it was Sally who finished her training. We don't know what these trainings consisted of, but we did see a change in Irina. Something about her seemed sturdier—as if she'd become a woman to reckon with. In short, more like Sally.

Whatever it was, Irina did her mentor proud, and soon they weren't just colleagues but friends. They started sitting at a separate lunch table in the cafeteria. They began going to Off the Record instead of Martin's for happy hour. On Mondays, they'd come into the office quoting lines from *Silk Stockings*, *Funny Face*, *An Affair to Remember*. When Sally would arrive home from a trip, she'd place little trinkets on Irina's desk: a Pan Am sleep mask, lavender-scented lotion from the Ritz, a squished penny from one of those machines on the Atlantic City boardwalk, a snow globe from Italy.

For Irina's twenty-fifth birthday, Sally had thrown her a dinner party. We'd never been to Sally's apartment—a one-bedroom walk-up above a French bakery in Georgetown—so we jumped at the chance when she placed the navy blue invitations on our desks. *Your presence is requested for the celebration of the birth of our dear friend Irina*, read the handwritten silver calligraphy.

When we asked about bringing dates, Sally told us that this party was for us gals. "It'll be more civilized," Sally said, laughing.

We wore our most fashionable cocktail attire, several of us even splurging at Garfinckel's for the occasion. "This is *Sally Forrester's* dinner party. You don't show up wearing a knock-off of last year's Dior," Judy said. "Besides, we can wear it for New Year's."

We took taxis instead of streetcars or buses so we'd arrive fresh-faced, with our mascara and lipstick intact despite the heavy snow. We ascended the two flights and at the top heard a song playing on the other side of the door. "Sam Cooke?" Gail asked.

Before we could knock, Sally opened the door, looking stunning in a gold satin wrap dress with tasseled belt. "Well, don't just stand there!" We trailed Sally into her apartment, her black stilettos wobbling on the plush pink carpet.

Irina looked lovely in her emerald-green skirt and matching bolero jacket. We wished her happy birthday as we pressed our small gifts into her hands.

Sally disappeared into the kitchen and Irina motioned for us to take a seat on the white leather sectional. To break the silence, we asked questions about the apartment's décor. With Sally busy in the kitchen, Irina answered for her.

"How'd she find this place?" Norma asked. "It's to die for."

"Saw an ad in the *Post*."

"These candlesticks! Where are they from?" Linda asked.

"Inherited. A grandmother, I think."

"Is that a real Picasso?" Judy asked.

"Just a print from the National Gallery."

"What did Teddy get you for your birthday?" Gail said.

"He told me to pick out something nice from Rizik's." She straightened her jacket. "Sally and I went today."

Sally emerged from the kitchen carrying a crystal punchbowl filled with fizzy pink liquid that matched the carpet. "And doesn't she look gorgeous?"

We nodded.

After two glasses of punch, we moved to the dining area, where a long table was set, complete with calligraphed nameplates, white calla lilies, and cloth napkins folded into fans.

"What a production!" Norma whispered.

After dinner, chocolate cake, presents, and a few more glasses of punch, we left Sally's thinking the party was a bit much for a birthday but agreeing she really knew how to throw a shindig.

Some may now say otherwise, but we never noticed anything off about Sally. Sure, the high attention she was paid by the opposite sex invited the occasional catty remark, but we all respected her. She never said "Sorry" or "Please" or "Just a thought." She spoke the way the men spoke, and they listened. Not only that, but she scared the hell out of a few. Her perceived power may have come from the tightness of her skirt, but her real power was that she never accepted the roles men assigned her. They might've wanted her to look pretty and shut up, but she had other plans.

Later, when Sally's name had been redacted from every memo, every call log, and every report, we tried to remember whether there'd been any clues about who she really was. But it wasn't until much later that we put the pieces together.

CHAPTER 18

~~THE APPLICANT~~

THE CARRIER

A week passed. Then a month. Then two. The wedding plans went ahead. Teddy and I would be married in October at St. Stephen's, followed by a small reception at the Chevy Chase Country Club. My cover would become my life.

Teddy's parents would be paying for the whole thing, but Mama insisted on taking care of the flowers, the cake, and my dress. Even before the engagement, she'd purchased the material for the gown—ivory lace and satin.

The day after Teddy proposed, she took my measurements while I was at the stove making breakfast. The dress—what she said would be her greatest work—was halfway done by February. But by March, she stopped making the gown, complaining she'd have to start all over again unless I put back on the fifteen pounds I'd lost since January. I told her she was being crazy, that I hadn't lost fifteen pounds, maybe five at most—and even then only because of the stomach flu, which was the excuse I gave when I couldn't get out of bed for a week following my dinner with Sally.

I couldn't hide anything from her. Despite my layers of sweaters and thick wool tights, Mama could see my body was shrinking. My skirts had to be safety-pinned not to fall off my hips, and I wore thick turtleneck sweaters to hide my jutting clavicle.

Mama responded by adding bacon fat to everything: to shchi, borscht, pelmeni, beef stroganoff, to blinis and omelets. I even caught her tipping grease from a frying pan into the plain oatmeal I ate for breakfast. She insisted I have seconds of every meal and watched my plate as she'd done when I was a child.

On the weekends, she'd bake multiple cakes, saying she was testing which to make for the wedding— honey, drunken cherry, Neapolitan, bird's milk, even a two-tiered Vatslavsky torte. She'd force me to take multiple slices of each, often spooning vanilla ice cream on top.

Mama wasn't the only one to notice my dwindling figure. Teddy asked if everything was okay so many times I told him if he didn't stop asking, things wouldn't be. He said he wouldn't ask again but hoped I wasn't trying some crazy new fad diet. He said I was perfect just the way I was, and his sincerity filled me with an inexplicable rage.

The typing pool also noticed. Judy asked what my secret was and said my waist was as tiny as Vera-Ellen's in *White Christmas*. The rest of the Pool acted like Mama and left doughnuts from Ralph's on my desk.

It wasn't that I didn't want to eat; I just had no appetite—not for food, not for anything. It was hard to sit through a movie. It was excruciating to be in crowds. I began walking to work instead of taking the bus, just to be alone. At parties, I didn't even attempt to make polite conversation. Even at the Sunday Company gatherings, where I used to enjoy the intellectual sparring and the feeling I was getting insider information, I chose to stand next to the wives instead of Teddy, where I didn't have to say much of anything except that I liked the confetti dip.

Teddy tried to pull me out of whatever I'd fallen into. He tried and tried, and I almost loved him for the effort. I tried to love him, I really did. He loved me more than anyone ever had. So why wasn't it enough?

I saw Sally twice during that time. Had she made herself scarce for my sake? Had she even thought of me for one minute? The first time, I was leaving the office and she was standing in the lobby as the elevator doors opened. I stepped out and we almost collided. I stepped right, then left. She mirrored me, then we awkwardly repositioned. She said hello and smiled, but

I saw her looking me up and down, and I knew from her expression that I must've looked terrible.

The second time, Sally didn't see me. I'd seen her sitting in the booth by the window at Ralph's, across from Henry Rennet—there in the front booth, at the window, for the world to see, midday on a Tuesday. And the world did see. When I returned to the office, it was all the typing pool could talk about.

"Think they're dating?" Kathy asked.

"Lonnie said she thinks they've been dating since New Year's. Saw them together at some party. Someone should warn her what an asshole he is."

"I'll volunteer," Norma said.

"Is it true, Irina?" Linda asked.

"I don't know."

"Well, Florence over in Records said she saw them whispering in the stairwell," Gail said.

"When?"

"I don't know. Few weeks ago?"

So that was it. She'd been interested in Henry the whole time. I was nothing but a passing fancy at best. The thought repulsed me. I could take not being with her, but I knew I wouldn't be able to stand seeing the two of them together.

Unbeknownst to Teddy or Mama or anyone, I spoke with Anderson that day about the possibility of a foreign posting. "Aren't you getting married?" He looked at my ring finger.

"This is a hypothetical question."

"Hypothetically, it's none of my business. But I'm sure we'd find a place for you."

"Keep this between us?"

He pretended to zip up his lips.

That evening, as the sun bathed E Street with that orange late-afternoon glow, I thought maybe by that time next year, I'd be walking down the streets of Buenos Aires or Amsterdam or Cairo. I relished the notion of shedding who I was, shedding everything, and becoming someone new. It was a delicious feeling, and for the first time in a long time, I smiled.

When I got home, the smell of bacon fat didn't greet me at the door. Mama was sitting at her sewing machine not sewing. She had a full cup of tea in front of her, the water black from her having failed to remove the teabag. "What's wrong, Mama?"

"I can't rewind my bobbin."

"That's all?"

"I've tried for hours."

"Is it broken again?"

"No. My eyes are."

"What do you mean?"

"I can't see out of the left one."

I went to her side. Looking into her eyes, I failed to see anything wrong. "What? When did this happen?"

"I woke up like this."

"Why didn't you say anything?"

"I thought I could fix it."

"With what?"

"Garlic."

"We'll get you to the doctor first thing tomorrow." I took her hand and felt it tremble. "I'm sure it's nothing," I said, trying to believe it.

The next day, I took Mama to an eye doctor, who she complained wasn't Russian and therefore would be biased. "Biased how?" I asked her. "Dr. Murphy is Irish."

"You'll see!"

The nurse called her name, and I got up to accompany her as I usually did, in case she needed help translating. But she told me no, she wanted to go in by herself. I agreed, sat back down, and flipped through *Time* magazines for an hour.

Mama came out, rubbing her arm where the doctor had taken her blood. When I asked what he'd told her, she said he didn't know anything. "I told you. He's prejudiced against Russians."

"He said nothing?"

"They took my blood and put me in an X-ray. He said he'll call when they know."

"Know what?"

"I don't know."

Two days later, there was no scene, no rushed trip to the hospital, no fall, no ambulance, no emergency; there was just a phone call from Dr. Murphy telling Mama what he'd already suspected when he first shone his tiny flashlight into her eyes. There was *a mass,* as he put it, and when I got on the phone for clarification, he said she needed to go back for more tests as soon as possible, and to discuss "paths of treatment."

"Paths?" Mama asked when I hung up. "What paths?"

"Treatments, Mama."

"I don't need treatments. I need to get back to work."

She went about the rest of her day as if nothing had changed. When I told her we needed to schedule the appointment, she said she'd be fine and not to worry, but it's all I could do.

The next few weeks, Teddy sprang into action, going about the task of getting Mama well the way he would approach a project at work: methodically, persistently, and calmly. He secured Mama appointments with the best specialists in Washington, then Baltimore, then New York.

But after going from doctor to doctor, specialist to specialist—including a Chinese herbalist who looked at Mama's tongue and gave the same diagnosis the others had—Mama told me she wanted to stop all treatments. "What will be, will be," she said one night as I was serving her the tuna casserole one of our neighbors had brought over.

I served her three helpings, even though I knew she had barely the appetite for a few forkfuls. "What do you mean, *what will be, will be*?"

"It means what it means. I'm done."

"You're done?"

"I'm done."

I set the Pyrex casserole dish down with such force that the glass cracked.

Mama reached for my hand, but I refused and stormed out.

When I came home later that evening, Teddy was gone and Mama was at the kitchen table. I went into my bedroom without saying a word. I was so angry at her, at the world, at everything.

In hindsight, I wish more than anything that I'd taken her hand that night in the kitchen and told her I was sorry. I thought there'd be time. Time to make amends, time to let her know I supported whatever decision she made, time to tell her how much I loved her, time to embrace her as I hadn't done since I was a little girl. But there wasn't. There's never enough time.

St. John the Baptist was filled with friends and acquaintances of Mama's I never knew she had. One person after the next gave their condolences and told me things about my mother I wished I'd known while she was alive.

We unveil ourselves in the pieces we want others to know, even those closest to us. We all have our secrets. Mama's was that she'd been generous to a fault. I discovered she'd clothed nearly our entire neighborhood for free: she'd tailored a secondhand suit for an out-of-work veteran with an interview to be a cashier at Peoples Drug, repaired the bridal gown of a woman who could only afford to buy one with a broken strap and a wine stain on the bodice from the Salvation Army, patched the coveralls of a bottling plant worker, and mended many socks for an elderly widower who just wanted some company.

And that yellow prom dress I'd helped Mama rebead a year earlier? It had been a gift, not a commission. Mrs. Halpern's teenage daughter wore it to the funeral, and the sight of her twirling to show it off made me dizzy with appreciation for the person my mother was.

Mama herself wore a black dress with intricate flower beading running down the sheer sleeves. The dress had been another secret. How long she'd been working on it I didn't know. But I did know she'd made it to wear at her own funeral, as I'd first seen it the morning she didn't wake up—pressed and laid across the rocking chair in her bedroom for me to find.

Inside the church, the Orthodox priest circled Mama's casket, swinging his incense, the scented smoke billowing out over his gold cassock and dissipating above his head.

I turned away for a moment and that's when I saw her: Sally had come. She was standing toward the back, wearing a short black birdcage veil. I turned back toward the priest, who was still swinging his incense—my thoughts on Sally instead of my mother. I wished she would walk down the aisle and stand next to me, take Teddy's place, then my hand. But she stayed in the back and Teddy by my side.

The funeral ended and I followed Mama's casket out of the church. As I passed Sally, she touched my arm. Her veil was askew and she had tears in her eyes. I kept walking. The procession made its way to Oak Hill Cemetery, where Teddy had arranged for Mama to be buried in a nice plot overlooking Rock Creek Park. Standing next to Mama's grave, I looked for Sally in the crowd, but she wasn't there.

After, Teddy tried in vain to comfort me. Days passed, then weeks. One night, when I couldn't sleep, I decided to call Sally. My hands shook as I dialed her number, but the line just rang and rang.

EAST

MAY 1958

CHAPTER 19

~~THE MUSE~~
~~THE EMISSARY~~
THE MOTHER

I woke from a dreamless sleep to Mitya standing over me. "Someone is outside," he whispered.

"Is it Borya? Did he lose his key again?"

"No."

I swung my legs over the bed and toed the floor until I found my slippers. "Go back to your room."

Mitya didn't move as I fumbled for my robe.

"Mitya, I said go back to bed. And don't wake your sister."

"She's already up. She heard it first."

Before I could ask what they had heard, there was a crash. "It's just a branch," I said, my voice as low and steady as I could will it. "That poplar has been dead

313

since last winter. I've told Borya we needed to cut it . . ." Another sound outside stopped me. It was quieter, muted. It was no falling branch.

The sound of the front door opening sent us both running toward the entryway. Ira was there, standing in the doorway, barefoot, her white nightgown illuminated blue with moonlight. The sight of her startled me. She was a ghostly angel—a woman now. "Ira," I said gently. "Close the door."

Ignoring me, Ira stepped outside. "Come out!" she called out. Mitya pushed past me to join his sister. I grabbed hold of Mitya's nightshirt, but he shrugged me off. "Show yourself!" he yelled, his voice cracking. Movement behind the woodpile at the side of the house sent both my children tripping over themselves to get back inside. I shut the door behind them and tested the knob to make sure it was locked.

"It's them," Ira said. "I know it." As she hugged herself against the wall, she no longer looked like a beautiful apparition; she looked like my little girl again.

"Who?" I asked.

"A man followed me home from the train station yesterday."

"Are you sure? What did he look like?"

"Like the rest of them. Like the men who took you away."

"I've seen them too," Mitya said. "They watch me from behind the fence at school. Two, sometimes three of them. They don't scare me, though."

"Don't be silly," I said, but I didn't believe my words. Mitya was prone to exaggeration, and his *very healthy imagination,* as Borya had put it, resulted in stories. He'd found a piece of Sputnik in the woods. He'd saved a little girl in his class from a wolf that had wandered onto the playground. He'd eaten a magical plant that gave him the power to jump higher than a trolleybus.

But this story I did not doubt.

Zhivago had been published in Italy six months earlier, and with each new country that published the book—France, Sweden, Norway, Spain, West Germany—I could feel more eyes watching us. With each foreign publication, questions arose about why the book had not been published at home. For now, the State spoke no word publicly of the novel. Its hand was steady, but a tremor grew. I knew it was only a matter of time before they'd act.

I'd never spoken to the children about the men who sat in their black cars at the end of the drive, or the men who followed me whenever I went into Moscow. Instead, I just waited for what felt preordained—I waited for them to come for me.

I had done my best not to alarm the children. I closed the drapes, complaining of headaches. I locked the doors, saying a neighbor's house had been broken into by some teenagers. I visited a kennel to see about getting a Caucasian shepherd, telling the man my son could learn some responsibility by taking care of a dog.

But my children were never fooled; they were too old for that. They knew to look for the truth not in my put-on smile or the words coming out of my mouth, but in my shaking hands, the bags under my eyes.

I did speak to Borya about my increasing fears, but he was distracted by the onslaught of letters from well-wishers, smuggled-in newspaper clippings of rave reviews from abroad, and requests for interviews. He was in demand—and I now had to share him not only with his wife, but with the entire world. The last time I spoke of the matter, we walked the path along Lake Izmalkovo. Borya was preoccupied with finding the right person to translate *Zhivago* into English. He answered my question about getting a guard dog by asking if I thought the English edition should include the poems at the end of the novel. "They're saying the rhyme detracts from the meaning," he said.

Everything was about the book, and nothing mattered more—not the fame the international editions had brought him, nor the looming threat from the State, nor his family, nor mine. He even put it above his own life. His book came first and always would, and I felt like a fool for not having realized that sooner.

As Ira held back tears and Mitya pretended to be strong, I was struck with the enormity of being utterly on our own. I gathered myself and peered out the window, but saw only the gentle sway of the poplars, their black shadows dancing on the gravel path.

Then movement.

The children jumped back, but I held still. I flung open the drapes.

"Mama!" Mitya cried.

"Come," I said. "Look."

The children looked over my shoulder. Outside, two red foxes stood atop a log they'd knocked loose from the woodpile. Their golden eyes met mine before they fled back into the woods.

We laughed until tears came, until our stomachs hurt. We laughed until it didn't seem very funny anymore.

"Are you sure there's nothing else out there?" Mitya asked.

"Yes." I closed the drapes. I kissed their cheeks as I had done when they were little. "Now back to bed."

The children shut their bedroom door, but I knew I wouldn't be able to sleep. In the dark kitchen, I put a kettle on. Not wanting to wake the children, I lit a candle and picked up a newspaper.

No picture was included with the article, but I had no trouble imagining the crush of white and tan fur, the tangle of hooves, the broken antlers with their downy fuzz singed off. TWO HUNDRED REINDEER STRUCK DEAD BY LIGHTNING ON THE PUTORANA PLATEAU. I brought the page closer to the candlelight to see if

I had read the number correctly. I had. Two hundred gone in a moment. The sky cracks open and—

The kettle's whisper turned to a howl and I removed it from the stove. I went back to the article. The reindeer had huddled together for protection, hence the large number of dead. A shepherd from Norilsk was the first to come across the casualties. He said they looked as if they'd been shaken up like backgammon dice and scattered across the snowy mountaintop. Leave it to a shepherd to also be a poet.

How many years would it take their bodies to decompose, their bones to bleach? Would the villagers collect their antlers and display them as unearned trophies on their walls? Why hadn't they broken from the herd and headed for lower ground? Or maybe they just did what they'd done for thousands of years. There's no telling when the sky will open up.

If it had been men outside our door, would I have barricaded us in? Or would I have opened the door and offered myself up? Would I have screamed Borya's name, knowing he couldn't hear me?

"Do we have anything to eat?" Mitya asked from behind me.

"Did I wake you?"

"Can't sleep anyway." He went to the cupboard. In the last year, Mitya seemed to always be eating. He'd grown almost five centimeters in six months; the stool he'd once used to reach the top shelf was now a plant stand. He pulled out a bag of stale sushki and I poured him a cup of tea. He dunked his snack and ate it in two bites.

"Did you really see men outside your school?" I asked him softly.

"I think we should get a pistol," he answered.

"A pistol won't do us any good."

"Two pistols, then," Ira said, coming into the kitchen and sitting down at the table. She took a sip from Mitya's teacup.

"Two pistols. Ten pistols. They won't help us."

"I'll learn how to use it," Mitya said. He made a gun with his hand and pointed it at his sister.

I placed my hand atop his and folded his fingers down. "No."

"And why not? Who will protect us? I need to do something. I am the man of the family."

Ira laughed, but my chest tightened. My boy.

"Are you excited for camp, Mitya?" I asked, desperate to change the conversation. He was to start his summer session of Young Pioneers the following week. For the last four summers, Mitya had so enjoyed his time in the woods. The summer I returned from Potma, he hadn't wanted to go, fearing that if he left my side, I'd be taken again. He'd sobbed as I dressed him in his white shirt and red neckerchief and boarded him onto the bus. As I stood with the rest of the parents and watched the bus drive away, he didn't even wave goodbye. But when he came home, he was full of stories of the friends he'd made, of playing Geese and Swans, raising the red flag, morning and afternoon calisthenics, and marching—he even liked the marching. For weeks he sang Pioneers songs and recited facts he'd learned about corn quotas.

Mitya raised his head. "I suppose."

"You don't want to go this year?"

"I'm sick of all those songs," he said. "And I wish you'd signed me up for the Young Technicians camp instead. I'd rather be building things than marching."

"I didn't know you wanted to—"

"It costs extra," he interrupted.

"I'm sure we could've worked something out."

Mitya reached for another sushka. "You would've asked him?"

"I would have thought of something."

"Why won't he marry you?"

"Mitya!" Ira slapped his arm.

"You've asked the very same thing," Mitya said. "Just not to Mama. People at school say things, you know."

"What do they say?" I asked.

Mitya said nothing.

"I've been married twice before and don't want to marry again," I said, knowing they could see right through me, as they could see through everything now.

"But you love him," Ira said. "Don't you?"

"Sometimes love isn't enough," I said.

"What else is there?" Ira asked.

"I don't know."

Mitya and Ira glanced at each other, and their silent agreement broke my heart.

When the house was quiet, I looked in at the children, both sleeping again. I put on my raincoat and left. I couldn't go to him; he'd be asleep. I walked along the green fence by the main road. As I walked, I thought of Mitya as a little boy, refusing to let go of my hand before boarding the bus to camp. I thought of him now saying we needed a pistol, being the man of the household. I thought of Ira, how she'd grown since that day the men took me. I thought of my children knowing, so young, that love sometimes isn't enough. A truck's headlights appeared in the distance. I wondered what would happen if the truck swerved off the road, if I didn't get out of its way. The sky cracks open and—

WEST

AUGUST–SEPTEMBER

1958

CHAPTER 20

THE TYPISTS

The Agency moved fast. After Irina's successful night in the Bishop's Garden, with the Russian manuscript now in our hands, there was no time to waste. In the time it took winter to thaw, the cherry blossoms to bloom and drop, and the dome of Washington's humidity to descend, *Doctor Zhivago*'s Russian proofs were prepped in New York, printed in the Netherlands, and shuttled to a safe house in The Hague in the back of a wood-paneled station wagon. Three hundred sixty-five copies of the novel had been printed and bound in blue linen covers—just in time for the tail end of the World's Fair, where we'd distribute the banned book to visiting Soviets.

But all that was only after a few hiccups.

The Agency's initial plan was to contract a Mr. Felix Morrow—a New York publisher with close ties to the

Agency—to arrange the layout and design of the manuscript and prepare proofs that couldn't be traced back to American involvement. Then the manuscript was to be shipped off to a yet-to-be-determined publisher in Europe for printing—another safety precaution to erase any Company fingerprints. A memo even stipulated that no American paper or ink be used.

Teddy Helms and Henry Rennet had taken an American Airlines flight to New York, then a train out to Great Neck, to personally hand the Russian manuscript to Mr. Morrow—along with a bottle of fine whiskey and a box of Mr. Morrow's favorite brand of chocolates to seal the deal.

But Felix Morrow proved to be a liability. A former Communist turned Trotskyite but now as American as apple pie, as he put it, the New York intellectual loved to talk—and talk he did. Even before the ink on the contract dried, he was telling everyone about the great book he had in his possession.

Norma even heard through her old New York literary contacts that Morrow had contacted several Russian scholars to review the manuscript, and soon everyone was talking about a Russian edition in the works here on American soil. She immediately alerted Anderson, who told her they'd take care of it. "No pat on the back," she told us. "Not even a thank-you."

Even worse, Morrow had also contacted a friend at the University of Michigan Press to explore the possibility of printing the novel in the United States—in spite of the exclusive world rights owned by the Italian publisher Giangiacomo Feltrinelli and likely to secure a nice amount of change. "I can publish anywhere I please," Morrow had told Teddy when confronted.

Teddy and Henry were again dispatched to Great Neck—to quiet Morrow with an even finer bottle of whiskey and an even bigger box of chocolates, and to halt his deal with Michigan. Morrow protested, but finally he agreed to be cut out of the operation—not because of the whiskey and chocolates, but because of the promise of an even larger compensation than he'd initially been given.

After the Morrow situation was put to bed, Teddy and Henry trekked over to Ann Arbor to stop Michigan from moving forward. They pleaded with the university's president to cease the publication plans. They told him the first Russian-language edition needed to appear to come from Europe in order to have the greatest impact on the Soviet reader and to avoid being dismissed as American propaganda. They also emphasized that the author, Boris Pasternak, could be put at risk if the book was connected to U.S. distribution. After some back-and-forth, Michigan had agreed to delay the publication until the Agency's edition appeared in Europe.

The Agency then worked with Dutch intelligence to finish the job. The proofs prepared by Morrow were sent to The Hague and a deal was made with Mouton Publishers, which was already contracted to produce the book for Feltrinelli in Dutch, to do a small run in Russian for the Agency.

After all that, *Doctor Zhivago* was finally on its way to Brussels and the World's Fair; if all went according to plan, it would be in the hands of Soviet citizens by Halloween.

To celebrate, Teddy and Henry arrived back in Washington just in time to catch Shirley Horn's second set at the Jungle Inn. They took a seat in the red vinyl booth farthest from the stage.

Teddy drank whiskey on the rocks and Henry sipped a dirty gin martini as they watched Shirley. They were so transfixed that they didn't notice Kathy and Norma in the booth next to them. Or perhaps they did notice the women but just didn't recognize them without their typewriters and steno pads.

"She's good, right?" Henry shouted over the din of the club. "What did I tell you? The real deal."

"Very," Teddy said, waving his hand to flag down the waitress.

"The real deal. Absolutely. Aren't you glad you came out tonight?"

"What's with the waitress?" Teddy asked. He loosened his tie. "We should've gone home to change. We look like a couple of feds."

"Speak for yourself," Henry said, dusting something invisible off his navy blue jacket. "And you know damn well that if we'd gone home first, you'd have just stayed in. What's with you lately, Teddy boy?"

Instead of answering, Teddy rose to get another drink, returning with two martinis, an extra olive in his.

"A toast?" Henry asked.

"To what?"

"The book, of course. May our literary weapon of mass destruction make the monster squeal."

Teddy raised his glass half-mast. "*Za zdorovye.*"

Kathy and Norma, still unnoticed, raised their own glasses to toast the victory.

The two men watched as Shirley dipped her head to her keys, looked up to the ceiling, then glanced over at a man wearing a black Stetson with a peacock feather sitting up front at a small round table.

"What's the story there?" Henry asked, nodding toward the man at the table.

"I'm not in the mood."

"Come on! For old times' sake."

"Husband," Teddy replied. "He sits and watches her every show. Or maybe . . . a lover?"

"No," Henry said. "Ex-husband. Watching her perform is as close as she lets him get."

"That's good, real good."

"Any chance of reconciliation?"

"No."

The two friends sat for a few minutes.

"You sure you're all right, Ted?"

Teddy finished his drink in two gulps.

"How's Irina?"

"She's fine."

"Cold feet's normal. Hell, I have cold feet now, and I'm not even dating anyone."

"It's not that. She just . . . she gets so quiet."

"We all have our quiet moments."

"Nah, this is different. And when I ask why she's quiet, she gets mad." Teddy looked around. "Where's the goddamn waitress?"

"So . . . to change the subject—"

"Thank you."

"Wanna hear a rumor?" Henry asked.

Kathy and Norma leaned back to hear better.

"Would I be in this business if I didn't?"

"You hear about the redhead?"

"Sally Forrester?"

Norma and Kathy shot each other a look.

"Bingo," said Henry.

"And?"

"About to be tossed. Damn shame, too. I loved seeing her coming, but not as much as I liked seeing her go."

"Why?"

"I've always preferred a nice ass."

Norma rolled her eyes.

"No, why's she going to be canned?"

"That's the best part. You'll never guess."

"Just tell me."

Henry leaned back in the booth. "Ho-mo-sexual."

"What?" Norma let out, unable to contain herself. The men didn't notice, but Norma and Kathy sank down in the booth a few more inches.

"What?" Teddy asked.

"Well, Ted, it means she prefers the company of other women."

"I mean, when did this happen? I thought you two had a thing or something?"

Henry sipped his drink. "Maybe some guy dumped her and she never looked back."

"Jesus Christ." Teddy lowered his voice. "I mean, how did you find out?"

"You know better than to ask for my sources."

"She's Irina's best friend," Teddy said. "I mean, they haven't been spending as much time together, but—"

"Maybe that's it. Maybe Irina found out Sally's little secret too."

"She never mentioned anything to me."

"All relationships are built on small omissions."

Shirley ended "If I Shall Lose You" and addressed the crowd. "Y'all stay put now. Order another drink to warm your soul, and I'll be back in a hot minute." She rose from the piano and sat down next to the man wearing the black Stetson. He kissed her and she pushed him away but held on to his wrist, turning it over to kiss its underside.

"Definitely a lover," Teddy said.

In late August there was a massive thunderstorm and half the District went dark. The morning commute was a mess, and the buses and streetcars ran late or not at all. Irina usually took the bus to work, but on that day, Teddy must've picked her up, because when we were getting our morning coffee in the break room, we noticed them still sitting in his blue and white Dodge Lancer. We tried not to watch, but that proved difficult, as the break room window overlooked the east parking lot.

It was already nine thirty, but the couple was showing no signs of hustling in. Instead, they sat, and we pressed our faces against the window until the glass fogged. By nine forty-five, we cracked the window, hoping we could hear something, but had to close it again when a gust of rain blew into our faces.

We could see Teddy slumped over the steering wheel as if he'd been shot, and Irina looking out the passenger window. Around ten, Irina got out and rushed into the office, her heels skidding on the slick sidewalk.

A few minutes later, Teddy drove off, fishtailing onto E Street, and we went back to our desks.

Irina came in, took off her raincoat, and took her seat. She rubbed her pink eyes and complained about the storm.

"You okay?" Kathy asked.

"Of course," Irina said.

"You look a little upset," Gail said.

Irina licked her fingertip and started flipping through her notes from the previous day. "I'm just a little frazzled this morning. The weather and all."

"Don't worry," Gail said. "We told Anderson you were in the ladies'."

"Anderson was looking for me? Did he say what he wanted?"

"No."

"Good." She opened her purse and took out the small metal cigarette case with her initials engraved on it that Sally had given her for her birthday. She brought a cigarette to her lips and lit it, her hands still red and shaky. We'd never seen Irina smoke, but that wasn't what we noticed first; what we noticed first was that her engagement ring was gone. "Well, I mean, I hate to be late," Irina continued. "Thanks for covering for me."

We wanted to ask about Teddy and the car. We wanted to ask about the missing ring. We wanted to ask if she'd heard the rumor going around about Sally. But we didn't. We figured we'd give her some time and ask for details the next day.

But the next morning, Irina was called into Anderson's office.

We knew that Irina was called into his office. We knew that when she came out she rushed into the ladies' and stayed a good long while. And we knew that after she left the restroom, she went home early, complaining of a stomachache.

Helen O'Brien, Anderson's secretary, filled us in on the rest.

"He told her the Agency needs to maintain the highest reputation, and she replied *Yes, of course.* Something about decorum in the office and at home. And she was like, *Yes, I agree.* He went on to say there'd been rumors of personal misconduct. And then there was a long pause. She asked if it was about her and said as far as she knew, she carried herself according to the highest Agency standards. And he was like, *Look—people are saying you might be a little funny, you know, in that way. And if it's true, that's a liability for us.* She denied it up and down. And I think she may have started crying, but I couldn't be sure through the door. He told her he was glad to hear it, and that he hopes the rumor doesn't come back to his desk like it did with another woman he had to fire the other day. She asked who it was, and he waited a few seconds. Then he said it: *Sally.*"

Irina didn't come in to the office for the rest of the week, and we never got a chance to ask her what was happening. That Saturday, she boarded a plane bound for Brussels and the World's Fair.

The following Monday, Teddy didn't come into the office either. Nor did he come in the rest of that week.

We met up for happy hour at Martin's to discuss.

"Maybe he went to Brussels to win Irina back?" Kathy suggested.

Norma held up an oyster twice as big as the others. She inspected it a second and tipped it back. "You old romantic," she said. "I heard he's locked himself in his apartment and refuses to get dressed or answer the door."

"Where'd you hear that?" Judy asked.

"Reliable source."

"I'm pretty sure he's just on assignment," Linda said, stabbing at an olive in her martini glass with an oyster fork.

"You're no fun," Norma said. She waved the waitress over and asked for another martini. "She needs another too," she said, pointing at Linda.

Linda didn't protest. "Or maybe he defected. Maybe it wasn't just his heart Irina broke."

"Now that's the spirit!" Norma said.

"Or maybe he's with Sally," Linda went on.

"But what about her being," Kathy lowered her voice, *"you know?"*

"But the timing makes sense. First Sally leaving, then Irina leaving." The waitress came and placed our martinis in front of us. "Maybe instead of Sally and Henry, Sally and Teddy were having an affair this whole time, and when Irina found out . . ."

Norma pulled Linda's drink away from her. "Now I think you've had too many."

We never did find out what Teddy was doing the week he didn't come into work, but we do know that the day he did come in, he approached Henry Rennet from behind as Henry stood in the lunch line waiting for chicken-fried steaks and instant mashed potatoes. Teddy tapped him on the shoulder and he turned. Without a word, Teddy punched his friend in the face. Henry tottered for a second, then fell. His green plastic tray hit the floor first, scattering the scoop of yellow corn he'd been served. His body followed, making contact face-first with the fallen corn and the black-and-white-tiled floor.

Teddy stepped over Henry, kicked his tray across the cafeteria floor, walked to the ice dispenser, got a fistful of ice, and left.

Judy was exiting the line with a cup of chicken soup when she heard Henry's face hit the floor, like the thump of raw meat on a marble countertop. It took her a moment to realize that the two white Chiclets that had scattered across the floor and come to a stop just inches from her patent leather kitten heels were actually Henry's front teeth. The woman next to her screamed, but Judy just sensibly bent down and collected the teeth, putting them in her cardigan pocket. "Just in case they could put 'em back in," she told us when recounting the story.

Those who hadn't seen or heard Teddy's fist connect with Henry's mouth thought Henry had fainted. "Get a doctor!" someone yelled. Henry sat up, dazed, as Doc Turner—not a real doctor, but an elderly cafeteria chef with a perpetually half-smoked cigarette hanging out of his mouth—emerged from the kitchen holding a frozen steak. "Here you go, buddy," he said, handing it to Henry.

Henry's mouth dripped red down the front of his white shirt. He put the steak to one eye, then the other, then his nose. It wasn't until he tasted something metallic that he realized his two front teeth were gone. His tongue explored the new hole.

Doc Turner helped Henry to his feet. "Must've did someone wrong, huh?"

"Who was it?" Henry asked. He looked at the semicircle of people gathered around.

"I just saw the aftermath," Doc said.

"Teddy Helms," Judy said. "It was Teddy."

Henry wiped a glob of bloody corn from his mouth, cut through the crowd, and walked off.

Norma said she saw Henry leaving Headquarters as she was coming in from a doctor's appointment. "You could see the imprint of Teddy's Georgetown class ring right under Henry's eye," she snickered. "Couldn't have done it better myself."

The next day, we got to work a few minutes early to see what the consequences of the lunchtime brawl would be. "Think he'll be fired?" Kathy asked.

"Nah, that's how the boys settle things around here. I wouldn't be surprised if Dulles encouraged it, even. They'll be back to normal in no time," Linda said.

We went to work trying to figure out what had provoked Teddy to send his best friend to the dentist. "Let's work backwards," Norma suggested one morning at Ralph's. "Teddy punched Henry, Irina left Teddy, Sally was fired."

"What's the connection?" Linda asked.

"Beats me," Norma said.

And while Teddy appeared in the office the next day, two Band-Aids wrapped around his knuckles, Henry never returned. Norma did come across a bit of intel about his whereabouts, though. How, we knew better than to ask. But she told more than one of us his location, thinking it might be useful at some point.

Two weeks later, Judy surprised herself when she put her hand into her sweater pocket and found Henry's teeth instead of the tissue she was expecting.

Three weeks later, we returned the wedding gifts we'd bought for Teddy and Irina, happy we'd saved the receipts.

A month later, Anderson brought in a new typist, and we realized Irina was not coming back.

CHAPTER 21

~~THE APPLICANT~~
~~THE CARRIER~~

THE NUN

Under a curtain of wet hair, I watched the black water swirl down the drain. The chemicals made me dizzy, and when I lifted my dripping head, the woman who came to make me into a new woman opened a window.

After wrapping my head in a white towel, she instructed me to sit on the old trunk that doubled as the flat's coffee table. She popped open her shrimp-pink makeup case to reveal a pair of shears peeking out from a purple velvet case, a variety of dyes, two tape measures, foam padding, makeup brushes, black and white fabric samples, and yellow rubber gloves.

She picked through the knots in my hair, combing it out until smooth, then pulled it back. After sawing through it with the scissors, she handed me a guillotined ponytail. I held on to it as she shook up the bottle of black dye she'd used on my head and delicately applied it to my eyebrows with a small brush. It burned more than the slight tingle she'd promised.

After wiping it off, she told me to stand and strip. I hesitated. "Don't worry, honey," she said. "I've seen it all." I'd managed to gain back some of the weight I'd lost after Sally ended things, but not much. She held the foam padding to my chest, then my behind. "We're gonna have to give you a little something extra."

As she took my measurements, she talked. She told me how she used to work in the Warner Bros. costume department, applying false eyelashes to a temperamental Joan Crawford, inserting shoe inserts to hike up Humphrey Bogart, and scouring every Hollywood beauty parlor to find the right shade of blond for Doris Day. She rambled on about the time she'd walked into a dressing room to see Frank Sinatra's head between the legs—*hat still on!*—of an actress she wouldn't name. "He didn't even look up," she said. "Just mumbled into her hoo-hah for me to come back in twenty minutes. I never pegged Ol' Blue Eyes as the generous type."

I said nothing as the woman told her stories. Normally, I would've found her highly entertaining, but I wasn't in the mood, and she was the kind of woman who could talk for forty-five minutes without realizing her audience had fallen asleep.

I'd arrived on a plane eight hours earlier and was exhausted. It was the first plane I'd ever been on, and when I stepped out onto the tarmac, even before my makeover, I became more than a Carrier—I became a new person.

I'd asked for it; now here it was. I had more than an assignment and a one-way ticket: I had a chance to become someone else, a clean slate. So I took it. Heartbreak can be freeing—the weight lifted, no one left to hurt or be hurt by. At least that's what I told myself.

The woman packed away her scissors and dyes and gloves. She swept my hair off the floor and put it into a small plastic bag, packing it away in her case. Before leaving, she told me a florist would deliver the nun's habit to me in a box meant for long-stemmed roses. She opened the door and turned back toward me. "Lovely meeting you, dear."

"You too," I said, even though we'd never even given our names.

I locked the door behind her and walked over to the cracked mirror hanging above the bathroom sink to see the stranger in its reflection. I ran my fingers through my few remaining inches of hair. Licking the tip of my finger, I rubbed a spot of black dye off my temple and told myself I could be anyone now.

As I dressed, the thrill dulled. What would Sally think of my transformation? What would Mama have thought? I cupped my hand against the back of my neck. Mama would definitely have hated it. Sally would say it was

341

a *statement*. Teddy would've said he loved it, even if he didn't.

After Mama's funeral, I didn't want to be alone, so Teddy stayed at my apartment, on the couch. On nights when I couldn't sleep, Teddy would read to me—essays in *The New Yorker* by E. B. White and Joseph Mitchell, short stories by men whose names I've forgotten. Once, on the night when I told him I couldn't marry him, he read to me from a stack of papers in his briefcase. He hadn't told me he was the one who'd written what he was reading until he finished, revealing that it was the first chapter of a novel he'd been working on for years. I told him I loved it, that he must finish it. "You really think so?" he asked. When I said I wouldn't lie to him, he asked if that was true.

I had trouble meeting his gaze, but forced myself to. "I can't marry you."

"We can wait. For as long as you need. You're still grieving."

"No. It's not that."

"What is it, then?"

"I don't know."

I could feel him holding his tongue, not saying the words hanging between us. "I think you do."

"I don't."

"Is it Sally?"

"What? No . . . I have trouble making friends. Real friends, anyway. She's been a good friend to me."

"Nothing has to change. I know—"

"I don't think you know me like you think you do."

"That's the thing. I do."

"What are you saying?" I asked.

"I'm saying I just want to be with you—whatever that means for you."

But I couldn't understand. I didn't want to understand. "What does it mean to *you*? What do *you* want?"

"A wife," he said. "A friend." He sniffed up a tear. "You."

"What do you think I am?"

He bowed his head. "Be honest with me."

I told him I was, and he asked that we sleep on it, to give it time before making any decisions. I had agreed, mostly to get away from seeing him like that, and we parted—him to the couch and me to my bed, where I spent the night listening to him tossing and turning in the other room.

The following day, a storm knocked out half the power in the District. As Teddy drove us in to the office, we didn't speak or turn on the radio. The only sound was the windshield wipers battling the driving rain. When we pulled into the parking lot, I slid off his grandmother's ring and put it on the dash. He slumped forward, and I left him like that. I had nothing else to say, and I feared anything else would either hurt him more or stop me from getting out of the car. I'd been the one to end it, but it felt as if I was breaking my own heart—not the way Sally had, but in a way that made me feel even more adrift, as though I'd cut the one tether still holding me to the ground.

Teddy didn't come in to the office that day, and I didn't see him before I left. He'd retrieved his suitcase and was gone before I returned to the apartment. The next day, I was called into Anderson's office and questioned about my relationship with Sally. I was told she'd been fired and that my relationship with her had been suspect, which I denied convincingly enough for Anderson to say he believed me. They were the ones who had taught me to become someone else, after all, to lie about who I was. And turning my new power back onto them felt good.

It was all too much to think about. And yet there in Brussels, looking at myself in a mirror halfway across the world, I still couldn't put it out of my mind. But I needed to. There was no turning back. The mission had begun.

＝＝◈＝＝

I wrapped my hair under a scarf and set out for the rendezvous point. Brussels was buzzing, the moon a half disc above the city. The streets were packed with fairgoers from around the world. Passing a crowded café, I overheard people speaking French, English, Spanish, Italian, Dutch. As I cut through La Grand-Place, a group of Chinese men and women stood in the square's center, gazing at the top of Hôtel de Ville while passing around a box of chocolates. Two Russian men passed so close that one brushed my shoulder. Did the one in the fur cap look at me a moment too long? I didn't turn around or quicken my pace. I just kept my gaze straight ahead and kept walking.

I arrived at the address my handler had given me on rue Lanfray, just off Ixelles Ponds. Standing in front of the grand Art Nouveau building, I was awed by its five stories of intricate inlaid wood and the swirling mint-green iron that climbed its façade like ivy. The entire house belonged inside an art museum. Ascending the curved cement staircase to the double front doors, I told myself I belonged there; or rather, the person I had become did. I pressed the gold buzzer once, counted to sixteen, then pressed again. I felt a light flush of perspiration at the nape of my neck. A man dressed as a priest opened the door. "Father Pierre?" I asked, in Russian.

"Sister Alyona. Welcome." The sound of my new name caused my chest to loosen.

I shook his hand firmly, as Sally had taught me. "Pleasure."

"We started without you." I didn't know his real name, nor did I know if Father Pierre was even Catholic. He wore the collar but had an ivory cashmere sweater draped over his shoulders as though he'd just returned from playing golf. In his early thirties, Father Pierre was blandly handsome with thinning blond hair, cerulean blue eyes, and a reddish beard. He ushered me in, and I followed him upstairs.

The flat was furnished with the luxurious but eclectic décor of someone who was new to money and had hired someone to give him taste. The mix of modern Danish furniture, seventeenth-century tapestries, and folk pottery gave the effect of wandering into a museum that had been shaken up inside a snow globe.

I was on time to the minute but the last member of our team to arrive. A man and a woman were already seated on a kidney-shaped couch, sipping cognac in front of a barely lit fireplace. The man known as Father David was the agent in charge of our mission. The woman, Ivanna—her real name—was the daughter of an exiled Russian Orthodox theologian and the owner of a Belgian publishing house that printed religious material. She was also the founder of *Life with God,* an underground organization that smuggled banned religious material behind the Iron Curtain. Her group had been working in conjunction with the Vatican since the fair had opened, and we were to follow her lead in how to most effectively distribute *Zhivago.*

Ivanna and Father David looked up when we entered but did not smile or stand. There was no need for introductions: they already knew who I was, just as I already knew who they were. I sat on the edge of a white linen lounge chair and they continued.

On the sleek black coffee table in front of them was an exact model of Expo 58, complete with blue-tinted mirrors representing fountains and pools of water, miniature trees, sculptures, flags of every nation, and the Holy See's ski-sloped, white-roofed City of God pavilion—the location where the mission would take place.

It had been Ivanna's idea to use the fair as a means of proselytizing, but it was Father David who took the idea and made it the Agency's own. He believed Expo 58 would be the perfect location to get the book back to the USSR, and with it, to incite an international uproar over why it was banned.

Father David was soft-spoken but commanded attention, steady and confident as Chet Huntley on the nightly news. He also looked more like a priest than Father Pierre did, with his Boy Scout haircut, delicate pink mouth, and long fingers that one could picture holding up the Host.

Father David pointed to the model, showing us the separate routes we'd take in and out of the fair each day. If we suspected we were being tailed, we were to duck into the Atomium—the fair's centerpiece, which stood a hundred meters tall and depicted the unit cell of an iron crystal magnified 165 billion times. We were to take the lift to the top of the aluminum structure, where there was a restaurant boasting a panoramic view of Brussels and a waiter ready to assist.

After giving us the overhead view, Father David moved the model to the floor and unrolled blueprints of the City of God. He pointed to the spot where Rodin's *The*

Thinker stood. "Father Pierre will be stationed here, circulating within the crowd to evaluate any Soviets who might make for potential targets," he said. "Once they are identified, he will signal Ivanna by scratching his chin with his left hand." He traced a path from *The Thinker* to the Chapel of Silence, his long fingernail scraping across the paper. "Ivanna will then usher them to the Chapel of Silence, where she'll screen them for propaganda interest. If a target is receptive"—his finger moved around the Chapel's altar to a small, unnamed square room—"she will escort them here, into the library, where I'll be waiting with Sister Alyona." He looked at me, then continued. "After a final assessment, the handoff will occur." He pulled his hand back from the blueprints. "Oh, and one more thing: from here on out, we will only refer to *Zhivago* as the Good Book." He sat back in his chair and crossed his legs. "Any questions?" When no one answered, he took us through the plan again from start to finish. Then he took us through it again.

With the plan cemented in our minds, we sat and talked, drinking red wine from teacups and smoking. Only then did I ask it: "The Good Book—is it here?" Ivanna looked at Father David and Father David nodded. "They were taken directly to the fair earlier today, but we have one here." She walked to the foyer closet and pulled out a small wooden crate covered by an old mat. She removed the mat and picked up a book. "Here," she said, handing it to me.

I was expecting it to feel illicit. I was expecting to itch with dissidence. But I felt nothing. The banned novel looked and felt like any other novel. I opened it and read aloud in Russian: "They loved each other, not driven by necessity, by the 'blaze of passion' often falsely ascribed to love. They loved each other because everything around them willed it, the trees and the clouds and the sky over their heads and the earth under their feet." I shut the book. I didn't want to think of her. I couldn't.

"Have you read it?" I asked.

"Not yet," Ivanna said. Father David and Father Pierre shook their heads.

Opening the novel again and turning to the title page, I noticed an error. "His name."

"What about it?" Father David asked.

"It should not be written as *Boris Leonidovich Pasternak*. Russians wouldn't include his patronymic. They'd only write *Boris Pasternak*."

Father Pierre puffed on his Cuban cigar. "Too late now," he said, and held his hands in prayer.

The following morning, I carefully dressed in my padded brassiere and underpants, then slipped on the shapeless black habit and veil with a stiff white band that framed my forehead. I was forbidden to wear makeup of any sort; the woman from Hollywood said I'd have to make do with a dab of Vaseline rubbed onto my lips and the tops of my cheekbones for shine. But I didn't even do that. Looking in the mirror, I liked how my face looked: raw, pale, maybe a little older. Stepping back to take in the full look, I felt sexless—and powerful.

At precisely 0630, I left the flat for my first day at the fair. If we did our jobs correctly, we'd have given out the last of the three hundred sixty-five copies of *Doctor Zhivago* by the end of the third day.

On the tram built to shuttle fair visitors from the city center to the Heizel Paleis, I spotted the Atomium. It was far larger than the model had prepared me for. The official symbol of the fair—printed on every poster, every pamphlet, and almost every postcard and souvenir—the nine-sphered Atomium was supposed to represent the new atomic age. To me, it looked more like a leftover set from *The Day the Earth Stood Still*.

The fair would not open for an hour, but throngs of people had already lined up outside the large iron gates. Impatient children pulled at their mothers' purses; American high school students stuck their hands and heads through the fence, one almost getting stuck; a young French couple necked in public without regard to anyone's stares; an elderly German woman took a photograph of her husband standing next to a woman dressed in the black skirt, black jacket, black tie, and black hat of a fair guide. It was a thrill to be surrounded by so many people while still feeling unseen. No one paid attention to the nun.

I joined the line of fair workers at the Porte du Parc gate, which led directly into the International Section. As I approached the guard, I took a deep breath and pulled out my Expo 58 badge. He barely looked at me as he waved me in.

It was extraordinary. The model hadn't come close to depicting the enormity of it all. It was the first World's Fair since the war, and an estimated forty million tourists from every corner of the globe were expected.

Except for the fair workers hustling to their positions and a brigade of broom-wielding women sweeping debris from the street, I had the main thoroughfare to myself. I passed the Thai pavilion and its multiple tiered roofs resembling a temple atop a gleaming white marble staircase. The U.K. pavilion bore a striking similarity to three white pope's hats. The French pavilion was an enormous modern basket woven of steel and glass. West Germany's was modern and simple, like something Frank Lloyd Wright might've dreamed up. Italy's resembled a beautiful Tuscan villa.

I quickly located the American pavilion, and I couldn't decide whether the building, surrounded with state flags, looked more like an overturned wagon wheel or a UFO. Immediately to its left was the Soviet Union's behemoth—the largest pavilion by far in the International Section. It looked as if it could eat the American pavilion. Inside there were facsimiles of Sputnik I and II, which I longed to see. I'd never admit it aloud, but when Sputnik was launched, I couldn't help but feel a twinge of pride. I'd never been to the Motherland, but as I looked up at the sky the night the satellite was shot into space, I felt a connection to the place of my parents' birth in a way I hadn't before. That night in D.C. was cloudy, and I knew you couldn't see it with the naked eye, but still I looked to the heavens, hoping to see a flash of silver streaking across the sky. So there, standing so close to the thing—or at least, a replica of it—I wanted so much to go inside Russia's pavilion and see it, touch it.

But I couldn't deviate from Father David's plan.

On the other side of the American pavilion was my destination: the City of God. The Holy See's white building, simple and sloping, appeared small enough to fit within just the lobby of the USSR's pavilion. I walked inside the quiet building, the clacking of my cheap black leather shoes echoing off the marble floors. Vatican workers scurried about, preparing to open. They mopped the floors, set out pamphlets, and refilled the basins with holy water. They said *Hello, Sister* as I passed, and I smiled the way I thought a nun might: with just the corners of my mouth.

Father Pierre was already in position—standing next to *The Thinker,* his hands behind his back, rocking on his heels. As I passed, his gaze didn't break from the famous sculpture.

Down the vaulted corridor and into the Chapel of Silence, two nuns were readying the small altar facing the pews. They looked me over, then continued lighting the candles. Had I passed the test? If I hadn't, the nuns revealed nothing. Nor did they react when I circled the altar and walked through the parting in the heavy blue curtains behind it.

"You're here," Father David said as I entered the secret library. He looked at his watch. "The public gates are open. You ready?"

I took my place on a wooden stool in front of the bookshelf filled with copies of the Good Book, each in its crisp blue linen cover. I was calmer than I'd expected, but Father David radiated nervous tension as he paced the small room. Four steps to the right, four steps back. I later discovered that it'd been two years since Father David had been in the field, the last time in Hungary, where he'd helped rouse the partisans to revolt against their Soviet occupiers.

We heard the first muted footsteps and whispers of visitors entering the City of God. I slowed my breath to see if I could hear what language the people were speaking. Was it Russian? Father David appeared to be listening too, his head cocked toward the opening in the curtains.

We waited on edge for our first targets to arrive, and I could feel small knots form between my shoulder blades.

Ivanna opened the curtain. Behind her stood a Russian couple, looking as if the Wizard of Oz's curtain had been pulled back only to reveal a priest, a nun, and some books instead of a man pulling levers. I hesitated, but Father David didn't. He greeted them warmly, in flawless Muscovite Russian. All nervousness gone, he'd transformed into the perfect priest—charming with a hint of power—whom upper-class parishioners would want to invite to Sunday dinner.

Father David asked the couple questions about their visit to the fair. *How are you enjoying it? What sights have you seen? Did you come to see the Rodin? Have you visited the model of an atomic icebreaker? An astonishing feat of science. There's a line to view it, but it's well worth the wait. Have you tried the waffles?*

In no time, Father David quickly ascertained the couple's story. The woman, Yekaterina, was a ballerina with the Bolshoi performing nightly at the Soviet pavilion; the older man, Eduard, simply described himself as a "patron of the arts." Eduard boasted of the woman's performance the night before. "She left the audience breathless. Even from the corps."

Father David jumped on this, telling the couple he had recently seen Galína Sergeyevna Ulanova dance in London. "It was life-affirming," he said. "As if the Madonna herself had kissed the soles of Galína's feet. She was the physical embodiment of poetry." The couple agreed wholeheartedly, and with that momentum, Father David seamlessly transitioned into a more general conversation about art and beauty—and the importance of sharing it.

"I couldn't agree more," Yekaterina said. From the rosy tint in her cheeks, it was obvious she was quite taken with the young priest and his passionate speech.

"Do you like poetry?" he asked her.

"We're Russian, aren't we?" Eduard answered.

The couple had come into the library only minutes earlier, and Father David was already turning to me to hand him a copy of the Good Book—which he in turn gave to the man. "Beauty should be celebrated," he said with a holy smile. The man took the book and looked at its spine. He knew immediately what it was. Instead of giving *Zhivago* back to Father David, he licked his lips and handed the book to Yekaterina. She frowned, but at his nod, she put the book inside her purse. "I believe you're right, Father," Eduard said.

When it was done, the couple had taken the book and Eduard had invited Father David to sit with him in his box for Yekaterina's evening performance. Father David said he would do his best to make it.

"It worked," I said when they were gone.

"Of course it did," Father David said, his voice steady.

Our targets came fast after that. An accordion player in the Red Army Chorus hid the novel in his empty instrument case. A clown in the Moscow State Circus stowed it away in his makeup case. A mechanical engineer who'd grown up hearing her mother recite Pasternak's early poems said she desperately wanted to read it but would likely do so only while at the fair. A translator who'd worked on the Soviet pavilion's brochure in multiple languages told us he'd always admired Pasternak's translations, especially his Shakespearean plays, and had dreamed of meeting him. Once, he'd seen the author dining at Tsentralny Dom Literatorov but had been much too shy to approach him. "I missed my chance," he said. "But I'm making up for my cowardice by having this." He held up *Zhivago*. Before he left, he gave me a copy of one of the Soviet brochures he'd translated. Inside was a map of the entire fairgrounds spanning two pages. I laughed as I noticed that the American and Vatican pavilions were markedly absent.

Speaking Russian again brought Mama to the forefront of my mind, and I longed to see someone who reminded me of her, even a little. But most of the Soviets who came were members of the intelligentsia—educated, well-spoken, and in favor with the State. Others were young and out of the country for the first time—the musicians and dancers and other artists performing at the fair. All were city people, their hands soft and uncalloused. They could afford to travel, and even more important, were given permission to. They dressed like Europeans, in their tailored suits and French couture day dresses and Italian shoes. And although I'd never been to the Motherland, these were Russians I didn't recognize; they were so unlike my mother, and the thought pained me.

In the afternoon, Ivanna came into the library to tell us there was an influx of Russians viewing *The Thinker* and she believed word had spread. "Should we slow down?" she asked.

"If anything, we should speed up," I said. "We won't have much time now that word has gotten out."

"She's right," Father David said. "Keep them coming."

When we'd given out a hundred copies, Ivanna stuck her head behind the curtain, holding one of the blue linen covers that had been ripped off the front of the novel. "They're littering the steps with them."

"Why?" I asked.

"To make them smaller," Father David replied. "To hide them."

———

We had planned to be at Expo 58 for three days, but we gave out our last copy of the Good Book midway through the second day.

Blue linen book covers littered the fair. A prominent economist removed the pages of an Expo 58 souvenir book and replaced them with *Doctor Zhivago*. The wife of an aerospace engineer concealed it inside an empty tampon box. A prominent French horn player stuffed the pages inside the bell of his instrument. A principal dancer for the Bolshoi Ballet wrapped the book in her tights.

Our job was done. We'd sent *Zhivago* on its way, hopeful Mr. Pasternak's novel would eventually find its way home, hopeful those who read it would question why it had been banned—the seeds of dissent planted within a smuggled book.

Father David, Ivanna, Father Pierre, and I parted according to plan. Ivanna would return the following day, staying at Expo 58 to distribute her religious materials. But the rest of us were to leave the fair and not return. There were no grand goodbyes, no pats on the back, no *job-well-done*s, no *mission-accomplished*s. Just some nods as we left the City of God one by one. No further contact was allowed. Where the Fathers were headed, I didn't know; but I was to board a train to The Hague the next day, where I'd meet with my handler for debriefing and my next assignment.

EAST

SEPTEMBER–OCTOBER
1958

CHAPTER 22

~~THE CLOUD DWELLER~~

THE PRIZEWINNER

Boris stands behind a split rail fence, tending a patch of earth where he had planted winter potatoes, garlic, and leeks. A visitor arrives, and Boris props his hoe against a birch tree.

"My friend," the visitor says, extending his hand to Boris over the fence.

"It's here?" Boris asks.

The visitor nods and follows Boris inside.

They sit across from each other at the dining room table. The visitor opens his rucksack and places the book, still in its blue linen cover, in front of its author. Boris reaches for his novel. It is much lighter than the hand-bound manuscript he'd entrusted to foreign hands two years earlier, and much different than the glossy published volume that had become an international bestseller in Europe—a volume he's seen only in photographs. He runs his dirty fingernails across its cover. His eyes fill with tears. "It's here," he says again.

The visitor takes out his second gift—a bottle of vodka. "A toast?" he asks.

"Who did this?" Boris asks.

The visitor pours himself a drink. "They say it was the Americans."

Boris takes his morning walk. It's raining, so he takes the tree-covered path through the birch forest back to his dacha instead of his usual route through the cemetery, over the stream, and up the hill. The few dead leaves still clinging to the forest canopy are enough to shield him from the rain. He's dressed appropriately for the weather, in his raincoat and cap and black rubber boots; but as he nears home, he feels a coldness soak through to his bones.

Boris hears them before he sees them. As he emerges from the wood, he sees cars parked along the narrow street, then the small crowd in his garden, under the cover of black umbrellas. A young man sits atop the section of fence with a rotted board. Boris wants to call out to him to move, but instead he stands as still as a deer who's seen her hunter before being seen.

He thinks of retreating back into the forest. But someone calls out his name and the crowd moves toward him like a large mammal. The man sitting on the fence jumps down and is the first to reach him. He pulls out a notepad and holds his pen at the ready. "You've won," he says. "You've won the Nobel Prize. Any comment for *Pravda*?"

Boris tilts his head to the clouds, letting the cold rain fall on his face. *Here it is,* he thinks. All laid out like a feast. His legacy engraved in gold. But no tears of joy mix with the rain running down his cheeks. Instead, fear comes over him like one of his icy morning baths.

He looks to the far end of his garden, where a gate was torn down twenty years earlier. He imagines his neighbor, Boris Andreyevich Pilnyak, coming through it, excited to share his onion harvest or the latest chapter of his novel. He remembers, later, after that novel was banned and Pilnyak accused of orchestrating its foreign publication, passing his friend's dacha on his morning walks and seeing him looking out the window, waiting. "They will come for me one day," Pilnyak had said. And they did.

A flashbulb pops. Boris blinks. He searches for someone familiar in the crowd—someone to hold on to—but sees no one.

"Will you accept?" another reporter asks.

Boris toes his boot into a puddle. "I did not want this to happen, all this noise. I am filled with a great joy. But my joy today is a lonely joy."

Before the reporters can ask more questions, Boris puts his cap back on his head. "I do my best thinking while walking, and I need to walk some more." He cuts through a parting in the crowd and continues back into the forest.

She will know to come, he thinks. *She will be waiting.*

He sees Olga's red scarf from a distance and a weight is lifted. She's atop the grassy knoll in the cemetery where the earth has yet to be broken, pacing the length of an invisible grave, her arms folded across her chest. Even now, Boris is still taken aback when he sees her. She's aged. Lines radiate from the corners of her eyes and her blond hair has become brittle. She's gained back the weight lost in the camps, but instead of settling back into her hips and thighs, it has gone to her stomach and face. Ever since *Zhivago* was published abroad, she no longer curls her hair or wears jewelry. Perhaps she no longer wants to stand out. Or maybe she is simply too tired to care. Regardless, Boris thinks her even more beautiful.

She runs to meet him. They embrace and he's enveloped by her, even though she's the one who fits neatly inside his arms. Her touch is a poultice.

Boris feels Olga holding her breath and rubs her back as if to prompt the exhale. She pulls away and confirms what her body has already told him she is thinking. "What will they do to us now?" she asks.

"It's a good thing," he says. "We should be celebrating. They won't be able to touch us. The world will be watching."

"Yes," she says. She looks around the cemetery. "They are watching."

He kisses her forehead. "It is a good thing," he repeats, trying to convince himself. He looks in the direction of his dacha. "The vultures are waiting. I must face them."

"You'll accept the Prize, then?"

"I don't know," he tells her. But he can't imagine not accepting. His life has led to this precipice; how can he not take this final step, even if into the abyss? If he retreats now, each time his beloved smiles, he will see the chip in her tooth from her days in the camps and will be reminded that it was all in vain.

Olga smooths the front of his jacket, her hand pausing at his heart. "Come to me when you can?"

He places his hand atop hers and presses it deeper into his chest.

The rain has ceased and the crowd has grown. Neighbors have joined the reporters, trampling his potatoes, his garlic, his leeks. A few men in black leather dusters mill about. Zinaida is standing on the side porch with Nina Tabidze, who is visiting from Georgia. They've placed two wooden chairs at the bottom of the steps to block entry, and Boris's dog, Tobik, keeps watch from underneath one.

Zinaida moves a chair to let Boris enter, but Boris pauses to talk to the reporters. Since his meeting with Olga, his spirits have brightened considerably, and although he doesn't fully believe what he's told her, the words have soothed him. The congratulations ringing out from the crowd are also a balm. A photographer asks for his picture, and Boris poses for the portrait, a genuine smile across his face.

Zinaida is not smiling. Her heavily penciled eyebrows make her look surprised, but her black frown says otherwise. "Nothing good will come of this," she says as her husband comes up the stairs.

"People on the streets of Moscow are already talking about it," Nina says, replacing the wooden chair. "A friend heard it on Radio Liberation."

"Let's go inside," Boris says.

Once inside, the smell of plum pie greets them and Boris remembers that it is Zinaida's name day. "My dear," he says. "I'm so sorry. In all this commotion, I've somehow forgotten."

"It doesn't matter now," she replies.

Nina touches Zinaida's shoulder, then goes to the kitchen to take the pie out of the oven.

The couple stands alone in the entryway. "You are not happy for me, Zina? For us?"

"What will happen to us?"

"What nonsense. We should be celebrating. Nina!" he calls to the kitchen. "Bring out a bottle of wine."

"It's not a time for celebrating," Zinaida says. "They'll want your head for this. First you give your manuscript to foreign hands, without its being published here? Now this? The attention, the outcry. No good can come of this."

"If you cannot bring yourself to muster congratulations, at least have a drink for your name day."

"What does it matter? You forgot it last year too."

Nina returns from the kitchen holding a bottle of wine and three glasses, but Zinaida waves her away and retires to her bedroom. Nina goes to comfort her friend, and Boris opens the bottle himself.

The next day, Boris's neighbor, the author Konstantin Aleksandrovich Fedin, knocks on the door, and Zinaida opens it. "Where is he?" Fedin asks. Without waiting for an answer, he bypasses Zinaida and takes the stairs up to Boris's study, two steps at a time.

Boris looks up from a stack of telegrams. "Kostya," he greets his friend. "To what do I owe this visit?"

"I am not here to offer you congratulations. I'm not here as your neighbor or friend. I'm here on official business. Polikarpov is at my house right now waiting for an answer."

"An answer to what?"

Fedin scratches his bushy white eyebrows. "Whether you will renounce the Prize."

Boris throws down the telegram he's holding. "Under no circumstances."

"If you don't do it willingly, they will force your hand. You know this."

"They can do what they want with me."

Fedin walks to the window overlooking the garden. A few reporters have returned. He slicks his hand over his widow's peak. "You know what they can . . . I lived through it as well. As a friend—"

"But remember, you are not here as my friend," Boris interrupts. "So what are you here as, exactly?"

"A fellow writer. A citizen."

Boris lowers himself to his bed, the simple metal frame creaking under his weight. "Which is it? A writer or a citizen?"

"I am both. And you are as well."

It was widely known that Fedin was next in line to serve as chair of the Soviet Writers' Union, so Boris thinks through his answer carefully. *"Inventas vitam iuvat excoluisse per artes."*

"From Virgil," Fedin says. "And they who bettered life on earth by their newly found mastery."

"It's engraved on the Nobel medal."

"Whose life have you bettered with this novel? Your family's?" Fedin lowers his voice. "Your mistress's? Or simply your own?"

Boris closes his eyes. "Give me time."

"There isn't any time. Polikarpov is expecting an answer when I return."

"Then take a long walk before you go home. I need time."

"Two hours," Fedin says from the doorway. "You have two hours."

But as soon as Fedin leaves, Boris gets up from his bed. He goes to his desk and composes a telegram to the Swedish Academy.

IMMENSELY GRATEFUL, TOUCHED, PROUD,
ASTONISHED, ABASHED.

—Pasternak.

WEST

October–December
1958

CHAPTER 23

~~THE SWALLOW~~

THE INFORMANT

There he was: standing in front of a bald tree wearing a cap and belted jacket, his right arm across his body, his hand just below his heart. The article accompanying the photograph was in French, but I recognized the word *Nobel*. "What does this say?" I asked my English-speaking waiter when he returned with my petit pain au chocolat.

"Boris Pasternak has won the Nobel Prize."

"Well, that'll spike book sales," I said. "Have you read it?"

"Of course!"

Everyone had read it. Thanks to my former employer, *Doctor Zhivago* had crossed the border undetected, finding its way back to the country where it was written.

371

The Nobel wasn't part of the Agency's plan—not as far as I knew—but I was sure they'd take credit for it anyway. I could picture them: standing in a circle, grins on their faces, celebrating with vodka shots. The only face I didn't imagine in that circle was Henry Rennet's. I knew he was no longer in Washington. In fact, I knew his exact location.

The day I arrived in Paris, I checked in to the Hotel Lutetia—not under the name Sally Forrester or Sally Forelli, or any other name I'd used before, but under the new name Lenore Miller. I then dropped a letter addressed to Sara's Dry Cleaners into a bright yellow post box. The letter contained the coordinates of Henry's location in Beirut and details of his new mission helping to launch a radio station to broadcast Western-friendly, pro-Chehab messages.

Giving up Henry was not my first plan. If Frank had been right about Henry's being a mole, I thought I could acquire enough information to ruin him through the proper channels. All those years that the Old Boys' Club thought I was just twirling my hair and giggling mindlessly at their dumb jokes, what I had really been doing was listening. But when Henry got word that I was poking around about him, he put a swift end to my Agency days. Oh well. Plan B.

Only Bev knew I'd left the country. She didn't ask where I was going, but when I told her I'd be buying a one-way ticket, my old OSS friend just quietly got up and left her kitchen, returning a few minutes later with an envelope fat with money. "His *gin rummy* money," she said, pressing it into my hands. "He'll never miss it." I said I couldn't possibly accept it, and she told me to stop being stupid. Then she slipped off the diamond tennis bracelet her husband had given her—an apology for yet another dalliance. "Pawn it."

My last night in Washington, I put on a record and got out my suitcase, still not knowing where I'd be going. I just knew that I needed to leave, to go some-place where I wouldn't know a soul—that there'd be no going back after I did what I was about to do. It wasn't until I removed my beige cashmere sweater from a drawer and discovered the Eiffel Tower print I'd planned to give Irina—still wrapped in butcher paper and tied with red string—that I made up my mind.

⸺◆⸺

They sent word by way of roses. Two dozen, white as a peace offering, placed on my vanity while I was out. I plucked the small card from the bouquet: *Nice to hear from you,* it read in Italian. I turned the card over. Blank.

It was unnerving to think they had been in my room, had gone through my things. The room was now certainly bugged. It was like seeing a spider during the day, then thinking you feel it crawling on you in the middle of the night. But after I gave them the intel on

Henry, surveillance was expected. I had no one to talk to, so it made me laugh to think of them listening to me listening to the Chet Baker record I'd purchased at a flea market. Perhaps they'd eventually tire of "My Funny Valentine" and listen in on someone else.

———⟺———

Weeks passed. The white roses wilted, their shriveled petals piling up on the vanity. The newness of the City of Light had worn off, and I was running out of Bev's money. And not knowing what, if anything, had become of Henry began taking its toll. When I thought of him— and I always thought of him—my insides felt as if they were filling up with cold, dark smoke. When I couldn't sleep, I'd lie on my back and picture the black smoke twisting out of my mouth and curling toward the ceiling.

To give my days structure, I began visiting every bookstore, bookstall, library, and bouquiniste along the Seine, seeking out copies of *Zhivago*. Though I longed to read it, I hadn't brought myself to do it. It was connected to them, to her, and I knew that to read it would bring back memories of things I didn't want to think of, things that would make my heart pound when I woke up and found myself halfway around the world, alone. Yet I sought it all over Paris, spending the last of my funds accumulating a small tower of copies.

When I could no longer afford books, I developed a new routine: sitting in my room all day, listening to my record, taking baths, and napping. I began subsisting on stale baguettes, apricot preserves, and warm Perrier. I kept the curtains drawn, and days passed without my even looking out the window.

Eventually I ran out of money and began returning my copies of *Zhivago* one by one. And it was there—waiting in line at Le Mistral—that someone tapped me on the shoulder. "Bonsoir," said the petite woman with finger-waved hair, dressed in an oyster-shell-pink pencil dress and black velvet pillbox hat. She picked up a copy of *Lolita* and smiled as if she knew me.

"Do you know where the travel section is?" the woman asked, switching to English.

"I'm sorry, I don't."

"I'm looking for a book. About Beirut. Do you know where that might be?"

She turned and left. I followed her out, tucking *Zhivago* back into my purse. I followed her past René Viviani Square. I wished I could stop and touch the famed locust tree for good luck, but we continued across la rue du Petit-Pont, past the church of Saint-Séverin, its Gothic gargoyles staring down at me. When we passed the church of Saint-Sulpice, I thought of Irina—what she must have looked like in that nun's habit.

I followed her into the Jardin du Luxembourg, and as we circumnavigated the octagonal basin, the woman spoke, her voice low and obscured by the fountain.

"He checked in to a hotel in Beirut under the name Winston, as you said he would. Within an hour, he checked back out of the hotel—with help from two of our bellmen." She paused. "We thought you might want to know."

What did Henry think when he heard the knock on the door? Did he have any sense of what was coming? Did he feel paralyzed? Did he scream? If so, did anyone hear him? I knew he hadn't, but I wished, oh how I wished, that he thought of me when they took him.

"That's all," the woman finished. She stopped to face me and kissed both my cheeks.

"That's all," I said when she had gone.

Back in my hotel room, the dead roses had been replaced by a fresh bouquet. I splashed water on my face and applied my red lipstick. I dressed in black slacks, a black blazer, and black leather kitten heels. I opened the curtains, blotted my lips, and assessed myself in the mirror.

I'd been trained to spot a double. Calm under duress, above average in intelligence, transient, easily bored. Ambitious, but with short-term goals. Unable to form lasting relationships. They often defect because of their own interests—money, power, ideology, revenge. I knew these traits, was trained to look for them. So why had it taken so long for me to recognize them in myself?

EAST

October–December
1956

CHAPTER 24

~~THE MUSE~~
~~THE REHABILITATED WOMAN~~
~~THE EMISSARY~~
~~THE MOTHER~~

THE EMISSARY

He won, he won, he won. My thoughts matched my steps as I paced Little House waiting for Borya to arrive. The Nobel was his. Not Tolstoy's or Gorky's, not Dostoyevsky's: Boris Leonidovich Pasternak was the second Russian writer ever to receive the Prize. His name would be marked in history, his legacy secured.

And yet, should he accept it, I feared what else might come. The Nobel win was already an embarrassment to the State, and Boris's accepting the Prize would be viewed as an even greater indignity. And the State did not like

379

to be humiliated, especially at the hands of the West. So once the world looked away, once the headlines died down, then what? Who'd protect us? Who'd protect me?

To still my nerves, I went outside to the small garden Borya had helped me plant. The morning rain had ceased and the clouds parted to reveal a light that bathed everything anew. Everything—how the magpies called out to each other, how a sunbeam warmed the neat row of seedlings, how the air felt against my exposed wrists and ankles—everything, every little thing, felt altered in the way it does when the world you've known is about to change.

Borya approached, hat in hand. We met midway down the path and he kissed me. "I've sent the telegram to Stockholm," he said.

"Saying what?" I asked.

"That I've accepted the Prize, and all that will come with it."

"You'll go, then?" I asked. "To Stockholm?" For a moment, I allowed myself to imagine this absurd dream: me in a black gown made in Paris, tailored to fit my body like a second skin; Boris in his favorite gray suit he'd inherited from his father. I'd watch as he'd stand to accept the Prize. And while he was at the podium, I'd let the cheers from the audience come over me like a wave. At the banquet, we'd dine on filet de sole bourguignon in the Blue Hall and he'd introduce me as the woman who'd inspired Lara, the woman the world had fallen in love with, just as he had.

"That's impossible," he said, shaking his head. He took my hand, and without another word, we went inside and to my bedroom and made love in the slow and steady way we'd grown accustomed to.

He spent most of the night with me, not leaving my bed until the blue light of morning peeked between my curtains. In that light, I saw new moles and black hairs and yellow marks on his back, then looked at my own skin. Our ages hit me as if jumping into a freezing river, and I wondered if we had anything left in us to sustain all that was to come.

As I watched him leave my bed, I was seized with a deep longing for something I hadn't lost yet, but knew I would soon.

***

After Boris sent his telegram to Stockholm, the Kremlin issued its official response to the Academy. "You and those who made this decision focused not on the novel's literary or artistic qualities, and this is clear since it does not have any, but on its political aspects, since Pasternak's novel presents Soviet reality in a perverted way, libels the socialist revolution, socialism, and the Soviet people."

Their message was clear: Boris's defiance would not be tolerated. And it would not go unpunished.

We were told couriers were going door to door, from Peredelkino to Moscow, summoning every poet, play-wright, novelist, and translator to an emergency meeting of the Writers' Union to address the issue of the Nobel. Attendance was mandatory.

Some writers were undoubtedly elated that the narcissist, the overrated Poet on the Hill, was finally getting his due. Some, we were told, said justice should've been served long ago, the questions about why Boris had been spared by the hand of Stalin during the Great Terror still unresolved. Other writers were apparently nervous, knowing they'd have to fall in line to denounce their peer, their friend, their mentor—hoping their protests would appear genuine when they were called upon.

Borya didn't read the newspapers, but I did.

They called him a Judas, a pawn who'd sold himself for thirty pieces of silver, an ally of those who hated our country, a malicious snob whose artistic merit was modest at best. They deemed *Doctor Zhivago* a weapon heralded by enemies of the State, and the Prize a reward from the West.

Not everyone spoke out; most just kept quiet. Friends who previously sat rapt at Little House listening to Borya read from *Zhivago* made themselves scarce. They did not send letters of support, nor did they visit, nor did most admit to having a friendship with Borya when asked. It was these silences, the taped mouths of friends, that cut the deepest.

One day, Ira returned from school with news that a student demonstration had taken place in Moscow. Borya was sitting in his red chair as Ira, still in her coat and squirrel hat, paced in front of him. "Professors told students that attendance was mandatory."

Borya stood up and put some wood into the stove. He faced the fire, warming his hands over the flame for a moment, before closing the metal door.

"The administration handed out placards for us to carry, but I hid in the toilets with a friend until they left." Her eyes looked to Borya's for approval, but he didn't return her gaze.

"What did the placards say?" Borya asked.

Ira took off her hat and held it in her hands. "I didn't see them. Not up close."

The next day, a photograph of the "spontaneous demonstration" appeared in *Literaturnaya Gazeta*. A student held up a placard with a cartoon image of Borya reaching for a sack of American money with crooked fingers. Another placard stated in black block letters: THROW THE JUDAS OUT OF THE USSR! The article also printed a list of names of students who signed a letter condemning *Doctor Zhivago*.

Ira held up the newspaper. "Half these students never signed it. At least they told me they hadn't."

That night at dinner, Mitya asked if it was true that Borya was now richer than the greediest American. "The teacher said so in school. Are we rich now too?"

"No, darling," I told him.

He rolled a kidney bean across his plate with his thumb. "Why not?"

"Why should we be?"

"He pays for our house. He gives us money. So if he has more, he should give us more."

"Where would you ever get an idea like that?"

Ira shot her brother a look and he shrugged.

"It makes sense though, Mama," Ira said. "Suppose you should ask him?"

"I won't hear another word of it," I told her, although I can't pretend I hadn't been thinking the same thing. "Now finish your dinner."

It had been raining for five days when they met in the great White Hall of the Writers' Union. With every seat filled, writers lined the walls. Borya was asked to attend, but I pleaded with him to stay home. "It will be an execution," I said. He agreed that his presence would accomplish nothing and instead wrote a letter to be read:

> *I still believe even after all this noise and all those articles in the press that it was possible to write Doctor Zhivago as a Soviet citizen. It's just that I have a broader understanding of the rights and possibilities of a Soviet writer, and I don't think I disparage the dignity of Soviet writers in any way. I would not call myself a literary parasite. Frankly, I believe that I have done something for*

literature. As for the Prize itself, nothing would ever make me regard this honor as a sham and respond to it with rudeness. I forgive you in advance.

The hall echoed with jeers from the crowd. Then, one by one, each writer went to the podium to condemn *Zhivago*. The meeting lasted hours, every last person speaking out against him.

The vote was unanimous, the punishment effective immediately: Boris Leonidovich Pasternak was expelled from the Soviet Writers' Union.

The next day, I gathered every book, every note, every letter, every early draft of the manuscript from my Moscow apartment. Mitya and I took them to Little House to burn. "They won't take what's mine again," I told my son, as we gathered sticks from the forest. "I'd rather destroy everything."

"How can you be sure?" Mitya asked.

"We're going to need more wood," I said, picking up a small log.

Borya arrived as we placed the rocks we'd hauled up from the creek in a ring. "Has it all been for nothing?" he asked, in lieu of a greeting.

"Of course not," I said, and dumped a bucket of dry leaves atop the wood. "You've touched the hearts and minds of thousands." I poured petrol onto the leaves.

He circled the fire pit. "Why did I write it in the first place?"

"Because you had to, remember?" Mitya said. "That's what you told us. You said you were called to do it. Remember?"

"It was nonsense. Utter nonsense."

"But you said—"

"It doesn't matter what I said then."

"When you handed it over to the Italians you said you wanted it to be read. Well, you've accomplished that."

"I've accomplished nothing but putting us in danger."

"You said the Prize would protect us. Do you no longer believe that? The whole world is watching, remember?"

"I was wrong. It's my execution that the whole world will watch." He raked his hands through his hair. "Am I what they say I am? A narcissist, someone who thinks—no, *believes*—fully believes, that he has been chosen for this task? That I'm fated to spend my life attempting to express what's in the hearts of men?" Borya paced frantically. "The sky is falling, and I sought to *write* instead of building a roof to protect myself and my loved ones. Has my selfishness no bounds? I've sat at my desk for so long. Is it true I'm out of touch? Could I even know what is in the hearts and minds of my countrymen? How could I have gotten it all so wrong? Why go on?"

"We go on because that's what we have to do," I told him. Before I could get another word out to calm him, he launched into his plan.

386

"It's all too much. I won't wait for them to come for me. I won't wait for their black car to arrive. I won't wait for them to drag me out into the street. To do to me what they did to Osip, to Titsian—"

"And to me," I added.

"Yes, my love. I'll never let them. I think it's time we left this life."

I took a step back from him.

"I've saved them, you know. The pills. I've saved the Nembutal I was given the last time I was in the hospital. Twenty-two. Eleven for each of us."

I didn't know whether to believe him. Boris had threatened to kill himself before. Once, decades earlier, he even drank a bottle of iodine when his wife, before she was his wife, had refused him. He'd confessed to me later that he'd only sought her reaction, not his actual death. But this time, something in his voice, how he remained calm, made me think he might be serious.

He reached for my hand. "We'll take them tonight. It will cost them dearly. It will be a slap in the face."

Mitya rose to his feet. He was now taller than I, and almost as tall as Borya. Mitya, gentle Mitya, looked him in the eyes. "What are you talking about?" He looked at me. "Mama, what is he talking about?"

"Leave us, Mitya." I said.

"I won't!" He reared back as if he might hit Boris.

For the first time, I realized that his was no longer the hand of a little boy, but of a young man. A well of guilt filled my chest. All these years, I'd put Borya first.

387

"Nothing will happen." I let go of Borya's hand and took my son's. "I assure you." I pulled a fistful of kopeks from my pocket and asked him to get more petrol for the fire.

He refused to take the money. "What is wrong with you? With both of you?"

"Take it, Mitya. Go and get the petrol. I'll be right along."

He grabbed the money and left, looking back to warn Borya with his burning stare.

"It will be painless," Borya said once Mitya was gone. "We'll be together." All this time, he'd been pretending the roaring whispers of condemnation weren't upsetting him—that the microphones we suspected were planted in his house and mine were something to laugh about, that the negative reviews had no merit. He'd been focusing on a speck of white light at the tunnel's end that, with the latest blow from the Writers' Union, had faded to black.

And he believed I'd follow him—that I'd take the pills, that I didn't have the strength go on alone. At one time, I might not have. In fact, I might have been the one to first suggest it. But not now. Now I could go on. I would go on. They could put him in the ground, but not me.

I told him it would just give them what they wanted— that it was a weak man's move. I said they'd gloat over their victory of the dead poet, the cloud dweller Stalin never finished off. Borya said he didn't care about any of it as long as the pain would stop. "I can't wait for their darkness to befall me. I'd rather step into the dark than be pushed," he said.

"Things are different now that Stalin is dead. They won't shoot you in the street."

"You haven't lived through it as I did. You didn't see them pick off your friends, one by one. Do you know what it feels like to have been saved when your friends were murdered? To be the one left behind? They will come for me. I'm sure of it. They will come for us."

I asked him to wait one more day, saying I wanted to say goodbye to Ira and Mama, that I wanted one more sunrise. In reality, I had one last plan—and if that plan didn't work, I knew he might still be talked off the ledge. And if *that* didn't work, I knew another sun would come up anyway, and I'd go on. It's what Russian women do. It's in our blood.

I found Mitya at the tavern near the train station, a small can of petrol at his side. I told him I'd never leave him. By the look in his eyes, I knew he didn't believe me. I wept, telling him I was sorry, so sorry, and he told me he forgave me. But I could tell he said it only to get me to stop crying.

I asked if he'd accompany me to Konstantin Aleksandrovich Fedin's dacha—step one of my plan. He agreed, reluctantly. We left the tavern and trudged up the muddy hill.

I knocked at the door of the grand home of the newly anointed chair of the Writers' Union, built from large logs stacked atop each other. No one came, so I knocked again. Fedin's young daughter answered. Without invitation, I barged in. Mitya waited outside. Just as Katya was saying her father wasn't home, he appeared.

"Make us some tea, Katya?" Fedin asked his daughter.

"I don't want tea," I said.

Fedin's shoulders rose, then fell. "Come." I followed him into his office, where he sat, swiveling in a leather chair. Looking like a snowy owl on his perch—with his white hair, his high widow's peak, his arched eyebrows—he gestured for me to sit across from him.

"I'll stand," I said. I was so tired of sitting across from men. I got right to the point. "He will kill himself tonight if something isn't done."

"You mustn't say such a thing."

"He has the pills. I've delayed him, but I don't know what more I can do."

"You must restrain him."

"How? It is you and the rest of the Central Committee who have done this."

Fedin rubbed his eyes and straightened his back. "I warned him this would happen."

"You warned him?" I shouted. "When did you warn him?"

"The day he won. I went to his dacha and told him myself that his acceptance would force the State's hand.

I told him, as a friend, that he must turn it down or face the consequences. Surely he told you of this."

He hadn't. Another thing he'd kept from me.

"Boris has created the abyss he stands at now," Fedin continued. "And if he kills himself, it will be a terrible thing for the country, an even deeper wound than the ones he's already inflicted."

"Nothing can be done?"

He told me he'd arrange for Boris and me to meet with Dmitri Alexeyevich Polikarpov—the same official from the Culture Department with whom I'd pleaded after Borya had sent his manuscript away with the Italians. We could make our case in person to him, with the understanding that Borya would apologize for his actions.

I agreed, and I was prepared to do everything in my power to convince Borya to agree to it. I'd tell him he was selfish. I'd bring up my time in Potma. I'd tell him they'd go after me again. I'd tell him he had never given me what I'd wanted most: to be his wife, to have his child.

But in the end, there was no need.

Before I could ask, Borya informed me he'd already settled the matter. He'd sent two telegrams: one to Stockholm, declining the Prize, and one to the Kremlin, letting them know. The Nobel would not be his.

"They're coming for me, Olga. I can feel it. Even when I'm writing in my study, I can feel them watching. It won't be long now. One day, you'll wait for me and I'll never come."

WEST

DECEMBER 1958

CHAPTER 25

~~THE SWALLOW~~
~~THE INFORMANT~~

THE DEFECTOR

According to my former employer, one can sum up the entire spectrum of human motivations with a formula called MICE: Money, Ideology, Compromise, Ego. I wondered how the other side would assess me. Did they have their own formula? Did they think through these things with more nuance?

The woman who'd told me about Henry hadn't yet appeared again, but I knew she would in time. Meanwhile, I sold off two of my favorite Hermès scarves and my remaining copies of *Zhivago*. I did keep one, though, the English edition I failed to return at Le Mistral—which I placed in the nightstand next to my bed, where one might find a Bible in an American hotel.

I no longer spent my days in my room; I no longer mourned the person I used to be. Mornings, I went to the Jardin des Tuileries—walking the gravel corridors of perfectly manicured trees, feeding the ducks and swans at the pond, pulling a green chair into a spot of sun to read. In the afternoons, as the days got shorter, I sat at every terrace on rue de la Huchette, sampling each café's selection of mulled wine. I made friends with the barman at Le Caveau just so I could sit on one of the plush red couches and listen to Sacha Distel croon night after night.

Wherever I was, she was never far from my mind. I kept waiting for the day when I'd wake up and my first thought wouldn't be of her. The worst was when I dreamed of her. How one moment we were together, only to wake and feel the loss all over again. Sometimes I'd feel a spark run across my body, convinced Irina must've been thinking of me at that exact moment. Silly.

On her birthday, I wanted to call—even just to hear her answer—but didn't. Instead, I opened the nightstand drawer, removed the book, and, for the first time, began to read.

On they went, singing "Rest Eternal," and whenever they stopped, their feet, the horses, and the gusts of wind seemed to carry on their singing.

His words grabbed hold of my wrist. I knew the way a feeling can linger after a song ends. I shut the book and went out onto my balcony, which was only big enough for a single chair. I sat and opened the book again.

When I read the part where Yuri reunites with Lara, in the battlefield hospital, and realized that this book—this novel they deemed a weapon—was really a love story, I wanted to close it once more. But I didn't. I read until the sun had faded into a purple halo over the tops of the buildings. I read until the streetlights turned on and I had to squint to make out the sentences. When it became too dark, I went back inside. Wrapping myself in my robe, I lay down and continued to read—until I fell asleep, my hand an accidental bookmark.

When I awoke, it was nearly midnight and I was hungry. I dressed and put the book into my purse.

As I crossed the hotel lobby, I saw the woman from the bookshop seated on a chaise longue, beneath a portrait of Flaubert. She was impeccably dressed in Chanel tweed, and her hair was still perfectly finger-waved, albeit two shades lighter than it was when she told me about Henry. When she saw me, she got up without making eye contact and left.

We walked for what must have been twenty minutes, the woman never looking back. Eventually, we came to a stop at the Café de Flore, on the boulevard Saint-Germain. The café's awning dripped with white Christmas lights. Its terrace was empty, and its snow-laden wicker chairs looked as if they were wearing white fur coats.

A torn red, white, and blue *Vive de Gaulle* banner hung from the wrought iron balcony on the second floor.

Inside, the woman kissed both my cheeks again and left, but not before pointing to a table in the back, where a man I recognized was waiting.

I knew they'd come, but I wasn't expecting it to be him.

He stood to greet me, the too-small tortoiseshell glasses he'd worn to Feltrinelli's party gone. *"Ciao, bella,"* he said, his Italian accent also gone, replaced with a Russian one. He reached for my hand and kissed it. "Pleasure seeing you again. I suppose you've come to have your dresses cleaned?"

"Possibly."

We sat and he handed me a menu. "Order whatever you'd like." He raised a finger. "One cannot subsist on pain au chocolat alone." He already had an open bottle of white wine and a silver tray of untouched snails in front of him, so I ordered a croque-monsieur from the crisp-collared waiter and waited for him to speak.

He drank the last of the wine and signaled the waiter for another bottle. "I prefer women to men and wine to both," he joked. Communist or capitalist, men are still men. "We wanted to thank you in person," he continued. "For your generosity."

"Did you find it useful?"

"Oh, yes. A talker, that one. Very . . . how do you say . . ."

"Social?"

"Yes! Exactly. Social."

I didn't ask for details about what happened to Henry Rennet, and I didn't want to know. For a year, I'd wanted revenge more than I'd ever wanted anything. And after he'd gotten me fired, I not only wanted to destroy him, I wanted to burn the whole thing to the ground. But I felt only a minor relief at the confirmation of Henry's fate. Anger is a poor replacement for sadness; like cotton candy, the sweetness of revenge disintegrates immediately. And now that it was gone, what did I have left to keep me going?

The waiter returned with my food, and as my new friend ate his snails, he laid it all out for me in as few words as possible.

"How long will you be in Paris?" he asked.

"I have no return ticket."

He dipped a snail into a dish of melted butter. "Good! You should do some traveling. See the world. There's so much a woman like you can do. The world is yours for the taking."

"Hard to take it with limited funds, though."

"Ah." He slurped down a snail and pointed his two-pronged fork at me. "But I can tell you are a resourceful woman. And one who deserves whatever she asks for."

"I'm not sure that's the case anymore."

"I assure you it is. You undervalue yourself. Maybe less perceptive men can't see it, but I can. As Emerson said, one must be an *opener of doors*."

Since arriving in Paris, I'd walked past the big black doors within the high cement wall enclosing the Hôtel d'Estrées several times. Each time, I'd look up and see the red flag with its gold hammer and sickle and wonder: What would it be like to walk in as one person and out as another? Here was my invitation to find out.

I thought of Henry Rennet dancing me through the restaurant lobby, then opening the coatroom door behind me. I thought of Anderson passing by, after, without a word—then seated at his big mahogany desk telling me I was no longer a *desirable asset* and how he hated to say it but I'd become *too much of a risk* to keep on. I thought of Frank passing me in the hallway as I left HQ for the last time without so much as a handshake.

I thought of Irina—the first time I saw her, and the last. I'd planned to talk to her after her mother's funeral, to comfort her, to hold her, to tell her everything. But instead of going to the cemetery, I went to Georgetown and sat through the second half of *The Quiet American*, alone.

I still had the note I'd planned to slip her after the funeral in my pocket. The words I wrote had worn completely away from constantly being rubbed between my fingers as I walked the streets of Paris. But I remembered what I'd written, the words I never gave her, the truth I'd kept to myself.

And then there was the truth I kept *from* myself. I'd boarded the plane to Paris convinced there was no alternative. But that first night, the *what ifs* surrounded me like a cloud of gnats. I imagined the whitewashed house in New England that Irina and I could've moved to—its yellow door and porch swing and bay window overlooking the Atlantic. I imagined us going into town each morning for coffee and doughnuts, the townsfolk thinking we were roommates. As I thought of all the paths I didn't take, the loss came over me like a lead blanket.

I thought of the book in the purse sitting next to me. How did it end? Do Yuri and Lara end up together? Or do they die alone and miserable?

The waiter took our plates and asked if he could get us anything else.

"A bottle of champagne, perhaps?" my new friend asked, looking at me, not the waiter.

I raised my glass. "When in Paris."

EAST

JANUARY 1959

CHAPTER 26

~~THE MUSE~~
~~THE REHABILITATED WOMAN~~
~~THE EMISSARY~~
~~THE MOTHER~~
~~THE EMISSARY~~

THE POSTMISTRESS

The first copies were passed from hand to hand in the parlors of Moscow's intelligentsia. After Borya won the Nobel, then declined it, copies of the copies were made. Then copies of those copies. *Doctor Zhivago* was whispered about in the bowels of the Leningrad Metro, passed from worker to worker in the labor camps, and sold on the black market. "Have you read it?" people across the Motherland asked each other in hushed voices. "Why was it kept from us?" The *it* never needed to be named. Soon the black market was flooded, and everyone could read the novel they'd been denied.

When Ira brought a copy home, I forbade her to keep it in the house. "Don't you realize?" I cried, ripping the pages up and tossing them into the bin. "It's a loaded pistol."

"You're the one who bought the bullets. You placed him above our family."

"He *is* our family."

"And I know what you're keeping hidden here. Don't think I don't!" She stormed out before I could respond.

The money was kept in a russet leather suitcase with a brass lock tucked behind the long dresses in the back of my closet. The bundles were wrapped in plastic, stacked neatly in rows under two pairs of trousers.

D'Angelo had arranged for the transfer—first from Feltrinelli to an account in Liechtenstein, then to an Italian couple living in Moscow. The Italian couple would phone my apartment and say a delivery for Pasternak was waiting at the post office. I would then collect the suitcase, take the train to Peredelkino, and store it at Little House for safekeeping.

Borya didn't want it. Not at first. With the State having cut off his ability to publish or make a living through his translations, he said we'd find other ways to support ourselves. I reasoned with him that it was but a fraction of what he was owed. Feltrinelli had sold so many copies, he'd already had to reprint it twelve times in Italian; it was a bestseller in America too. The film rights had even been sold to Hollywood. In the West, Borya would've been a very wealthy man. When he said we'd make do with what we have and we should be grateful we have each other, I asked him to imagine what would become of me and my family once he was gone.

He eventually came around.

To say I pushed him to accept the foreign royalties would be an understatement; to say I had anything in mind other than ensuring my family would be taken care of, a lie. But why not get something for myself? Why not? After everything I'd done. After everything I'd been through.

But with the money came even more surveillance. They were still watching. I saw no one but always felt their eyes. I shut the windows, closed the drapes, and obsessively checked the locks to Little House. At night, every branch breaking, every gust of wind rattling the door, every screech from some distant car made me jump. Sleep was out of the question.

Seeking relief, I left Little House to stay at my Moscow apartment. It was difficult to be away from Borya, but for the first time in my life, I was glad of the five flights of stairs, the onionskin-thin walls, and my many neighbors who lived on top of one another. If something were to happen, surely someone would hear it and come to my aid. Wouldn't they?

I was also glad to be with my family. I was seized with the feeling that I needed to be near my children, something I hadn't felt so strongly since they were young. But Mitya and Ira stayed out of the apartment, making excuses about friends and school. When they were home, they treated my mother with the respect they denied me. Mitya, who had always been such an obedient child, began acting out. Not coming home when he said he would, sometimes smelling of liquor. Ira choose to spend most of her time with a new boyfriend.

Borya was warned by friends to leave Peredelkino for the safety of the city, but he refused. "If they come to stone me, let them. I'd rather die in the country."

The first night I spent back in Moscow, a neighbor knocked on our door and told us that Vladimir Yefimovich Semichastny was giving a speech on television about Boris. Ira and I followed her back to her apartment and stood with her family around the tiny television propped up on a cold radiator. The black-and-white picture flickered in and out, but we could hear the leader of the Young Communist League loud and clear. "This man went and spat in the face of the people," Semichastny railed. "If you compare Pasternak to a pig, a pig would not do what he did, because a pig never shits where it eats." The camera panned to the crowd of thousands. "I am sure the society and government will not place any obstacles in his way, but would, on the contrary, agree that his departure from our midst would make our air fresher." The audience erupted in applause. Khrushchev himself, sitting on the dais, stood and clapped. Ira looked at me with fear in her eyes. I took her hand and led her back to our apartment.

Later that night, Mitya woke me. A drunken party had gathered in front of our building. I wrapped a shawl around my shoulders, went to the balcony, and looked down. Three men wearing dresses, no doubt sent by the KGB, were dancing and singing "Black Raven," an old drinking folksong I'd always hated.

> *Raven black, why are you wheeling,*
> *Over my head circling low?*
> *Ever will your prey elude you.*
> *Raven black, I am not yours!*

The noise had also awoken my neighbors, who joined me outside on their balconies and yelled for them to shut up. The men dressed as women looked up and laughed. One pointed in my direction. Then they linked arms and sang even louder.

> *Why do you spread wide your talons,*
> *Over my head circling low?*
> *Or do you sense prey beneath you?*
> *Raven black, I am not yours!*

"You can't tell from up here," Mitya whispered, "but they're wearing wigs. Bad ones. One has lipstick smeared across his mouth like a clown."

409

Take my shawl, now stained with red blood,
To my darling, dearly loved.
Say to her that she is free now:
To another I am wed.

"Crazy drunks," Ira said. She placed her hand on my shoulder. "Come inside, Mama."

"Nothing will be enough for them," Borya said after I told him what happened. "I'll have no peace until I'm in the grave. I've already penned a letter to the Kremlin, asking for your permission to emigrate with me."

"You asked them before you asked me? What if I don't want to go?"

"You won't?"

"That's not what I said."

"I haven't sent it yet."

"That wasn't my question."

"I can't leave without you. I'd rather be sent to the camps."

"What about my family? What would they do?"

He told me we'd find a way. What I didn't know was that he'd already discussed the matter with his wife. He didn't ask me the same question he'd asked her until she'd told him she'd never leave, and while he was free to go, she and their son would have to denounce him once he was gone. "You understand," she'd told her husband.

The following day, he told me he'd torn up the letter to the Kremlin. "How could I look out another window, in a foreign city, and not see my birch trees?" he asked.

It was his stand: not to let them drive him from his home.

I should have known that leaving was never a real option for him. In spite of everything, he'd be lost without Mother Russia. He could never leave his trees, his snowy walks. He could never leave his red squirrels, his magpies. He could never leave his dacha, his garden, his daily routine. He'd rather die as a traitor on Russian soil than live as a free man abroad.

They banned Borya from receiving mail, cutting off one of his only lifelines from the world. Shortly after, letters began appearing under my apartment door. Some were stamped, some not; some had return addresses, some not. Each morning, Ira and I would bundle the letters, wrapping them in butcher paper like cuts of meat. We'd take the train to Little House, where Borya would be waiting to read them. I had become his postmistress.

He received letters from Albert Camus, John Steinbeck, Prime Minister Nehru. He received letters from students in Paris, a painter in Morocco, a soldier in Cuba, a housewife in Toronto. His demeanor brightened as he opened each envelope.

One of his most treasured letters came from a young man in Oklahoma. The man wrote of his recent heartbreak and how much *Doctor Zhivago* had touched him. The man had addressed his letter to *Boris Pasternak, Russia, in a small town outside Moscow.*

Borya took his time replying to each, his soaring handwriting covering page after page in purple ink. He wrote until his hand hurt, until his back ached, but he refused to dictate his replies when I offered to help. "I want my hand to touch theirs," he said.

But he received other letters too, letters to which he did not respond. Letters from detractors, letters from the State, letters meant to intimidate. Despite his renouncing the Prize, they wanted to see the cloud dweller brought back down to earth. They wanted him on his knees. They wanted him to grovel, to bow down. He would not, but neither would he confront them. His inaction was seen as weakness, both by those watching the affair unfold from afar and by me.

If he wasn't going to do something, I would. I couldn't wait for them to come to my door.

I met with the head of the authors' rights division of the Writers' Union, Grigori Khesin, an old contact of mine from *Novy Mir.*

He barely listened to me as I stated Borya's case, and when I was finished, he said there was nothing to be done. "Boris Leonidovich is no longer a member of the Union and thus has no 'rights' to be upheld." I stormed out of Grigori's office and was immediately approached by a man offering another solution.

This man, Isidor Gringolts, was a distant acquaintance. I recalled having seen him at poetry readings but barely knew him. Young and handsome, Isidor had wavy blond hair and dressed like a European. For some reason, I found myself nodding as he told me he'd do anything in his power to help Boris.

We went to my apartment, where a plan was set in motion. After hours of debate with Ira, Mitya, and a close circle of friends, Isidor told us the only thing to do was to pen a public letter from Boris to Khrushchev, asking for forgiveness and not to be expelled from the Motherland. I balked, thinking Borya would never sign his name to such a thing or allow this stranger to put words in his mouth. But he was convincing, and in the end, we decided it was the only way.

Isidor wrote the first draft himself, and I adjusted the voice to sound more like Borya's. Ira delivered the letter to Peredelkino. They'd worn him down so much that when Ira asked if he'd sign it, Borya could no longer raise his voice; all he could do was raise a pen. "Just let it be over," he told her.

He offered only minor revisions. "Olya, keep it all as it is," he'd written me in a note. "Write that I was born not in the Soviet Union, but in Russia." Ira said his hand shook as he ended the letter with his own addition: *With my hand on my heart, I can say that I have done something for Soviet literature, and may still be of service to it.*

The next day, Ira and a friend from school took the revised letter to 4 Staraya Square. A guard outside the gate of the Central Committee building saw them approach. With a cigarette clenched in his teeth, he looked them up and down and asked what they wanted.

"We have a letter for Khrushchev," Ira said.

He laughed, almost spitting out his cigarette. "From whom? You?"

"From Pasternak."

The guard stopped laughing.

Two days later, Polikarpov phoned to say that Khrushchev had received Borya's letter and that his presence was requested immediately. "Put on your coat and meet us on the street. You will be accompanying us to fetch the cloud dweller."

Ten minutes later, a black ZiL idled outside my apartment building. Inside, Polikarpov was waiting. Already in my coat, I looked out the window, then at my clock. I waited fifteen more minutes before leaving the apartment.

As I approached, Polikarpov stepped out of the car. He was wearing a thick black jacket that came down to his ankles, the cut of it foreign, the wool heavy and luxurious. "You've kept us waiting."

I didn't apologize. My anger mimicked a bravery I could not contain. He ushered me into the backseat of the car. He sat in front with the driver, whose eyes never left the road. The car took the middle lane, reserved for government vehicles. As we sped through traffic, civilian cars pulled over to the side.

"What more do you want from him?" I asked.

Polikarpov turned to face me. "This whole affair, which he has brought unto himself, is not yet finished."

"He declined the Prize. He renounced *Zhivago*. He begged forgiveness. What more do you want? This ordeal has stolen years from him. He's an old man now. Sometimes I barely recognize—" I stopped myself. Polikarpov didn't need to know more.

He turned back around. "We do thank you for your help in getting Pasternak to sign the letter. We won't forget it."

"It was Boris's letter, not mine."

"My friend Isidor Gringolts—I believe you know him? He told me personally it was you who wrote most of the letter. His work on the matter has also been recognized."

Of course Gringolts had been sent by them. How could I have been so stupid?

"We're now relying entirely on you to put this matter behind us," Polikarpov continued.

Big House was dark, except for the light in Borya's study. The car pulled up and I saw his silhouette in the window. The light shut off and the downstairs light turned on. I wanted to go to him but did not dare leave the car. I could see another figure walking back and forth, shorter and hunched. Zinaida wouldn't allow me even to stand on her porch.

Borya emerged, wearing his cap and jacket, an odd smile on his face as if he were about to embark on a holiday. The driver got out and opened the door for him. He didn't register any surprise at seeing me in the back-seat. Nor did he express worry when Polikarpov confirmed we were indeed on our way to meet with Khrushchev. The only uneasiness Borya relayed was that he wasn't wearing suitable trousers for the occasion. "Should I go back inside and change?" he asked, when the car was already headed down the road. Polikarpov chortled. Even stranger, Borya joined in, laughing hysterically. His laughter infuriated me and I shot him a look, which he pretended not to see, which infuriated me even more. At a stoplight, I felt like opening the door and getting out, leaving these men to deal alone with what they'd wrought.

We arrived at Entrance No. 5 of the Central Committee building and followed Polikarpov through the gate. Borya stopped at the heels of a guard. "Identification," the guard said.

"The only identification I had was my Writers' Union membership card, which they've just revoked," said Boris. "Thus I am without identification completely. Worse, I'm without proper trousers." The guard, a young man with full lips and freckles across his cheeks, chose not to engage and waved us through.

Polikarpov left us in a small waiting area, where we sat for an hour. Borya touched my gold bracelet, which he'd given me three New Years earlier. "Should you be wearing this?" he asked. He brushed a piece of my hair behind my ear. "And the pearl earrings? And the lipstick? It might give the wrong impression."

I opened my purse. Instead of taking off my jewelry and wiping off my makeup, I took out a small vial of valerian tincture and drank it down to calm my nerves.

Finally Borya's name was called and we stood. "You are not needed," the guard said to me. Ignoring him, I took Borya's arm and we walked down a long corridor and into an office where Polikarpov sat waiting. The strong scent of aftershave greeted us. Polikarpov appeared to have showered, shaved, and put on a new suit. He acted as if he had been waiting all day for us. It was another intimidation tactic; we would not be meeting with Khrushchev at all. He cleared his throat as if to give a speech. "You will be allowed to remain in Mother Russia, Boris Leonidovich," he said.

"Why did we have to come here when you could have told us this hours ago?"

He ignored me and raised a finger. "There is more." He pointed to two chairs. "Sit."

I could hear Borya grind his custom-made teeth. "There is nothing more!" he exploded. Finally, the anger I'd longed to hear. He was standing up for himself at last.

"You have caused so much anger from the people, Boris Leonidovich. There is little I can do to calm them. You have no right to muzzle them. They have a right to express themselves. Tomorrow, *Literaturnaya Gazeta* will include several of these voices. There is nothing we can do about that. The people have their right. Before you will be given permission to stay, you must first make peace with the people. Publicly, of course. Another letter is needed posthaste."

"Have you no shame?" Borya asked, his voice still raised.

"Come," Polikarpov motioned toward the chairs again. "Let's sit and talk like gentlemen."

"There is only one gentleman here," I said.

Polikarpov chuckled. "Would the great poet's wife agree?"

"I will not sit," Borya continued. "This meeting is over. You speak of *the people*. What do you know about *the people*?"

"Now look, Boris Leonidovich, this whole business is almost over. You have a chance to make things right with me and with *the people*. I've brought you here to tell you everything will soon be right again as long as you cooperate." He came around the desk, placing himself between Borya and me. He put a hand on Borya's shoulder and patted him as one would a good little boy. "Goodness me, old fellow. What a mess you've landed us in."

Borya shrugged his hand off. "I am not your underling, some sheep you can direct to pasture."

"I am not the one who has stuck a knife in the back of my country."

"Every word I've written was truth. Every word. I am not ashamed."

"Your truth is not our truth. I am only trying to help you rectify things."

Borya started for the office door.

"Stop him, Olga Vsevolodovna!" Polikarpov's bravado disappeared. He looked pathetic and desperate. It was clear he'd been ordered to quietly put an end to the whole affair but had wanted to puff out his chest first and was now failing at the task.

"You must first apologize for speaking to him like that," I said.

"I apologize," he said. "I do. Please."

"End this now," Borya said, still standing in the doorway. "I beg of you."

The next day, twenty-two letters authored by "real" Russian people appeared in *Literaturnaya Gazeta* under the headline SOVIET PEOPLE CONDEMN B. PASTERNAK'S BEHAVIOR. Each one parroted the party line: *Judas! Traitor! Fake!* A construction worker from Leningrad penned that she had never heard of this Pasternak before, so why should we pay him any mind at all? A garment worker from Tomsk wrote that Pasternak was on the take from the West, funded by capitalist spies who'd made the writer a very rich man.

Polikarpov decreed that one last letter of apology, addressed to "the people," was needed. I wrote the first draft, edited it to Polikarpov's specifications, and persuaded Borya to sign it.

The night the final letter was printed in *Pravda,* he came to Little House wanting to make love. But the shining brave poet was gone. In his place stood an old man. He touched my waist as I stood at the sink peeling potatoes. And for the first time, I moved away.

WEST

SUMMER 1959

CHAPTER 27

~~THE APPLICANT~~
~~THE CARRIER~~
~~THE NUN~~

THE STUDENT

Most of it was waiting: waiting for the intel, waiting for the assignment, waiting for the mission to begin. I waited in hotel rooms, apartments, stairwells, train stations, bus stations, bars, restaurants, libraries, museums, laundromats. I waited on park benches and in movie theaters. I once waited for a message at a public swimming pool in Amsterdam for a full day, and left so sunburned I had to wrap aloe-soaked gauze around my shoulders and the tops of my thighs.

Nine months after the World's Fair, I waited yet again—in a hostel in Vienna, for the seventh World Youth Festival to begin.

Set for late July, the festival would be ten days of rallies, marches, meetings, exhibitions, lectures, seminars, and sporting events. There'd be a Parade of Nations, the release of a thousand white doves, and a grand ball at the end—all dedicated to promoting "peace and friendship" among tomorrow's leaders. During the fest, the expected twenty thousand international students attending from Saudi Arabia and Ceylon to Cambridge and Fresno could take part in union-led tours of an electrical plant, hear presentations from leaders in the voluntary work camp movement, or attend lectures on the peaceful use of atomic energy.

The Kremlin had invested an estimated $100 million to ensure the festival's lasting influence on its participants.

But the Agency had other plans.

After *Doctor Zhivago* popped up across the USSR and Pasternak's notoriety skyrocketed, the Soviets began searching for the banned book in the luggage of citizens returning to the Motherland after being abroad. It was a propaganda coup for the Agency, and as a result, they decided to double down—to print and disseminate even more copies. This time, instead of the blue-linen-covered edition printed in the Netherlands, we'd made a miniature edition ourselves—printed on thin Bible stock, small enough to fit in a pocket.

I'd gone to Vienna early, to await the arrival of two thousand copies of the tiny book. *Animal Farm, The God That Failed,* and *1984* were also designated for distribution, and dozens of us awaited the arrival of the books that would fill our "Information Booths" throughout Vienna, ready to hand off to student delegates taking in the sights. It was the Agency's own way of spreading *peace and friendship*.

My hair had grown out a bit since Brussels and was dyed back to a brassy shade of its former blond. And I dressed as if on my way to a poetry reading: black turtleneck, black clam diggers, and black ballet flats. I'd become a student again.

My first location was to be the Wurstelprater. I was to scout out the amusement park prior to the start of the festival, to determine the most trafficked spot from which I could hand out the most books before inevitably being asked to leave.

After passing the ghost train, merry-go-round, bumper cars, shooting galleries, and biergartens, I decided the foot of the Wiener Riesenrad would be the most advantageous spot, as I could envision every student tourist wanting to take a ride on the world's tallest Ferris wheel. Plus, I got a small thrill from standing so close to the ride featured in one of my favorite movies, *The Third Man*.

With my location set, my next step was to visit a dry cleaner on Tuchlauben, where I would tell the clerk I'd been sent to a retrieve a suit for a Mr. Werner Voigt and ask if I could pay in Swiss francs. I'd then be given the bagged suit with a ticket noting the address where the first batch of miniature *Zhivago*s would be located. Dissemination would begin the following day.

But first, I was hungry. I decided to stop and buy two plate-sized potato pancakes before leaving the park—one for dinner and one for breakfast. The food stand was strategically placed next to the Riesenrad, a trap for everyone waiting in line. It was there, standing in line for food behind an American tourist wearing unflatteringly tight lederhosen, that I saw her.

She was there, in line to ride the Ferris wheel, her back to me.

Sally was wearing a long green coat and white gloves, her red hair cut a bit shorter than I'd last seen it. Even from behind, she was beautiful. It reminded me of the first time I saw her in Ralph's. How the first thing I saw when I turned around was her hair.

It was strange seeing her like that, in a place where I was no longer myself, where she was no longer herself. Reality had shifted. And so much time had passed. Over the last year, I'd let myself come to believe I'd gotten over her. Maybe, I'd told myself time and again, there was never even anything to get over.

But there she was. She'd finally come for me.

Sally tilted her head, as if she could feel me notice her. She didn't turn around to see if I'd seen her, but she didn't have to. She knew I would. Of course I would. Should I join her in line? Run up from behind and put my arms around her? Or wait for her to come to me?

I got out of the food line and shifted a few steps over to the line for the Ferris wheel, cutting in front of a group of French-speaking students who paid me no mind.

I inched forward, several spots behind Sally. When she reached the ticket booth, she removed her wallet from her purse. But just as she was handing her money to the woman in the booth, a tall man with salt-and-pepper hair came up and plucked it out of her hand. He paid and she kissed his cheek.

She didn't even have to turn completely around for me to know.

I watched as the man with salt-and-pepper hair opened the door to the enclosed red gondola for the person who wasn't Sally. I bought a ticket anyway and boarded by myself. I looked up to see if I could see the Sally look-alike again, hovering somewhere above me. I couldn't. The ride rocked as we left the ground. I leaned out the open window and watched as the world below became quiet and small.

———

I saw her again and again. Long after I'd handed out my last copy of *Zhivago* in Vienna and gone on to the next mission, and the one after that. Our time together had been brief, but that didn't matter. I'd see her for years to come: hailing a rickshaw in Cairo, her red manicure a flash of color in the dusty street; boarding the last train in Delhi, her matching luggage held by a man twice her age; in a New York bodega, petting a cat who was standing atop a stack of cereal boxes; in a hotel bar in Lisbon, ordering a Tom Collins with extra ice.

And as the years passed, her age always stayed the same, her beauty sealed in amber. Even after I met a nurse in Detroit who opened doors inside me I hadn't known I'd locked. Even then, I'd still see Sally sipping coffee at a diner counter, or sticking her arm out of a dressing room for another size, or in the balcony at a movie theater watching a picture by herself. And each time, I'd feel that same inner gasp, that exquisite anticipation—that moment the lights go down and the film begins, that moment when, for just a few seconds, the whole world feels on the verge of awakening.

EAST

1960–1961

CHAPTER 28

~~THE MUSE~~
~~THE REHABILITATED WOMAN~~
~~THE EMISSARY~~
~~THE MOTHER~~
THE EMISSARY
~~THE POSTMISTRESS~~

THE ALMOST WIDOW

He was all apologies when he arrived late at Little House. "All is forgiven on your birthday," I said, helping him off with his coat.

He joined our friends in the sitting room and I brought out another bottle of the Château Margaux I'd purchased on the black market, reasoning that Borya's seventieth birthday made a fine excuse to crack open the brown suitcase. I'd also purchased a high-necked red silk dress—the finest I'd ever worn.

We ate and drank and Borya held court as in old times. He was in high spirits. He'd begun writing again and told everyone about his new project: a play he was tentatively calling *The Blind Beauty*. He laughed and smiled as he opened his presents and telegrams from well-wishers around the world. I watched him from across the room, warmed by the light he radiated, a light rekindled after all that time languishing in the dark that had settled over us both. It was the same glow that had first attracted me to him so many years earlier.

Our guests stayed late into the night. When they finally left, Borya made a show of begging them to stay. "Just one more glass," he said, blocking the coat rack.

Once we were alone, Borya sat back in his big red chair, holding an alarm clock given to him by Prime Minister Nehru, who'd voiced his support of *Zhivago*. "How late everything has come for me," he said. He put the clock down and reached for me. "If only we could live forever like this."

I held on to that night. How healthy he'd looked on his birthday, how happy. But his light began to dim almost as quickly as it had returned.

His appetite went first. He began accepting only tea or broth when he came to dinner at Little House. He complained about leg spasms that kept him awake at night and a numbness in his lower back that made it hard to sit.

Exhausted, he had trouble concentrating on his play and couldn't respond to the hundreds of letters that still came to him. His bronze complexion faded to a bluish gray and his chest pains became more frequent.

One night, as I was cooking mushroom soup, he came to Little House with his unfinished play, pleading for me to take it for safekeeping. He looked so sickly I told him he must see a doctor immediately. "Tomorrow, Borya. First thing. How could your wife not see . . ."

"There are more important matters." He held up the play manuscript. "If something were to happen . . . This will be your insurance. Something to support your family when I'm gone."

When I told him he was being dramatic, he pushed the play into my hands. When I refused it, he broke down and sobbed. I rubbed his back to calm him, shocked at the feeling of his spine underneath my hand. It both repulsed me and filled me with a new tenderness, the kind reserved for an ailing parent. I promised to take the manuscript. He straightened and took me in his arms, kissing my cheek and neck. We retired to my bedroom, eager to shed our clothing, to feel our skin against each other's, his skeleton against my flesh. At the beginning of our courtship, I'd always kept the lights on, pleased with his seemingly never-ending surprise at my body. Now, so many years later, I turned off the light.

I hadn't known it would be our last time. If I had, I wouldn't have rushed it. From the bedroom, I could hear the soup boil over onto the stove, so I moved my hips in the way I knew would cause him to finish.

After he dressed and went home, I dined alone. It would be the second-to-last time I'd see him alive.

The last time, I almost didn't recognize him. He was an hour late for our meeting in the cemetery, and when he approached, I first took him to be a stranger. He walked so slowly—his footing unsure, his back bent, his hair uncombed, his skin even paler. Who was this old man coming through the gate? As he approached, I hesitated before embracing him, partly because I was afraid of hurting him with my touch, but, shamefully, more because I realized in that moment that my lover was gone for good. This was not him; how could it be?

Sensing my hesitation, he stepped back. "I know you love me. I have faith in it," he said.

"I do," I assured him. I kissed him on his chapped lips as if to prove it.

"Do not make any changes in our life, I beg of you. I couldn't live through it. Please, do not return to Moscow."

"I won't," I said, squeezing his hand. "I'll be right here."

We parted after making plans to see each other at Little House that night. He never came.

It was his heart. Like Yuri Zhivago, it was his heart in the end. Throughout his life, when confronting illness, Borya was always melodramatic, convinced his end was near. But this time, he remained unconvinced his latest ailment would prove fatal. Bedridden, he wrote me that this setback would pass, that he'd be up and finishing his play any day.

He wrote again the next day, saying they'd moved his bed downstairs to more easily care for him and that it pained him to be so far from his writing desk. He said not to worry, that a nurse had come to live at Big House, and his dear friend Nina was visiting daily. He also asked that I not come, saying his wife had warned against it. *Z, in her foolishness, would not have the wit to spare me. But if things worsen, I'll send for you.*

Days passed, and when I didn't receive another letter, I sent Mitya and Ira to Big House to report back. They saw a young nurse coming and going, but the drapes had been drawn, so that was all they could tell me.

Another day passed. I still hadn't received word from him, so I went to Big House myself, convinced Zinaida was keeping my letters from him. It was early evening and a light was on in his study. Who was upstairs? His wife? One of his sons? Were they going through his books and papers already? Would they find my letters hidden inside his books, or the flowers I'd picked, pressed between the pages? When he died, would there be anything left to mark our time together? When the study light shut off, I began to cry.

The young nurse exited the house. She was a pretty girl, and I felt a stab of jealousy knowing she was the one bending over his bedside, spooning broth into his mouth, holding his hand, telling him everything would be okay. She looked startled when she saw me standing on the other side of the gate. "Olga Vsevolodovna," she said. "He said you would come."

"Has she no decency to let me see him?" I asked. "Or is it he who does not want me to come?"

"No." She looked toward the dacha. "It's that he can't bear for you to see him."

I just stared back at the nurse.

"He's sick, very sick. Skin stretched over bones, and without his false teeth now. He says he's afraid you'll no longer love him if you see him in that state."

"Rubbish. Does he think me so superficial?" I turned my back on the nurse and the house.

"He's told me how much he loves you. It's embarrassing how he goes on about it." She lowered her voice. "With his wife in the next room."

The nurse said she had to catch the train into Moscow, but she promised to keep me updated if he took a turn. I remained at my post. Around midnight, when I hadn't come home, Ira and Mitya brought me tea and a thick blanket.

My presence outside Big House did not go unnoticed. Zinaida would look out the window through a part in the curtains, then quickly close them.

I kept vigil outside the gate for days, getting updates from the nurse. He'd had a heart attack, and the only thing they could do was keep him comfortable. I pleaded with her to tell Borya I was outside, that I needed to say goodbye. She said she'd pass on my message.

When cars carrying journalists and photographers joined me at my post, I knew my vigil had turned into a death watch. I left and returned wearing my black dress and veil. Hours passed. I wore a path in the new spring grass with my pacing.

And still he never let me in.

Only after he was gone was I allowed inside Big House. Zinaida opened the door without a word and I rushed past her to his still-warm body. They'd just cleaned him and replaced the bedsheet, but the room still smelled like antiseptic and shit.

We were alone for the last time. I held his hand. His face looked like a sculpture and I imagined the death mask they'd soon make of it. The last weeks, I'd attempted to prepare myself for what it would be like; but it wasn't anything like how I thought it would be. The air hadn't changed, my heart kept beating, the earth kept spinning, and the realization that everything would go on, that the world was ever ongoing, felt like a horse's kick to the chest.

As I held his hand, I could hear talk of the funeral arrangements in the adjacent room. I told myself this would be the last time we'd ever be alone together. I kissed his cheek, straightened the white sheet, and left.

I had no body to tend to, no funeral arrangements to make, no reporters to ward off. All that was left to me was to remember.

I thought of the first time he reached for my hand, how I had no idea my body could vibrate from the inside out. I thought of him reading me early pages of *Doctor Zhivago,* how he'd pause at the end of each paragraph, anxious to see how I was responding. I thought of the afternoons spent walking Moscow's wide boulevards, how I felt the world expand each time he looked my way. I thought of the many afternoons making love, and the many nights he said he didn't want to leave my bed.

I also thought of him leaving my bed after I'd begged him to stay. I thought about pulling in to the train station after my three years at Potma—how, when I saw he hadn't come, I felt like turning around and going back. I thought of the many times he told me it was over and the many terrible things I said to him in response. I thought of his oversized ego in his prime, and the diminished man *Zhivago* had left behind.

They dressed him in his favorite gray suit and laid him in a box of virgin pine. I waited outside his dacha while *Panikhida* was offered inside. The great pianist Sviatoslav Teofilovich Richter played in Boris's music room, his notes drifting out the open window.

The music ended and they carried his coffin out and paused near his beloved garden. I stood beside Borya, opposite Zinaida: his widow and his almost widow. I wailed, and Ira and Mitya held me up by my arms. But Zinaida stood there, silently, with grace.

The procession filed down the hill and up to the cemetery to the grave site Borya had picked out for himself, under three tall pines. His death notice in the newspaper was but a line or two, and yet they came. Hundreds, maybe thousands, followed the coffin. They were old and young, neighbors and strangers, workers and students, peers and adversaries, factory workers and secret police dressed as factory workers, foreign correspondents and Muscovite reporters. All had gathered around Borya's final resting place; the one thing they had in common was that they'd all been changed by his words.

They made speeches and recited prayers, and I stared into the open coffin, which was covered in wreaths and branches from lilac and apple trees. From the back, a young man cried out, reciting the closing stanza to Borya's poem "Hamlet":

> *But the plan of action is determined,*
> *And the end irrevocably sealed.*
> *I am alone; all round me drowns in falsehood:*
> *Life is not a walk across a field.*

By the last line, others had joined in. Then a man announced, with booming authority, that the funeral was over. "This demonstration is undesirable," he said, and motioned for two men to bring forth the coffin's lid. I pushed my way to the front of the crowd and kissed Borya's face one last time. I was moved aside and the lid was secured. People protested the abrupt ending but were silenced by the sound of hammers driving nails into wood. Each crack of the hammer made me shiver, and I pulled my coat tighter.

As they lowered his coffin into the earth, chants of "Glory to Pasternak!" rose up and carried across the crowd. I was reminded of the first time I saw him read so many years ago, when his fans could not stop themselves from finishing his poems before he did. How I sat in the balcony, hoping he could see me through the bright lights. How he did see me, and how my world was forever changed.

I wouldn't see Zinaida again after the funeral. She did her best to erase me from his history, and her family took on the same cause after her death. I fought it for years. But could I blame them? I knew what they called me, what rumors persisted. And even if I was forever branded an adulteress, a seducer, a woman after money and power, a homewrecker, a spy, I was content knowing at least Lara would survive me.

On the morning they came for me for a second time, two and a half months after Borya's death, I was sitting in my dark kitchen sipping tea. I'd brewed it too bitter for the third day in a row.

I heard the slow churn of gravel under tires, and I didn't need to get up to know a black car was making its way down my drive.

I finished my tea and put the cup and saucer in the sink. I thought of Ira, still asleep in her bedroom—how she would later see the teacup with a brown ring and have to wash it, knowing it was mine, and that I was gone.

The sound of car doors opening and closing set me in motion. I went to Mitya's room first, but saw his bed was empty. "He didn't come home last night," Ira said, startling me from behind. She went to the window above Mitya's desk. "There are two cars now."

I watched as four men leaned against their cars, smoking and chatting nonchalantly, as if waiting for their girlfriends. I watched as one put out a cigarette in one of my flowerpots and another washed his hands in my birdbath. I closed the curtains and went to the telephone. "Get dressed," I said. Ira left the room.

Dialing Mama's number, my hands trembled terribly. "Mama?"

"Are they there?"

"Yes. Are they there too?"

"Yes."

"They are just trying to intimidate us again. You have nothing to worry about."

Ira emerged, dressed in her most conservative outfit: a long beige skirt and matching jacket. "Is Mitya at Babushka's?" she asked.

"Is Mitya there?" I asked Mama.

"He came last night. Drunk again. He's too young to drink like he does—"

"Mama."

"He's up now. I told him to stay put."

"Good. Keep him there."

Three hard knocks on the front door shook the floorboards. Ira grabbed my arm. "I have to go, Mama."

I walked to the entryway with Ira holding my arm like a small child. A man wearing an expensive-looking trench coat cut through the four men in the cheap black suits, leaving muddy tracks across my grandfather's Akstafa rug. "We finally meet."

"Welcome," I said, poised as a hostess.

"You were expecting us, of course," the man said as his smile grew. "No? You didn't imagine your activities would go unnoticed?"

I forced a smile to match his. "Care for some tea?"

"We can help ourselves."

I knew what they were looking for—and they wouldn't find it at Little House, nor at my Moscow apartment.

The day after Borya was put into the ground, the money—the foreign royalties that would prove I was guilty of crimes against the State—had been given to a neighbor who never asked what was inside the brown suitcase.

Hours passed. Eventually, one of the men, the one with a small scar down the center of his bottom lip, carried a dining room chair out into the drive where Ira and I waited. He asked if we wanted to sit. Ira replied no and the man shrugged, took a seat, and lit up a cigarette. He barely looked at us as we stood and watched the others continue to tear apart our home.

We heard a bicycle approaching. Midway down the drive, Mitya hopped off his bike, letting it crash to the ground. "You have no right," Mitya cried, his voice cracking.

The man with the scar continued smoking. I went to Mitya and took him by the hand. "Hush," I said, noticing his sour smell. Looking at him, I could see his shirt was stained with vomit. "Where is Babushka? I told her to keep you there."

The three of us huddled together as we watched the men emerge from Little House carrying boxes filled with our possessions. When they came out with stacks of journals belonging to Ira—likely filled with musings on school and boys and broken friendships—she stiffened next to me but didn't say a word. And when the man in the trench coat came out and stumbled on a loose board, Ira squeezed my hand instead of laughing. The image of him tripping would stay in my head later, after he became my interrogator.

I went willingly—without struggle or protest. The man in the trench coat didn't even have to ask. He just pointed to the second black car. I kissed both my children goodbye and got inside.

My children didn't look as I was driven away. Ira stood in the doorway, surveying the damage the men had done. Mitya sat on the top step, his head resting upon his knees. I closed my eyes and didn't open them again until we'd arrived at the big yellow building.

"What's the tallest building in Moscow?" the driver asked me when we stopped.

"She's heard that one before," the man in the trench coat said as he opened my door. "Haven't you?"

Without answering, I got out of the car, straightened my skirt, and let them take me.

Dear Anatoli,

I woke to the sound of my daughter wheezing. My dear Ira. They say she helped me conceal foreign money, and now she sleeps in the bunk across from mine. She is ill. A fever. They've allowed me to stay with her until she shows improvement. But I don't want you to worry, Anatoli. She's fine. I'm fine. I just thank God they left my Mitya alone. At least there's that.

Although I last wrote to you so many years ago, I've never stopped writing. Letters composed in my head while I bathed. Letters composed when I could not sleep. Letters penned somewhere deep inside myself. But now I can no longer keep the words from coming out.

I traded knit socks for this pen and paper. I want to purge what is inside me. Now, where was I?

I wonder where you are. Why were you not the one to meet me at Lubyanka and continue our late-night chats? Have you been replaced? Have I been? Do you ever think of me? Does my name ever cross your lips? Perhaps you stayed away this time because I am older now than I was before. Perhaps my company was more pleasing then.

The first time, I was pregnant. I lost my baby. Now I am older and becoming infertile, the man who fathered my unborn child buried. Time is a terrible thing.

I have been here before. And yet, in a way, I never left.

The ink on my sentence has dried. I will spend the next eight years at this place—the first three alongside my daughter, an innocent. I suppose I always knew they would find the money, or at least say they had.

It is March 1961, month three of our sentence, and our surroundings are still a blanket of white, the horizon gray. It is night, and I write under a gas lamp turned so low I can only see the paper in front of me and the shadow of my daughter's slender back as she sleeps on her side under two woolen blankets—one of which is mine.

Earlier, Ira and I worked at the pit digging a new latrine. Her hands are blistered and cracked and she can barely lift the pick, so I dig harder and faster. I don't say it aloud to anyone, but part of me has missed this work—putting the shovel to the earth, stepping on it with both feet to penetrate deeper, exposing the soil underneath, dark against the white snow.

I am exhausted, and yet I do not want to sleep until this story is told. I'm pressing the pen harder now. It is fading. I think the woman who is wearing my socks lied to me for the trade; the pen's ink is almost gone. There is so much more to write. Maybe the rest of this letter will be written in the indentation the pen's tip makes in the paper. Maybe you will have to read it like braille.

As it is, my story no longer belongs to me. In the collective imagination, I have become someone else—a heroine, a character. I have become Lara. And yet when I look, I don't find her here. Is that how they will know me when I'm gone? Is that the love story they'll remember?

I think of Borya's own ending for his heroine:

One day Larisa Feodorovna went out and did not come back. She must have been arrested in the street at that time. She vanished without a trace and probably died somewhere, forgotten as a nameless number on a list that afterwards got mislaid, in one of the innumerable mixed or women's concentration camps in the north.

But Anatoli, I am no nameless number. I will not disappear.

EPILOGUE

THE TYPISTS

In the winter of '65, *Doctor Zhivago* premiered on the big screen. We went together. Some of us were still at the Agency, but most had left by then. A typist's shelf life isn't very long. New typists came and went. Many men had risen through the ranks, and some of us had too. Gail had even been awarded Anderson's position after he died of a heart attack while accompanying his teenage daughter to a Beatles concert at the Coliseum.

We'd married, or not. We'd had children, or hadn't. We were all a little older—fine lines appearing when we smiled or frowned, our figures no longer quite the lithe young things we used to hide behind our desks.

It was good to see each other. The last time had been at a wedding in '63. After the *Zhivago* mission, Norma left the Pool to pursue her master's in creative writing at Iowa, and around that same time, Teddy began to pursue her long distance. They got hitched once she'd graduated, and Teddy left the Agency for a job at another secretive company just down the road from Langley: Mars, Inc. The wedding was an informal affair held at the outdoor dance hall in Great Falls Park with a barbecue reception and chocolate fondue fountains donated by Teddy's new employer. His parents seemed aghast, but the rest of us had a great time. Henry Rennet was not there, and no one missed him. After Norma tossed her bouquet—which Judy expertly dodged— Frank Wisner gave a toast to the happy couple. It would be the last time we'd see our old boss; he'd take his life two years later, in the fall of '65, just before *Zhivago*'s premiere.

Hugs and cheek kisses were exchanged outside the Georgetown Theater, its neon sign bathing us in a red glow. Tickets were purchased, and while we waited in line for refreshments, Linda showed us photos of her twin boys sitting on Santa's lap at Woodies and Kathy pulled out snaps of her Hawaiian honeymoon. We talked about how much we wished Judy could've made it. She'd moved to California to become an actress, and although she'd yet to hit it big, she did land a bit part on *The Dick Van Dyke Show.*

We took up the entire third and fourth rows of the Georgetown. The lights dimmed and popcorn and Raisinets were passed around as the newsreel played, showing footage of America's military escalation in Vietnam. Those of us still at the Agency remained stoic as the camera panned to show downed planes, burned fields, and collapsed roofs. They knew more than those of us no longer at the Agency, and those of us on the outside knew better than to ask.

When the theater went dark and the music started, a few of us exchanged looks and hand squeezes. And when Lara appeared on the screen in a white blouse and black tie, sitting behind a desk, we all thought the same thing: *Irina*. Actually, it was Julie Christie. But still—her hair, her eyes. It was our Irina on that screen.

We got chills when Yuri first saw Lara from across the room. We sniffed back tears when he told her goodbye for the first time. We held out hope that the movie would depart from the book and end with Yuri and Lara living in that country house until their dying days. And even though we knew it was coming, we let the tears flow when they said goodbye for the last time.

As the credits rolled, we dabbed our eyes with our hankies. *Doctor Zhivago* is both a war story and a love story. But years later, it was the love story we remembered most.

Three years before the Kremlin lowered its Soviet hammer and sickle and replaced it with the Russian tricolor, *Doctor Zhivago* came to the Motherland for the first time—legally, that is. Gail sent us a postcard from her trip to Moscow. The postcard was an advertisement for Sotheby's *Bidding for Glasnost '88* auction, and her note said our novel was everywhere. The following year, Pasternak was reawarded the Nobel, his son accepting the Prize on his behalf.

We're ashamed to admit it, but some of us still hadn't actually read the book at that point. The few of us who knew Italian had read it back when it was first published. Others had read it in the years following the mission, some waiting until after seeing the film to sit down with the Russian tome. But not all of us had gotten around to it. And when we finally did get around to reading *Doctor Zhivago*—to reading the words the Agency had viewed as a weapon—we were struck by both how much the world had changed, and how much it hadn't.

Around the same time, Norma wrote a spy thriller, dedicating it to Teddy. It was her first published novel, and while it received only lukewarm reviews, we still lined up to have her sign our copies at Politics and Prose. The Agency put out a statement distancing itself from the novel's content—the story of a female agent provocateur who took down a double—but we thought it rang pretty true. Those of us who remain use computers now: desktops and laptops and smartphones purchased by our children for our birthdays and Christmas, their uses taught to us by our grandchildren.

"You have to move your finger like this, Grandma."

"Just hold down the *Shift* button."

"That's because you're on *Caps Lock*."

"Don't worry about that button."

"A selfie is when you take a picture of yourself."

The keys click now, not clack. There is no ding. Our words-per-minute count isn't what it used to be, but we can do extraordinary things with these machines. Best of all, we can keep in touch. Now, instead of memos and reports, we forward each other jokes and prayers and photos of our grandchildren, and some great-grandchildren too.

We're not sure who saw it first—we all seemed to see it at the same time. It was an article in the *Post* about an American woman held in London on charges of espionage, awaiting extradition to the United States. What caused such a stir was that the woman was eighty-nine, her crimes of leaking information to the Soviets decades old. The talking heads debated what should be done in such a case.

But our interest in the article was its photo.

Although the woman's face was covered by her cuffed hands, we needed only a glimpse to know who it was.

"As I live and breathe."

"It's her."

"Not a doubt in my mind."

"Never lost her figure."

"Is that the same fur Dulles gave her?"

The article said the woman had been living in the U.K. for the last fifty years—above a rare books shop she'd owned for three decades, along with a nameless woman who'd passed away in the early 2000s.

We look for the other woman's name in other articles but can't find it.

Although the success of the *Zhivago* mission became Agency legend in the years to follow, our record of Irina's career became spotty after Expo 58, her file ending with a brief memo noting her retirement in the '80s and nothing more.

Our fingers fly across the keys.

"Was it her?

"Was it them?"

"Could it have been?"

Secretly, we hope so.

AUTHOR'S NOTE AND
ACKNOWLEDGMENTS

Many books made this one possible. First and foremost, Boris Pasternak's *Doctor Zhivago*, a novel as relevant and vital today as it was when it was first published by Giangiacomo Feltrinelli. I'm forever in debt for the brave gift he gave the world.

For my research, Peter Finn and Petra Couvée's *The Zhivago Affair* proved an indispensable asset. In 2014, thanks to Finn and Couvée's petitioning, the CIA released ninety-nine memos and reports pertaining to its secret *Zhivago* mission. And it was seeing the declassified documents—with their blacked-out and redacted names and details—that first inspired me to want to fill in the blanks with fiction.

Throughout the novel are many direct descriptions and quotes, including excerpts of conversations, as documented in first-hand accounts. Olga Ivinskaya's autobiography, *A Captive of Time*, and Sergio D'Angelo's memoir, *The Pasternak Affair*, shed light on what it was like to have lived through many of the events described in my novel.

I'm also grateful for Elizabeth "Betty" Peet McIntosh's book *Sisterhood of Spies*, which exposed me to a world of real-life heroines, including the author herself. Monuments should be built in these women's honor.

The Lavender Scare by David K. Johnson tells the lesser known history of the United States' Cold War persecution of LGBTQ people. Countless people were forced out of their jobs, reputations were publicly destroyed, and many lives were lost. Their stories must not be forgotten.

Some of the other books I consulted were *Inside the Zhivago Storm* and *Zhivago's Secret Journey* by Paolo Mancosu; *Legacy of Ashes* by Tim Weiner; *The Agency* by John Ranelagh; *The Cultural Cold War* by Frances Stonor Saunders; *The Georgetown Set* by Gregg Herken; *The Very Best Men* by Evan Thomas; *Hot Books in the Cold War* by Alfred A. Reisch; *The Spy and His CIA Brat* by Carol Cini; *Finks* by Joel Whitney; *Washington Confidential* by Jack Lait and Lee Mortimer; *Expo 58* by Jonathan Coe; *Feltrinelli* by Carlo Feltrinelli and Alastair McEwen; *Lara* by Anna Pasternak; *Safe Conduct* by Boris Pasternak; *Poems of Boris Pasternak* translated by Lydia Pasternak Slater; *Boris Pasternak: The Tragic Years, 1930–60* by Evgeny Pasternak; *Boris Pasternak: The Poet and His Politics* by Lazar Fleishman; *Boris Pasternak: A Literary Biography* by Christopher Barnes;

Boris Pasternak: Family Correspondence translated by Nicolas Pasternak Slater and Maya Slater; *Fear and the Muse Kept Watch* by Andy McSmith; *The Novel Prize* by Yuri Krotkov; and *Inside the Soviet Writers' Union* by Carol and John Garrard.

In addition to books, I could not have written my novel without the help of many people and institutions. Thanks to the Keene Prize for Literature, the Fania Kruger Fellowship, and the Crazyhorse Prize for the support. Thanks to the Michener Center for Writers, for giving me the time and resources to start my novel and the mentorship to finish it. Specifically, thank you Michener directors Jim Magnuson and Bret Anthony Johnston, for giving us weirdos a place to forever call home. And thanks to Marla Akin, Debbie Dewees, Billy Fatzinger, and Holly Doyel for keeping the whole thing afloat. I owe a debt of gratitude to my teachers, careful readers, and mentors, including Deb Olin Unferth, Ben Fountain, H. W. Brands, Edward Carey, Oscar Casares, and Lisa Olstein. Special thanks to Elizabeth McCracken, whose guidance, pen, and advice were invaluable. And of course, to my friends and fellow classmates, especially: Veronica Martin, Maria Reva, Olga Vilkotskaya, Jessica Topacio Long, and Nouri Zarrugh, for reading my work, pushing me to do better, and for making me laugh.

I'm beyond grateful to everyone at Knopf for having faith in this book and guiding it to fruition, including: Sonny Mehta, Gabrielle Brooks, Abby Endler, Emily DeHuff, Nicholas Thomson, Kelly Blair, Nicholas

Latimer, Sarah Eagle, Paul Bogards, Katherine Burns, Andrew Dorko, and especially to my amazing editor Jordan Pavlin, who strengthened every page with her careful pen and encouragement.

And to everyone at Hutchinson for their devotion, keen-eye, and creativity. Thanks to Jocasta Hamilton, Najma Finlay, Susan Sandon, Rebecca Ikin, Sarah Ridley, Amber Bennett-Ford, Mat Watterson, Claire Simmonds, Glenn O'Neill, and my brilliant U.K. editor Selina Walker.

Thank you to my incredible agents Jeff Kleinman and Jamie Chambliss, who saw the first twenty-five pages of the novel—years before it was completed—and believed. You have changed my life. And to Melissa Sarver White and Lorella Belli for helping bring my book to the world.

To all my friends—from Greensburg (the Motley Crew!) to D.C. to Norfolk to Austin and beyond: I don't know what I'd do without you.

To my family—Sara, Nathan, Ben, Sam, Owen, Grandma, Uncle Ron, all my aunts, uncles, and cousins, Janet, Hillary, Bruce, Parker, Noah, Scout, and Clementine—thanks for always being by my side.

To my parents, Bob and Patti, for naming me Lara and showing me what love can be.

And above all, to Matt, my first and last reader. Not only did you encourage me to pick up the pen, you made each page of this book stronger. I owe you everything.

A NOTE ABOUT THE AUTHOR

Lara Prescott recently received her MFA from the Michener Center for Writers at the University of Texas, Austin. Before that, she was a political campaign operative. Her stories have appeared in *The Southern Review*, *The Hudson Review*, *Crazyhorse*, *BuzzFeed*, *Day One*, and *Tin House Flash Friday*. She was awarded the 2016 Crazyhorse Fiction Prize for a version of the first chapter of *The Secrets We Kept*. She lives in Austin, Texas.

A SPECIAL NOTE TO
WATERSTONES READERS
FROM THE AUTHOR

—◆—

I have my parents to thank for naming me after Boris Pasternak's heroine in *Doctor Zhivago*. My mother had loved David Lean's masterful film adaptation of the novel, and as a child, knowing nothing about either the film or the book, I'd wind up her musical jewelry box again and again to hear it play "Lara's Theme".

Over the years, each time I've read *Zhivago*, I've taken something different from it. As a girl, I was most interested in the love story. Later, I was most taken with the sheer brilliance of Pasternak's poetic sentences. On my more recent readings, what has struck me most are the ways in which Pasternak conveys the importance of free thought. Through the life of Yuri Zhivago, the author demonstrates that the yearning for freedom remains an indestructible force—in spite of political systems that seek to repress it. Indeed, *Zhivago* is chiefly about individuals who think and laugh and love for themselves, no matter the cost.

And in 1950s Soviet Russia, that was about as subversive an idea as one could convey. At the time, Boris Pasternak was one of the most famous living Soviet writers. His poetry readings would sell out packed auditoriums. Fans would stand and shout lines from his poetry, unable to contain their excitement. *Doctor Zhivago* was to be his first novel—and one the Soviet Union knew people would want to read.

When the Kremlin got word of *Zhivago*'s themes—as well as its critical depictions of the October Revolution and the Russian Civil War—it decided it must keep Pasternak's first novel and life's work from reaching its citizens. A message about the importance of the individual over the collective from such a renowned figure would certainly sow seeds of discontent. Thus, the Soviet censors banned *Zhivago*, blocking its publication both at home and abroad.

Meanwhile, in the United States—fresh out of WWII and now firmly in a new, Cold War—political leaders were looking for ways to demonstrate American superiority over the East. And what better way, thought the newly formed Central Intelligence Agency, than through art and literature?

Indeed, art and literature can be powerful tools; they've certainly changed my own life. My parents instilled within me a lifelong love of reading from an early age. Growing up in a small town in Western Pennsylvania, I would go with my mother to the Greensburg Hempfield Area Library once a week to pick out a stack of books to take home. And as a teenager, one of my first jobs was at a bookstore. It was from those early experiences with books that I first realized that beyond the borders of my own life, there are new worlds out there waiting for me to explore, new people from different cultures and backgrounds waiting to meet me.

Throughout my life, so many books—like Edward P. Jones's *The Known World*, Toni Morrison's *The Bluest Eye*, J. M. Coetzee's *Disgrace*, and Patricia Highsmith's *The Price of Salt*, to name just a few—have all had a hand in changing the way I view the world. To me, there is no greater way to create empathy than storytelling. Books allow us to experience others' lives, visit other time periods, walk the streets of places we've never been. They build connection, creating a shared experience.

So it's no surprise that governments—seeking to control how their citizens view and experience the world—have always used words as weapons. Today, tweets, bots, fake news, and Facebook posts do the job; but sixty years ago, the Soviets and Americans both used books.

I write about this in *The Secrets We Kept*, through a character named Teddy Helms—a young, idealistic CIA officer with a background in literature:

*Teddy would pour us whiskeys from the bottle
he kept in his desk and wax poetic about the
role he believed art and literature played in
spreading democracy, how books were key
to demonstrating that great art could come
only from true freedom and how he joined up
with the Agency to spread that message. He'd
say Russians valued literature as Americans
valued freedom: "Washington has its statues of
Lincoln and Jefferson," he said, "while Moscow
pays tribute to Pushkin and Gogol." Teddy
wanted the Soviets to understand that their
own government was hindering their ability
to produce the next Tolstoy or Dostoyevsky—
that art could thrive only in a free nation, that
the West had become the king of letters. This
message was akin to sticking a knife between
the Red Monster's ribs and twisting the blade.*

Thus, the Agency began smuggling banned books behind the Iron Curtain.

I first learned about this effort in 2014, after my father sent me a *Washington Post* article he'd read about newly declassified documents that shed light on the CIA's Cold War-era "Books Program". What had caught his eye was its discussion of *Doctor Zhivago* as one of the books the Agency had used, and to great success.

With my interest piqued because of the connection between the novel and my name, I devoured the incredible true story behind *Zhivago*'s publication—a story brought to life through Peter Finn and Petra Couvée's nonfiction book, *The Zhivago Affair*.

As Finn and Couvée discovered, the CIA had obtained the banned manuscript of *Zhivago* (rumored to have been provided to the Americans by MI6), clandestinely printed it, and smuggled it back into the USSR. As part of their research, the authors had successfully petitioned the CIA to release ninety-nine documents detailing its *Zhivago* mission (codename AEDINOSAUR)—documents which I then scoured with great interest.

The initial internal CIA memos on *Zhivago* described the book as "the most heretical literary work by a Soviet author since Stalin's death," saying it had "great propaganda value" for its "passive but piercing exposition of the effect of the Soviet system on the life of a sensitive, intelligent citizen."

Here's what I write about those early *Zhivago* memos in *The Secrets We Kept*:

> *The memo passed through SR faster than word of a break room tryst during one of our martini-soaked Christmas parties and spawned at least half a dozen additional memos, each seconding the first: that this was not just a book, but a weapon—and one the Agency wanted to obtain and smuggle back behind the Iron Curtain for its own citizens to detonate.*

That, of course, is a fictionalized account. But it was seeing the actual memos and so many other declassified documents like them—with all their blacked-out and redacted names and details—that first inspired me to fill in the blanks with fiction.

So, in Elizabeth McCracken's workshop at the Michener Center for Writers at the University of Texas, I wrote a short story centered on the Agency's secret mission to obtain and print *Doctor Zhivago* and smuggle it back into Russia.

The first voice that came to me was that of a group of fictionalized (and mostly unnamed) women CIA typists working in the Agency's Soviet Russia division.

Years before pursuing my dream to become a novelist, I'd had a successful career as a political consultant, living and working in Washington, D.C. I knew what my own experience in that world had looked like—marked by sexism and inappropriate behavior, surrounded by powerful men with big egos—and imagined what it must have been like for these women in the 1950s, long before women's liberation, more than half a century before #MeToo.

With that background, as I began writing my *Zhivago* story, I imagined all the idealistic Ivy League men at the CIA working on the mission—and behind them, the women in the typing pool. While most eyes gravitate toward the famous men in the spotlight, I've always been more intrigued by the women in the background.

As I sat down to write, I chose to focus my story on those women, telling the story first through their voice:

The men would arrive around ten. One by one, they'd pull us into their offices. We'd sit in small chairs pushed into the corners while they'd sit behind their large mahogany desks or pace the carpet while speaking to the ceiling. We'd listen. We'd record. We were their audience of one for their memos, reports, write-ups, lunch orders.

Sometimes they'd forget we were there and we'd learn much more: who was trying to box out whom, who was making a power play, who was having an affair, who was in and who was out.

Sometimes they'd refer to us not by name but by hair color or body type: Blondie, Red, Tits. We had our secret names for them, too: Grabber, Coffee Breath, Teeth.

They would call us girls, but we were not.

We came to the Agency by way of Radcliffe, Vassar, Smith. We were the first daughters of our families to earn degrees. Some of us spoke Mandarin. Some could fly planes. Some of us could handle a Colt 1873 better than John Wayne.

But all we were asked when interviewed was "Can you type?"

And even beyond having been inspired by my own experiences in the political workplace, the typing pool's voice echoed some of my own thoughts and insecurities from when I was a younger woman living and working in D.C. As one example:

> *Sure, [our parents] were proud when we graduated from college, but with each passing year spent making careers instead of babies, they grew increasingly confused about our state of husbandlessness and our rather odd decision to live in a city built on a swamp.*

This was the voice I first hit upon in my short story—the story that, over the course of three years, I expanded into *The Secrets We Kept*, using the CIA's typing pool as a kind of Greek Chorus to drive the narrative.

But as I dove deeper into my writing, I realized I was missing half the story by focusing only on the women of the early CIA.

I subscribe to the thought: "Read a hundred books, write one"—which was certainly part of my process. I pored over book after book about the Cold War, propaganda, CIA history, Russian history, Boris Pasternak, Washington, D.C. in the 1950s, and much more. Then, one book in particular caught my attention. *A Captive of Time* is the autobiography of Olga Ivinskaya, Boris Pasternak's mistress and muse for his character Lara. Ivinskaya also played a pivotal role in Pasternak's writing process, and in helping bring *Zhivago* to the world. In fact, she was twice sentenced to hard labor in the Gulag for her involvement with him. And yet, she stood strong.

Seeing through Olga's eyes what it was like to stand by the love of her life no matter the cost, I knew that I couldn't just tell *Zhivago*'s story through women in the West; there had to be an Eastern thread to my novel as well—one told through Olga's lens. Over the years, Olga's story and reputation have been suppressed by those wanting to protect Pasternak's legacy. Above all else, I wanted to give her a voice once more.

I also wanted to give a voice to the long-forgotten women spies of the early CIA—women to whom monuments should be built to mark their courage and contributions.

During the Second World War, women had served as intelligence officers in the OSS (the precursor to the CIA). But after the war, those same women were stuck behind desks. As I write in *The Secrets We Kept*:

> *There was Betty. During the war, she ran black ops, striking blows at opposition morale by planting newspaper articles and dropping propaganda flyers from airplanes. We'd heard she once provided dynamite to a man who blew up a resource train as it passed over a bridge somewhere in Burma. We could never be sure what was true and what wasn't; those*

old OSS records had a way of disappearing.

But what we did know was that at the Agency, Betty sat at a desk along with the rest of us, the Ivy League men who were her peers during the war having become her bosses.

We think of Virginia, sitting at a similar desk—her thick yellow cardigan wrapped around her shoulders no matter the season, a pencil stuck in the bun atop her head. We think of her one fuzzy blue slipper underneath her desk—no need for the other, her left leg amputated after a childhood hunting accident. She'd named her prosthetic leg Cuthbert, and if she had too many drinks, she'd take it off and hand it to you. Virginia rarely spoke of her time in the OSS, and if you hadn't heard the secondhand stories about her spy days you'd think she was just another aging government gal. But we'd heard the stories. Like the time she disguised herself as a milkmaid and led a herd of cows and two French Resistance fighters to the border. How the Gestapo had called her one of the most dangerous of the allied spies—Cuthbert and all. Sometimes Virginia would pass us in the hall, or we'd share an elevator with her, or we'd see her waiting for the number sixteen bus at the corner of E and Twenty-First. We'd want to stop and ask her about her days fighting the

Nazis—about whether she still thought of those days while sitting at that desk waiting for the next war, or for someone to tell her to go home.

They'd tried to push the OSS gals out for years—they had no use for them in their new cold war. Those same fingers that once pulled triggers had become better suited for the typewriter, it seemed.

In my novel, the characters Sally and Irina are very much inspired by real spies like Elizabeth "Betty" Peet McIntosh and Virginia Hall.

And Sally and Irina's love story was very much inspired by real events as well. A little-known aspect of American history is the Lavender Scare, which began in the 1950s. Just as it became standard practice for the federal government to fire suspected communists during the Red Scare, the Lavender Scare saw suspected LGBTQ individuals removed from their government positions. Thousands lost their jobs, with many even taking their own lives after being publicly outed.

In *The Secrets We Kept*, we see Sally living through the Lavender Scare:

I'd had friends who were picked up during their late-night walks in Lafayette Square, locked up, their names printed in the newspaper. I'd had friends who were fired from their government jobs, their reputations destroyed, disowned by their families. I'd had friends who convinced themselves the only way out was to step off a chair, a noose wrapped around their neck. The Red Scare had dwindled, but a new one had taken its place.

So at the same time the United States was working to show Soviet citizens that their government was censoring and persecuting them, it was persecuting employees within its own ranks. (In fact, the U.S. government didn't end the practice until the 1990s and still has much work to do to ensure equal rights—but that's another story.)

The Secrets We Kept is so heavily based on these pasts—in the East *and* West—and my historical research. But it wasn't just books and memos that I used to write my novel.

In addition to my more traditional research methods, I also had the opportunity to travel to Russia, D.C., London, and Paris while writing *The Secrets We Kept*. It's one thing to *read* about the history, but it is another to explore the same Moscow streets, walk the same village paths, see what Boris and Olga saw sixty years ago. It was truly a magical moment getting off the train in Peredelkino, outside Moscow, and taking the same route Pasternak had walked to his dacha on the hill so many times. Visiting his gravesite and its modest tombstone was an incredibly moving experience that I'll never forget.

As well, I procured many historical artifacts over the course of my writing—including a miniature copy of *Doctor Zhivago* produced by the CIA; original articles on Pasternak and *Zhivago* from the late 1950s, as the events were unfolding; souvenirs and maps from the Brussels World's Fair where *Zhivago* was first disseminated; and many items related to early women spies. I believe there's a power in objects and felt a certain magic when holding these items. I surrounded my writing desk with them, hoping some of that magic would rub off.

The result of my process is a polyphonic novel that's driven by strong female voices, and that—like *Doctor Zhivago* itself—is about war, propaganda, persecution and above all else, love.

It's about the experiences and feelings we all share—no matter what time or place we come from. It's about using history as a tool to understand our present. As Boris Pasternak once wrote, "It's past; you'll understand it later."

And in a time where there is so much talk of building walls and vitriolic rhetoric emphasizing all that makes us different, it is almost a revolutionary act to imagine what makes us similar. That's the power of books, the power of storytelling. It's a power that's been used by governments in the past, that's still used by them today. And it's a power that, as individuals, we too can use in pursuit of a better future.